The Day I Clean My Last Toilet

J. R. Warnet

PAGE PUBLISHING, INC.
New York, NY

First originally published by Page Publishing, Inc. 2019

ISBN 978-1-64350-658-6 (Paperback)
ISBN 978-1-64350-659-3 (Digital)

Printed in the United States of America

This book is dedicated to me. I'd like to thank
myself for all the hard work, determination and
fortitude to finish such a daunting task.
Thank you again, me; this could have
never been possible without you!

Synopsis of the Book

S o here's the deal. How many people do you know hate their job?

It's not a trick question. It's one of the most critical questions posed today, yet not many people want to admit they actually hate what they do for a living. I'm not talking about the 5 percent of workers who wake up yearning to go in to the office. I'm referring to a vast majority of Americans who get out of bed, drive to work, and wonder how the hell they got to this point in their life.

This topic is personal to me, as it is to millions of college graduates who find themselves without hope, purpose, or a relevant job once they graduated. It's why I decided to write this book. Well, one of the reasons. I needed a creative outlet so I didn't go mad trying to make sense of the mess.

I recently read a statistic that almost three thousand people default on student loans each day in this country. That calculates to the largest debt crisis ever to hit America. The main reason, as I found out over the past decade, is because all of us followed our dreams that eventually turned into a nightmare. My story in a nutshell: I went to college, graduated with a BA in creative writing, and now I clean toilets to pay back my tremendous student loans.

I wouldn't necessarily call it a happy ending. But I did what I thought was right at the time. Millions of people have done what I did. They went to college or a trade school only to find out their dream position has about ten thousand applicants already waiting for an interview. So what did they do? They took a job to get by. Twenty years later, they're still working a job for a fraction of what they could've made had they landed the "perfect" job.

After swinging a mop for nearly two decades, it's time to spill all. I'm ready to tell my stories to anyone who's in the same boat as I am. This book is for the eighteen to forty-five age group who share my pain, who work at a place they loathe because they can't go anywhere else with their résumé. I'm talking about the college kid with a master's in culinary arts who has to work a hot dog stand at a minor-league baseball field. Think about a skilled craftsman who can build an entire house from the ground up but now runs a checkout line at Home Depot. And think about all those times you worked a job you despised because your kids needed braces or your partner needed the medical coverage for an operation.

We've all been there. That's why this book can relate to all of us in some way or another. These tales come from numerous people I've worked with and countless situations. Some of these stories are real, while some are a figment of my imagination. A good number of them are so real it might remind you of your neighbor or a coworker. I hope you don't have coworkers as weird or insane as I do, but if you do, I'll pray for you.

Just a word to the wise: this book is raw. It's told from the point of view of a disgruntled worker who can't believe what he sees on a daily basis. Some of the content is very vulgar, extremely blatant, and above all, bitterly honest. I don't hold anything back because I can't hold it back anymore. The musings of an enlightened school janitor are what I like to think of this book as. Picture Anthony Bourdain's *Kitchen Confidential* but with a mop instead of a frying pan. Throw in some dirty humor and behind-the-scenes information of a public school, and you've got the basics of this book.

So enjoy reading it, and try not to laugh, cry, or relate to it too much.

J. R. Warnet

Chapter 1

Call Me Janitor

For those of you who think your job sucks, you obviously have never worked as a janitor before. Spend a little time mopping puke for years on end, and you'll think middle management at some accounting firm isn't so bad after all. It's torture here. Children are mean and filthy. Teachers are equally mean and filthy with an added level of smugness only found at a Jaguar dealership. And don't even get me started on the bosses.

Think you're in a dead-end job? The highest I can go is head janitor. That's like being the tallest midget in the room. You're still a midget no matter how much taller you are than everyone else. If the term *midget* is too harsh for you, then think of being the brightest lighthouse in the harbor or sharpest crayon in the box. It's not a privilege to be head janitor; you still clean up crap at the end of the day. That's my point.

Each time I think I've seen it all, I get smacked with a whole new level of carnage. Things only created in a mad scientists' lab get put in front of me all the time. If I didn't know any better, I'd think I was being followed around all day by people wearing hidden cameras. This job makes you think there is no hell, only another year of work. Try being the guy who has to clean up after five hundred screaming children on a daily basis. Not to mention thirty neurotic teachers and seven or eight stuffy upper-management members. They all hate me, by the way. They think I can't hear them laughing or calling me Mr. Mop when I turn my back. It's embarrassing to work here.

Whenever I tell people I'm a janitor, they usually have mixed reactions. Most people start to look for those telltale signs of a mop swinger: The long hair with matching thin mustaches or goatees. Dirty fingernails and the faint smell of sour milk for cologne. I even get asked if I live in the boiler room and cook grilled cheese sandwiches on a radiator. To those people, I usually laugh and make some reference to *Half Baked* or *Good Will Hunting*. Sometimes at a party I'll run into someone who looks absolutely mortified when I tell them I'm a janitor. Usually their mouth is agape, and if you listen close enough, you can hear the needle scratch on a record in the background.

"You're a janitor?"

"Well, yes," I say. "I'm a custodian at a school in—"

"How did you get *that* job?" This is almost always followed by a grotesque look on their face while they contemplate if I'm semiretarded or not.

"Well, I applied and got hired."

"Hmmmm. Okay."

They always seem like they want to say something inappropriate like "Hey, are you a child molester?" or "Does your family approve of your lifestyle?" Often enough I'll run into a person who says they know someone who works as a janitor, just to make conversation. "My uncle Sal is a janitor in Rahway…" And they say it in the same tone if they had told someone they were dying of brain cancer. Over the years, I've come to expect this from people. I believe they say it either to make me feel better about my profession or they mention it as a knee-jerk reaction. I guess most folks aren't as accepting of janitors as they should be. Imagine your teenage son telling you he wants to grow up to be a janitor when he gets out of high school or college. "It's either that or quarterback for the Washington Redskins, but I haven't made up my mind yet."

It's not as glamorous as it's portrayed in movies or on Broadway. This job is no cakewalk to say the least. I've been told several times how I should be lucky to have a job in this economy. I've been doing this for over two decades, even before the economy took a shit, and I still wish I had joined AmeriCorps or learned how to fix transmissions. I come to work each day thinking of ways to get fired because I can't stand working here anymore. After years of watching countless slap-in-the-face tactics, I'm convinced I'll end up like that old guy in the *Shawshank Redemption*. One day I'll be feeding pigeons from a park bench, and the next, I'm swinging from the ceiling wondering what the hell happened to my life.

Perhaps the only reassuring benefit of this job is you are never short of stories to tell. Being a janitor almost guarantees you'll meet new and exciting people on a daily basis. Each time you walk into work, your coworker, foreman, or immediate supervisor could potentially be a different person. It's a well-known fact that the custodial arts has a high turnover rate due in part to the amount of fuckups who work here. I've seen a ton of people waltz through the door only to see a majority of them take the high road out of Dodge. Some realize this is the end of the line, submitting to the darkness. Others stay long enough to witness their breaking point, leaving once they've been scarred deep enough. Still, a handful of lifers, such as myself, stay on because we are institutionalized. The thought of a real job scares us, so we slink back into our caves known as janitor closets. Before long, the months turn into years, and everything just turns into a blur from there.

You run into a wide variety of characters when you clean toilets for a living. Most of them are foreigners who talk in their native tongue every time you walk by. I know they're talking shit about me, and I couldn't care less, but you'd think they would try to disguise it. A dead giveaway is when they talk in their language and the only word in English is my name. We have a true United Nations of cleaners over here too. The Serbs only talk to the Serbs, the Mongolians avoid the Chinese, and the Spanish guys avoid all contact with the Mexicans and the Puerto Ricans completely. For the few English-speaking workers here, it's a battleground whenever you sit down to lunch: either you eat with the Mexican who steals your newspaper or the Yugoslavian who calls you a stupid cunt in whatever language they speak.

Nobody stays unless they have given up completely. If you're in it for the long haul, you know the drill, like the first few weeks of boot camp. Not many people work as a janitor for a few months and decide to leave on their own will. "Maybe I'll take up the violin and join the orchestra next year." Like prison, there's only two ways out: death or parole (a.k.a. fired). We had one lady whose husband died a few years ago. Apparently, he had a big insurance policy when he fell off the roof. "Poor Morton, he was up there fixing the gutters, and I heard this big thud on the ground." Personally, I think he took a header off edge because she, his wife, was insane. Whatever the case, he left her about six hundred thousand dollars. A year and half later, she was back scrubbing toilets after spending most of it on porcelain teacups and trips to Las Vegas. Deep down I know she missed the cold embrace of this job and needed it back in her life. It happens to everyone who works here long enough. You have a feeling in your gut as if you want to throw up but nothing else comes out. That's what being a school janitor feels like every day.

The turnover rate in this place is remarkable to say the least. I came into work one Monday to find the rest of the crew, consisting of two full-timers and three part-timers, had drastically changed within days. One guy died, which to his credit was probably the best way to leave the job given the circumstances. Another guy moved back to the motherland, as he called it. Two ladies who used to be good friends had a fistfight in the parking lot right before their shift was over. Both were canned regardless of who swung first. Not sure what happened to the last guy, Michael Keaton. He looked and sounded like Mr. Keaton, hence the name. Everyone gets a code name here; it's just the custom. One of the little things I do because this job needs some spicing up sometimes. So I had five new coworkers just like that.

There's something wrong with a vast majority of my coworkers. No, I'm not talking about handicaps or disabilities. I'm referring to their mannerisms, attitudes, dispositions, and demeanors. They are here for a reason, and that reason is because they are crazy. I met a guy once who claimed he was a certified member of MENSA. He showed me his credentials, which consisted of a certificate (*certificate* was spelled wrong on his paper) stating he was a genius with an IQ of 290. He actually took the time to print a piece of paper and sign it. I asked him how he got into the exclusive club, just so I could hear his story.

"They asked me over a hundred times, and I kept telling them I was busy and shit," said George, who, at that moment, was jamming a pencil eraser in his ear to get the wax out. "I told them I just wasn't ready for that kinda pressure."

"So… when was the exact moment you knew you'd been accepted into MENSA, George?" I said.

"It was fucking priceless, pal! The head guy came to my house with a big check like they do in those Publisher Clearing House commercials and a big-ass bunch of balloons too. He comes up to me and practically begged me to join, so I said, 'What the hell, I guess I'm just that fucking good, eh?' He told me I was selected out of millions who applied each year to be in their smart group, so I had to say yes! I guess you just can't run from the limelight, ya know?"

Most janitors aren't alone when it comes to success. I've met several "millionaires" within the system. A few told me they only did this to pass the time while their stocks surged uncontrollably. They never disclose how they got their stacks of cash, although I found many of them drive a bike to work, so their fortunes must be in environmental endeavors. One asshole said he had almost three million dollars in the bank, and when I asked to see proof, the stock market took perhaps the most devastating fall since Black Tuesday. "Oh, man, I lost it all over the weekend. Goddamn pork bellies fell through, and now I'm stuck here until I can raise up my empire again."

Most people here are the last rung of the work ladder, bottom-dwelling scum suckers who can't cut the mustard on the outside. I say outside because this place is most definitely a prison. Everybody says that about their job, but this place is full of criminals like any correctional facility across America. In fact, some of the best workers here are actual felons out for good behavior. This place is the last stop on the Fuckup Express. Most people here can barely function as a human. Can you imagine if you had them working at Barnes & Noble or Arby's? I know at least half of them would shit their pants if you asked for extra Horsey Sauce at the drive-through.

On the plus side, I've meet a handful of people who care about the job and take responsibility for doing the best they can. These same workers are the ones who pay taxes, never violate the law, and tuck their children in at night. Once in a while, they'll have a drink at parties or accrue late fees at the library, which is the deepest their debauchery goes. But they're outnumbered here ten to one by the seriously deranged workers.

Mind you, not many people here are competent by any stretch. I've seen thirty-two workers go to the hospital for mixing bleach and ammonia, and two of them did it on two different occasions, which is truly beyond me. That's like the golden rule of janitoring. You never mix bleach and ammonia, but damned if these window lickers do it all the time. These are the people who get promotions or become bosses. Common sense does not reign supreme here.

Speaking of bosses, let's address all of them. We have three kings in this regime, the three stooges. Over the years we had several different starting lineups, so I'll address the current batting order. By the way, these fuckers are complete degenerates. All three of them have the combined intelligence of moldy bread, yet they are the powers that be in the department. I'd rather take orders from a dead hamster than listen to these morons, but such is life. The head supervisor has his entire office covered in certificates showing how great a leader he is. The second-in-command barely graduated high school and suffers from little-dog syndrome. And the third, he's just a fall guy and probably won't be around much longer. I'd be surprised if he still has his job by the time I'm done writing this chapter. It happens here quite often. The big bosses, the ones who watch the teachers, sub out my departments bosses all the time. They don't want anyone getting too comfortable in their positions.

There's not much to being a school janitor. Throw in some bags of garbage and a few stained ceiling tiles, and you've got the gist of it. I'll be outlining the whole process over the next few chapters. You'll meet incredible coworkers, hear things you don't want to believe are true, and hopefully come away with a different perspective of the guy who sweeps the hallway. In any case, if you don't like the stories, then that's on you. I'm just here to give you a little chuckle and relieve some of my own stress at the same time.

Chapter 2

A Day in the Life of a School Janitor

I think it's about time I told you what I do on a daily basis. You know, not many people know what a janitor does once they strap on the olive-drab jumpsuit. I'm guessing most of you don't give a shit what the janitor does, but I'm gonna tell you anyway. You know why? Because I want you to see what I go through so you can feel my pain. And because it's my fucking book.

They say you can't judge a man until you walk a mile in his shoes. Try jogging in my boots, covered in chewing gum and school cafeteria pudding, then we'll talk. It is a dirty job, and yes, someone has to do it. I don't like doing it, but I need money, just like all of you. If I knew how to make money that didn't involve swabbing out pissy toilets, I'd so jump on it. But alas, I'm not the banker or accountant type. I wouldn't know how to rebuild a transmission or fill cavities or even take an order in a drive-through. I blame the American education system for my current employment position. "Go to college," they said. "Give yourself a chance to compete in the new millennium," they said. Fucking college was a sham. A lot of good forest ecology and beginning guitar does now with eighty thousand grand of debt and a ten-year-old F-150 with a smoking tailpipe.

The life of the janitor is a calling; not many people have the intestinal fortitude to sweep dried, dead skin cells off the floor. That's what those hair ball–looking things are, you know. If you've ever seen a gray fuzzy creature in the corner of a hallway, odds are it's mostly people jerky. The human body sheds something like thirty thousand dead skin cells an hour just by walking around. Hair follicles, dried sweat and dirt particles, microscopic laundry detergent remnants, lint balls, etc., they all fall to the ground when you move your limbs. Once your skin cells flake off, they combine with other people's skin cells to make a disgusting toupee of filth.

I'm the guy who wrangles them into a mountainous pile to sweep into the trash. Yup. Glamourous work all right.

Think about how many dust bunnies you've stepped over during your lifetime. All those furry beings are about 90 percent skin from dirty people you've never met. You can be hopping along in a public area like a mall and inhale someone's dirty feet crumbs. Bet you didn't know you were wafting in other people's dandruff flakes each time you breathe?

Now imagine doing that with 1,400 people in a confined area without a proper air circulation. That's public schools for you. We have the same ventilation system as an oven in Sobibor.

Think about how many nasty little children are running around in a school just spitting, sneezing, and puking all over the place. It's a fucking catastrophe is what it is! I go home each night smelling like pencil shavings and ass, covered head to toe with half a million dead skin cells stuck to me like Velcro. I can't get the water hot enough in the shower anymore.

Anyhoozers…

So what does a school janitor do during a typical shift? Good question. It depends on what job title you have. The day janitors don't do a fucking thing. Seriously. Most schools have a day janitor. You probably know him as Mr. Jaime or Ms. Miranda. Not that all places have a Spanish-speaking/looking janitor, but I'm painting a picture here, so just go with it. Some places call them head custodian, day head custodian, lead custodian, blah, blah, blah. He or she is the person who unlocks the school in the morning, turns on the lights, then takes a nap. Once the school buses drop off their passengers, the day janitor finds a cozy place to take a siesta. Day janitors are fucking lazy fucktards who avoid work like the plague.

I've seen one guy put caution tape around a pile of shit on the bathroom floor. Instead of disinfecting the area so no one can get sick, he made a crime scene out of the dookie with a note saying, "Clean me up!"

How in the hell can you leave a pile of crap on the floor for hours on end? I mean, it took longer to get the caution tape, rope off a four-sided ring around the poop, and then write a note as what to do with the fecal matter. Mind you, a day janitor's job is exactly the same as mine. If you see shit on the floor, you clean it up. That's kind of what we do. Starbucks baristas make espresso drinks. Burger King burger flippers turn beef patties over, right?

Day janitors think doing janitor work is beneath them. "I've been promoted" is a line I've heard before. "I'm the boss... You work for me!" is another line. Truth is, day janitors got their jobs because they're older than the pyramids of Egypt. These relics from the past have a good forty years in, so the bosses think they're the best. Kind of like "Fake it till ya make it." Honestly, most of the day janitors are practically in heaven's waiting room anyway, mere seconds away from stroking out midsentence.

I have to give them credit though: all day janitors are really good at hide-and-seek. They've been flying under the radar for years dodging work. The whole "out of sight, out of mind" concept is in full effect here. Just because someone has been silent for four decades does not make them a good worker. Crafty, yes. A good worker? Not so much. I call day janitors Top-Step Divas because they've reached the top of the pay scale and don't want to work anymore. Being a day janitor is also considered semi retirement. It's a few minutes away from a nice pension and free medical. As long as you don't drop dead or punch a kid in the mouth, you've got yourself a sweet little setup.

Another thing they're good at, other than nap time and hide-and-seek, is pushing work onto someone else. Kind of like your job when your boss dumps a pile of paperwork onto your desk and says, "Can you do me a favor?" Yeah. It happens to us all. At least at your job, the boss doesn't plop a heap of shit onto your desk. (Okay, so I don't have a desk per se, but you get what I'm saying.) I have a closet. The janitor closet. I get notes taped to the door, sometimes written in crayon, telling me what to do. Yup. Fucking crayon. Written by a man, who has the same level of education as the children walking the hallways with him. That's my boss. One of them anyway.

All tasks the day jerk-off doesn't want to do gets pushed back onto me, the guy in charge at night. I'm what you would call a night head custodian, night lead janitor, head moron in charge when the sun goes down, etc. I assign work, check on work, and above all, do work. I'm really just a fall guy, and no one listens to a goddamn word I say. My crew, consisting of anywhere between two and fourteen people given the night, does what they want, when they want. Sometimes they sweep the floor. Sometimes they have sex with their girlfriends in the boiler room. A real mixture of souls is what I have to work with.

By the way, have you seen a school janitor lately? They aren't what one would consider a normal person. It's a gaggle of hardened criminals, degenerates, psychopaths, and mentally unstable ruffians. Basically anyone who either can't work around the public or who isn't *legally* allowed to work with the public anymore. You've filled out a job application before. You know those boxes you read and reread carefully so you don't check *that* specific box? Things like the following:

- Have you ever been convicted of a crime?
- Are you legally able to work in this country?
- When was the last time you checked in with your parole officer?
- Do you talk back to the voices in your head?

Well, all those individuals found a home.

Society's outcasts wash up on the shores of Janitorland, where we take any moron with a limp, a police record, or a mental instability. This is a place you work only if all other viable options are off the table. Would you ever in a million years say to yourself, "Ya know what... I feel like scrubbing mold off a student's desk today. Maybe I'll work in a public school, where children carve detailed penises and swastikas on lockers."

A vast majority of my coworkers chose this over something even less appealing, like funeral embalmer or Walmart cashier. Let's just say at least one former employee has been fired for exhibiting unprofessional behavior (his name was Charlie, and he's not allowed within one hundred feet of a morgue or graveyard anymore). These helpless stunods have reached the end of the road in employment, having been terminated from every other reasonable job. Any normal person with half a brain stem doesn't apply to be a janitor, unless they're hiding from the mob or can't function in public without screaming uncontrollably.

Years back, one of the more infamous psychiatric wards in the area closed due to budget cuts. The newspaper said most of the residents were turned loose on to the streets, kind of like releasing white doves at a wedding ceremony. A long-standing joke is that one of the bosses took one of the tart carts from the bus yard, drove down a local highway, and picked up any vagrant with a half-decent smell. Funny thing is, we had a couple of years where we had some truly terrible people working here, just around the same time the nuthouse was shuttered. Like people you wouldn't want to be trapped in a broken elevator with.

Imagine having fifty heavily medicated loonies being told, "No more happy pills for you, Samuel. You're free now! Go run and terrorize the neighborhood." I'm positive most of them were given a job here.

Some of these people though, who the hell knows how they got here. My educated guess is some did illicit drugs, some used to steal cars, while others were hired simply because they were able to spell their name correctly on the job application. The only prerequisite here is stumbling into the HR office without pissing yourself during the interview. Even then, if you can demonstrate an ease of cleaning up that piss, you might have a shot.

The most common worker employed is the retired thug. He's the guy who's been in and out of our correctional facilities since the age of fourteen. He doesn't have a pension from the penal system even though he's been there longer than I've been alive. Since he's got a record, no one will hire him, except, you guessed it!

One guy did time for window shopping as he called it. "I used ta walk by department stores in the city, tro a brick through the winda, and grab whatever looked expensive." That's how he spoke, by the way. Like he had a sixth-grade reading level and was raised by demented hoodlums. This is the guy, and many more like him, I have to convince to not steal thirty laptops when I turn my back. Especially when they are right there out on the open, without a barrier of glass to deter him. When the repeat offenders come to my post, I usually let them do whatever the hell they want to do. They didn't get that teardrop tattoo under their eye because they cry a lot. No, they got it because they murdered someone, and I sure as hell won't be next.

Then comes the junkies, the ones who steal anything they can stick in the pants or up their ass. Due to their excessive drug use, not a single one of them is worth anything. I can't get them to listen to me because they're too busy twitching from withdrawal. I guess it's hard to focus when all you think about is your next hit. Oddly enough, all of them volunteer to clean the nurse's room. Gee, I wonder why? I'm not a police dog by trade, but I can sniff out an addict trying to poach pills from the nurse's closet any day. I had to convince the school's security officer to put a camera on the nurse's room because we've had multiple druggies raiding the medicine cabinets.

Then comes the professional thieves. Pickpockets, watch snatchers, jewelry jammers, with sketchy eyes and fidgeting fingers. No lie, I've had to call the cops because one girl tried to crack open a safe in the principal's office. I found this bitch with a crowbar trying to pop open the safe like a Pringles container. Really? She thought she could muscle her way into a tiny vault with a pry bar from her trunk? No stethoscope or titanium drill bits, just strength and determination for this girl!

When I caught her, she tried to assault me with said crowbar, spouting something about needing money. "I need a fucking fix, you fat bastard! You call the cops and I'll end you!" For a tiny, little thing, she had a tremendous amount of energy. I guess running out of black tar heroin will amp up the adrenaline.

Multiple career criminals work here, but old habits die hard. Eventually the urge to "borrow" a teacher's purse takes hold of their easily lead minds. I've had to call the police more times than a normal person should. It gets so bad the 911 operators know me by name. "What is it this time? Did Julie get into a fistfight with Harry again?"

One night, I found some guy passed out while eating a ham sandwich. Turns out he wasn't sleeping. He croaked right there with half a boar's head hoagie in his hands. I don't even remember his name. Mike or Joe or some shit like that. The sad part is, I didn't even flinch when I discovered he was dead. I'm so jaded from this place things like finding a corpse while making the rounds don't faze me anymore. I was more pissed off because I had to do the rest of the work he didn't finish. Fucking guy. Who did he think he was dying like that on my watch?

I'm truly a horrible human being because the whole time I saw him sitting there, with his eyes closed and rigor mortis setting in, I was thinking about that poor uneaten ham sandwich. There it was resting comfortably in his hands getting stale. That's where my mind is from working here. I feel more for cold cuts than I do for my coworkers.

Not all our employees are crooks or turn up dead. The ones who don't have a police record aren't exactly angels either. How do I say this delicately. We have a lot of problematic workers. The rest of the custodial crew members are either mentally impacted or have some kind of deficiency. I'm not talking about physical attributes like half a leg or a cleft pallet. I'm more focused on the head cases who'd melt the place to the ground with everyone inside and not even bat an eye. A tremendous number of workers like to carry on conversations with themselves. You know the type. The kind you see bopping down the street mumbling gibberish, which later turns into violent screaming and arm flailing?

These are the ones you got to watch out for. I call them kooks. They are the loopy bastards you don't want to become unleashed. Never, and I mean never, turn your back on a kook. Experts say if you turn your back on a lion, they attack because they know you're not watching them. The same law of nature applies to a person who constantly flips their tongue around in their mouth. Unpredictable at best. And they blurt out the most awkward shit. Half the time I think the demons inside of them take control of their voice box just to fuck with me.

I'll give one of the wet brains a work assignment for the night, to which they will say something extremely random. "Do you know my dog, Fluffy, once ate a snapping turtle? She ate the whole damn thing, shell and all!"

Wow. And I have to say "Wow" inside my head. If I say it out loud, the nutjob might start yelling about how he has the power to shoot laser beams out of his ears like a superhero. You think I'm joking here, but I've actually had this conversation happen with a very disgruntled wacko. He didn't last too long here. Just long enough to scare the bejesus out of me. God, how can one person be so deranged? He's still locked away in a state-run facility, probably drooling from a forced Lexapro ingestion. I hope that motherfucker never gets loose.

Anyhoo, let me run you though a basic night as a school janitor. We show up around 4:00 p.m., when all the sane, rational people have left for the day. Nobody wants to be bothered by a horde of mental cases, so management pulls us in when the school is abandoned. It's usually for the best. My coworkers deserve to be locked in a dungeon, kept away from the prying eyes of Joe Q. Public. Kind of like Frankenstein or Shrek. At 4:00 p.m., a school is quiet most of the time. A quiet place is a recipe for disaster when dealing with jabber heads. It's my burden to get them organized, like how a cameraman waves a toy in front of a distracted infant during formal pictures.

As ringleader of the night janitors, it's my job to rope them together and assign work. Keep in mind, if any one of them is off their meds, they might set the others off too. Depending on the post, some schools have three employees, and some have fifteen. Larger schools like middle and high schools get more people because they have a shit ton of after-school activities. That's usually where I'm posted, assigning work to whoever the hell shows up.

I start my shift counting bodies, hoping I have enough to get the job done. Nine times out of ten we're short. Double work for everyone!

I survey the lineup like a drill sergeant calling to check for bunk inspection. "You! Private Jailbird, hit the garbage cans now! And you, Private Crossed Eyes, start sweeping the hallways fucking ASAP!" It's imperative to talk to them like this so they know I mean business. If they detect the slightest hint of fear, I'm toast. On rare occasions, the workers do the work assigned, and everyone goes home with a sense of pride and satisfaction. Truth is, most days I have trouble. If I'm slated to have, say, ten workers, maybe seven will show up. One called out sick, one had a nervous breakdown, and the other violated probation. Most times the number of employees out is higher.

Once I get a head count, I assign work. That's when the fun starts. "I ain't doin' that shit!" says the crackhead from Bayonne. "I don't do toilets, you feel me? Fuck you, honky! I'll slap yo ass if you make me scrub shitters!" Here we go. Now I have to call the supervisor, who is just as afraid of a strung-out junkie as I am. I don't confront the cons here. I've been threatened about a hundred times. Most are idle threats, but I have had a gun pulled on me once. I let the big bosses, the fuckers who make a hundred grand a year, handle confrontational employees.

After some yelling, the boss fires said crackhead, cutting our numbers again. There goes another worker sent home for the night. Down to almost half the proper number of staff, and the shift just started.

I'll have another employee complain about their personal life. These ones tend to be harmless, just annoying. "My boyfriend got drunk last night and punched the wall in our trailer. Now we have a hole, and rain is pouring into my living room!" Judging by her face, he almost punched a hole in her skull too. There goes another employee, leaving to either patch up the wall or bail out her future wife-beating husband. So that leaves me with five bodies to do ten people's work.

Here's where it gets interesting. The other four remaining workers are normally stressed out and tend to get mouthy when you change their routine. If I tell Betty to do more work than I assigned her an hour ago, she goes ballistic. "Oh, fuck this place!" she says as she hurls a broom across the hallway. "I'm so sick and tired of doing this shit! My sciatica is acting up… Go ask Henry to do extras. Fuck off!"

For the record, that's the second employee to tell me to go fuck myself and we're not even halfway through the evening. (Remember the Bayonnian crackhead?) In her defense, Betty is normally crazy, so her response is routine. Now I have to tell Henry to pick up some work, which doesn't go so well. "Hey, I'm already doing enough as is," said Henry, who is currently sitting on his ass stirring a cup of Wawa coffee. "I'll have to call my union rep to see if he wants me to be doing all this extra work…"

Also, just for the record, that's the second time I've been threatened on the night. Albeit a nonviolent union thuggish response, but still. You can't threaten your boss when he tells you to do a job, can you? I'm in the same union as Henry, but Henry's juiced in. His brother-in-law is a union rep at another post, so he has a get-out-of-jail free card.

Henry makes a phone call, and minutes later a Pinkerton wannabe shows up and hands me a pamphlet on workers' rights. "Our union brothers and sisters will not to be overworked… It's our right to unionize to fight oppression!" You'd have thought I put the guy in shackles, for Christ's sake. "The union denounces your attempt to overwork this man. He has rights!"

Motherfucker, I know the rights here. I'm just the asshole who assigns work. Boom, there's yet another reason why this place sucks out loud. I can't make workers do more than they feel comfortable doing. What kind of horse shit is that? If you don't want to exert yourself, you don't have to. Your rights are protected by the union, even though the work you're currently doing is well under the minimum amount.

Great. Henry and Betty flip me off. Now I have to talk to the other two guys, who don't speak a word of English, supposedly. Pancho and Miguel play stupid when I tell them to pick up a few rooms. "*Que*?" (Huh?) Yeah, right, you speak English, *bendejo*! You know what the fuck I'm saying. So I say it in English *and* in Spanish. Still nothing. I'm fluent in both languages, by the way, but I guess these two guys are still befuddled. "Miguel, *trabajo*? Pancho, me *el hefe.* Me… *el patron? Comprende?*" I get nothing. They both keep staring at the floor hoping I just walk away.

Maybe I'll learn Dutch or Swahili in order to communicate properly in the future.

Around the halfway point of the night, I get to interact with teachers. Not because I want to, but I have to. You see, teachers, in general, are lost little puppies. I'm tasked with moving boxes from one room to another or help move a teacher's desk a quarter of an inch to the left. A slave with a really large set of keys is what I amount to. These fuckers can't be bothered to learn my name, but they sure can scream "Hey, janitor!" down an empty corridor. I've only worked in this shithole for almost twenty years, but hey, who the hell cares what the janitor's name is anyway? It's not like I'm a real live human or anything.

Later in the evening, I run into the really depressing teachers who have nowhere else to go. Most of the staff have left by now, but we have a few teachers who stay because they're avoiding something at home. One teacher has a cheating husband, so while her marriage is crumbing in front of her very eyes, she decides to post up at the school until we kick her out. Good-looking lady too. I guess her husband has a wandering eye, or maybe she's a shitty wife at home. If I have to escort you out of the building each night because your marriage is over, it's a damn shame. Time to face it, sister, and hit the bricks so I can sweep out your classroom in peace.

We have another younger teacher who thinks her future husband will walk into her empty classroom and whisk her off her feet. At least that's what I think she's doing in there all alone. I'm sure she read it in one of her romance novels, where Prince Charming trots in on a white horse to take her to never-never land. She looks so goddamned sad sitting behind a gunmetal gray desk patiently surveying anyone who dashes past her open door. I kind of feel bad for her. She seems nice, but you know as well as I do that this lady is probably toxic. There's a reason she can't keep a man from sprinting out of the Applebee's on a blind date.

I have a couple of real nasty teachers who bother me every fregging night. They complain it's too hot in the building, then it's too cold. I've already explained the crappy ventilation system to them, but they do not care. I don't know, wear a jacket or something.

Tonight, we have one teacher who is afraid of black people. This crotchety bitch says a janitor keeps staring at her. "I want him out of my sight! The one with the afro... he keeps look at me like he wants to have sex with me! Tell him to stop looking at me!" I mess with her a little by telling her we have two employees with an afro. "Is it a short afro or a big afro? The one with the big afro is much more confrontational than the short afro."

She doesn't stay too long after she finds out we have two possibly aggressive black guys who may or may not want to have sex with her.

With about three hours left in the shift, and little under half the work left, I start to panic. It's my ass if the work doesn't get done. That's all I know. When I ask the remaining stiffs for help, they blow me off. "You're the asshole in charge... you deal with it!" So I got no help from the people who are supposed to listen to me. Ya know, like any other fucking job in the world.

In addition to basic daily cleaning of a school, we have to set up for activities. Typically, a school is jam-packed with things like board meetings, township meetings, parent-teacher conferences, after-school clubs, sports of every fucking kind, dog and pony shows, the circus, mass ritual sacrifices, etc. Now I have to convince the remaining scumbags to meet me in the library to set up tables for a bake sale in the morning. "I ain't doing that" is the general consensus. Why do these people still have jobs? I'd like to smack each one of them with a tube sock full of rusty bolts, but I have to be nice so they help me get the work done.

In between trying to beg for some help, I'm stopped by a woman in the hallway, squawking about something. Yet another job perk: I get yelled at by some whored-out soccer mom who asks why her son's game was cancelled. "Hey, janitor! Where the hell is the basketball game? It's supposed to be here at 7:30 p.m.! Why isn't there a game here tonight? It says so on the school's Facebook page! I want to know right now where is the goddamn—"

Yeah, I've been yelled at enough tonight. In a moment of rage, I spout out, "The fuck do I know, lady? Do I look like I give a fuck?"

I normally say those things in my head, like one of the crazies I work with. I guess my internal filter turned itself off.

Appalled, she dashes out the door with her phone in her hand. Minutes later, I get a call on the radio about the incident. Of course, a union rep comes back over, along with another supervisor, to have a powwow over why I cursed out a taxpaying citizen. "You're just lucky she doesn't want to sue us for verbal abuse!" says the useless supervisor.

By the end of the day, about 20 percent of the work isn't done. I run out of steam around 11:30 p.m., leaving a note to the day janitor in blue ink, not canary-yellow Crayola, explaining the situation as best I could. Shortage of staff, worker rebellions, bullshit meter on overload—same shit, different aroma. The day janitor, in turn, writes me up. The next time I come in for my shift, I have two bosses and a different union rep asking me why the work isn't getting done.

I'd like to say I'm exaggerating. I wish I could say that. But this is a typical Tuesday at my job. I'm stuck between several massive dicks getting gangbanged like one of those weird German pornos you see floating around online.

This brutal ass fucking happens each and every day I come to work. I guess that's why no one ever wants to do this job. I'd have an easier time wiping burger grease off a flat-top grill than dealing with this mess. Why do I do it, you may ask? Why on God's green-and-blue earth would I subject myself to this carnage instead of manning a cash register at Target? That's a good fucking question. Truth is, I don't know why I do it. Maybe because I'm used to being treated like dog crap. I guess I've got a case of Stockholm syndrome or some shit. Who the fuck knows anymore.

Chapter 3

The Rusty Chain of Command

As a school janitor, you must always keep the following thought in the back of your mind: everyone is your boss. You, my mopping friend, are the pond scum of the lake. Hell, we're treated worse than pond scum, but I can't think of anything lower than pond scum at the moment. From the top of the shit ladder all the way down to the last rung, you are an insignificant piece of dog feces, at best. Pick any job in a school district except a janitor, and you would be my overseer.

I don't mind it, though. I've spent so many years at the bottom of the food chain I wouldn't know what to do if I had a chance to feast at the top. All these sons of bitches think they're better than us moppers because they went to college. Just because someone has a spiffy piece of paper hanging on the wall doesn't make them superior. It just means they were dumb enough to pay eighty grand for a special job title. I spent years in college as well, and I've got those papers too. Doesn't give me the right to talk down to another human being because they empty a trash can for a living.

I imagine you have the same separation of classes at your job too. It's okay. You can admit you're smarter than your boss even though they make five times the amount of money you do. That's the way that stale cookie crumbles, Chief. What separates me from you is a green jumpsuit and a pair of rubber gloves. That, and odds are you don't have to clean the shitter in your bosses' office. I do, and I fucking hate it.

Let's go from the top and work our way down to me, the lowly janitor. First up, we have administration. They consider themselves like the gods in Greek mythology, mighty titan slayers casting down judgment from Mount Olympus. I consider them the biggest bunch of jackasses on the planet. These people are borderline retarded. I'm not saying that in a negative tone. It's just administration, at my job, are nonthinking half-wits who got the job because they know somebody.

Think about administration as being the head honcho, the tippy top of the heap where all the laws are thought up. These under-educated, overpaid fuckers make all the decisions from school budgets to pay raises. They golf more hours in a week than they work, all on taxpayers' tab too. In fact, administrators do very little work. Most of their paperwork is done by their secretary, who signs their name using a rubber stamp. I guess making two hundred thousand dollars a year isn't enough to make them physically put pen to paper.

Most administrators know someone or have family who knows someone. That's how they got their job. It wasn't because they were valedictorians or put in years of hard work and dedication. The head bosses either blew somebody or muscled their way in.

Don't be fooled by their cunning display of work ethic. Administrators are always sprinting off somewhere pretending to talk on their phones about how much work they need to get done. "I need those annual budget reports on my desk immediately! I have to review them now before the next board meeting." I've heard this phrase a thousand times echoing down the halls by numerous bosses. I'm not sure how many annual budget reports a school has to have, but these guys sure need to review a lot of them on a daily basis.

As soon as they see someone like a janitor, they give the illusion of work to get out of making small talk. The only thing more obvious would be faking a cough and running the other way with a Kleenex over their nose. "I'm sorry, I can't talk right now. I have the Ebola, and I'm late for my doctor's appointment."

I saw one administrator talking on his phone last week. He was walking so fast it looked like he had fire sparking out of his asshole.

He was just jabbering away looking all flustered, making sure I saw him speaking diligently into his cell.

"Yup... yup... I understand you completely," he said. His leather wing tip shoes made that clip-clop sound, which drives me nuts. "Yes, indeed. I'll have those figures over to your department right away." He hangs up the call as he passes me. "Ugh, so much to do! I feel like I need to be split into two halves just to get any work done!"

Yeah, right, motherfucker. You're probably late for teetime, you prick.

School administrators spend a good chunk of their time making or pretending to make phone calls. True, the phone rings a lot in their office, but it's mainly to find out when the whole lot of them head out to lunch at the local pub. We had one guy years back who showed up to every board meeting crocked. Now picture this: a shiny-faced guy reeking of whiskey, slurring his words in front of taxpaying citizens. Fucking guy practically spit on the microphone when he spoke to the public, blabbering on about unnecessary spending. "We need to cut those electric bills, people. These kids leave the lights in the classrooms on all day, for crying out loud!"

Most of the bosses in my school district are either crooked or covering for a crooked buddy. Each one is eviler than the last, always scheming behind one another's backs like a half-assed version of *The Sopranos*. I imagine closed-door meetings to resemble something out of a mob hit scene. "You know, Bobby No Nuts didn't seal that construction contract on the new school. I think it's time to send him to the farm." The *farm* usually meaning being demoted back down to principal or gym teacher if they really fuck up.

You can't get a boss job without several degrees (those expensive pieces of paper), so either they rigged the records or they know how to schmooze the public into thinking they are the best candidate for the job. It's amazing how they can lie like a rug and still get you to believe they are telling the truth. I had the unfortunate pleasure of attending a board of ed. meeting years ago for one of my college classes. Let me tell you it's a goddamn shame how these criminals still have a job. Some of them are so fucking dumb they make shit up as they go. It doesn't take much to look busy in the eyes of the public. Just write a bunch of notes down in front of the townsfolk all while robbing the township blind behind closed doors.

If they last five years in the same job title, they will probably retire a wealthy person, all on the taxpayers' dime. The dumb ones, the stunods who get caught filtering money through side businesses, almost always go out on a medical or get promoted to a better job in some other school district. It's like a miserable dance back and forth all while saying it's "for the benefit of the students." Recently one of the bosses was caught sleeping with his secretary. Instead of being fired, like you or I would have been, the board gave him a superb letter of recommendation to continue his exploits at another district. And his secretary, you ask? She went out on maternity leave and followed him to the same school after she had the baby.

Once administration takes a dump, it leads down to your administrative lackeys (i.e., principals, vice principals, heads of departments, etc.). Of course, they have the educational documents to show you they are leaders, but anyone can print a degree from a website. You wouldn't believe the amount of fake degrees these shitheads have stuck to their office walls. It's like they all went to Phoenix Online when they had a two-for-one special on masters and doctorates. I bet if you look closely at the degree, it would say: "From the hallowed halls of the University of East Bumfuck, where character counts!"

Most of their degrees are from some obscure online college founded in some guy's basement. I had problems with one principal years ago who brought me into his office like I was one of his students. I guess he figured it would intimidate me. It didn't. He complained that I wasn't working hard enough, saying I had an attitude problem. While scanning the walls in his office, I noticed he had a degree from Belford University.

"Hey, isn't that the online college who got busted by the government for selling fake diplomas?" I said with a coy smirk.

He left me alone after I kept asking what field he got his doctorate in.

School principals observe and report back to administration. Basically, they pussyfoot around all day monitoring teachers to evaluate their performance. The only time the principal or vice principal does any real work is when an entire class fails a standardized test. You remember them, right? Those bullshit bubble answer papers that can only be filled out with a no. 2 pencil? It's a state test to see if little Jonah can go on to middle school. If a class passes those tests, the principal is free to roam the school handing out detention slips for the rest of the school year. If not, they have to make sure the teachers know how to do their jobs right by having pointless meeting after meeting.

School principals also play an intricate role in putting those inspirational posters on the walls so students have a comforting environment. Truth is, the lazy bastards usually make a janitor tape the "Reach for the stars" signs to the wall. Sad irony, huh? The dirtbag janitor is the guy giving your kids the inspiration to be the next president of the United States.

Principals and vice principals find ways to outdo one another in the public eye. If test scores are failing, the principal holds a bake sale to take the attention away from the mess. Everyone turns a blind eye to bad test scores as long as they have brownies and cupcakes to eat. Of course, the proceeds from the bake sale are supposed to go toward new school supplies. Wrong answer. A majority of school supplies are actually paid for by the state through your taxes. Sad fact is, the money you pay for baked goods goes toward a new cappuccino machine in the faculty lounge. Or maybe a leather Ottoman for the principal's office.

A principal's main job is to babysit the teachers. I'd do that job for $120,000 dollars a year. Wouldn't you? That and answer a few phone calls or have meetings if your child is throwing food in the cafeteria. That's it. That's all they do. Most of their work is done by their secretary, just like their idols, the administrators. I guess no one likes to do paperwork around here except the secretaries?

After the principal, the next rung on the doo-doo ladder is teaching, the department with the most people on payroll. Since they only work ten months a year and don't have a shred of common sense, fuck 'em. If they spent more time taking business administration classes in college instead of doing bong hits out of an apple, they'd be a little further up the ladder. I like to call them the common senseless. I'm dead serious with this one. I haven't met one single teacher who has a fleck of common sense. If it isn't taught at college or found in a textbook, teachers probably wouldn't know it. If it requires general thinking, like how to change a tire, forget about it.

Teachers love to stay in their classrooms all day like prisoners on lockdown. They toil away after school like trolls digging for diamonds in the mountainside. Maybe they just like their little comfort zone of solitude. Perhaps they are dedicated workers who devote hours on end to grading tests or beefing up their portfolio. I'm just guessing here, but I'd say teachers are more like obsessive-compulsive zombies who have nothing to go home to but a bottle of Xanax and a cat named Mr. Waffles. Seriously, get the fuck out already! I know you hate when a janitor comes in to dump your trash, but I got a job to do, lady! You don't see me sweeping the floor when you're trying to teach algebra, do you? Instead of spending quality time with a family member after school, they spend most of their lives putting smiley-face stickers on ugly drawings. That and messing around with other teachers or students. More on that later.

And I hate to break it to you, but most teachers don't give a shit about your child. If you ever heard what these demons say about your kids when the bus leaves, you would hate them as much as I do. The language they use to describe students is deplorable. "Holy shit, that kid is dumb! Why can't he remember the capitol of Idaho?" Walking down a school hallway after hours is similar to overhearing the cool kids in high school gab about the nerd table at lunch. You would think less of a teacher if you really knew what they were talking about before you come in for parent-teacher conferences.

Teachers, or expensive babysitters, complain the most out of all the people who work for a school district. "I didn't have the full twenty-seven minutes for my lunch break... I need to have more than two months off during the summer to prepare myself for teaching... Why do *I* always have the stupid students?" Jesus Christ, I've never seen such whiny group of pussies in my life. Every day they complain about students or the job or state tests or whatever else pisses them off. I had a teacher complain to me she doesn't have enough wall outlets to run her Keurig and mini fridge at the same time. Really? This ain't your college dorm room. Why are you so concerned over the amount of noneducational electrical gadgets you can have in your classroom? Do you need to have a fresh latte with your toasted muffin while teaching the youth of America?

Teachers are paid to educate your child. I get a check for cleaning up puke, while a teacher gets a check for teaching kids how to finger paint. True, some teachers do the job they get paid for, but there is a widening group of teachers who don't give a fuck if your kid knows how to count. These are collectively known as the teachers who reach tenure. After a certain amount of years, a teacher cannot be fired for something you or I would be fired for. Infringements like failing test scores have no effect on a teacher who has passed tenured age. They become untouchable for most offenses. Unless Mrs. Siegfried beats a student to death with a stapler, she can keep her job until time stands still.

Think about in another light: tenure means they have passed the timeline of being fired for not educating anymore. It would be like a receptionist answering the phone for about five years and then one day saying, "Well, I answered the phone years ago. Do I have to pick that phone up today?" Most jobs require you to do the job properly every single day. Not teaching. They can turn on the TV and let the class watch *The Lion King* if they don't feel like opening up the teacher's manual that day.

If an entire class of twenty-five kids can't spell the word *cat*, I think the teacher shouldn't get his or her paycheck. You'd get fired if you worked at Burger King and everyone who ate your burgers got ptomaine poisoning. The same results should apply to schools where educating future world leaders is part of the job. But with teachers, once you pass tenure, you can coast until retirement.

Next, we have the IT department. Yup, those glasses-wearing, iPad-juggling computer dorks who look down on you because you don't know how to write code for websites. If you have a technology problem, they stare at you, silently judging your every move. "Is the computer plugged in? Did you unplug it then plug it in again?" Really, Dilbert? That's all you got? How hard is it to make sure a computer runs an antivirus program? That's the most work they do. These bookworms make astronomical amounts of money for updating your Windows XP to Windows 10. As if any trained circus monkey couldn't click a mouse a few times.

I'm not too worried about this group. Angry, yes, but not worried. Within ten years, the students at the schools I clean will have enough technology practice to take Dilbert's career away in a heartbeat. I don't know what Java is, but I bet it will be obsolete in a few months, just like their jobs.

Guidance counselors? Fuck them too. These counselors think every kid has been groped by Uncle Dean at a family pool party. Here's a tidbit of knowledge for you: guidance counselors have the highest rate of prescription drug usage of anyone working within the public school systems. Do you know why? Because they talk about feelings all day. They need something to numb the pain of hearing how little Mikey hates doing homework. Or how little Jinny doesn't want to be a hairdresser when she grows up.

When did a guidance counselor ever tell you a goddamned thing worth remembering? I can't remember a thing any guidance counselor ever told me in middle school, high school, or college. They're fucking useless! They might have a higher degree than teachers, but they can't really do anything for your child. If a kid says he wants to murder his eighth-grade class, the counselor hits the Red Flag button. They call the cops and let a real professional handle the situation. All a counselor does is pick out the deranged students and rat them out to the police. A therapist snitch is a better term than a guidance counselor.

A school nurse? A boo-boo kisser, you mean. Stick out your tongue and put this thermometer under it. And slap a Band-Aid on it if it bleeds. Bang. I just did a school nurse's job. Just think, a school nurse probably has less education than the local clinic nurse. Anything above their pay grade, like the flu or measles, and they call the EMTs or have the kids' parents pick them up. You don't even want to know how much a school nurse gets paid to do that job. It's ridiculously high.

How about a school lunch lady? A culinary artist's worthy of molding government cheese into something hallway edible. Have you seen what schools are serving your kids nowadays? I'd put more faith in hospital food or the stuff we send to third world countries as refuge aid. Little Jeffie's art project looks better than the slop that comes out of a school lunchroom today.

Now we've discussed most of the staff, I think it's time you meet my other bosses: the support staff. In other words, anyone else who is not a teacher, principal, or administration or abovementioned stooge. This includes substitute teachers who were smart enough to pass community college but not big-boy school. The list also has people like crossing guards, bus drivers, secretaries, delivery guys, mailmen, any child's parent, and/or voters. Pretty much any asswipe who enters a school thinks they can boss the janitor around. Just because I wear Dickies and carry a set of keys doesn't make me your bitch.

If you look at the whole thing like this, it puts everything into perspective. Since the janitor is best known for cleaning up shit on a regular basis, it would seem almost fitting to get all the shit once it stops rolling downhill. There's nowhere else for all that dung to go except the bottom, so we get used to being crapped on each day. That's where I come in. When a teacher floods the school because they broke a toilet, I'm here to save the day. When an administrator wants his desk moved a quarter inch to the right, I'm there with a helping hand. I'm the poop man. I clean up all the shit from the shitheads above me.

Years ago, we had a meeting for the sole purpose of telling us where we fall on the ladder of success. All the departments sent a few emissaries to take notes, and since I'm one of the only janitors who can spell his name, the boss sent me. So there I was, a flag bearer for Team Dirt sitting next to the rest of the departments.

The schmuck giving the PowerPoint presentation started rambling on about how each of us played an important role in the wheel of progress. "Each one of you makes this system run…" I lost interest three minutes into his speech until he had trouble loading the

PowerPoint. Here's a guy who makes around 140,000 dollars a year and he can't get a simple PowerPoint to work. After a minute or two of futzing with the projector, the tech guy looked at him and said, "Is it plugged in?"

So the Mexican standoff began: Dilbert from the tech department sitting in his chair watching the presenter sweat it out. The whole time, the administrators watched Dilbert not doing his job. These two were exchanging words, nice, office-lingo words like "Did you try rebooting the program?"

I was smack dab in the middle losing patience with each passing moment. Finally, after seeing an opportunity to make both of them look like dummies, I went over to the laptop and fixed the problem. As I walked back to my seat, I felt the eyes watching me. Pure silence as both Dilbert and presenter guy stared at me in disbelief. Sure, they should have known how to fix the problem, or maybe they didn't feel like fixing it. Just another example of big paychecks, little ambition.

I sat down to see all these lovely faces looking at me as if they just found the cure for cancer. "Holy shit, the janitor knows how to use a computer!"

Nonetheless, the slideshow started. Random happy-faced people smiling in the workplace with words like *teamwork* and *helpful* being either highlighted or italicized. Whoever made this PowerPoint probably makes around ninety thousand dollars a year and produced the same quality slideshow sixth graders make for a book report.

I took two things away from this meeting: One, I hate everybody I work with. And two, I was the only one in the room who knew exactly where I fell in the food chain. I was the very last link of that chain, and every department around me made me aware of that fact. From the dickhead administrators all the way down, I was, indeed, the last stop on the Fuckup Express.

Now, I know what I was getting into when I signed up for this gig. I know I'm the butt of everyone's jokes, including little kids who throw pencils at me as I walk by. But to know each department you work with thinks you're handicapped is unacceptable.

It kills me to know this each time I walk into work. I have more of an education than a vast majority of the people I work under.

My college degrees actually came from *real* colleges, not some online flunkies school. I'm extremely overqualified and underpaid. Yet I take directions from people who couldn't navigate their way out of a wet paper bag.

I've come to enjoy my shit existence, as morbid as it sounds. You know exactly what you're getting with shit. No two thoughts about it. If it smells like shit and looks like shit, well, it is what it is.

Chapter 4

SuperMop Tyrell Jones

Throughout my career as a janitor, I have seen various personalities. Many of whom wish not to be named in my journal entries. One guy, whom I spent many years with swinging a mop, said it was okay to use his likeness in print. In fact, he told me specifically if I didn't use him as a lead character, he'd whoop my sorry white ass for not using a prolific personality such as his. I'm referring to the one, the only Tyrell Jones.

I'd heard of this guy soon after I got the job but didn't meet him until a staff in-service day. Basically, when your kids get off from school for a holiday, the janitors come in to learn about chemicals. They can't just give us the fucking day off like teachers and bus drivers. We have to sit in a little auditorium and stare at cleaning supplies all day. The seats are made for little kids, yet the bosses expect grown adults to be comfortable for hours on end.

Anyway, I took a seat all the way in the back so I could use my iPod and fall asleep. That's right, an iPod. Think about how long ago it was when people used iPods instead of using their phones to listen to music. That's how long ago it was when I met Tyrell. I never got a chance to put my headphones on, though. Seconds after I sat down, in walks Tyrell, with his arms extended toward the ceiling. He was singing The Temptations' "Just My Imagination," waiting for the crowd to chime in. When they didn't sing back, he stopped, put his arms down, and said, "Fuck all, y'all squares. I'll sing it myself!"

Who the hell was this black dude singing his ass off? And why did he look like a pimp, belting out a doo-wop song? At the time,

I was new myself, not yet accustomed to the ways of the janitoring world. So I glanced around to gauge everyone's reaction.

Most people, including the stuffy bosses, shook their heads or rolled their eyes. A slow grumble and murmurs came from the rest of the workers.

I'd been told about Tyrell. How he was a nutjob, he was crazy as hell, blah, blah, blah. "You'll never seen anyone else like him at the meeting!" someone told me. Sure enough, he was one of a kind, all right.

He looked exactly like everyone said he would: think of a fifty-year-old Urkel from the hood, complete with Gucci glasses and a pimp limp. He sauntered into the auditorium wearing old-school white pants with a fake Rolex and a straight-brimmed Yankees hat. His shoes were laced up Air Jordans with the tag still on them. If he had dreads, he could have passed for an old Rick James stunt double. But he was bald as hell under his hat. Like a black Kojak.

Tyrell said hello to the whole group and swaggered in. "The king is back, y'all! Better give it up for yours truly!" Man, was he loud! His soprano voice pierced right through you. Judging by his attitude and attire, I was a little anxious to see what he was like in person. I figured he was either an asshole or a barrel of fun.

Tyrell walked over to the cookie tray next to the coffee urn, so I decided to walk over to grab a cup as well. Just before I filled the cup, Tyrell stopped humming to himself and stared at me. He was taken aback for a second, slowly eyeing me up as if I had stolen his car.

"Uh... uh... who is you?" he said as if he knew me from somewhere. "Dig this man, I know you. You used to live down on Jamaica Boulevard in Brick City, right?" He shook his finger at me like he was an old man trying to discipline his dog for shitting on the carpet.

"No... no. We've never met. I work over at—"

"Yeah, yeah. I know you! You that sucker who sold me a broken Zippo at the flea market. Hey, man! You owe me ten bucks. That shit don't work!"

My first impressions were a bit rocky. I was defensive for a minute trying to decide what to say next. What was up with his voice? Was he being serious with me? I couldn't tell at first. Turns out, he was nuttier than a holiday fruitcake, which I admit is a line I stole from him.

"I never sold you a Zippo," I said. "I think you have me confused with someone else."

"Nah, man. I know you, man! You didn't have that goofy-ass beard back then, but I remember you. Hey, dig this… didn't you used to work the train yard at Penn Station? Whatchu doin' working here?"

I started to tell him who I was just as his cellphone went off. I was interrupted by the sweet sounds of Bobby Brown as he sang "It's My Prerogative," to which Tyrell put his left hand up with a smile on his face. "Oops, there it goes again. Must be one of my girlfriends calling for some after-hours lovin'! I got to take this, man. I got these females waiting on me!"

Weirdest first impression ever. It boggled my mind how this dude talked; the way he held himself was ridiculous. He was so confident and free with his speaking. He didn't give two shits about anything job related. I'll admit, most of what people said was true about Tyrell: he was vulgar, bitterly honest, and unruly. Just the type of person I could relate to.

As I finished filling my coffee cup, Tyrell was talking loudly into his phone about some late-night rendezvous with a lady. He didn't care who was listening about how he was "goin' to slide them panties off like a champ." A few women in the audience were listening to Tyrell with prissy smirks on their faces. Most of the men were smiling or laughing, except the bosses. They were eyeballing him something fierce. Since I was standing next to Tyrell, I was guilty by association. Great way to make a first impression of my own. Everyone who watched Tyrell thought I was his sidekick, a portly fellow with the same lack of respect for the job. Not a good way to start off my career.

Later after his explicit phone conversation was over, Tyrell bounced over to an empty seat in the front row, sat down with a plate full of stale oatmeal cookies, and proceeded to chew loudly. I had known the guy for thirty seconds and surmised he had all the attributes of a new best friend. I never forgot that day. I worked with the guy for eighteen years on the job, and I still smile when I think our first conversation. He accused me of selling him for a broken lighter, insulted me, then simply walked away after having phone sex in front of the entire department. Who does that?

Tyrell had a way about him that no one can explain, not even Tyrell. For all my years pushing a janitor cart, I've never met some-one even remotely like Tyrell. All the shit he did, and got away with, could only have come from him. The situations, the awkward con-versations with coworkers. Picture a *Seinfeld* episode where Jerry is replaced by Homie the Clown, and you've got a day in the life of Tyrell.

I asked a coworker about Tyrell, and he started cracking up. My friend, who helped get me the job, knew everything about everyone. He was my unofficial information officer / nosy Rosy. "Why do you want to know about *that* weirdo?" he said. "You really want to know about that crackpot?"

A few minutes later, I knew all about Tyrell and his illustrious career as a school janitor. He started back in the day when the school district was hiring full-time employees for a building boom. The dis-trict needed a new crew to fill custodial positions, so they hastily hired as many applicants as they could. Pretty much anyone with the ability to hold a mop. The bosses didn't research if Tyrell could do anything other than hold the mop. They assumed since it's not open-heart surgery that anyone with half a brain can clean toilets.

The truth was, Tyrell was the worst janitor who ever strapped on a pair of coveralls. Everything he did was the exact opposite of what a normal person should do. He couldn't clean to save his life. Not that he gave a shit, but still. Everything he touched somehow became worse after he touched it. The floors were always sticky like flypaper. If you walked down a hallway he "cleaned," your shoes made a funny squeaking noise. You could write your name in the dust of any classroom he worked in. His bathrooms smelled like someone just pissed all over the place. Everywhere Tyrell worked, you could see baby sagebrush blowing down the hall like an abandoned Wild West town.

All Tyrell did was bullshit all day long to whomever would be dumb enough to listen. If you followed him during a standard work shift, you would see an older black man without a care in the world, chatting up a storm about nonsense. A typical janitor does things like empty a garbage can or sweep a floor. Not Tyrell. His version of throwing out trash encompassed him waltzing in and out of rooms, with his cell phone on his ear, talking to some random floozy. Sometimes as he walked, he picked up a garbage can to dump it into a larger garbage can. Not all the time, though. If he was deep in conversation about some sexual position, he'd bypass entire rooms without so much as looking in them.

I'm sure you've seen a janitor mop a floor before. It doesn't seem too difficult, does it? Perhaps a man with only one arm can achieve this task, if need be. Tyrell had very poor mopping technique. Instead of a side-to-side motion, Tyrell would drag his soaking-wet mop behind him, again with one hand on his phone, texting or sexting with some broad. God forbid he put the phone down for a few seconds to properly do the tasks at hand. You know, the job he was getting paid to do?

If someone interrupted Tyrell while he was on the phone, he'd nod dramatically while scooting past them. Eyes closed and all, still talking away on his phone. That was his version of someone miming the jerk-off motion. If they continued to bother him, Tyrell would put the phone to his chest and say, "I'm on the goddamned phone, sucka! Can't you see that! I'm busy, bitch!" He said this to people like teachers, principals, bosses, you name it. He didn't give two fucks about it either.

Most school janitors do a decent job cleaning. They scrub walls and desks to mirrorlike perfection. Tyrell, on the other hand, didn't take his job that seriously. "If they don't like the way I mop dis floor, then let them hire some other asshole to replace me. Please… I'd love to see someone do what I do for the money I does it for!"

It is a fact Tyrell had the worst track record of any janitor ever in this district. He has the most complaints, the most safety violations, the most sick days off (not including workman's comp.), and the most enemies of any employee. Not to mention his utter and total lack of respect for anyone who works "above him." Anyone not a janitor in a school district is technically your boss. Even the part-time lunch ladies can order you around if they so desire. My buddy Tyrell thinks that's bullshit. "Let me tell you something, Jack!" (That's what he called everyone, even women.) "If you think I'ma let you tell Tyrell how to do his job, you fucking crazy. Ain't nobody tellin' Tyrell how to work!"

I forgot to mention he loved to talk in the third person. It got confusing from time to time, but you'd get used to it.

Our bosses, didn't know what to do with Tyrell. When the bosses finally believed they had enough evidence to fire him, he came back with a marvelous story or defense. One time two bosses had photos of Tyrell's work performance, or lack thereof. Tyrell took one look at the photos and said, "You kiddin' me, right? How you gonna take pictures of some dirty-ass floors and try to pin it on me? Do you have a reference point in these pictures? How do I know that you ain't take them pictures at another school or even printed that shit off the internet?"

He did have a good point. Two days later the dismayed bosses came back with more photos, this time with reference points in the background. Tyrell's inner lawyer came out once again. "Let me get this straight… you think a couple painted walls in the background is enough to get rid of me? Mothafucka, please! You so stupid 'cause these pictures don't have a time stamp on them. They could be from six years ago, for all I know! Next time, try taking the picture with today's newspaper in the corner."

And just like that, the bosses were roadblocked yet again. It turns out the union had to agree with Tyrell on most of the issues. Years ago, a teacher filed a complaint saying Tyrell called her a hoe. "Do you mean to tell me this woman is claiming I called her a derogatory comment? Well, where's the proof? Does she have a witness to said story or maybe a signed affidavit from any witnesses? Or does she have a video or audio clip proving I said such atrocities?"

Tyrell turned many issues away with simple logic. Most of the time he talked as though he never completed the eighth grade. When it came to defending himself, he had a PhD in self-preservation. "I am shocked and appalled this woman would defame my character this way! I have half a mind to press slander charges!"

Most of the time it wasn't worth it to go after Tyrell. He gave new meaning to the term *slick*. To be honest, the bosses we had in the board of education weren't too bright themselves. On some occasions, a few administrators gained enough courage to try for Tyrell's termination. Whenever the heat got too much for Tyrell, he started playing his ultimate trump card. "Here we go again," said Tyrell. "A few *white men* coming after the black guy! I have rights in today's America, gentlemen. If you continue to harass me about my work performance, I will be forced to call my attorney… and the Reverend Jesse Jackson!" As for the union, they were so afraid of being sued they didn't get involved. They knew when to back off and let administration take the fall.

One hard-assed administrator tried with all his might to get Tyrell fired. It didn't end so well for Mr. Bossman. Tyrell was fired on a Friday evening for poor work performance. That Monday morning, the protestors showed up. The first time Tyrell called the NAACP, he had protestors marching in front of the board office waving signs and singing. Right in front of the crowd, with a megaphone, was Tyrell himself, leading the charge. "What do we want? Equality! When do we want it? Now!" Newspaper reporters, TV news vans, civil rights activists, and even some hippies showed up in Tyrell's honor. Within hours, he had his job back and an apology from administration. As for Mr. Bossman? He left two weeks later to work at another district.

You should've seen the reception for Tyrell when he got his job back. "Oh, my brothas and sistas… thank you so much for your support!" There was Tyrell on the local evening news standing at a podium, blowing kisses to the crowd. "I put my faith in the system, and my faith has been restored!" Tyrell was a showman when he needed to be. Most of the time, he weaseled out of work by being an excellent strategist. "Five steps ahead, my young, bearded friend," Tyrell would say to me, all while holding up his right hand to show his five fingers wiggling in the air. "Five steps ahead of anything these stupid, punk-assed, stiff, white-collared mothafuckers can throw at me!"

He might have been ignorant, lazy, vile, and outspoken, but had balls the size of casaba melons. That's why I liked him. "I called the NAACP, the AFL-CIO, the Teamsters, the *Daily News*, the *New York Times*, Channel 7 News, and my friends in Newark to help get the word out," he later told me. "Fuck these racist-ass bitches! Goddamn honkies!"

I reminded Tyrell I was indeed a honky myself. "That's okay, baby. I won't hold it against you! You all right, anyway. You not a honky to me."

That was the kind of relationship I had with him. We didn't see color; we saw compatriots working a job we despised, united in our fight against the board of ed. He was the hood-raised ebony to my trailer-park-grown ivory.

During the whole time with Tyrell, I amassed a volume of stories, tales, adventures, and mishaps most writers can only salivate over. Like the time Tyrell took a year off from work, stating he was going back to college to finish his degree in horticulture. First off, I don't think he graduated high school. But anyway, Tyrell returned to work, sans degree. But he did have a story and a brand-new Audi.

I asked what happened to his degree in horticulture. "Yeah, I didn't do that shit," said Tyrell. "I was helping my cousin sell weed in Paterson for six months. I messed with some plants now. Yeah, man… we had all sorts of primo shit growing. Made mad loot all the way. Then shit went sour, and Tyrell had to lay low for a little while." Technically, he was working in horticulture, just not on a collegiate level. "My cuz and I split the profits, bought me that new sports car over there caaaaaassshhh money."

Everyone had their own personal Tyrell story, many of which weren't too flattering. One of the maintenance guys said Tyrell had been stealing his tools piece by piece. Tyrell had apparently started with the smaller items and progressed to larger battery-operated tools over the course of a few weeks.

"That son of a bitch stole my wrenches! I know it's him. You wait until I catch his thieving ass!" Tyrell denied the allegations, of course. Years later in conversation, I asked him if he really stole the guy's tools. "Fuck yeah I took 'em," said Tyrell. "I traded with the super in my apartment building for a new dishwasher. That asshole maintenance guy don't need all them tools. How many fucking screwdrivers do you need anyway?" I can picture Tyrell stashing the power drill and Sawzall in his trash can to drop off to his car when no one was looking. Tyrell was crooked, but bitterly honest too.

A bus driver once told me Tyrell asked her if she was good at driving stick shift. "Yeah, I know Tyrell. That sick fuck asked me if I could play with his knob and throw his engine into gear. Dirty prick."

He loved to talk about ladies, though. If my math is correct, Tyrell must've had sex with over one thousand women, many of whom still call out his name in the middle of the night. "I'm tellin' you, I got several hundred satisfied women who still sweat when they hear the name Tasty Tyrell!"

The bosses told him several times not to talk to coworkers inappropriately, but he never listened. All he did was nod his head with his mouth open and say "Huh" real loud. The sound of him saying "Huh" resembled a goose honking. It was a bold, ear-scratching bellow he uttered when he was done listening to someone. A true fuck-off, conversation-ending phrase. Tyrell said he was hard of hearing when asked why he kept interrupting a boss during conversation.

Tyrell started working only a few years before I came to work here. He had been transferred about seven times within the first three years of working. That's when I got to work with him. Management transferred him to my building a few months after we first met. I remember when the night-shift boss at my building found out Tyrell was our next crew member.

"If you transfer that crazy bastard to this school, I swear to Christ Almighty I'll quit!" This guy was flipping out, calling people, urging them not to move Tyrell. "How dare you put me in this situation? That guy is a walking clusterfuck and you know it. You put him here, and I'm out!"

Tyrell made his migration anyway, and they moved the night boss to another building. Within hours of Tyrell coming to my post, I knew he was going to be my next buddy. We got along so well after he finally realized I wasn't the guy that sold him a Zippo.

I knew he was a fuckup soon after we started working. Yet somehow, I liked him. He had a way about him words can't describe. He was always telling me how he knew he fucked up in life, but he couldn't change the past. "Don't do what I did, man. You never wanna steal TVs to sell for crack. They always get you in the end."

I'm not completely sure who they are, so I'll just have to say either a drug dealer or the man.

Even though we came from different eras and backgrounds, he had a lasting impact on me. Tyrell spent most of his childhood in and out of foster care. He told me this in depth over our lunch hour each day. In fact, I can recall multiple days where we ate lunch for hours chatting about everything. I guess Tyrell just loved to talk and I enjoyed listening.

Tyrell had grown up in the projects of Newark, Brick City as he called it. During his younger years, Tyrell got into selling and using crack through high school. "Yeah, man, my first job wasn't flipping burgers at McDonald's. Nope. I stood on the corner near this old bodega slinging rocks." After being locked up for a few smaller charges, Tyrell found a steady gig as a security guard at a halfway house. He spent almost ten years being clean until he started using again, which cost him his job and pension.

You would think given his bad work ethic, lack of respect for authority, and all-around defiance, he would have been axed years ago. But then again, the normal rules of physics don't apply here. Slackers get rewarded, while hardworking people get shit on. Like the slippery eel, Tyrell always got away, even when his number was up several times over. He did the dumbest shit while working, sometimes just to fuck with people. While mopping, he would forget to put out a Wet Floor sign. Seconds later, a teacher would bust their ass and sue the district for big bucks. Instead of firing him, management would recommend he take classes to learn the basics of workplace safety. Weeks later, Tyrell would report the district to the state for not properly training him when he was hired. "I think they didn't train me on purpose," he said. "Maybe it's because *I'm black* and they don't want a *black man* to be safe while on the job!"

What made Tyrell so famous was his lack of common sense. It's a simple rule that if you see something dirty, you clean it up. I mean, that's the job. It's not like we work in a library and reshelf books all day. For those who don't know the standard operating procedure of a janitor, we do three things: take out garbage, sweep floors, and clean bathrooms. Apart from a few other subtleties, that's what janitoring is all about. I don't think your average person needs to be trained as a janitor. Not according to Tyrell, though. He made the bosses retrain him every six months. He stated because of a learning disability, he never fully grasped the concept of mopping. "You mean, Mr. Boss, I have to move the mop to the left, to the right, then *back* to the left again? That sounds awfully complicated to me."

Tyrell would contemplate each move made. Did he really want to bend over to pick up that piece of paper? Probably not. It depended on what mood he was in. If he had sex earlier that day or drank a few 99 Bananas Schnapps on lunch, chances are that paper would stay there until the sun froze. Same went for garbage overflowing in the teachers' lounge or shit on a toilet bowl.

Most people were offended after speaking with him for extended amounts of time. He was very blunt and spoke his mind to whoever was listening. One time he got transferred because of a lewd con- versation with one of the cafeteria aides. He told a Dominican girl she had the fattest ass he had ever seen. She didn't speak very much English, but she knew what "Why don't you break me off a piece of that booty?" meant. Another time he threatened to smack a gym teacher in the parking lot. The whole fight revolved around who had the better jump shot, Jordan or LeBron. Tyrell, being old-school, of course, went with Jordan. When the teacher said LeBron was the all- time greatest, Tyrell went bonkers. "Is you crazy or just plain stupid! I ought to knock some sense into your lopsided dome!"

Tyrell had no filter. He said whatever he felt whenever the thought popped into his head. He once told a coworker to eat his ass at a company picnic. I almost spit out my potato salad when I heard it. He caused a scene near the grill, Tyrell yelling about who cut whom in the hot dog line. It escalated into a pushing match where the unlucky coworker was shoved onto a table, right into a big bowl of baked beans. Like most infractions in Tyrell's life, it eventually ended in a full-on riot. "I'll smash this mothafuckin' Fanta over yo head if you take another step, Jack!"

According to Tyrell, he was the only person on the job who had spent time running the streets. "I'm the only true thug in this place," he said numerous times. "Not one of these fools has been in the trenches of life, you feel me?" His stories about his past were outrageous. Jesus Christ, this guy could spin some tales! He once told me he met James Brown in Atlantic City playing craps. Tyrell said he asked Mr. Brown, the Godfather of Soul, if he could be his hype man. "James told me himself he wanted me on his payroll. Next thing I know, his ugly-assed bodyguard started pushin' up on me. That's when I had to get real on his ass and shove that goofy fuck to the ground. Then security came, next the cops. In a matter of minutes, man, I had the whole Atlantic City Police Force shutting down the Showboat Casino!"

Tyrell also insisted he had sex with Mariah Carey on the Sky Ride at Six Flags Great Adventure. He elaborated on his rendezvous with the pop star: "She told me her boyfriend was a real ass clown, ya know. I remember, as a matter of fact, that our sweet love session was when she was filming that *Fantasy* video, where she was on that roller coaster and shit. So there we was, just a rockin' that little red box back and forth, to and fro, in the air. Sheeeeeeit… I'm lucky to be standing here right now tellin' you this because I don't know how we didn't shake the bitch off the high-wire!"

I was fascinated by his choice in apparel. Even though we're supposed to wear a uniform, Tyrell insisted on wearing his own stylish clothing. He had Roca Wear, Tommy Hilfiger, Ecko, FUBU, Coogi, Nike, Under Amour, and Puma shirts, pants, socks, and underwear. Some days he wore so many different colors he looked like a ghetto rodeo clown. Then came the shoes. He told me he got all his shoes on discount. "When you this good-lookin', your feet need to represent," said Tyrell. "They got to be fresh, you know what I'm sayin'?" I'm not sure why anyone would wear a 250-dollar pair of shoes to scrub toilets, but to each their own. One day he came to work on a Friday wearing these ridiculous shoes. I'm talking absurd.

I asked him what the deal was with his serious sneaks.

"Are those alligator shoes, Tyrell?" He shot me a look as if I just questioned his entire existence.

"Pa-lease! Those shits are haggard compared to my shoes, baby." Tyrell showcased his feet like a fashion show, detailing each inch as if he was one of Bob Barker's Beauties. "These are stingray, my brotha. You ain't never seen no kicks like these! I bought these off one of my supersecret connections in the city. Costed me a week's pay too. I'm meeting a very special lady tonight after work, and these bad boys will send her senses into overdrive, know what I mean?"

What do you say to a man who spends six hundred bucks on a pair of shoes for one date? He proceeded to do a little dance number next to his janitor cart, pulling his mop ever so close to his face. You have to picture a fifty-three-year-old man shaking his legs wildly in a school hallway, gyrating inches away from a filthy mop. In exotic fish-skinned dress shoes, no less.

"That's right, sweetie pie," Tyrell said while addressing the mop. "I'ma dance you right out those panties and shake your tree loose!" Tyrell dipped the mop as if he magically transformed into a sexy Latin ballroom dancer. He stopped just as he was about to plant a kiss on the piss-soaked mop and smiled up at me. "Tyrell know how to make them panties soppin' wet. Like eating biscuits and gravy, baby!"

Some days he looked more like a butler than a school janitor. Those were the special once-a-week occasions when Tyrell took a lady out on the town. Most of the time, when he didn't have a date or a drug deal to complete, he dressed like someone headed to a 50 Cent concert. Each day he had some type of jewelry on to match his eccentric clothing. I've never owned a Movado watch, but if I did, I sure as hell wouldn't stick it in a toilet to pull out a clog. His diamond earrings, or icy spotlights as he called them, made him look like a strung-out Deion Sanders from his rap video days.

This guy had a stellar hat collection to accentuate his thug-in-spired ensembles. One day, he would come in with a purple-and-yellow Lakers hat followed by a camouflaged New York Giants hat the next. On special days like holidays or Fridays, Tyrell would wear an old-style chimney sweep hat or something like the Irish immigrants used to wear working the docks back in the 1920s. I was waiting for him to wear a sombrero one day, but it never happened.

Regardless of his age and his looks, Tyrell always thought he was the bomb diggity. Each week his date card was maxed out, filled with an infinite line of women who all needed their Tyrell fix. He once claimed his address book (dubbed the Pussy Portfolio) held over four hundred numbers from his past exploits. In the last ten years, he must've had at least one hundred different ladies show up at work. To be honest, I thought he was goofier than hell. He had that high-pitched voice combined with a Southern drawl worthy of a William Faulkner novel. I guess women like that sort of thing. Maybe he makes them laugh or perhaps he studied the *Kama Sutra* thoroughly. I gave up trying to figure out his sexual secrets years ago.

Problem was, Tyrell was addicted to sex. He always said he replaced the crack in his life with another type of crack. "Yeaaaaah, baby, I gave up the glass dick. Now I smoke ass and pussy, ya heard me?" I used to joke with him when he brought a hideous female to work. He'd only shrug his shoulders, winking at me as he left for the night. "Well... sometimes you bite the bullet and let that hood rat eat some cheese," he'd say.

One thing's for sure, he always talked about sex to whomever would bend an ear. It's not appropriate workplace speech, especially in a school, but Tyrell spoke like he was fluent in snatch. Whenever teachers would stay late to grade papers, he would turn on soul music: Marvin Gaye, Luther Vandross, Teddy Pendergrass, etc. He was convinced each female teacher wanted to sleep with him. "Oh shit, baby!" Tyrell would yell down the hallway when a special song came on. "Tyrell gonna let the tiger loose on some of y'all bookworms!"

I was there the last few months when he really started to mess up on the job. And I mean, like, completely fuck up. Something tells me the bosses finally used their brains to set him up. It was only a matter of time until they had enough dirt on him. In the last six months Tyrell worked, he must have had eight union meetings, all with photos, videos, and signed grievances against him. Finally, after a few suspensions, the head boss came to take his keys on a Friday, just before he was ready to head out on a date with some skeezer. As a janitor, when someone takes your keys, it's like the pink slip. Tyrell took his walk of shame out to his car, and I never saw him again. Eighteen years with the guy, and he walks out on me without saying goodbye. I tried his phone, his house phone, nothing. My guess was he was too ashamed to be done in. Perhaps it was just time for him to go.

I was extremely sad when they shit-canned him. How could I not? The man was a legend among janitors. The truly wicked Tyrell Jones and all his exploits can never be forgotten. After you work with someone for almost two decades, you get to know them as a person, not just another coworker. To me, I didn't particularly like many of my coworkers. They either infuriated me or confused me. No gray area between us cleaners of the night. Tyrell was different. He was the only coworker I would consider a close friend, not just some dude you help cleaned floors with.

Tyrell taught me a lot about his past life in Newark, and being from a small trailer park in South Jersey, I learned a hell of a lot about not believing in stereotypes. I had spent much of my life always being afraid of places and people like Tyrell. And yes, I do mean the hood and black people, in general. I'm not racist. It's just I didn't feel comfortable in big cities and I lived a sheltered life in my little neighborhood. But after spending time with Tyrell, I had gotten over my phobias to know a truly amazing man. Someone whom I considered better than what the gossipers labeled him as.

We had talked about so many different things over the years, but I'll never forget one of our first conversations:

"So dig this, man, why is you cleaning schools for a living? You done some time back in the day too?" said Tyrell.

"Nah. I just spent too many years in college and I can't find a job," I said. "I got this job because it was flexible around my classes, and after I graduated, I couldn't find anything steady."

"What you go to school for? You look like you would be some sort of accountant or businessman."

"I went to school for marine biology originally."

"What the fuck? You wanna talk to Flipper and shit? You think you some sort of Jack Cousteau or something?" I started to laugh. Tyrell had a way of putting life into perspective, and he knew how to get his point across.

"Of course, I do!" I said. "That's what I love in life, but it doesn't pay the bills. Most of the jobs are for minimum wage, feeding seals at aquariums. I figured I'd just stick it out here and collect a pension. I got a ton of student loans coming in, so I need this job."

"I heard that, man. I got bills out the ass with these credit cards maxed out. They bleed me dry each fucking month. Shit, I might need a second job just to pay for taking the ladies out on the town." Tyrell looked at me with a grin. "So that's what you love, huh? Playing with fishes?"

"Yes, I do, Tyrell. It's my passion, my dream."

"Damn...," said Tyrell. "That's deep, my brotha."

"What do you love, Tyrell? What are your dreams?" I said. He sat there for a few seconds, tilting his head upward pondering my questions.

"Welp," he said. "I love crack and pussy. They got college degrees for that?" For once, Tyrell was serious.

"I don't think so," I said. A full smile came across my face as I tried not to laugh my ass off. Only Tyrell would say something like that and mean it.

"Oh, well, back to clean these here fucking toilets," said Tyrell. Then he started giggling. The kind of gut busting giggle you get once in a blue moon.

"What?" I said. "What are you laughing at?"

"Listen here, man... you ever find any sea creatures in the toilet bowls at work?"

No, Tyrell. I can't say that I have.

Chapter 5

Your Tax Dollars Hard at Work!

Y ou want to know why your property taxes are so high? Take one look at the defunct public school system, and you've got your answer. Here's the scoop on why taxes are off the charts. A majority of your tax dollars don't go to education of students. It goes to fat cat raises and political endorsements of the assholes at the top of the list. Much like the government, school boards take care of the head cheeses by giving them a ridiculous salary. Why in God's green earth does a school principal have to make 130,000 for 10 months work? In turn, why are those jerks further up the trough like administrators making 250,000 a year? A typical head honcho in this school system makes around 10,000 dollars every 2 weeks. Think about it. You can buy a gently used Chevy Malibu for 10,000 dollars. You get to keep the car forever, not just borrow it for two weeks.

A damn good hooker would rock your world for 10,000, and I can guarantee you'd get more bang for your buck with the prostitute. To be fair, a school administrator fucks the taxpayers all year round for their salary, so I guess you get more value with a superintendent than with a moderately priced call girl. Each time the school board "has a meeting," it really means "spread the ass cheeks of the Joe Public just a little further apart." If the taxpayer knew exactly where their taxes went, they'd shit a brick. A very small portion of a school tax budget goes directly to the students' well-being. Something like 12 percent of all that tax budget goes to things like new books or pencils. The rest goes to administrative costs like high balls on the golf course or paying lawyers to defend them and their cronies.

The numbers vary across the country, but in my neck of the woods, 70 percent of tax dollars go toward public schools. Of that money, 90 percent of those taxed dollars go toward paying for educational expenses. You know, vital things like 100 dollars' worth of Italian pastries for a supervisors' meeting. I don't know about you, but I can't function unless I eat seven chocolate chip cannoli. Other important things like multiple computer training classes for members of administration because they don't know how to use a laptop. A kindergartener knows how to use an iPhone. Why doesn't a school superintendent? If I'm not mistaken, being proficient in all forms of technology was a requirement, yet two bosses still can't answer emails on their smartphone.

That's not counting behind closed-doors deals that taxpayers are oblivious to. All these so-called school improvement projects are by far the worst. Years ago, one of the schools needed a new roof because the old one rotted away. Each time it rained, the roof would leak, causing thousands of dollars in damages to the stuff directly under the roof. Things like computers, furniture, and almost an entire library of books were ruined.

Instead of fixing it all at once, the board decided to patch it up as need be. So they got new carpeting, new books, and everything else to replace the old stuff you could ring out like a sponge. The masterminds on the school board went with some fly-by-night roofing company who botched the roof repair. A week later, after repairs were complete, the roof collapsed from being completely saturated. Thank the heavens no one was under it when it fell. Guess what happened to all those new books they just replaced? Yup. The taxpayers had to fork over twice the amount of money to replace the same items purchased earlier. In the end, the board of ed. wrote it off as faulty maintenance. They fired a bunch of full-time janitors to offset their losses.

It would blow your mind if you knew how much money a board of education spends on tax writes off per year. Anything and everything can be written off if it's deemed necessary for educational purposes, which, oddly enough, never goes to the progression of students. The board of ed. paid $360 in parking tickets because a vice principal parked in a handicapped spot three days in a row. He wasn't disabled, unless you count utter stupidity and arrogance. When asked why he parked in a clearly handicapped spot, he told the board his normal parking spot was having the lines painted on it. Instead of simply parking a few spaces further from the front door, this numbskull thought to himself, "Well, why should I have to take a few extra steps? I don't see anyone in a wheelchair who needs this spot at the moment."

We had one brazen administrator order a full-body electric shiatsu massage chair because she complained her job was too stressful. "I need something to take out the kinks in my neck due to the amount of workload I have." Are you fucking serious—1,300 dollars for a leather recliner to rub your spine? Jesus, this thing was gorgeous, I'll give her that, but come on! I highly doubt any town taxpayer would approve of this purchase. Especially when a good number of parents in the district lost their jobs in the recession and are on a fixed income. In one of the most flagrant misuses of power I've ever seen, the board of ed. hid the purchase, saying it was for new curriculum books. Fact is, these new books they say they purchased were hidden in a spare room for three years, still with plastic wrap on them. I know this because my boss had me take the books out of storage and I had to move the new chair into this twat's office on the same day.

Principals also destroy a school budget for buying the dumbest shit. One guy in my building gets paid to walk around and evaluate the decor. This dude should be handing out detention slips, not playing interior decorator. On most school days, you can find him reviewing paint splotches or arranging his desk to make the room flow better. "I need my file cabinet to match the shelves, and ultimately I'd like to get bamboo blinds to really set the room up perfectly." School principals are supposed to be focused on important things such as standardized tests. Not Bob Villa over here. All he cares about is getting his office to look like something out of *Better Homes and Gardens*. You should see him on back-to-school night. It's like some half-assed masquerade ball from hell. "The new Hopi pottery display case has to have more lighting on it. Can we get some antique lamps and hang them from the ceiling?"

I personally have thrown away thousands of books. I didn't want to because I know how many school districts are dying for book donations. But once the boss man says "Chuck it," it's time to trash it. One summer, my coworkers and I threw away an entire dumpster full of new and slightly used books. Brand-new history books that were never opened! These books were probably three years old, at most. We were told to throw them out at night so no one would see the school flushing money right down the drain. It backfired on them in the end because the dump truck broke its hydraulic lift trying to pick up the dumpster in the morning. Quite a few parents asked questions at the next board meeting as to why a school was throwing away pallets full of unused books. As usual, they told the public it was because the books were outdated or were damaged. I'm pretty sure a book on the American revolution hasn't changed for over 230 years, but who am I to judge?

These jackass teachers waste just as much as the bigwigs. Do you know how many keyboard keys I've swept up from juggled laptops? A bunch. Every time they drop their laptop, I can play Scrabble with the remains. It racks up 1,100 bucks of loss with each oops. One of the storage rooms in a smaller elementary school has about 700 of them just sitting in boxes waiting to be recycled—700 broken laptops. Why don't they just give teachers a sledgehammer. It'll be faster.

We had a colossal fuckup several years ago when the board upgraded all the teachers to new laptops. Because, sure, why not give them new laptops to toss around like those guys who throw salmon to each other in Pike's Market. Some brainiac thought it would be a great idea to switch all the laptops in the district to new MacBooks. Sounds good in theory, but all the school programs were running on PC platforms and couldn't be used with the new Mac systems. So the board had to buy all new software for Macs, thus spending another 150,000. Now the district has the same software for Mac and PC even though they can't use half of it.

The kitchen department throws out all the food they don't sell at the end of the day. Thousands of dollars literally rotting in a landfill. You figure all those uneaten pizzas and hamburgers could have been donated to local soup kitchens or homeless shelters. But there's a caveat: due to school board rules, anything that is considered trash cannot be donated because it was paid for by the taxpayers. Instead of doing something meaningful with edible, perfectly fine food, the school district would rather toss it. I don't know about you, but that shit pisses me off to no end. Do you know how many people die each year because they don't have access to basic nourishment? It's not like the food is poisoned or spoiled. They didn't sell it that day. Nothing else is wrong with it.

Believe it or not, hundreds of pounds of uncooked food expires at the end of the school year. I've seen boxes of hot dog rolls and tater tots go bad. Instead of ordering quarterly or even monthly, the school district places a massive order once a year. Pounds of sausage and Steak-umms hibernate in cold storage only to be discarded months later. Half the order is destroyed each June because by the time the next school year rolls around, there's no room to freeze the new shit they ordered.

All departments in a school district are guilty of wasteful spending. You would assume someone from the technology department would have a bit more intelligence than your average house cat. Wrong again, my friend! Apparently starring at computer screens all day warps the mind faster than free basing Adderall. Three people make up the tech department here, and they all look like Dilbert from the comics. Dilbert 1 is the head computer inspector. Minus the upward-facing tie, Dilbert 1 is in charge of two other geeks. Dilbert 2 looks exactly like Dilbert 1 but about ten years younger. Then there's Dilberta, the girl techie who had bad asthma and wheezes all the time.

During the summer, I had a run-in with one of the Dilberts over a laptop delivery. The day after the shipment, Dilbert 2 approached me. This guy had a look of utter disgust.

"Ummm… excuse me, Mr. Janitor? Do you know what happened to the empty boxes we threw out yesterday?" I hate when people call me Mr. Janitor.

"Well…," I said, "my guess is one of those big red garbage trucks came and took whatever was inside the dumpster to a landfill."

"Are you serious?"

"Oddly enough, I am. You told us they were garbage, so we threw them out."

"You mean all those boxes are gone? Where did they take them?"

I wasn't sure if he was pulling my leg or just trying to make sarcastic banter. I took one look at a bead of sweat racing across his brow and figured out something important must have been in those boxes.

"Usually that's what happens when someone empties a dumpster," I said.

"You're absolutely positive they took all the trash, right?" Before I could answer, he walked away toward the dumpsters to see the news for himself. I watched him jog back and forth as he talked into his phone. Not quite sure what he was saying, but he had his hand attached to his forehead in an "Oh, fuck" posture.

Minutes later, Dilbert 1 drove up in his Prius and had a conversation with his coworker. They got pretty animated out there, standing around an empty dumpster gyrating arms up and down. I walked away to do my job when I passed by the tech office only to find Dilberta yelling into her phone, "It wasn't my fault! I unpacked them just like I was told."

When the district received a brand-new laptop shipment, someone forgot to check the boxes before they threw them out. Common sense would implore you to make sure each box had nothing in it before you threw it out. Turns out all 1,800 laptops were accounted for, but not one of them had a charger.

Sure enough, a day later the board had to order all new chargers to go with their brand-new laptops. Take one wild guess as to where that money came from? You guessed it. The board laid off more janitors to cover the cost of 1,800 laptop chargers.

If you think I'm making this up, by all means, look it up for yourself. Attend a board of education meeting sometime. See where your money goes. Most school administrators roll up to a board meeting in a car worth more than my house. BMW, Mercedes-Benz, we had one guy park a new Maserati in the first space of the parking lot in a "Fuck you, taxpayer!" gesture. You ever take a Jaguar for a test drive? Hell, when's the last time you bought a new car, for that matter? But these crooks and their cohorts squander tax dollars each time they sign a document supposedly for the betterment of the children.

Chapter 6

The Tale of Mad Maggie

All this time I've been telling you about the nutjobs and I forgot to mention the craziest janitor ever. Literally, she was the battiest broad of them all. In my eyes, everyone is a crazy person here, so when I tell you this one is the ringleader, I would take notice. Margret Maya Thompson, or Mad Maggie, was the single most troubled person ever to don the mop. She makes all the rest of the weirdos look normal. All jobs have someone like Maggie, and if you can't figure out who it is, you're probably the psychopath at work. Mad Maggie was the mental patient everyone tried to avoid. Like "walking fifteen minutes around the building to use another door so you don't run into her" kind of person. Her story is complicated, complex, and above all, completely screwed up. Buckle up, cupcake, this one's a real doozy.

I guess Mad Maggie was human at some point before she started to work here.

Sure, she can vocalize and move her appendages like you and me, but that's where the similarities end. Everything about her made you want to curl up in a ball and cry yourself to sleep. Her hair made you think she was auditioning for a role in a new *Blair Witch Project*. Those eyes of hers, good lord. What a set of peepers! She looked like one of those weird paintings where the eyes follow you. Try to imagine someone who drank an entire urn of coffee. It's like she could watch you from any angle with her freakish fish eyes.

All her mannerisms were alien in form. Her body language was inhuman, almost as if she was a half frog person or something. When she walked, or more like skittered, her body convulsed like an addict finding a fix. It was a combination between someone with the hiccups, a bad limp, and a nervous twitch all at the same time. Think of a broken robot break dancing. Her voice made you want to stuff cotton balls in your ears. My god, that high-pitched screech sounded like alley cats being maimed. Maggie looked like someone let Charles Manson out of prison and gave him a sex change.

Regardless of her downfalls, I'd still put Maggie on the top of the list for best workers. I've never seen someone so infatuated with cleaning toilets before. I don't know what it was about those shitters, but she never stopped cleaning until the porcelain came off. "I've got to get this mess off here," she says. "Nobody likes a dirty toilet, do they?" Maggie worked nonstop, always picking up more than her share of the load. Mad Maggie took cleaning to a whole other level, like a janitorial Matrix of sorts. Doing a job good wasn't enough for someone like Maggie, whom perfection was a must. "Gotta do a perfect job," Maggie always used to say. "No sense doing something bad when it can be done perfect!"

Maggie joins a long line of freaky cleaner ladies. If there ever was an all-star game of janitoring, Maggie would bat cleanup. The rest of the team would be comprised of foreigners and OCD old ladies.

There's Demetria the Greek, who specializes in dust removal. She once spent an entire week moving each object in her section to dust. Every goddamn thing from books to desks.

Then we have Kata, who hates all forms of dirt. Kata sees dirt and goes nuts, making a big stink until she has eradicated it. I think she holds the record for the most workdays without a sick day. All she wants to do is clean. Kata wanted to come in on Saturdays to work for free because she said the dirt was forming each minute she wasn't there.

The fastest cleaner by far has to be Monica. Her big thing was she had to have each room completely cleaned within seven minutes. From top to bottom, Monica was like a NASCAR pit crew all by herself. I used to watch her dash around the room cleaning like a crazy little spider monkey. And who could forget the two old Yugoslavian ladies both named Mary.

Mad Maggie outdid them all with one swing of her broom. Maggie cleaned so well she gave the Russians a run for their money. Believe me, that ain't no joke. I heard one Russian lady talking about Maggie when she first started. "Look at her, crazy lady working like dat. She no stop for nothing! I no see her stop to drink water or eat sandwich. Who she think she is? In old Soviet Union, we no work dis hard!"

You'll have to take my word for it when I say no one cleans better than a woman from behind the Iron Curtain. These ladies are known for their sweeping skills. They won't acknowledge Maggie is the best cleaner, but those casual sneers tell the whole story. "Ack! Look what she do now? She cleaning ceiling tile! Who do dis? Not me. No Russian woman ever clean ceiling tile before!"

Maggie has never told anyone a thing about her past. In this job, if you don't tell us about your past, some asshole usually makes one up for you. One guy said she used to work at Home Depot selling hardwood flooring. My night boss said Maggie was a crossing guard in the Trenton School District for fifteen years before she came to work with us. I even heard one of the grounds guys say he saw Maggie working at a Sonic Car Hop years ago. There were so many rumors about Maggie that I decided to find out the truth for myself.

I spent a good deal of time working on research files when I started college. It was sort of a training course for anyone who wanted to be a Lit. major in school. English professors gave their class about a hundred hours of research to weed out lazy students. If you passed the first few weeks of looking for pointless shit in the library, it usually meant you were smart enough to get a degree in English or literature. I had a knack for finding out useless information, so I decided to use my skills to dig up the dirt on Maggie. Glad I got something out of that waste of time called a higher education!

Maggie's story goes something like this: she used to work as a neurosurgeon at a hospital in Philly. No bullshit here. That's the God's honest truth. She wasn't a Stop sign holder or a hardwood floor specialist. Margret, as she was called back then, was one of the best brain surgeons on the East Coast. I found old newspaper articles about how she saved patients with bad brain injuries. She was a god among surgeons, according to Google. She could weave the inner workings of the human brain like a maestro playing a Stradivarius. Her track record was impeccable, over three hundred surgeries with a perfect success rate! It's uncanny to come close to such a feat, let alone do it repeatedly with perfect results.

I didn't believe what I had found until I saw photos of Margret from back in the day. She didn't look like she does now with her wildly combed gray hairs set around a weathered face. Margret took care of herself back then and looked like a normal woman in her late twenties. Everything about her was perfect, her smile all the way down to her perfectly kept scrubs. To think Mad Maggie used to smile was a real kick. She never smiled unless you count the time one of the Yugoslavians called her the cleaning machine. Margret Thompson had notoriety, money, and above all, the respect of everyone she worked with. She was one of those people who you saw in newspapers and magazines, in the fame sections. I saw one picture of her online standing next to a Porsche 356 Speedster in an interview titled "Most Successful Bachelorettes of Philly." People loved Margret, and the amazing work she did for her patients was something out of a fairy tale. Until one day things started to fall apart.

Margret found out the hard way that nothing in life is perfect every time. Sometimes things don't go as planned. Her track record of flawless surgeries was broken one day. Margret was a perfectionist, and it bit her in the ass once she lost her first patient. She had a motorcyclist who hit 120 miles per hour going over the Betsy Ross Bridge. Something went wrong in the ER, and he flatlined on Maggie's watch. It's unclear if it was her fault, but she took it to heart. "I did the surgery as I always have... Why did he die?" One failed surgery turned into a two and then three. She had lost her touch, and it snowballed from there.

The hospital revoked her license a few days after the alleged Play-Doh Incident. Apparently, Margret took one last surgery after several botched operations. The result was a tragedy; she had messed up so badly that the patient's brain looked like wet Play-Doh after she was done. The police were called after she went batshit, throwing bits of brain around the room screaming at the nurses. "I can fix it! Look, see? It's all better now!" She cracked like an egg right there in the OR. Maggie smeared this poor guy's brain on her face like war paint and ran through the hospital whooping like an Indian. The cops dragged her away to the paddy wagon while she sang, "One little, two little, three little Indians!"

After a long trial, the courts gave her a year in the pen for "violating human remains" according to the press. The media started calling her the Brain Butcher, which is probably not a good term to call a neurosurgeon. Any little shred of life left in her vanished when she lost her job. She disconnected from life all together. Years of being the best brain surgeon in the Tri-State Area gone in a flash.

After she was released from prison, Maggie simply disappeared. Her colleagues went on record to say they thought she moved to some third world country to do surgeries again. I don't think I could picture her in Botswana fixing someone's brain in the jungle, although she had the whole witch doctor look down pat.

Maggie went off the grid for several years before coming back to civilization. From what I found, I think she ended up in Southern Jersey living in an abandoned apartment complex. For any of you who have been to Southern Jersey, I think you will agree going off radar for years is completely doable. There's people down there that would make *Deliverance* look like a Disney movie.

Several police reports from the area mentioned a crazed person attacking local bird feeders. Who knows why Maggie would be vandalizing bird feeders, but they do look like human heads from a distance. From what I can gather next, she was living in transient homes until the she was removed for disruptive behavior. You know you're completely screwed up when other bums kick you out for being too crazy.

Anyway, Maggie had become increasingly OCD, trying to clean all the homeless people from head to toe. "Just because you're homeless doesn't give you the right to become a pig," she was quoted as saying. Reports from a local shelter said someone was trying to organize all the shoes from cleanest to dirtiest while giving random health checkups. Once Maggie started to wear an old pair of scrubs she found in a dumpster, the bums got wise and gave her the boot.

I don't know how the hell she got the job here. Odds are she probably stumbled into the office while walking down the street and my boss hired her without any questions. That's my theory anyways, but it sure does feel like the boss hires screwballs by the truckloads. Once hired, Maggie made it her mission to rid the school of dirt. She took off down those corridors with lighting speed and laser precision. It was like witnessing the Six Million Dollar Man in action for the first time. Maggie was natural janitor, a whirlwind of washing with the just right amount of talking to yourself. I imagine her looking something like the Tasmanian Devil when he gets all hopped up, mops and rags flying around in a dust cloud tizzy. She made that sound too, sputtering and spitting all over the joint.

Mad Maggie was a cleaning juggernaut if there ever was one. A Terminator for dirt. The minute she walked in the door, Maggie would pick up the classroom keys. I'm sure she had food or a bottle of water somewhere because she never brought it in with her. What kind of person doesn't bring in lunch or even a magazine to read on break?

Maggie never stopped to talk to people as she passed them in the hallway. Just a quick nod, and she was off. One time a boss stopped her to ask how she was doing. He got as far as "So how's the new job working for you?" until he realized Maggie wasn't in front of him anymore. She kept on pushing the broom down the hallway speaking in short, one- or two-word phrases. "Can't talk," she said. "Gotta run, bye now!" The only time I saw Maggie stop was when two bosses cornered her in a classroom to tell her what a fine job she'd been doing. Even then she was rocking back and forth like a runner trying to keep the heart rate up while checking their watch. "Sorry, I have to work," said Maggie as she picked up a rag and sprinted down the stairs to another room.

Once you walked into her section, you knew it was unlike anything else you'd ever seen. Every single item was cleaned and sterilized like a one of those ultra clean science labs. From the shiny terrazzo floor tiles to sparkling tabletops, you could literally eat off the surfaces in Maggie's section. Any surface at all. It's like no children had ever stepped foot into those rooms! No pencil marks on the floor, no scummy handprints on the windows. My god, even the teacher's desk was dust free and neatly organized. When I first walked into her classrooms to investigate the scene, I felt as if I should be wearing a white smock and plastic booties on my shoes.

The real treat was walking into one of her bathrooms. Maggie spent hours polishing every inch until everything shined like diamonds. It smelled clean even after those little bastards pissed on the floor. I don't know how she did it, but Maggie worked her ass off until her section was the talk of the district. It was amazing to see all the other workers marvel at her accomplishments. They all complimented her on how good a job she did: "Maggie, oh my lord! Your section is so clean and pretty!" "Look how clean those walls are!" "You must be so proud of your area, Maggie." Each time, Maggie would say "Thank you" and continue to work full steam ahead.

As a janitor, you come to hate three times of the year: summer work, Christmas play, and the spring concert. Summer work is when we clean the entire school to get it ready for the next round of kids to fuck it up all over again in September. Personally, I hate this time the most because no one gives a rat's ass about how hard we work. The Christmas play is usually a bitch too, because everyone takes vacation and the remainder of the crew is stuck working ungodly hard. But the spring concert is the time when all the parents come in to watch little Susie and Timmy singing their lungs out in front of the whole school.

On the night of the spring concert, all the janitors finished their work early to help clean up after the concert was over. You know, folding chairs to put away, running a Zamboni over the floor to sweep up all the empty candy wrappers, crap like that. Maggie has never worked a concert, so we told her to watch us and pick up the trash near the door entrances. In the middle of the cleanup, I noticed Maggie talking to one of the parents by the exits. Me being nosy and wanting to get out of the real work, I made my way over to them to eavesdrop. After I heard what they were talking about, it all made sense to me.

"Margret? Margret Thompson?" said the parent. "Is that you?"

"Hi, umm. Hi," Maggie said as she rocked slightly from side to side.

"Wow! It's so nice to see you! Do you remember me?"

"Not... not really. I... have... I..."

"It's me! Sheila Reynolds. We used to work together at the hospital. Oh my god! How have you been?"

"I'm good. I'm good. Ummm..."

"I'm just here to watch my daughter in the concert. She plays the flute in the school band. It's been so long! Are you... working here now?" Maggie was standing near the doorway holding a bag of garbage listening to the lady talk.

"Ummm... well...," said Maggie with a blank expression on her face.

"So you're not in the medical field anymore? I didn't know where you went after..."

"Yeah, I'm here now," said Maggie. "I work here."

"You're a... janitor now?" said Shelia. "I thought you'd be working in another hospital somewhere? You were amazing as a surgeon. What happened?"

I didn't tell anyone what I found out while researching Maggie's past. The rest of the crew, working diligently at folding up chairs, were now eavesdropping what they could from the conversation. They all looked baffled watching Maggie talk to someone as if she knew them. For all they knew, Maggie's past was a mystery, much like as Maggie herself. I kept pretending to work at mopping a juice stain on the floor while inching closer to the conversation.

"So...," said Sheila. "How's it going, Maggie? The last time I saw you, I was coming off a shift at the hospital."

"I'm good. Just doing good, I... I guess," said Maggie.

"Are you okay, Maggie? We didn't know what happened after you left."

Maggie was quiet. She didn't move from side to side like she always had. She was focused on looking at the lady who was asking questions about her. By this time most of the parents had cleared out of the concert and it was starting to quiet down. As I mopped,

I noticed the rest of the crew watching Maggie's movements too, waiting for her run around like a crazy person. It was as if time was slowly coming to a halt, moving people started to slow down as if freezing in place.

"Margret? Margret, are you okay?" said Sheila. Like a runner waiting for the gun at the beginning of the race, Maggie was transfixed in position staring off into space. Then it happened. One of the crew dropped a folding chair onto the tile floor, creating a bang sound. Maggie snapped back from whatever daydream she was having with a few blinks.

"I gotta run," said Maggie. "Gotta clean those toilets." Maggie dropped the bag of trash and jolted off to her section. The lady continued to call her the name "Margret," but it had little effect on the now-sprinting Maggie. By the time we had realized what had happened, Maggie was jogging down the hallway toward her section, never stopping to say goodbye to an old acquaintance. I stood there swinging a now dry mop on the floor while everyone else on the crew stood in place with perplexed looks on their faces. Even Sheila had a dumbfounded look as she started to walk toward the doorway.

"What the fuck was that?" whispered one of the coworkers.

"I don't know," I said. "It's Maggie. Who the hell knows anything with her?" But I knew. I knew exactly what transpired between them. It was only a matter of time until she went rouge again. Once something triggers an insane person, they snap right back into Pyschoville, population: one.

As the rest of the crew finished cleaning up from the concert, Maggie was on full tilt back to her section. I guess she had to clean something to blow off steam from what just happened. I didn't get it. It's not like the lady embarrassed her or anything. From what I could hear, she really didn't say much about the whole "brains on the wall" incident from Maggie's old job. I'm guessing here, but I'd say the sight of an old face from a jilted time sent Maggie back into a dark place.

I had to lock up the building that night, so as I made my way down to Maggie's section, I could hear feverish scrubbing abound.

And a louder than usual talking to one's self emanating from a bathroom.

"Hi... I'm... Hi... my name is...," muttered Maggie's as I walked past the bathroom. The sound of an abrasive cleaning pad buffing a urinal was all I could make out. I peeked my head in to check on her, but as I got closer, the scrubbing sound seemed to get louder and louder. I spoke softly so as not to scare her, but she kept on cleaning and talking.

"Maggie? Maggie, are you okay?" I said.

"Hi... my name... my name is... Hi... I'm fine..."

"I'm locking up the school now. We have to leave in a few minutes, okay?"

"I'm good... I'm fine... fine... I'm... Hi..." Maggie's voice was elevating as I came closer, as did the volume of the scrubbing. I felt her talking louder was like a dog growling over bone. If I had come any closer, she might've bit me.

The next day Maggie was extremely fast-paced as she came in for her shift. Like, extremely fast, even for her. Normally she would walk in a straight line. She made erratic movements with her arms raised slightly as if she had invisible scrubbing pads in her hands. I noticed the talking under her breathe was considerably louder too. What once was a vague whisper morphed into an audible rant. Maggie also picked up the same noticeable blinking many high-strung people have. Maggie's new twitch looked as if she had epilepsy.

A week after the concert incident, Maggie hit rock bottom. We found her on the tile floor of a bathroom with a plunger in one hand and a scrub pad in the other. She was convulsing on her back staring at the ceiling while mumbling gibberish.

I felt bad for Maggie as I saw her rolling around on the floor like a turtle on its back. To me, she looked like a robot who went haywire. My boss took one look at her and said, "Call the police. This lady needs help." Hell, I could've told you that!

As she was loaded into the ambulance to be carted off to the funny farm, I saw glimpses of her past flash across her face. I saw her smile, although her face went from smile to smirk and back to smile within seconds. Yeah, she was fucked up, all right. Maggie was crying and laughing at the same time as the ambulance doors closed. It was the end for her. I think everyone including Maggie knew this was her last time in public. Being trapped by a fragile spiderweb of sanity is no way to live. Perhaps if she didn't run into that lady, she might have lived out the rest of her life as a humble janitor?

Her downfall was that she spent both her careers cleaning a mess she didn't create. I hope one day she realizes she can't clean everything up. There is always going to be a broken brain or a dirty toilet somewhere.

Chapter 7

The Adventures of Drunk-Ass Leonard

Have you ever had a coworker whom you knew would do something horrible? I mean, like, really bad? Well, I get that feeling about multiple coworkers. My buddy Tyrell pops into my head, with all the shit he pulled. We had a couple of other delinquents who stole laptops and various other infringements. These all pale in comparison to what happened one Saturday night. I'm referring to Drunk-Ass Leonard, and his tale is a real clusterfuck.

So years ago an older guy named Leonard Borkowski worked here. He didn't really work, per se. Let's say he was employed for several months. Lord knows how he got here, but I do know he worked everywhere else before he landed with us. You see, Leonard had a taste for the sauce, hence the name Drunk-Ass Leonard. (I usually give really detailed nicknames, but in Leonard's case, it's cut and dry.) He was a babbling, useless buffoon who came to work crocked almost every day.

He didn't seem like a bad guy when he was sober. You could talk to him about regular everyday stuff as if he was a functional member of society. But as soon as he had a few cocktails in him, he turned into the biggest drunken douchebag. Leonard didn't have beer muscles—he had beer bazookas just waiting to explode. I'd say Leonard got shitfaced at least three times a week, with Friday being his complete train wreck day. He'd show up pie-eyed in his rusty Toyota pickup, and I'd wonder how the hell he made it to work without killing himself.

Leonard was born in 1956 in Sayerville, New Jersey. His childhood was normal enough, from what he's told me, but it all fell apart during his last year of high school. Leonard was a good-looking guy back in the day, a typical red-blooded American teenager with piss and vinegar in his veins. He showed me an old picture shortly after I met him that he just so happened to have in his wallet. By the way, why do people have old photos of themselves on them at all times? It boggles my mind how someone tries to relive their glory days like when a girl puts an old photo on a dating website. Ah, you don't look like that anymore, Lisa!

Anyway, things went south when Leonard turned eighteen, the legal age for drinking back then. He replaced the piss and vinegar in his veins with gin and tonic. Once he discovered the sweet taste of hooch, Leonard wanted to have as much as possible. Halfway through his senior year, he was thrown off the football team for showing up to practice drunk. It's kind of ironic the team mascot of Sayreville is the Bombers because Leonard was bombed all the time.

"It was all downhill from there, chief," said Leonard to me one day, with the smell of Lairds on his breath. "After I got tossed from the team, I flunked out of school. Who needs that bullshit education anyways... I learned enough in school to know when I'm done learning!"

Leonard was 6 feet, 2 inches, 290 pounds, with a salt-and-pepper moptop. It was a far cry from what he used to look like. His blond curls and washboard abs were long gone. Now his gut stuck out 2 feet from his body. His skin was dried out, much like someone who's been suntanning for about 40 years straight. If you look closely, you could see a yellowing of his skin, a clear sign on serious liver damage. Have you ever met someone who burped all the time? That's Leonard. He's one of those people who always burps. I'd see him swaying down the hall constantly tapping his stomach, gently exhaling years of consumed booze. And he's always chewing gum. Probably to mask the smell of whisky or vodka wafting out of his mouth.

I'd never seen Leonard with a clean set of clothes. Every day he'd come to work with stained, dirty jeans and a hole-ridden work shirt. Mechanics have a cleaner wardrobe than this guy, and they work in grease all day. I'd bet Leonard had worn a set of clothes for three or four days in a row at times. He looked like he'd been rolling around on the floor of some scummy bar for hours on end. I wouldn't doubt it if he woke up some mornings on the same barstool from the night before, calling the bartender for another round.

I've never met a coworker with so many problems before. It's like this guy had a never-ending black cloud over his head. But then again, if you drink for twelve hours a day, a little collateral damage is expected. Listening to Leonard's stories could make anyone's problems seem insignificant. It's a good way to feel better about yourself, even if you're going to hell for it. Mad about a flat tire? Don't worry about it. Leonard's old truck was stolen by a homeless person who took a shit on the dashboard. Feeling sad about not having enough money? Leonard once sold his Labrador retriever for a pint of Jägermeister. I wanted Leonard's stories to have a happy ending, but each one was worse than the last.

Some days Leonard would open up about anything, hoping maybe someone would listen and offer some guidance. "Did I ever tell you about my third DUI?" said Leonard as he stumbled into the break room. "Jesus Christ, that fucking cop had it in for me since the last two DUIs he caught me on. Talk about prejudice!"

Leonard wasn't black, nor any other minority. Just a drunken Polish guy with a bad case of alcoholism. I don't know how he passed the job interview. If the boss opted for a Breathalyzer instead of the standard interview, Leonard wouldn't have made it past the front door. This guy couldn't tie his shoes without getting lost halfway through the process. Leonard told me he's been fired from every job he ever had. "This job is the only place to take a chance on poor old Lenny," he said while tears slowly gathering in his eyes. "I'm gonna put both feet forward for this job and go those extra miles!"

I'm taking a wild guess here, but something tells me he was drunk each time he got canned. "I used to work at the steel mill out by Trenton," said Leonard. "But that son-of-a-bitch Max ratted on me! He told the boss I was drinking on the job. Hell, I wasn't drunk! What the hell did he fire me for? I could still operate the crane with a few drinks in me."

In the first month, I discovered a lot about Leonard. For starters, he's been married four times, and each wife left him because of drinking. He has five kids, and they all hate him, even his youngest

THE DAY I CLEAN MY LAST TOILET

son, who's only nine. You know you're a fuckup when a fourth grader calls you a loser. Leonard has had about one hundred jobs in his life, and I wish I was kidding when I say one hundred. "I've been fired so many times I lost count after forty-six," said Leonard. "It's a big-ass number, I can guarantee that!"

According to Leonard, he's been fired from every chain store in the Tri-State Area: fast-food joints, convenience stores, food shopping centers, auto repair shops, and about thirty construction companies. The only bright spot in his career is a world record for being fired in the fasted time. He lasted six minutes at a liquor store in Manalapan. "I went to the back to get a special order for a customer. That's when I noticed the beer tower just sitting there. I chugged a whole twenty-four-pack of Bud as fast as I could. By the time the boss found me, I was on the floor pissing myself near the empty cans. Boy, that was the best job I ever had!"

His insatiable need for booze caused him to lose everything. He's lost his license at least eight times, and I don't think he has one at the moment. Car insurance companies laugh in his face when he calls for a quote. From what I can estimate, Leonard has been in a dozen car accidents, all of them involving liquor. It's a bloody miracle how he hasn't killed anybody yet. The belligerent bastard still thinks it's okay to get smashed and play destruction derby in traffic.

"Since no one will give me insurance and I lost my damn license, I say 'Fuck it' and drive without them," said Leonard.

"Aren't you afraid of cops, lawyers, court fees, and other stuff, Leonard?" I said.

"Fuck no!" he said. "The judges keep allowing me to post bail, and I keep changing my address all the time. Hell, I owe so many people for lawsuits and claims. Fuck 'em all! I ain't got no money for them. Maybe if a job would keep me for more than a few weeks, I could pay some people back."

Everyone knew Leonard was a lush, but we dealt with him as best we could. Me and the other coworkers stayed away from him, but he kept following us around the building. One night, Leonard drank a few brewskis and threatened to wrestle the crew. "I bet I could power slam anyone of you right here right now on the gym floor." Mind you, I work with three older women, so I'm guessing his invitation was mainly for me. His third week here, he challenged the night supervisor to a bare-knuckle boxing contest. "Loser buys the winner anything he wants out of the vending machine, like six or seven candy bars, okay?" said Leonard.

After Leonard's first month, the problems started getting worse. I heard a story around town about some asshole who'd go to Taco Bell wearing a full-size eagle costume.

Apparently, someone got all tuned up, put an Eagle costume on, and ordered a ton of food at the drive-through. This doesn't sound like a big issue, but the mystery customer caused a huge scene each time. Allegedly, Leonard would honk the horn as he ordered to screw with the teller or make bird noises into the microphone, squawking uncontrollably.

"Yeah, I'll take a bac, bac, bac, bac burrito and a side of becaaaaack!"

The manager of Taco Bell said Leonard fell asleep while ordering, causing a twenty-minute delay in the drive-through lane. Old Lenny must have been really sauced because the manager had to physically shake Leonard to wake him up. Once the manager saw the name of the school on the mascot's costume, he called the school board the next day.

As I've said before, it's damn near impossible to be fired from this job. Between the union and labor laws, a worker has about fifteen strikes before they're out. I'm sure if one of your coworkers got drunk and caused a scene at a fast-food joint, they'll be fired. Here, you get a verbal warning.

The real massacre was when Drunk-Ass Leonard got completely trashed. Leonard's version of drunk is unlike what most people consider drunk. Think rampaging maniac with a beer gut. I've seen some real fucktards work here over the last two decades, but Drunk-Ass Leonard has to be one of the top three biggest assholes. The first time I found him completely bombed, he was playing with the instruments in the band room. I heard noises coming from the back hallway one night. When I walked down to investigate, I found a belligerent dumbass pounding away on a drum set, drunkenly singing his lungs out.

"Sweeeet Caarroolllinnee!" *Bom bom baaaaaaa!* He was smashing symbols and bass drums completely out of tune, flailing his arms like someone having a seizure. "Good times never seeeeemed soooo good… So good! So good!"

"What the fuck are you doing, Leonard?" I asked. I really didn't know what to expect for an excuse.

"Heeeeeey, buuuudddy!" said Leonard, with a few teeth missing in his smile. "I'm… I'm reliving my youth over here!" Leonard held both hands up with drumsticks and began hissing a sound similar to applause at a concert. "I never, ever made it to… to… my prom so… I'm having my own right here in this little room!"

We've all been drunk a few times, but this asswipe was beyond drunk. He was swaying from side to side while sitting on the drum stool. For a moment he looked like one of those inflatable arm tube guys you see at car dealerships when they have sales. So I stood in the doorway of the band room watching him waiting for Leonard to make his next move. I didn't want to piss him off by screaming because he might charge like a rhino. Ten seconds later, after his drum solo, he went in for the encore.

"Here we go! One… two… three… Sweeeeettt Caaarrroolllinnneee!" *Bom baa.* His tirade was interrupted when he projectile vomited. As he went in to smash the symbols, he puked on the hi-hat and the snare drum. Jesus Christ, he threw up so much so quickly! Halfway through puking, he fell forward onto the drum set, spewing as he fell. Within seconds, Leonard went from rock god to drunken-ass clown.

Have you ever watched something in real time but it seemed like slow motion? That's exactly what Leonard tumbling into the drums looked like. A few seconds after the noise stopped, Leonard began mumbling something about one of this ex-wives. "Aaaaaah… stupid… stupid fucking bitch. She took my… my house." A very disgruntled, dirty, and sleepy Leonard lay on the drums, a broken and filthy man. I casually reached for the hand radio to call the boss. By the time the boss got there, Leonard had shit himself and was singing "Sweet Caroline" again.

"Oh, what the fuck!" said the boss. "What the hell happened to him?"

"Why don't you ask Neil Diamond when he stops shitting himself," I said.

The boss asked me to help Leonard up. "Not my job," I said and walked away. My luck, he'd puke more or fall on top of me. So the boss called the police and the union leader to make sense of the situation.

When the smoke cleared, Leonard wasn't arrested or fired, which still blows my mind. The police reached an agreement with the union to drop him off at the drunk tank for the night and the union would work on a solution the next day.

I figured Leonard was good as gone once he pulled a stunt like that. The laws of normal thinking don't work at this job, as I told you many times before. Once Leonard woke up the next morning, he walked home from the police station and called the union. Turns out if an employee asks for help with a drug or alcohol problem, the job has to offer some form of assistance. Instead of being terminated, Leonard was enrolled in a twelve-step program, free of charge. The union paid for everything, with others' employee union dues, I might add. All Leonard had to do was watch a few instructional videos and swear he'd never do it again.

This is the kind of bullshit that gets my blood pressure off the charts. Had I pulled a stunt like this, I'd be locked up, then fired as soon as I posted bail. I don't know how he did it, but Leonard knew enough to call the union to set this whole thing up. I guess after spending countless hours in court, a repeat offender like Leonard picks up a few tricks.

A few days later, Leonard walks into work with a chip on his shoulder, giving me the business for ratting him out. He walks up to me with a smirk, being all self-defensive.

"You don't have to worry about me, buddy. I'm sober, and thanks a lot for calling the police on me. I won't forget that one, guy. And you won't be seeing me drunk again, I promise you that!"

"So… it's my fault you downed a bottle of Smirnoff and spewed on a drum set, huh?" I said.

"I'm going through a tremendous amount of stress right now," said Leonard. "My problems are under control. I'm working to find a solution."

This wasn't Leonard or the booze talking. It was a rehearsed speech most likely written by the union, or something Leonard read from the back of AA pamphlet.

"I would appreciate it if you were more supportive of my struggle in my time of need," said Leonard, all with a smug look on his face. Leonard didn't need support. He needed a swift kick in the ass or a two-by-four to head, not compassion.

I kept my distance from the newly reformed Leonard, always watchful of his next move.

With scumbags like Leonard, you have to ignore them knowing it's only a matter of time before they screw up. Leonard was a perpetual drunk. It wouldn't be long until the liquor took hold of him again.

It took about two weeks until Leonard fell off the wagon, just as I predicted.

One night, with the smell of booze in the air, I walked down the hallway to find Leonard sitting in a kindergarten room. There he was on an alphabet letter rug eating cookies and drinking milk. Let me reiterate. Leonard, the grown-ass loser, was sitting on a rug eating small packages of chocolate chip cookies and drinking small milk cartons. From the looks of it, he'd been at it for quite some time. This dumb ass was drunk again, smiling to himself with tons of empty cookie and milk containers all over the floor.

"What are you doing now, drunky?" I said. Leonard was laughing to himself, trying to make coherent words.

"I'm having a little snack! Hahahaaaa!" said Leonard with smeared chocolate on his face.

"Those don't belong to you, Leonard. Those are for the kids!"

"Aaaaahhhh… I bought these from the store," he said. "These are… these are my cookies."

"No, they're not," I said. "You can't eat little children's snacks, ya drunken mess."

"You're… you… you're not being very sup… supportive in my time of need," said Leonard.

A typical drunk, always blaming others for their mistakes. He became confrontational when I threatened to call the boss again, stating he would beat the shit out of me when he was finished with his last pack of cookies. This guy didn't look like he could get off the floor, let alone fight. Instead of sitting there arguing with a slob, I took out my phone, snapped a few glamour shots, and walked away.

I've seen too many jerk-offs like Leonard pull a skit like this. How many times can the union stick up for people who take advantage of the system? In total, he ate thirty-seven small packs of cookies and drank twenty-two tiny cartons of milk. A good forty-dollar snack was what Leonard had all while not doing the job, yet again.

Another union deal was struck, keeping Leonard's job as long as he paid back the money for the snacks. As you can see, this job is all about second chances. After this travesty, I washed my hands of the whole thing. I would keep documenting the weekly exploits of Drunk-Ass Leonard until he did something so heinous they'd have to get rid of him.

We had the union leaders come down a couple of weeks later to talk with Leonard after he sexually harassed a coworker. Gene, who's all of seventy years old and sweet as can be, called the boss saying Leonard kept following her around talking dirty to her. "Yeah, you know you want it, Grandma" was a line he used a lot. "Let me get up in the arthritis ass, baby" was another. Poor Gene is the picture-perfect old woman who never bothered anyone. Drunken and now perverted Leonard followed her around for three days asking if he could put those veiny legs behind her gray-haired head. Not even sexual harassment can trump alcoholism. Leonard begged for his job, telling the union and boss he's lonely, that he'll never do it again. "It's the booze talking! I'm sorry, I can't help it!" said Leonard.

Sure enough, old Lenny wasn't done terrorizing the job just yet. Three weeks later, Leonard got fucked up again and drove his janitor cart off the roof. I don't know how he did it, but the stupid bastard pulled a bunch of cleaning equipment and other items up onto the roof, where he proceeded to launch them into the air.

I went outside to dump trash on the night in question and found shrapnel littering the parking lot. A loud whistling sound came from above me, kind of like a bomb falling from a plane. Damned if it wasn't a highly intoxicated Leonard heaving a mop bucket from two stories up. *Neeeeeeerrrrrruuuuuuuummmmmm booooommmm!* There he was flinging anything in arms reach onto the parking lot in front of him. He got good distance with his janitor cart, which is astonishing because those things are pretty heavy.

Again, I called the union and my boss to get this lunatic down before he started catapulting kids. In total, Leonard broke approximately eight hundred dollars in cleaning equipment, including fifteen jugs of soap and an old microwave from the home ec. room. This time, he ran out of chances. No more booze-filled excursions or he'd finally be fired. Leonard was suspended two weeks for his shot put extravaganza, and I was promised by several union leaders that Leonard was on his last leg.

Things ran smoothly for those two weeks and continued to be smooth when the formerly Drunk-Ass Leonard came back. Much to my surprise, he seemed to be turning a new leaf. Leonard didn't have a grudge against me, and he stopped chasing poor Gene around the building asking her some "fine Granny lovin'." I hadn't smelled liquor on him since the night he hurled all that shit off the roof, so perhaps he learned his lesson.

Leonard was calm, seemingly sober. He had a defeated look in his eyes though, as if all the crap he did while drunk finally caught up with him. On break, Leonard ate his lunch, talking calmly with the rest of his coworkers. Typically, Leonard would wander around the school, being out of his mind shitfaced. The new Leonard didn't do those horrible things now.

It was nice to not babysit Leonard. No calls about disorderly school mascots, no verbal challenges to coworkers. It was easy sailing. I mean, that's all anyone wants, right? A quiet, easy day at work. That's all I've ever wanted at my job—just come in, do the tasks at hand, and go home.

If I've learned anything in this cesspool called a job, it's to never trust a dull moment. With the clowns I work with, you can expect a carnival of stupidity when things get a little too quiet. Leonard's final act was coming. You could feel the anticipation lingering in the air.

The second to last time I saw Leonard was on a Friday night during the winter. It was his turn to work overtime the next day, on the Saturday shift. We have weekend sports activities like basketball and wrestling that stay until about 9:00 p.m. or 10:00 p.m. Old Lenny seemed humdrum when he left Friday night, walking to his truck like a lost zombie looking for a fresh brain. He seemed down and out, you know, sadder than usual. With all the shit that's gone wrong in his life, I'd be a depressed lump of shit too. I didn't think anything of it until I got a call from the head boss late Saturday night.

"Hello?" I said.

"It's me, Mr. Polotski. I need you to come to the school as soon as possible."

"Why? What's the matter?" I said, all while thinking Leonard forgot to lock up the building after overtime.

"Just come to the building, please. What's left of it anyways." And then he hung up.

What's left of it? What the fuck did that mean?

A wide variety of things ran though my head as I drove to the school. Maybe Leonard finally snapped and took the school's basketball team hostage? It's easy to rig a homemade bomb nowadays with recipes on the internet. As I pulled into the parking lot, I saw several fire trucks, police cars, ambulances, and a handful of reporters with camera crews on scene. The school was almost completely in ashes with most of the building in rubble.

Then I saw Leonard, sitting on the back of an ambulance truck away from the smoking pile of concrete with half his clothes singed off. He had an oxygen mask on with EMTs standing over him. Located next to the ambulance was a small group of people: my boss Mr. Polotski, two night supervisors, the union leaders, the fire chief, a few officers, and a handful of reporters and cameramen. Everyone was involved in several conversations, all of them trying to talk at once.

Here's what happened: Leonard left the building around seven o'clock to get a cheeseburger. Instead of going directly back to the school, Leonard hit the liquor store and picked up a bottle of Popov

Vodka. Not a shooter or a pint, but a 1.75-liter jug of doom. I think the building might still be there today had Leonard drank in his truck, like most people. Getting wasted in your car isn't as bad as getting wasted in a school full of witnesses. Instead, he hid in the copy paper room, drank most of the bottle, and opened a window to let the cigarette smoke out. Half an hour later, Drunk-Ass Leonard nodded out from drinking, dropped a cigarette, and the room went up like a fireworks display.

This jackass couldn't have picked a worse spot to smoke. Twenty palettes of paper went up as if they were dowsed in gasoline. By the time Leonard realized what was happening, it was too late. The fire alarm went off, and everyone evacuated the building during the championship basketball game. Leonard, coming out of a drunken stupor, thought he was in the flames of hell. He ran out of the building, well, more like stumbled out of the building, and dropped to his knees outside. A fireman found him stopping, dropping and rolling, shouting, "Save yourselves! I'm sorry, Lord! Please don't take me... I'm not ready to go yet!"

The union couldn't save him even if they wanted to. Leonard burned down a two-story middle school worth about thirteen million dollars. Given his numerous second chances, and the complete destruction of an entire school, Leonard was fucked. After being arrested and charged with negligence, Leonard was given nine years in the New Jersey State Prison. The sentence would have been less had he paid all the fines from years of previous accidents, DUIs, and back child support.

Somehow, I don't think Leonard was upset with the outcome. Anything of value Leonard had, had already been lost to drinking, so he didn't have anything left to lose. Burning down a school was the proverbial icing on the booze cake for Drunk-Ass Leonard.

Ever since his early days of indulgence, Leonard had been in a slow descent leading up to his incarceration. It seems like a fitting end for someone who chose to drink himself into oblivion. He's probably happier than he's ever been in prison. Now he can make toilet wine all day long without having to drive to the liquor store to get it.

Chapter 8

Love, Sex, and Debauchery in the Public School System

Love is perhaps the one emotion you wouldn't expect to find while working as a janitor. Not many fairy-tale wedding stories begin with "So we met near the steaming pile of shit in the boys' locker room… I had a bucket, and she had the mop…"

True love stories are reserved for office workers in San Diego or Starbucks baristas who meet before grad school. The chances of meeting your soul mate as a school janitor are damn near impossible. Between the barrage of trash and the endless puddles of piss, a loving embrace doesn't seem to fit in. The term "a couple who mops together stays together" doesn't have a pleasant ring to it.

Teachers, and other school employees, seem to find love frequently, though. Late nights at board meetings or parent-teacher conferences seem to get the love juices flowing. It's common to see a pair of teachers get married and live a happy little existence. But it doesn't always end well. In fact, when love between educators goes awry, it can get pretty fucking ugly.

I met what seemed to be a lovely couple at one of the first schools I worked at, the Haversmiths. Boy, they were cute as cute could get. They were the perfect little team, complete with the same round Harry Potter glasses and matching khaki messenger bags. They would caress each other's hair with a quaint little smirk during PTO meetings. Mr. Haversmith would leave apple-shaped Post-it notes on her desk that said "Miss ya!" while the wife would blow kisses to her honey bear when passing in the hallway. These two were so lovey-dovey it made normal people sick. It was the kind of over-affectionate cow shit that made you want to smash a soldering iron into their eyeballs.

It got so damn sickening people stopped thinking it was quaint and started getting annoyed as all hell. I think they pissed off a few higher-ups, who kept sending out memos stating, "Please, no PDAs during school hours. We don't want to send the wrong signal to the students."

Soon enough, the Haversmiths' emotional displays caught the attention of the union, who agreed with administration about work-place etiquette. Good thing, because the single teachers, the ones who couldn't buy a date, were about to skin the two lovebirds alive. Mrs. Haversmith was transferred to another elementary school, much to the chagrin of her Romeo.

You should've seen this guy! "Why are they pulling us apart, my love?" I'd be damned if I had to work with my wife *and* see her each night at home. We'd kill each other within a week.

I felt bad for the guy, but I got real tired of making small talk when I saw him in the halls.

"Hey! How's it going, Mr. Haversmith?" I said.

"Oh, not good," he said. A look of vulnerability and anguish cascaded over him.

"Oh, I'm sorry to hear that. How is Mrs. Haversmith?"

"Well… I guess she's okay. I haven't seen her in a while. They took my love muffin away from me!" Then he'd start crying. Like, crying a lot. I felt uncomfortable standing there talking to him. Do I give him a hug? Why did he sound like Eeyore from *Winnie the Pooh* when he spoke?

This guy was bumming me out big-time. I almost thought I'd walk into his classroom one evening and find him hanging from the ceiling with little "Goodbye, my love!" Post-it notes all over his tweed jacket. Don't get me wrong, I have compassion, but a person who works with kids shouldn't be seconds away from blowing his brains out during a spelling bee.

I don't think Mrs. Haversmith took the move as hard as her husband. She made friends quickly at her new school. Word is, she spent a ton of time helping other teachers get their work done, if you know what I'm saying. Soon she started making after-school play-dates with many of her new buddies.

Long story short, Mrs. Haversmith cheated on her husband and got a divorce three months after the transfer. She now goes by her maiden name, Ms. Rouple, and is currently banging Mr. Jorge, the gym teacher, and Mr. Klein, the science lab teacher. Probably at the same time from what I heard. What about Mr. Haversmith, you ask? Well, he doesn't smile as much as he used to. No more adorable fruit-shaped stickies for this guy! Poor dude is the laughing stock of the school, and he's not even a student. You should see this chump shuffling down the hallways after school with his hands in his pockets. He's the saddest sack of shit you'll ever lay eyes on. Good thing teachers have great insurance because those prescriptions for Zoloft and Ambien don't come cheap.

Most of the teachers have families or hobbies outside of work. You know, like stamp collecting or visiting Civil War reenactments on the weekends. Mr. Shinner was a fourth-grade teacher who always kept to himself. He was a good-looking, shy, quiet person who always had a no-tooth-showing grin on his face. Those are the ones you have to watch out for.

He was forty-three, was single, had no children, and spent a lot of time traveling. Red flags were popping up all over the place. Unless you're a twenty-two-year-old hipster with a goatee and a trust fund, you shouldn't be traveling all over the country. No one thought much of him until he got arrested late one night at a rest stop outside of Philly.

Mr. Shinner spent a great deal of time on the road because he was a lot lizard. For those of you who don't know what a lot lizard is, it's a cross-dressing prostitute who goes from truck stop to truck stop selling sexual favors. He was caught in the sleeper cab of a Freightliner wearing a blond wig, six-inch heels, and a red leather skintight miniskirt. I saw his mug shot on one of those community alert websites after I heard the news. Could've fooled me! If I didn't see the Adam's apple and it was dark, hey, I don't know.

What he was doing there in full drag with a trucker from Ohio is none of my business. Pennsylvania State Police didn't think he was "meeting a friend for coffee" as he said he was, so they booked him on prostitution charges. Yup, the reason Mr. Shinner traveled so much is because he was blowing interstate travelers for quick cash. And all this time I thought teachers made pretty good money!

The teachers' union thugs tried to sweep it under the carpet saying he had a mild case of ADHD and he was under a doctor's care for depression. (There's that stellar insurance again!) Regardless of his mental state or sexual depravities, the board let him go quietly over the summer break. Nobody's heard from his since, but I can guarantee he's probably working a truck stop outside of I-95. Maybe wearing a leopard-print pantsuit with cat ears on.

I had him pegged from the beginning. Once you've seen the gaggle of nutjobs I've seen, they all start to stick out like sore thumbs. Telltale signs like one too many cats or being way too friendly with the children sends up my antenna. Janitors, we're all fucked in the head, so it's hard to tell who's insane and who's just a guy trying to make ends meet. Teachers and principals have a few quirks you can spot from a mile away.

For teachers, it starts with staying after school late. I've seen plenty of teachers stay an hour or so to grade papers. No biggie. But if you're shift is done and you're hanging around for hours at a clip, then you might need some counseling. I don't know about you, but I can't wait to get the fuck out of this place when my shift is up. When I see teachers staying an extra eight hours plus, or I have to kick them out when I lock up the building for the night, then we got a problem.

Keep an ear out for the ones who talk to themselves too. Basic mumbling is common in the workplace. Hell, I do that too. But full-on conversations? With no one else is the room? That's got serial killer written all over it.

I'm telling you it's all because of a lack of a love life. We've all been there. No sex for weeks or even months does something to a person. Now try dealing with thirty little screaming morons day in and day out. It's a recipe for a full-on nervous breakdown.

A couple of years ago, one of the teachers got into some trouble during a bad breakup. Mr. Jacobs, a fifth-grade history teacher, had an ex-girlfriend who called in a bomb threat. That's bad enough, but his ex-girlfriend was Ms. Sanchez, a sixth-grade Spanish teacher at the same school. This bitch called a bomb threat from her classroom! That's a special kind of crazy.

This lady went *loco* and threatened to blow the whole place up if Mr. Jacobs didn't come outside and tell her why he was sleeping with her sister. She's a teacher, for Christ's Sake! I'd expect that sort of behavior from an UPS truck driver. But a school? That's a line you don't cross.

She made a whole scene in the courtyard during lunch one day, screaming about how he used her for sex. She had a megaphone too. Ms. Sanchez planned ahead for this little show-and-tell session. She had Polaroids of the two of them in lewd and lascivious positions— ya know, things you're not supposed to be flaunting in front of perceptive children.

The cops, fire department, EMTs, and a few detectives were called in and put the school on lockdown for the rest of the day. Didn't matter to me, I got to sit in a room all day, doing nothing, while police tried to talk her out of it. I got to shelter in place playing cards with Miguel and Steve instead of sweeping floors. The batty teacher was bum-rushed by the school security guard after she started tearing the photos to pieces. Cops took her away after they found out it was a hoax. The whole emotional display wasn't fake, just the plastic bomb she had strapped to her stomach.

This wasn't Mr. Jacobs's only brush with crazy chicas at work. A year later, he had another teacher, Ms. McMichaels, the fourth-grade math teacher, threaten to cut off his penis. Out of nowhere during an assembly on the solar system, Ms. McMichaels whipped out a butcher's knife and chased Mr. Jacobs across the room. There he was running for his life being tracked by a redhead with a mini machete.

"You arrogant piece of shit!" she said as she sliced wildly at his crotch. "Who the fuck do you think you're dealing with?" Mind you, this was an elementary school. Not a high school with older kids who might have heard such words before. But a grammar school with young children who have probably never heard phrases like "Who else have you been fucking, Danie?" or "I'll cut your prick off and feed it to a stray dog!" I was sure some of those kids would develop some kind of trauma-related affliction.

The two of them were wrestling with a video about Saturn playing on the big screen above the stage. Talk about excitement! Eventually the samurai lunatic was subdued by the same brave security guard, but not before taking a few chunks of fabric out of Mr. Jacobs's pants. Who knows what could've happened if she really laid into him.

Now who do you blame here, the man whore who keeps banging deranged women or the crazy cunt who pulled a knife in front of kids? Both were fired after the incident, which I'm sure won't stop Mr. Jacobs from screwing psycho teachers.

One of the most infamous cases of sexual craziness came to light about five years ago. You may have heard about it on the news. Some of the younger teachers were caught operating a sex ring inside one of those retirement villages. Yup, folks, you heard that right! Fourteen very attractive entrepreneurs set up a prostitution network on the weekends to make some extra bucks.

It all started a year or so before the case made local news. A group of young teachers fresh out of college began working for the school district in September. Picture new, happy teachers ready to take on the world and mold the future leaders of this great country. That is, until they got their first paychecks.

Imagine the disappointment a new teacher has when they realize they went to school for four-plus years, then a year of on-the-job training, to make less than an assistant manager at Target. When you first start out, it doesn't pay to be a teacher. All those top-step divas who've been here twenty-some years make great money. But you need to be here twenty years, plus have advanced degrees. Beginning teachers make fucking peanuts compared to the veteran teachers.

Now, think about all those hefty student loans with their so-called low interest rates. Where does the government get off charging you 15 to 29 percent interest on college loans? You'd be better off taking a loan from Louie, the pawn broker, than having a federal loan payment.

I'd be mad as a hatter wondering where in the hell I was going to get 1,100 dollars a month for a student loan. That's called a mortgage payment where I'm from. And you pay that shit back for like ten years, at least. You could get a sweet-ass Lambo for that much.

Faced with the inevitable choice of armed robbery or organized crime, a small group of first-year teachers made a business decision. Instead of working as a waitress at Chili's, the teachers started their own rub and tuggery.

One of the teachers had a boyfriend who worked the gate at a retirement village. That's all they needed to get the ball rolling. He offered the maintenance guy at the clubhouse a piece of the action. In two moves, the fledgling business had a lookout and a place to conduct transactions. Now they needed a lineup of pretty merchandise to entice the Johns. Honestly, some of these teachers were hot as hell. It was a no-brainer. If you're an old pervert, you'd love to have sex with a young, pretty, flexible teacher. Their services practically sold themselves!

A few posts to Craigslist, in code, got the teachers their first clients. Then it was all word of mouth—literally. Guys at the local cigar shops, bars, and other frequently used social clubs started getting the word out about the new joint. Those teachers were working their sweet little asses off! From what the newspapers say, they took in something like $350,000 in the first six months. Sure beats teaching geography for a little-above-minimum wage.

Things went undetected for about eight months. Most of the clients came from outside the retirement village. They would use a password at the gatehouse to get buzzed in. From there, they drove to the clubhouse, where they were let in a side door. It was all protected too. The maintenance guy at the clubhouse planted bushes near the entrance to hide their activities. It ran like any shady side hustle. People got in on the action. Everyone had their own task to perform. It was all going great from a business standpoint. A few of the hooker teachers had minored in business in college. They had their own flourishing small business, complete with a schedule, client list, appointment times, and payroll.

A few nosy retirees started asking questions about why they couldn't use part of their own clubhouse. Word got out that it was a place of sin, but guess what? The old guys who lived there started using the services too! Yes, indeed. Grandpa Jim cashed his Social Security check and spent it on pussy. The old dudes told their wives they started a poker league. Pretty good cover if you ask me.

The death blow came when one of the wives caught her husband smelling like a French whore with body glitter all over his crotch. She nosed her way into the clubhouse and caught them in the act. She called the owner of the retirement village, the local newspaper, and then finally the cops. The business probably would still be operating today if one nosy old hag didn't spoil it for everyone.

Needless to say, the teachers all got busted for prostitution and lost their jobs. The only positive was if the teachers played their cards right and hid the money, they'd be able to pay off the student loans in no time. Just as soon as they served their time in a federally funded institute.

Sometimes the teachers aren't the only ones who have a hankering for sex. One of the administrators was caught cheating on his wife several years ago. Mr. Franklin was head of some educational department in the administration complex, or millionaires' row as I like to call it. Starting salary is around two hundred thousand for the entry-level shitheads. You work here long enough, like most of the management buzzards, you can afford an expensive house with a wrought-iron gate around it. Maybe a couple of gargoyles perched above the driveway.

Anyway, Mr. Franklin was an older gentleman with gray hair and a potbelly who smelled as if he dumped a bottle of Old Spice on his pants. Picture your drunk uncle who told racist jokes during the holidays. He was a longtime employee who had a tendency of flirting. And by flirting, I mean sexual harassing anything with a vagina and boobs. I think over his career, Mr. Franklin had around fifteen sexual harassment suits filed against him, ranging in severity from a simple "Hey there, sugar dumpling" to full-on groping.

By some miracle, each case was dropped right before it went to arbitration. Somehow the women who accused Mr. Franklin of derogatory remarks were promoted within days. It's weird, kinda crazy if you think about it. Each person who made an accusation against Franklin soon got a nice pay raise and a new job title. One secretary accused Mr. Franklin of grabbing her ass and yelling, "Honk, honk!" A week later, she had her own secretary and a company car.

This one chick whom everyone called Bubble Tits must have given some good head because she skyrocketed right up the corporate ladder. She was an entry-level file clerk who wasn't too bright but did have a nice rack. I guess that's why Mr. Franklin was drawn to her. A couple of weeks into her employment, she filed the first lawsuit—supposed breast groping. (Shocker, right?) After the first time, she dropped the charges. She went from a part-time nobody to a full-time secretary overnight. Usually you must work a year or so before you get full-time. Not Bubble Tits.

Two weeks later, Bubble Tits became *his* secretary, answering directly to Mr. Franklin. Again, they were marvelous melons, so I can't blame Franklin for his crimes.

Three months after that, she became head of the secretary department, leapfrogging about ten other people. This broad couldn't spell *secretary*, let alone be in charge of them. Rumors started to fly about their relationship until late one night during a board of education meeting.

I heard it on the district handheld radio that police and ambulance were dispatched to the administration complex. A few minutes later, they called for backup, not a good thing to hear in a school district. I thought maybe someone dropped dead at the board meeting, but it was much worse. The story goes Mr. Franklin and Bubble Tits were having sex in his office late one night until his wife walked in on them. Apparently Mrs. Franklin received a call from her insurance company earlier that day saying they couldn't fill Mr. Franklin's Viagra prescription. "My husband doesn't take Viagra!" said Mrs. Franklin, who soon realized why her husband was staying late at work all the time.

After driving to his office and having Philippe, the janitor, let her in, Mrs. Franklin walked in on her husband screwing his secretary on the copy machine. Like, right there on the glass screen with the machine on. Copies must have been shooting out all over the floor.

She flipped on the lights and let out a terrible scream, according to Phillippe. Mr. Franklin, who was all hopped up on Viagra, had a massive heart attack as soon as she flipped on the lights. Can you picture this scumbag, all sweaty and stinking of Old Spice, clutching his left arm with a hard-on that wouldn't go down?

Mrs. Franklin didn't even address her husband. She went after the secretary and started to slap the daylights out of her. Phillippe tried to do the honorable thing as he called 911. Too bad he spoke terrible English. All the dispatcher heard was "Naked lady getting hit, naked man grabbing his pee-pee and chest!" The police thought it was a prank until they heard a woman screaming in the background: "You two-bit whore... Get off my husband, you big-tittied tramp! I'll wrap those tits around your neck!"

After calling the police, Phillippe grabbed the walkie-talkie and tried to call the boss for help. "Come quick, come quick! Two people... they fighting and one guy... he dying on the floor!" It sounds funnier in a broken English-Filipino accent.

When all was said, Mr. Franklin was given an early retirement due to a heart condition. The whole incident was swept under the rug, like most of the stuff around here. Mrs. Franklin divorced her husband and took half his shit, but that too was covered up and soon forgotten. What about Bubble Tits, the voluptuous harpy of a secretary? Well, she is doing just fine in another school district. That's the thing about women with big knockers: they always land on their feet, even if those feet spend a lot of time up in the air on top of a Xerox copier.

Chapter 9

Some of the Weird Stuff I've Seen

I don't want to get all philosophical on you, but I've seen some incredible things at this job. You wouldn't think the life of a school janitor was all that glamorous. Hell, most of the time, it isn't. It's downright boring. On occasion, things tend to get real weird. Yeah. *Weird* is a good word choice. Let's go with that.

I've never seen a unicorn while cleaning, but let's say some paranormal activity has been witnessed. And honestly, the paranormal stuff is easier to explain than the rest of the crap.

Let's start with the paranormal shit and go to the real loco stuff later. Yes, ghosts are real, and they've scared the shit out of me. I've been yelled at, messed with, and even touched through another dimension. I guess if you were a prankster in this life, you keep up your shenanigans in the afterlife. In all my occurrences, I've never felt as if I was in danger, like a poltergeist or what have you. More like "Hey, let's mess with the janitor and see what he does" kind of apparition. See what I deal with? Even the phantoms make fun of the janitor.

When those entities manifest into visible forms, that's when the real fun begins. Most times I felt the hairs stick up on the back of my neck or a cold spot out of nowhere. You know when something is around you. It's a feeling you'll never forget.

Some of these schools were built in the 1930s, with most of them constructed around the sixties and seventies. That's a long time to gather residual energy from any poor individual who croaked here. Three janitors died in the line of duty: one in 1949, the second in

1985, and the last guy in 1999. The first guy was named Mortimer Johnson. He was working on the boiler when it blew up. Best-case scenario from this tragedy was, he was the only guy in the school when it went up like a powder keg.

This dumb fuck hit the wrong lever and turned the boiler into a giant bomb. Back then they never had safety commissions or work laws, so any nimrod could operate a boiler. When Mortimer reached for a lever, he pulled the gas valve, instead of the water valve, thus adding a shitload of gas to a big flame. Poor old Morty never saw it coming.

The second guy who kicked the bucket was named Stephen Ronkos. Big Stevie was what his coworkers called him. This dude was six feet, nine inches without boots on. This massive, corn-fed, country boy always wore flannels shirts and carried a thermos of coffee under his arm. Good worker from what I've researched. A little wet behind the ears or perhaps *simple* is a better term for the big guy. His wide smile made him hard to miss. That and his big-ass head. Big Stevie must have caused his mother excruciating pain during childbirth. From the photos I've seen, he looked like a life-size lollipop, skinny body with a humongous cranium. This guy was always bonking his head on overhanging pipes or doorframes. Pictures showed him with gauzes on his dome or a fresh bruise above his eyebrows.

His death was a little more gruesome than the first guy. Instead of it being quick, over in a second like Morty, the human bomb, Stevie suffered a little. During a renovation, Stevie was on the loading dock when a pipe broke off, impaling him in the middle of his forehead. He was cleaning up an oil spill on the dock when wham! Right through his skull. From the stories I've heard, he got skewered like a cocktail weenie. That humongous head didn't stand a chance against a steel scolding metal rod. Sad thing is, had Stevie been average sized, the pipe would've flown over his head, not through it.

Our third contestant in the janitor death game was Mark Milberg. He had a heart attack while working on a Saturday shift. This guy was an easy four hundred pounds and in very bad health. I don't know whose idea it was to make him cut the grass in the courtyard during a heat wave, but he did it. Fat people and high temperatures don't mix, trust me.

Come Monday morning another janitor opened the school to find Mark dead on a ride on lawnmower. There he was, all four-hundred-plus pounds wedged into the seat with his eyes and mouth wide open. It's fucked up to think about, but I bet he died on the lawnmower and just kept going around in circles until the gas ran out or he hit a wall.

Don't feel bad for the guy. He was a real prick. Anyone who eats four thousand calories a day is bound to kick off sooner than later. I'm sure his fat-assed ghost was responsible for a least one of my spiritual encounters.

I met this tub of shit about a year before he bought the farm. Mark made my life hell by riding my ass from the minute I walked in. "You better keep your cleaning up, son. If I see you slackin', I'll be on your ass like flies on shit." Then he'd cleared his throat with a wheezing, dry cough. You know, to move all the excess food out of the way of his windpipe.

That fat fuck always gave me trouble when I worked at his post. When I heard he died, I kind of felt relief. At least I wouldn't have to put up with his shit if I ever worked at that school again. The first day I went there after he died, I was having a good day. No screaming land whale up my butthole all the time. It was a rather pleasant day. That is, until someone or something yelled at me from out of nowhere.

I was sweeping out a classroom by myself in an empty hallway. My other coworkers were on the other side of the building, probably about a couple of hundred yards away. My stomach started to bother me, so I ran to the bathroom to take a quick dump. While sitting on the bowl, I heard a faint noise from outside the door. Didn't think anything of it until it got louder and sounded like someone whispering behind the door. Have you ever heard someone talking but it's muffled? Like they were holding their hand over their mouth? All of a sudden, I heard a raspy, dry cough come from outside the bathroom door. Well, when I heard that, the hair spiked up on my back.

It was the same cough Mark made all the time. Mark had a throat-clearing cough from years of cigarettes and Big Macs. If you've ever heard Mark's dry cough, you know it's not a common sound. Mind you, he'd been dead for over two weeks at that point.

I've never wiped my ass with such speed in my life. Boy, I got the hell out of there as fast as I could! That son of a bitch was standing outside the bathroom and was probably yelling at me to hurry up. "It doesn't take that long to shit, boy! Git your lazy ass out here and mop this hallway!"

Nobody else was anywhere near me when the incident occurred. When I finally found someone, they were all the way on the other side of the building. Could they have stood by the bathroom door coughing and then ran to the other side of the building? Maybe. But it was illogical and no one was out of breath from running when I saw them. The first thing someone said to me was, "You look like you've seen a ghost!" I nodded my head yes and never went back to that school again.

A couple of years later, I had another altercation with Casper. This time at a different school. Everyone loves Saturday overtime at my job. A Saturday overtime day consists of opening the building, letting the sports groups in and cleaning up when they are done. A solid twelve-hour day with very little work involved. I'm basically there to make sure the boiler doesn't malfunction and kill everyone.

Halfway through my day, I went to the library to take a nap. Don't judge me. It's a long day to sit there and do nothing, so I got a little sleepy. Anyway, as I dozed off in a recliner, I started to get a weird feeling, as if someone was standing over me. I'd open my eyes to see nothing, so I dozed back into dreamland. Well, soon enough as I entered a deep sleep, my mind drifted into the land of passion. As I lay there, dreaming about some hot chick, it felt as though someone was rubbing my leg. Then what I thought was a hand moved up my leg toward my naughty zone. Things were getting good. You know what I'm talking about.

Much to my dismay, I awoke. But I still had the feeling of someone rubbing my body. For about ten seconds, with my eyes open and being fully awake, someone was still touching me. Probably one of the best *and* worst experiences in my life. I could see the outline of hand moving up and down my leg and other parts.

I specifically remember jumping out of the chair and sprinting out of the library, with a boner no less. Good thing no one was around to see me when I got up! How in the hell was I supposed to explain that shit? A rather portly chap power walking around a school with an erection. Somehow telling the boss I was sexually assaulted by a ghost wouldn't have been the best course of action.

Another Saturday, at a different post, I felt as if someone was directly behind me. While sweeping a long hallway, I was startled by what felt like someone running up behind me. If you've ever had someone running behind you, you'd know the feeling. I turned around suddenly to see nothing but air and an empty hallway.

No one was in the building, of this much, I'm sure. I was finishing up cleaning after a basketball tournament. The last person walked out about an hour before the incident. Not another person in the place, yet I felt like someone was about to run right into me. Remember when you were a kid and you'd stammer your feet behind somebody to make them jump? Yup. That's what it felt like.

People say you're not supposed to turn around if you think a ghost is behind you. I guess they can get aggressive and try to harm you or something. I tell you what, it didn't feel like a ghost. It felt like someone was right up my ass, about to touch my back. That's how real it was.

One night, while locking up the same school after hours, I followed a ghost down an empty hallway. After pep rallies, we sometimes have people who get lost in the building. I'd find them wandering around calling out for help, as if they were deep in the Amazon jungle trying to navigate a way to freedom. One evening, I saw a man with a black jacket and black pants walking down the gym hallway. It was a little strange because the game ended around 9:30 p.m. and it was almost midnight when I saw him. He was walking away from me at a normal pace, about fifty feet in front of me. I called out to him to get his attention.

"Sir? Hello? Do you need some help?" Nothing. No stop in motion or turning to face me. Just the same straight forward walk. So I called out again.

"Excuse me... are you lost? You can't go down that hallway. There's no exit over there." He kept walking straight ahead without disruption. My luck, he was an old deaf guy who turned his hearing aids off or something. As I followed him for another ten seconds or so, I walked into a cold spot out of nowhere. There went that hair on the back of my neck again. I stopped walking and called out one more time.

"Hello?" I was standing still, but he continued to walk onward reaching the end of the hallway and disappeared into a wall. Dead fucking serious. This guy just disappeared into a cinder block wall.

At that point, locking up the rest of the school was not an option. I proceeded to jog to my truck and drove the hell out of there. Of course, I took some flak when the boss yelled at me the next day for not locking up. Instead of explaining my incident, I made up a story about getting a stomach bug and leaving early. A couple of harsh words are a hell of a lot better than finding out what vanished into that dead-end hallway.

There have been other instances with strange noises or falling items in classrooms. I've seen a few books fall off shelves with no one there to push them. Nothing was thrown at me, but I have seen small objects move by themselves. Spooky things like toys in the kindergarten room or piñatas in the Spanish room. Maybe it was the ghost of a kid trying to play with an Etch A Sketch or smash that piñata in half to get some candy? I'll never know, and part of me doesn't want to find out.

At least with ghosts you can sort of explain it to someone. Some folks have heard of a ghost tale or know of someone whose seen some stuff. This next story is not easily explained. In fact, I don't even know how to explain half this shit because it's so fucked up it's beyond explanation. But I'll try my damnedest.

A school parking lot must have some fantastic appeal to weirdos. People flock to them once the sun goes down. It's like the creepers think no one can see their exploits after the school buses leave. I've counted tons of kids getting high behind the school or cars parked away from prying eyes so they can get their groove on.

But one guy showed up like clockwork each week, and his saga is a real doozy. It started about a year into my long career as a professional mopper. It's almost twenty years ago this month, as a matter of fact. After I was finished with my work for the night, I took a walk out to my truck to get some change for the vending machine. The snack machine in the faculty lounge sells these packs of Big Texas Cinnamon Buns, and damned if they aren't great with a nice cup of coffee. Like Cinnabon style, only not as good. Not as much icing, if you ask me.

So as I walked back from my truck, I saw this car parked ominously behind a dumpster. It happened all the time here, so I just ignored it and went inside. Those tasty buns were calling my name, and my coffee was getting cold.

A week later the same car came back and parked in the same spot. Again, it happened all the time at a school. It was not my job to chase away the freaks. My luck, I'd get shot interrupting a drug deal or something.

Another week later, on a Friday evening at 8:30 p.m., the same car drove into the parking lot and parked behind the same dumpster. Now I was getting nosy. Was this a detective sent to spy on me? I owed a shitload of student loans to Uncle Sam, so I got a little nervous from time to time.

I wander around the school to see what was going on. With catlike evasion skills, I slip into the classroom located in front of the car to see what was going on. Cautiously, I peeked around the wall to look out the window only to find a bald man feverishly jerking off. I immediately regretted my decision to investigate. Jesus H. Christ, what the fuck was this guy doing masturbating in an empty school parking lot? How crazy do you have to be to rub one out here!

I was just glad this guy didn't see me. If we made eye contact, I'd never be able to sleep at night again.

My initial reaction was to call the police. Like any normal person, I don't want a pervert doing that shit near children.

But it would be a hassle to call the cops. Just hear me out for a minute, okay?

If I called the police, I would have to explain what this guy is doing, ID him when they showed up, have to point him out in a police lineup, and eventually testify in court. "Yes, Your Honor, that's the guy over there. He was cranking off behind a scummy dumpster on school property late one evening."

The last time I was called to court, I lost three weeks' pay. Fucking jury duty. I know it's my civic duty and all, but this case was a true shit storm. For three god-awful weeks I listened to Asshole A complain about how Asshole B's tiny fender bender altered his life forever.

My job doesn't offer payment for jury duty, so I got fucked out three weeks' money. It may not sound like a lot to you, but when you live check to check, it's a big deal. Sure, that five-dollar-a-day check from the county court might cover lunch, but I got bills, man.

So I made the decision not to call the cops on Petey the Pervert. Why the hell should I have to waste my time and money for this schlub? It was not like I did anything wrong here. Yet I'd be the one who'd get screwed because of some dirty old man who wanted to get his nut in front of a school.

Sometimes doing the right thing will fuck you in the end. That's a life lesson you can take to the bank. I decided to ignore the problem and hopefully it'd go away. If the police caught this guy on patrol, then so be it.

But the cops never came.

Week after week, I'd see this beige sedan drive into the parking lot, do his thing for about twenty minutes, and leave. At first it bothered the hell out of me. Not only was it repugnant to think about, but this asswipe was putting my job in danger. If I turned a blind eye and something bad happened, then I'd be held accountable for someone else's mistakes. That's all I needed: some after-school Girl Scout troop walking up on this guy while he's pulling his pud.

I thought of ways to stay on the other side of the building, hoping some do-gooder would report him and free me from my dilemma. Weeks turned into months, and before long, Mr. Jerkinstein was a regular fixture at my job. No one noticed the car at all. None of my coworkers saw him. Shit, maybe I was seeing things? This dump of a job had me second-guessing myself all the time, so perhaps this guy was just a figment of my imagination?

But I know he was real because I couldn't get that image of him jerking off out of my head.

For whatever reason, the entire carrot waxing scene was stuck in my mind visually. Traumatic incidents tend to stick with a person for a while, kind of like how alien abductees still remember those lights and anal probes.

To cope with the situation, I let my morbid mind go wild. Nothing says "Fuck it" more than a sick sense of humor. As the days went on, I figured I would at least give the guy a name, for shits and giggles. I called him Jacob. He looked like a Jacob. He's was in his midforties, average height and weight. He was bald, just like his little tally whacker, and he was dressed like a businessman or office worker. He looked like a stereotypical average middle-aged white guy, only sweatier because of the whole masturbating thing.

Being the fucked-up guy I am, I began making up short stories about Jacob the Jerker. Maybe this guy was going through a rough divorce and his ex-wife was taking half his money for child support? Or maybe his ex-wife, who left him, taught first grade at this school, and this was the only way in his messed-up head he could be with her? Perhaps Jacob had anxiety issues about giving presentations at his job, the accounting firm, and jerking off was his way to release some stress?

I felt it best to leave well enough alone with poor Jacob. As long as he didn't start flashing his meat at anyone, I was fine letting him do whatever he was doing out there. Who am I to judge anyone, right?

Ultimately, I felt sad for Jacob. I mean, how low do you have to be in life to be doing this sort of thing in an abandoned school parking lot.

After the sixth or seventh month, my feelings of sadness turned into anger and frustration. This guy was obviously in need of a helping hand and not in that way. Jacob needed to pick himself up and get on with life. Everybody loves a comeback story! Jacob just needed some guidance, someone to say, "I believe in you, Jacob." I was almost tempted to bang on his window one night and say, "Hey, man! Stop doing that shit and go see a shrink or something!" I decided against it just in case he had a heart condition. Sneaking up on an older guy and banging on his car while he was choking his chicken didn't seem like a safe thing to do.

Obviously confronting Jacob in person wasn't going to happen, so I got inventive. One morning, I had a visit at home from the Jehovah's Witnesses. Normally I would have turned the hose on him, but I took some of his pamphlets. I then went to work on that Friday and taped them to the side of the dumpster, the one facing Jacob's car where he parked. Maybe seeing one of those pamphlets would give him the idea to go talk to someone about his problems. A church perhaps, or maybe a priest? Shit, go speak to a rabbi. Just stop doing this shit behind a dumpster, Jacob!

That night, Jacob didn't see the papers because he ripped into his dick like he normally did, finished, and drove off like a champ. I'm thinking Jacob was in the zone and never saw the literature taped nonchalantly to the side of a dirty dumpster.

A week later I tried another tactic. I found a Neighborhood Watch sticker in my junk drawer, so I stuck that to the dumpster. Come Friday evening the same result occurred. My pal Jacob wasn't interested if the entire community was watching. Now I'm getting pissed. I wanted this guy to turn his life around and I don't even know him. Subtle hints weren't doing the trick, so I took an old can of spray paint from the boiler room and wrote "I see you" on the side of the dumpster on Thursday night.

Jacob still didn't get the hints I was leaving. He did his deed and took off. Now I was being more than nice letting Jacob work out his problems, but enough was enough. If someone leaves you signs about something and you don't get it, perhaps you need a reality check. Or maybe Jacob was into the whole "someone watching him" thing. What started out as subtle hints now turned into a voyeurism game. Great, now I was turning the pervert into an even bigger pervert.

So how did I deal with Jacob in the end?

Well, I was a coward and ratted his ass out through an anonymous tip. I went to the corner store up the road to get a couple of snacks and a big cup of coffee right before Jacob showed up. I dropped the dime on him. I called the police from a pay phone outside the corner store and drove back to work. Yeah, it was a long time ago. Hence the pay phone outside of the bodega.

When I pulled back into the parking lot, the cops were taking Jacob out of his car with their lights on. He was crying while the cops put him in handcuffs and slid him into the back of the patrol car. They took him away that night and impounded his car on the spot. As I was getting out of my truck, one of the cops came up to let me know the situation. "Wow! Oh my god," I said. "I didn't know he was there, Officer! I just got this tall cup of coffee up the road."

Jacob never parked his beige sedan in the parking lot ever again. Had he showed up, he probably would have been locked up for coming within so many feet of a school zone. Nobody wants to see someone have their life ruined by being arrested like that. But then again, I guess if you're doing what Jacob did in the first place, I'd say you've got bigger problems. I blame myself for letting this guy do what he did for so long. He was masturbating in a school parking lot for almost an entire school year. That's a lot of jizz, my friend. Should I have called the cops as soon as I first saw him? Indeed. But unless you want to pay my bills for three weeks while I testify in court, I'd shut the fuck up and enjoy the story.

Chapter 10

Bobby Benz

Well, I got moved again at my job. Second time this month. Now I was in some hole in the wall halfway across town. This place smelled, like, really smelled. Something must've died in ventilation shaft and nobody knew where the shriveled corpse was. I was sure the scent would go away. Maybe the people who worked here just didn't smell it? But I could smell it. Smelled like death.

I was transferred after an altercation at my previous post. And by altercation, I mean another janitor tried to club me over the head with a feces-laden plunger. I'd like to say it was the first time I'd been accosted with a plunger, but I'd be lying. Long story short, the boss moved me because the other guy was Russian and most likely a former KGB operative. That's what I think, anyway.

A piece of paper in my work file says I was disruptive, but I was moved so the Russian wouldn't cry discrimination. I never liked him or his snide remarks about taking me out with a broken bottle of Stoli. He said that line to me verbatim. The boss didn't believe me, so now I was hitting the road again, off to meet new coworkers. While my transfer was a pain in the ass, I did get a chance to meet yet another wacko in the line of duty.

My new coworkers were something of an odd couple. My superior was named Kata. She too was from the former USSR and knew the last guy I worked with. First time I met her, she mumbled something foreign before looking me dead in the face. "Oh, you know Demetri, eh? So do me…" Then she stood there eyeballing me with her cold gray peepers. Great, another pissed-off Commie. I've racked up quite a list of people who hate me. To the best of my knowledge, most of them come from Stalin's old regime.

Kata's English was bad. I mean, like, "How did you pass the interview?" bad. I'd been called a piece of shit in a few different languages, but Russian seemed to be a fan favorite. For the life of me, I can't understand why all these Russians hate me. I didn't know what else to say other than "Hi" and "Bye." Kata seemed offended to be in my presence. I bet you Demetri told her some bullshit about me.

A few days passed, and we began the formalities of getting to know each other. We'd talk, somewhat, about the job and other mindless chatter. "So you raised goats, lambs, and hens in your old country? That's nice." I wasn't being an asshole. Just trying to make conversation so I wouldn't get transferred again. "I've never smelled that kind of cheese before… You say you made it from what kind of milk again?"

She would smile and nod politely all the while waiting for me to turn around before she grumbled something unpleasant. Kata and I had an understanding after the initial meeting. During lunch, I'd leave her to knit some god-awful sweater while I read a book or surfed eBay on my laptop. We were like two countries separated by a menacing wall, but we kept our guns down most days. Even though Kata would have liked to see me dragged behind a mule cart, she wasn't the worst person at my new post. Kata and I united only in our hatred for our other coworker: Bobby Benz.

His real name was Michael Rivers. A tall, slinky young kid. Typical punk from New York, complete with blasting speakers when he pulled into the parking lot. This guy was a complete train wreck. Kata told me he had something wrong with him in her own way of speaking.

"He got brain diseases or something," said Kata.

"What do you mean?" I said.

"There's something wrong in his head. He's got ADD or ADHD. I don't know. As long as he do job, I no care what the fuck he do. He talk about him car *all* day. He love that thing and will talk your ears off. He thinks him ladies' man too. Truth is, he just stupid idiot like all the other stupid men. He thinks he got million of dollars and a girl on every block."

I had seen this kid in the hallway but figured I'd run into him eventually. I mean, it was only the three of us at night, so I had to meet him eventually. I spotted him the first night I was there, walking real fast with his head down, laughing to himself. Another winner! Finally, after saying hi here and there, he came over to start jabbering away. Never said two words to me before.

"Hey, do you know any good dojos around these parts, bro?" said Bobby.

"Ummm… what do you mean?" I said.

"You know!" He made a tsking sound after he said it. "Like an MMA ring or a place where they teach you to fight people."

"Not really…," I said. "I don't do that kind of thing."

"What?" he said. "Are you for real? You should try it, bro. I've been training for years to fight in the octagon. I'm gonna become a fighting machine one day and destroy all my opponents."

Before I could piece together a response to his weird comment, he was gone. Down the hallway he went, almost in a sprinting manner with his head hung low. What the hell was I supposed to say to something like that? Was that a threat or just ramblings of a mentally unstable individual? Did he just put me on notice about his superior warrior fighting skills?

He never officially introduced himself but rather made a serious statement and then walked away.

Here we go again. Another creep with a brain malfunction. I'd seen this stuff a thousand times at this godforsaken hellhole. Crazy one-liners from a former insane asylum resident. Most of the derelicts here either came from the local looney bin or took meds to stay out of one. I didn't know whether to call the cops or start carrying a set of nunchucks in my back pocket.

Bobby looked like a normal twentysomething-year-old until I watched him closer. He walked down the hall either fast or extremely slow, depending on the day. These were obvious signs of a tweaker, a former or current drug addict fiending for the next fix. This job's full of them—pill poppers, vein injectors, powder sniffers, you name it.

This guy didn't act like a speed freak, so I had to keep studying him until I got a sense of what I was dealing with.

Some days Bobby slowed it down a bit, you know, a slowed reaction time, walking like he's stuck in mud. Then I saw his hand-writing one day in the break room on his timesheet. It was extremely small and incoherent. And there it was, ladies and gentlemen, a cer-tified Ritalin or Adderall user. Bobby was a kook, a crazy person masquerading as a normal person until you took their pills away.

I know what you're saying, and you can call me an asshole if you want. Have you ever worked with a kook before? Sometimes you get the feeling they'll snap and kill a room full of people at a moment's notice. Bobby most definitely had murderous tendencies as our short conversations continued. A few days later, he came walking up to me again and asked if I had a few cans of Red Bull. Yes, you heard correctly. A few cans of Red Bull. Sure, I'd gladly give some jackass a four-pack of jet fuel so he could chug them and rip my arm off in a death match. Who the fuck asks for a few cans of Red Bull anyway? A jittery mass murderer, that's who.

When I told him I didn't drink the stuff, he stared me down like a lion stalking a gazelle. "What do you mean you don't drink the stuff? Are you some kinda loser or something?" said Bobby, who, at that time, had his fists clenched tightly. I was legitimately afraid for my safety at that moment.

"How can you not drink Red Bulls?" said Bobby. Notice the word Bulls, meaning plural. "I mean, who doesn't like the taste and effects of Red Bulls? It's, like, the best shit ever, bro!" This guy kept going on and on about how Red Bull was awesome and how he felt invincible when drinking it. There was a brief time during Bobby's tirade when I thought I should have taken some sort of defensive stance, just in case. I might have stepped back while trying not to make direct eye contact. It's best not to rile these kinds of people when they get worked up about something. I hate to use the term *retard strength*, but I kind of feel this situation warrants its usage.

During the two-minute-long speech, I reminded Bobby that I didn't have any Red Bulls, even though seeing him without a super-charged energy drink was probably far worse than if he had it. Picture a six-foot Eminem-looking kid, with crazy eyes, yelling how much he loves to drink several Red Bulls a day.

"Dude, you need to start drinking Red Bulls… It's amazing when you're lifting mega amounts of weight in the gym," said Bobby. I'm not sure, but consuming multiple Red Bulls and working out right after is the very best way to have a heart attack. Bobby didn't see it that way. He was thinking Red Bull replaced steroids and he'd ultimately look like a bodybuilder. Seconds later, the animal inside his feeble mind began to cool down. Realizing I had nothing to give him, Bobby turned around and strolled down the hallway like he did during our initial meeting.

After our energy drink debate, I didn't see Bobby for a week. He was off from work, which made me believe he suffered a caffeine stroke when he finally got his hands on some Red Bulls. Maybe he was locked up in some cage in Upstate New York trying to regain his sanity? Much to my dismay, the following week Bobby showed up, but with a calmer disposition. I saw him in the break room all dazed trying to open a can of SpaghettiOs. Yes! He was doped up! Someone shoved a few pills down his throat just in the nick of time. At least I wouldn't fear for my life today with Bobby tranquilized.

This pattern of schizoid talk, followed by weeks of medication-induced slumber, sums up the whole time I worked with Bobby. He'd go nuts over something miniscule, only to be zonked out of his mind for weeks straight.

The slightest thing would send Bobby into his dark place. Kata, Bobby, and I were sitting in the break room silently having our dinners on an otherwise quiet night. Bobby was eating a prefrozen pizza while Kata ate her homemade goat stew. The silence was broken, however, when Bobby took out his phone to start a blasting rap on speaker. Kata did not approve.

"Hey, stupid man," she said. "Turn off that crap. It give me headache all the time!"

"Don't tell me what to do, Kata!" roared back a now-enraged Bobby. "This is my favorite song, and I'll blast this shit all fucking night if I want!" Bobby had a bottle of Mountain Dew in his hands and pointed it at Kata in a stern gesture. Much like a bank robber pointing a revolver at a teller.

"No, you don't! I trying to eat and that stuff make my ears bleed. No one wants to hear that ruckus!" Kata screamed back, proving in my mind no one wins an argument better than a Russian. Bobby's fist clenched around his soda. In his head, it was probably Kata's throat he was symbolically crushing because Bobby was that fucking crazy. I was halfway across the room watching their quarrel. You know, a safe distance in case I had to dart toward an exit door if Bobby went berserk. It was impressive to see the color change in their faces when they screamed at each other. Reminded me of the autumn along coastal Maine.

"Let me tell you something, Kata! This music is part of my youth," said Bobby with his forehead rapidly gathering sweat. "I listened to it every day for weeks until I memorized each line. This music… my music, keeps me calm. Don't fuck with my calm, Kata!"

"Yes, definitely! Let's not disturb the monster's peace," I said to myself. "Don't provoke the demon, Kata. Please. For the love of Christ, don't piss off the hellhound!"

"You listen to me, crazy man! Turn it off now or I call Bossman." Kata was pointing at him with her wrinkled finger. "No one wants to hear garbage you play all the time!"

I didn't think it was a good idea to call him a crazy man, or point menacingly, for that matter. One thing you learn throughout life is to never to call a crazy person crazy.

At this point, they both stood up, mere feet from each other. I pushed back on my chair. If anything was going down, I sure as hell didn't want to be in their range.

Seconds later, Bobby was waving his arms frantically screaming how his music was his savior and without it he'd be nothing. Kata and Bobby exchanged viewpoints for about five minutes until Kata called the night boss.

"That's it! I call boss, you crazy, punk shithead!"

Bobby flipped the fuck out. Before Kata could grab the phone, he went into beast mode. He smashed his iPhone on the ground. Boy, he spiked it like he just caught the winning touchdown in the Super

Bowl. Then he began shaking his head from side to side, sort of like a dog when they swallow a hornet and get stung in their mouth. I did what any rational person would do—I took off like a scared rabbit. From down the hall, I could hear what I thought was a heinous crime scene unfolding. Poor Kata. It was my belief Bobby had picked her up and launched her into the vending machine. If Bobby killed Kata, I'd be upset. But I sure as hell wasn't sticking around to save her. She's got feet. She should've known to start running once Bobby started frothing from the mouth.

Turns out Bobby didn't kill Kata. He overturned some tables and completely obliterated one iPhone 6. Two cars pulled into the parking lot soon after Kata put down the phone, Bossman and Bobby's mother. I hoped one of them had a dart gun to sedate the maniac. His mother brought a full bottle of whatever magical drugs he took. It must have been some good shit too, because he went from raving lunatic to drooling baby in minutes.

Here's the kicker: instead of being fired or put in a padded cell where he belonged, Bobby was sent home for the night. He was told to take a few days off to clear his mind.

Are you fucking serious? Not for nothing, had I gone bonkers on the job, I'd be terminated. Not Bobby. Hell, this fucker goes apeshit, and the boss lets him take a vacation from reality. This was yet another bullshit unwritten rule at work. If you're "special," you get special treatment. If Bobby or any other kook went nuts, the bosses wouldn't fire them. Legally they can't due to the Americans with Disabilities Act. If these chowder heads have a preexisting condition, legally they must be coddled like an infant. "It's okay, Bobby. Because God gave you a fucked-up brain, you have the right to bounce a microwave off a coworker's head."

Fuck that. I think that's horseshit! Why do they get a pass to cause mayhem because their brain is a little screwy? Half the time I think these kooks do it on purpose to see how far they can push the envelope. If Bobby ever dismembered a coworker, he'd probably get a trip to Tahiti free of charge. Just as long as he agreed to take his pills after he disposed of the body.

Soon after his visit to Lithiumland, Bobby came back to work like a bat out of hell again. This time he was in search of a female companion. After weeks of ignoring me, he walked up to me with a grin on his face. This couldn't be good, I thought to myself.

"I need a new bitch to bang this weekend," said Bobby with his new iPhone blasting T-Pain. Super. Someone got him another phone to smash to smithereens during his next tirade.

"Excuse me?" I said.

"I'm heading to a ballin' club in the city this weekend, and I need a fine bitch to bang after I get all fucked up."

"Well," I said, not knowing what else to say. "I guess you could go online to find a girlfriend?"

"Nah, nah, nah, nah. Me and online girls don't go together too well," he said. I was afraid to ask what he meant by that last line.

Before I could answer, he rambled on. "I don't need no hugged-up girlfriend. I just need to use her without her getting all sappy."

"Ummm. I don't know what to tell you. I don't know any single girls… sorry."

"Bitches. You mean bitches, bro. All women are bitches," Bobby proclaimed then stormed off again.

This encounter was less violent though distressing none the least.

Since I wasn't going to get away from this cretin anytime soon, I decided to examine my adversary. "The best way to defeat an enemy is to learn their habits." You may have thought Bobby said that last line, but it was me. This crazy train had gone on long enough. I was done being hunted down each time Bobby had a thought process. It was time to evaluate my opponent.

I started with his clothes to see what kind of psychopath I was dealing with. He was wearing the angry-teen-rapper outfit, complete with a silver chain about the size of a tow rope. A hefty cross hung from it with fake diamonds studded around the depiction of Jesus. Not sure if our Savior wanted to be flanked by cubic zirconium in his final moments, but Bobby thought it was "pimpin'" and he later put it. His shoes were abrasive, Nikes with god-awful colored shoelaces.

Baggy jeans most days except when he wore skinny emo jeans to be trendy, with a fake Gucci belt.

Then came the shirts. He had several layers of clothing, all in alternating sleeve lengths. Starting from the inside out: a designer guinea T, followed by a long-sleeved black T-shirt underneath another tighter Affliction-style T-shirt. He never wore a uniform, and the bosses didn't seem to care. My guess is they knew how unstable he was and decided not to question a man who could go haywire at the drop of a hat.

Most of the time, he looked like every other wannabe suburban thug on MTV, but with braces. Not gold fronts, but actual braces. He's over twenty-one, I know that, but from the fables he told he could be anywhere from twenty-one to forty years old. And skinny like a twig yet he claimed he could lift several hundred pounds in a bench press. I bet those multiple Red Bulls come in handy with a couple of hundred pounds from a dead lift. He reminded me of a cross between Kanye West and Gilbert Grape.

The more I studied him, I discovered he was a compulsive liar, on top of being a kook. In the off chance he could actually hurt someone, I kept my conversations short. I quickly learned which phrases to avoid so he wouldn't decapitate me. First and foremost, never ask Bobby to turn off his music. Several people found out this tidbit of information the hard way. One night, after complaints from several teachers, he turned his music off in style. He picked up the radio he had, an old ghetto blaster, and smashed it on the terrazzo floor, stomping on the pieces while grunting heinously.

Then he went from room to room asking the teachers if it was quiet enough for them. "Are you happy now, lady? My music's off, and it won't be bothering you anymoooooore!" said Bobby, who was sweating profusely again. Some of the teachers were crying after his nutjob rampage. Cops were called to the school this time and so was Bobby's momma with a fresh bottle of his relaxing Skittles as she called them. I don't know how the hell the bosses didn't fire him that time. I guess if you've got a serious mental illness, you can get away with highway robbery if you produce a doctor's note.

This guy was beyond hope as far as I was concerned. After a weeklong hiatus, Bobby stumbled down the hallways for another month or so seemingly in zombie mode. Then one fine evening, Bobby went cray-cray yet again. Never said a word to me for two months after the radio incident then walked up to me asking about women.

"Hey, bro… do you have a single sister or somethin'? I need a date for this amazing party in New York this weekend, and I need some arm candy to walk in with."

Nope. Can't help you there, buddy. Who in their right mind would set this joker up with a family member? Unless you didn't mind seeing her picture on the side of a milk carton.

This guy must have mixed some hardcore meds if he thought I'd be his personal pimp. Why wouldn't he just leave me alone? Go ask Kata if she has a granddaughter or something! I kept my answers simple while avoiding eye contact again. In the back of my mind, I felt a bad confrontation with Bobby would resemble a tiger mauling deep in a Punjabi jungle.

Suddenly he took off again, sprinting down the hall after hearing I couldn't help him. In studying Bobby, I found a simple one- or two-sentence answer while looking slightly downward was the best course of action. This way I didn't provoke an attack. I felt like a safari tour guide when confronted with a charging elephant—ease them back while cautious not to make any sudden movements. Had I raised my voice to Bobby, he might have unleashed a goblin or two. I wasn't afraid of the guy. I was afraid of what the voices in his head would say if they felt threatened.

The next few weeks were surprisingly quiet for Bobby. His psychiatrists must have upped his dose, causing Bobby to smile a lot. Ever see a serial killer grin uncontrollably? Well, it ain't pretty. I guess it's better than having to fend off an unhinged mongrel seeking energy drinks or women. There isn't enough mood-elevating drugs in the world to control Bobby's urges.

I came into work one afternoon to find Bobby staring at me as soon as I walked through the door. He had his arms folded, perhaps concealing ninja throwing stars, waiting for me to come in. This was it. This was how my life was going to end. As I slowly ventured inward, Bobby stopped me with a series of sentences. "Would you ever date a Victoria's Secret model?" asked Bobby. "I have this friend who may be setting me up with a runway model."

Oh fuck! Now what? My feet were not three paces into the doorway when I was bombarded. Should I turn to run back out the door? Or chance it by pushing my way past him? "You only live once," I said to myself. So I used my snarky wit as a wild card option.

"You should totally go for it," I said. "I'd definitely check her out and see if she's hot." Why did I say that? He was going to freak out and smash my face in with a twenty-ounce Red Bull can! But alas, he did not.

"Yeah, bro. You got that right!" said Bobby with his crazy eyes now seeming relaxed. "What could it hurt, ya know? I mean, she's already a model and probably loaded, so what do I have to lose?"

Good god, it worked. Instead of blowing up in my face, Bobby was somehow calm, resisting the urge to meltdown. My quick wit somehow satiated the devil in his quest for answers. For the first time, being a smartass helped me instead of getting me in trouble. I was studying Bobby too hard for the past few months. The most basic of human emotions, sarcasm, was the ticket. Once I told him what I thought he wanted to hear, Bobby backed down. He smiled at me, walking away with a slow head bob.

This scientific breakthrough was something of an epiphany. Anytime Bobby asked me something, I gave him the exact opposite answer of what a rational person might say.

"You say you're having a threesome with twins later this evening, Bobby? I think that's awesome, bro. Make sure you give yourself a high five for me while you're doing it."

"Some guy cut you off in traffic the other day? Fuck that shit! You should've put him in a choke hold at the next stoplight."

I was giving Bobby answers only a deranged drifter would say, which in his mind was the perfect solution to his many daily problems.

Since my experiment of using sarcasm worked so well, I decided to go full force with it. I'd be the sounding board for whatever weird shit came bouncing into Bobby's head. "Do you think that teacher in room G14 has a sex slave?" asked Bobby. "Have you ever seen a Sasquatch before?" he asked on more than one occasion. "What's the highest level you ever made it to in World of Warcraft?" My answers came from the part of your brain you've always wanted to use but feared the results. To put it another way, I had no filter to stop asinine shit from coming out.

"I think most teachers in this school have a sex slave, Bobby. Especially the older ones."

"No way! Really?" Bobby's eyes got large and sparkly.

"Oh, without a doubt, bro," I said as fiendish thoughts raced through my head. "As for a Sasquatch, I've seen them quite a few times. And not to brag, but I've beaten World of Warcraft several times over, son. I've been over to China to play with a whole bunch of my teammates online. It was sick, bro!" I couldn't stop making shit up to say to Bobby. Who knows what I said half the time. I just wanted this creep to back off.

Did I feel bad about messing with a half-wit like Bobby? Of course. But it's better than living in constant fear all the time, wondering when the juggernaut will snap. Part of me was thinking I was an evil bastard for what I was doing. But I wasn't trying to make fun of him. All I wanted was to do my job and go home. Why do all the freak shows seek me out? No matter where I worked, at whatever post, these bizarre fuckers have to talk to me about the dumbest shit.

Bobby, who felt comfortable around me now, started to talk about his car. He drove this early-nineties beat-up Mercedes-Benz all souped up as he called it. Crackling window tint, rusty wheels, massive speaker system in the trunk, you know you've seen these shit boxes on the road before. To Bobby, his Benz was his pride and joy. Instead of chatting about random women or video games, we now talked about his car. Each and every day I would have to endure listening to the latest German-car happenings.

One day after a big rainstorm, Bobby said his car was unstoppable. "My Benz can do 140 in that shit, no problem."

"No doubt," I said. "You should always drive superfast in the rain."

"Fuck yeah, bro! Just last week I drove my Benz in a storm for over twenty minutes weaving in and out of traffic until those fucking pigs pulled me over," said Bobby, feeling like a popular kid for the first time ever.

"Whaaaaaat? Dude, you should've flipped them off and resisted arrest," I implored to Bobby. I wanted to see how far he'd go with his lies.

"Bro… that's exactly what I did! 'Cause I'm a super star! My car and my women need to be fast as fuck. These goddamn cops ticketed my shit. Told me they could impound it for what I done."

"No way! I would've made them catch me. If it was me, they'd still be chasing me down the highway," I said, all while watching Bobby's tiny face light up like the Fourth of July.

"Well, they said I was doing ninety in a sixty-five. I told that stupid fuck I had my Benz well over one hundred twenty. Fuck them! Then they hit me with a noise pollution ticket 'cause my tunes were up too loud and a front-window tint ticket too." Bobby was on a roll trying to go overboard with his comments. We exchanged nonsense for another minute until I ran out of extreme things to say. The whole time Bobby was getting amped up, trying to outdo me with more extravagant lines.

Bobby started telling me about his other violations, which I knew were bullshit the minute he mentioned jail time. According to Bobby, his license has been revoked twelve times, he had over one hundred tickets, and he's spent multiple nights in prison, where he met gang members who wanted him to be their leader. He also had several Mafia connections, but he didn't want to talk about that because then he'd be back in the Witness Protection Program.

"Them damn agents got me on surveillance 24-7, bro," said Bobby. "I don't want to alarm you, but I think they might try to raid this place and lock me up for several unrelated incidents last week."

Discussing illegal street racing with Bobby bored me to death once the novelty wore off. I found it hard to keep up with his enthusiasm, partly due to his infatuation with Red Bull. He was all jazzed about what new engine part he installed or how many times the cops followed him through his development. Listening to his mindless drivel made me feel like I was babysitting a teenager who played too much Grand Theft Auto. Enough with the shoot-outs and high-speed chases already!

I'd made it a point to avoid seeing him all together at work. Ducking behind garbage cans, using back hallways to random exit doors, it was tough to hide from a guy who was always focused due to his medication. Most nights I would've welcomed conversation with Kata regarding her childhood village in Stalingrad. Then it hit me: talk normal to him and see if he wigs out again. At least then he might do something really fucked up, like drive his car through the cafeteria walls.

A few minutes into my next shift, I saw Bobby walking toward me with a car parts magazine. I went back to simple one- or two-word answers while looking at the ground. It drove him nuts.

"Bro, have you seen the newest superchargers for Mercedes? I bet I could beat a Ferrari with that shit under my hood!" said Bobby as boyish laughter slide out of his mouth.

"No, I haven't seen it," I said.

"Huh? You gotta see this new part! It's like… insane or something!"

"Nah, I'm not interested," I said. Bobby's internal flame began to flicker.

"Yo, what the fuck? Are you kidding me right now? I'm… I'm sure you know how awesome my Benz would be with this awesome part in it."

Then I dropped the bomb on him. "Sorry, don't care about your car, bro."

Bobby's face went from overjoyed to confused to bitter hatred in a matter of seconds. I thought I heard a bolt of lightning strike in his head. Bobby went fucking bananas, ripping the magazine in half. He started to shake uncontrollably while a vein popped up on his brow.

"Yo… that's… that's fucked up, man. Why would you say something like that? How… how can you not like my Benz, bro?" It was the final straw for Bobby. He started to pant heavily like a rabies-stricken dog, gyrating.

At this time, Kata heard his loud voice and came running down the hall. "Why he do that?" she said. "What he all crazy man like dis?" I told her Bobby started freaking out over nothing.

"I don't know!" I said. "He must be pissed about something. You have to call his mom or someone before he starts breaking stuff again!" Too late. Bobby started a fast walk down the corridor flipping over anything in his way. Once he made it to the trophy display case, near the gym, he took each trophy out and proceeded to slam them onto the ground. Then he found a baseball bat someone forgot in the gym.

By the time the night boss made it to the school, Bobby's mom was pulling in as well. It was too late for them to help cover up his warpath this time. We had to call the cops soon after Bobby started smashing windows. Damn near thirty windows when all was said and done. The police took Bobby away in the back of a squad car, but not before they Tased him three times to get him under control. I told you, those damn Red Bulls were his favorite. He probably chugged a case before he came to work that day.

A lot of good a bottle of meds does when the guy's already off the deep end. This time the bosses had to fire Bobby, who was in the back of a real cop car for probably the first time in his life. Okay, I feel like crap having gotten the kid fired. In fact, I wished I never started to antagonize him in the first place. Was I about to step up and explain why Bobby went off like a tank? Nah, I don't think so. I needed this job too much. Even though I hated each day I come to work, I needed the money just like everyone else. Besides, I was minding my own business from day one. All I ever wanted was to be left alone. It was not my fault this kid's chemical imbalance got the best of him.

The next week, the boss moved a replacement over to fill Bobby's spot. Another kook, no doubt, who also had some sort of mental defect. At least this one wouldn't confront you in a violent manner. Not yet, at least.

Think about it this way, now Bobby can play Xbox all day while sucking down as many Red Bulls unemployment could buy. Unless the courts locked him away in a dungeon, with the rest of the monsters.

Chapter 11

Brother Wade Johnson

We had a guy here who loved Jesus more than life itself. His main goal each day was to praise him and follow his every command, while trying to do the least amount of work possible. On the outside, he was a saint. But I'm telling you the God's honest truth: I believe he was the Antichrist with a mop.

Wade Johnson, or Brother Wade as he liked to be called, started working here about five years ago. He was hired as a part-timer to fill in for someone who had a stroke. The guy Wade was replacing died two weeks later. Tough luck, I guess. Another one bites the dust.

So Wade got promoted to full-time. My boss gave him a set of keys and said, "You've got the job!" No lengthy job evaluation to see if Wade could actually do the job right. No one bothered to check if this guy was the devil incarnate, which I later believed him to be. Right before Wade was given the job permanently, the boss asked him if he had any questions or comments about the position. Wade's response, like all weirdo faith people, was, "I'll do the job as if Jesus himself asked me to clean!"

It's pretty much a given these asshole bosses never check if someone can do the job properly. "Would you consider yourself a good worker?" would be my first question, followed by "Do you know what a mop does?" In my department, the only job necessity is to stay afloat if you fall in a toilet while cleaning it. I mean, this isn't a complicated gig at all, but at least see if the guy can push a broom without difficulties before giving him a job.

The moronic tendencies aren't limited to my department. We had one supervisor who got the job because his brother wrote his résumé. Bob Jenkins, the math department manager, found out his wife was screwing one of the social studies teachers. He moved his family out of state to try to rectify the problem. When his job came up for bid, he suggested his brother, Tim Jenkins, take it. When it came time to review Tim's résumé, the department hired him on the spot. The powers that be never looked if Bob's old résumé was exactly like Tim's new résumé. The guy could barely count, let alone solve a single math problem! It took a whole year to figure out Tim was full of shit when his department's budget was over by about seven million dollars.

Speaking of dipshits, Wade gave me the chills from the get-go. Not because he was religious or because of his choice in moral thinking. I took one look at Wade and knew he was a phony. You know the feeling I'm talking about? The one where you look at someone and say to yourself, "Boy, I bet that person is a real asshole." Once I got to know Wade, I knew my gut instinct was correct.

For starters, he looked exactly like one of those bizarre holy rollers. Blonde hair, blue eyes, and wore his shirt tucked in. Some people like a shirt tucked in, but this guy was over-anal-retentive. He kind of looked like an albino or a leper. Maybe the Lord doesn't allow his followers to sunbathe?

Wade's hairdo resembled something Johnny Cash would sport, complete with the gel-slick wave ever so popular in the fifties. I can't remember a time when Wade had a hair out of place. That dome piece of his looked like it was a placed on his head with a spatula each morning. Those big wide eyes of his looked like he was frightened all the time. I'm guessing he saw the Holy Ghost each day and it scared the crap right out of him.

Wade was a neat freak deluxe. His tan khakis matched his loafers, and they both matched his skin tone. The guy looked like a window mannequin from LL Bean. I don't know what it was about this dude, but his very presence made me ill. I even hated his walk. It looked as if he was jogging while trying to lean back as far as he could while swinging his arms. Wade resembled a religious version of

Yogi the Bear except, instead of picnic baskets, Wade was constantly on the lookout for the Lord.

My first Wade encounter came a few days after we were introduced. That pompous asshole stopped me in the hallway to ask if I had seen him lately. When I said, "Who?" Wade rolled his eyes, in a judging manner, and tried to hand me a bunch on pamphlets. The last thing I needed in my life was some albino zealot, who walked like a cartoon character, to start blabbing about "making it right with the man upstairs."

When he spoke, he sounded like a preacher addressing a congregation. Wade's voice seemed to boom as if he was at a pulpit. Extra pronunciations with an emphasis on words like *we* and *perhaps*. All Wade talked about was how much he wanted to please Jesus. Within a week, I wanted to drive him off a mountain. I couldn't care less what anyone does in their personal life, but don't start trying to get me to drink the Kool-Aid too. Once I started using Wade's pamphlets for scrap paper, he got all uppity. That's the thing about people like Wade: once they know you aren't joining their cult, they treat you like a heathen.

Then the dark side of Brother Wade started to rear its ugly head. I would notice him whispering to other coworkers when he thought I wasn't looking. Soon enough I had dirty looks from the people I had known for almost four years. Once he found out I was in charge at night, Wade took it upon himself to make my life hell.

None of the teachers thought Wade was a bad worker. He had them brainwashed, thinking he was a good little Christian boy who always did the job perfectly. Truth was Wade didn't really work while at work. He came in early to make coffee for teachers who stayed late, and he listened to a nightly religious channel on the radio. That's about all he did. He prayed a lot. Manual-work-wise? Not too much in the way of scrubbing or taking out garbage bags. Just praying, listening to his tunes, and brewing coffee.

Wade's janitor cart was perfectly clean, though. That wheeled bucket and mop holder were immaculate, not a spot on it. Anyone with a little common sense would know if something looks brand-spanking-new, it probably hasn't seen a lot of use. Two months into the job, my night supervisor asked me to check up on Wade, so I did. As I walked down to his area to have a little chat, I found him standing in his janitor closet polishing the broom handle with the radio on. It was tuned to station WGOD, "Where Jesus rocks all day and all night!"

"Hey, Wade. The boss asked me to—"

"Whoa, whoa, whoa, mister! That's the word of God you're interrupting, my brother," said Wade. He looked me square in the eye. No smile, no mouth movement or any other facial expressions. Just a blank, milky-white pie face. I remember seeing those neon-blue eyes pierce me like daggers. I felt as if I was looking at a meth head ready for that next jolt. Normally I would continue to talk, but he caught me off guard. I stood there waiting a few seconds to see his next move. Boy, this guy was creepy, like a toy clown sitting in the corner of a dark room.

"Ha ha!" said Wade while his face cracked a smirk. "I was just fooling with you, my friend."

"Ummmm… Okay. Like I said, Wade—"

"Excuse me… Can you please call me 'Brother Wade'? I am more receptive to that name, if you please."

"Look, the boss wants me to check in on you, all right, pal? To see how you're doing. That's all." A fire began to swirl inside Wade's ridiculously large eyes once he heard me call him pal. He stopped polishing the broom handle as a demonic look started to fill him. He just stood there, eyes gleaming at me.

"Do you have any questions about the job, Wade?" I said. "Like, anything about the area you have to clean or duties you have to complete each night?"

"I am perfectly fine with my work task, my brother. Jesus has shown me the way of the mop, and I am content with the work I have been given…"

Here's a little secret for any of you future janitors in a school district: if you really want to get out of work, start talking about our Savior. Once you open that can of worms, it's practically illegal to fire you. Anything you do can be scapegoated by saying you believe in a higher power. It's almost as good as saying you have a disability or have a pending workman's comp. case. I'm not advising you go around kicking students because Jesus wants you to, but religious choice at this job means you have an invisible Kevlar bubble around you at all times.

"Well, Wade, the boss told me your hallway was dirty for the last three days and garbage was left in the same room for almost a week. You know it's part of the job to do those things, right?"

"I am sure I cleaned those items to our Lord's liking," said Wade. That freak show started looking toward the ceiling after he spoke. It's been a while since I've been to church, but I'm guessing our Savior isn't a set of rusty asbestos pipes. That's the only thing I saw up there.

This guy had a biblical an answer for everything. When asked about the leaky faucet in room B-55, Wade told me he would "fix the water like Moses parting the Red Sea." I told him to dust the window ledges more often, to which Wade replied, "I shall clean those surfaces like the Lord cleansing Sodom and Gomorrah."

I left Wade to do his work after seeing I couldn't get a straight answer out of him. Two days passed, and more complaints followed. That prick never fixed any of the problems I talked to him about. A week later, my boss showed up to investigate the situation. Only problem was the little saint threw me under the bus during the meeting. Wade denied I ever said anything to him about improving his work. He also told my boss I wasn't a good communicator and I should take a few hints from his pastor about how to speak to people. Now I defended myself and told the boss Wade was full of shit, but it was no use. That albino demon had convinced my boss I was the problem in the first place!

"All I am saying, Mr. Polotski, is that I was never shone the light of my cleaning difficulties," said Wade. "I feel my cleaning duties are up to the Lord's standards, my friend."

"Look, Wade," I said. "I asked you nicely to clean the section. I never yelled at you or spoke down to you. All I did was ask you to do the job."

"I did not hear those words from your mouth, my brother. All I have ever done was—"

"Stop calling me your brother! You're lying your ass off!" I said.

By the end of the meeting, Wade had my boss believing I was at fault for everything. This son of a bitch denied everything I said to him and kept calling me brother like I was in his congregation. I admit, I lost it and called him a motherfucker, which I shouldn't have. I also called him a Jesus freak, which is a big no-no at my job. My boss took Wade's side and gave me a write-up for being combative.

I had to apologize to this ass clown and take an online course in proper workplace speech.

This is the exact shit I'm talking about. Each time I try to do my job, someone comes along and fucks me over. Now I've got a Bible Thumper riding my ass like a rodeo bull, all because I wouldn't call him Brother Wade. I'll be the first to admit I am somewhat aggressive, but only after being messed with first. Now half the department thinks I'm harassing this guy over his religion. It's bad enough I have a sorted history with the Serbs, Russians and Mongolians, but now I have an entire army of Christians and Catholics talking shit about me.

My problems with Brother Wade continued to escalate as the days passed. Occasionally he would wave from his section of the building, smiling like he just met the pope. That scumbag acted like everything was perfectly fine! Never thought to himself, *Boy, I really screwed that guy over. I don't know why he hates me so much?* I don't know if this guy was a robot or he was trying to egg me on somehow. I finally told Wade to stay more than a hundred feet away from me at all times because I was afraid his Jesus vibes would infect my soul.

Of course, the little pussy called the boss, complaining I was creating a hostile work environment. So we had another shitty meeting. This time, I was told to allow Wade to express himself as he pleases at work. No one bothered to hear me out, yet again.

I had given up trying to explain my side once Wade started to sob uncontrollably. "All I was trying to do was make him see the light of Jesus... Why won't he let it in?" While he boo-hooed to the boss about how much he tried to be my friend, I kept my silence. I wanted to clobber him while reciting Marilyn Manson lyrics, but I couldn't. This was the second time management believed Wade's tall tales. This guy had everyone snowed with his boyish charm and holy appearance. To the outsider, Wade appears to be the all-American role model. If he had a little more meat on his bones, I'd say he might have been a high school quarterback and prom king. Granted, I'm no angel by any means. But this fregging guy had me up the creek bad.

The outcome of the meeting was if I had another altercation, I was to be moved to another building. That's what these dickheads do here: they move an innocent person while the real problem sticks around unscathed.

Weeks went by without a hitch until the entire crew had to set up for a Christmas play. It's standard operating procedure when you work in a school. These kids make hideous decorations us janitors have to set up like we're stage hands on Broadway.

I told Wade it was his job to the move the manger from storage to the stage area. I figured he'd like that sort of thing. The entire time Wade was rattling on and on about how much he loves this time of year. "It's our Savior's birthday celebration, my brother! Won't you help move the manger with me?" So I did. It's Christmas, and I figured if I worked with Wade, he'd lay off trying to get me fired.

Turns out since Wade is all of 120 pounds soaking wet. He couldn't hold the weight of the display. The entire manger, with Baby Jesus and all, spilled out on the floor, causing Wade to have a mini meltdown in front of the whole crew. He went batshit crazy in front of the principal and play director, blaming me for the whole damn thing.

"Oh, my dear Lord! You dropped him! You broke the crib of Jesus on purpose! How could you do such a thing!" said Wade.

"No, I didn't!" I said. "You dropped it! I had my end and—"

"Silence, you blasphemer!" Wade got all red in the face with his childish hands covering his mouth. I noticed he no longer said "brother" like he did before. Fucking bastard set me up. There I stood holding the end of the manger with Christ Almighty rolling around on the stage.

"I am so sorry, my Lord!" said Wade. "This vile man doesn't appreciate you like I do…" Wade was on his knees trying to cradle that plastic baby, all the while acting out an epic monologue. Nobody caught Wade's evil little smile when he stopped to pray for my soul. Once I saw that, I lost my cool and let fly.

"You stupid fucking cunt! I'm tired of you acting like I'm the problem here!" I figured since I looked like a moron standing there holding half a manger, I might as well relieve myself of the burden. The principal later reported that I threw it across the stage, nearly killing two people in the process.

"He's got all you suckers fooled, man! This guy has been lying his ass off since he got here. Ask him what he did. Ask him about all the lies he's been spinning trying to make me look like a sadist. I am so sick of this weirdo blaming me for everything *he* does wrong around here! Watch out for this guy! He's a fucking demon, and he's dangerous, man…"

A coworker later told me I tried to take Wade's head off with one of the wooden camels on the side of the stage. Oddly, I don't remember much else from that altercation. I might have called Wade and the play director a cocksucker. I have no clue why I started yelling at the director. He was probably just standing there with a stupid look on his face.

It was suggested at my union meeting that I was to be fired on the spot. Since I had a long history of supposed aggression to other coworkers and had a couple of incidents with Wade before, the head honcho wanted me terminated. As luck would have it, the union stepped in and worked out a negotiation to move me to another post as long as Wade signed a deal to not prosecute me for the whole wooden camel decapitation attempt. Wade, being the forgiving, loveable hero in this situation, agreed to spare me.

"We all must learn to forgive and forget, my brothers and sisters!" said Wade. The bosses ate that shit up with a spoon.

I later heard he was commended for his acts of kindness. Management made him the night supervisor at that building and was given a new raise for his conduct as well.

When I look back on the whole thing, I laugh. If I think about it too much, I might go nuts trying to make sense of it all. Wade played his cards right the entire time by painting me as the villain. If I hadn't lost my cool, I might still be working at that post. It was a cake job too. One of the easiest schools to clean, and only ten minutes from my house. Now I'm stuck in one of the filthiest schools in the district, busting my ass every night.

I'll tell you what, though. In a strange turn of events, Wade got what was coming to him shortly after I left. Turns out our little angel was handing out literature to some of the students who stayed for detention. Wade was busted for chatting to kids about staying on the right path. Some of the kids' parents complained to the school board, and within a week they fired him. You're allowed to have your own religious freedom, but it's illegal to try converting a minor in a school setting. I heard Wade was crying his eyes out, saying he was only trying to help them be better people.

Two months later, I read in the newspaper about a strategic sting operation involving one Wade Johnson, aged thirty-nine, of 152 Sycamore Street. Apparently, police found more literature in his apartment with a couple of not-so-flattering videos being shared online. From what I heard, he had other motives for working in a school, if you catch my drift.

After he was arrested for child endangerment and other atrocities, Brother Wade Johnson's reputation was destroyed. Everyone loved him so dearly, though. He was a model employee, remember? Not our Wade, the guy whom everyone trusted. Can't be the squeaky-clean guy.

No one believed me when I said he was a bad person. I told everyone he was evil, but even I couldn't predict how truly fucked up this guy was. He had people thinking he was a good guy until they found naked pictures of kids on his laptop. Good old Brother Wade, known now by inmate number J5HGD7789N.

The saddest part about it was no one apologized to me. I mean, thank God he didn't get to diddle any kids. But what about me? He screwed me! Don't I get to be vindicated?

"Hey, you were right! That guy really was an asshole." Nope. Never got recognition for calling him out in the first place. Like always I got the shaft. Well, now my buddy Wade would be getting the shaft for the next ten to fifteen years. Maybe he could pray at the chapel of his new home—a state-run corrections facility!

Chapter 12

Tyrell's Greatest Hits

From time to time, my buddy Tyrell really outdid himself. We were all used to him breaking a broom or cracking a sink faucet, but on some occasions, he took the word *accident* to extremes. Every four months or so, Tyrell would cost the taxpayers a couple of thousand bucks for miscellaneous fuckups. A snow blower burning out because he forgot to add oil would be another two grand. A busted ventilation system in the art room would run almost fifteen grand. Then on days when he was feeling extra creative, Tyrell would do things guaranteed to destroy everything in his path.

I'm not sure how he survived this long because some of the stuff he did was extremely hazardous. Then again, Tyrell was the most dangerous man I ever worked with. Things like selling crack in Newark or carjacking thugs in Camden were typical Wednesday to him.

For a former criminal mastermind like Tyrell, the public school system was a breeze. "This place is a fucking cakewalk from what I used to do to make dough," said Tyrell. "Ain't nobody shooting at cha here!"

No matter how bad he screwed the pooch, Tyrell would manufacture the perfect defense. "Listen, man, I know it looks like I threw that TV out the winda, but I'm tellin' you, it fell down like that. Piece of shit almost crushed my head! I had to jump out the way, and thankfully it went through the window instead of takin' my damn head off!"

Tyrell later claimed the TV tried to commit a hate crime by attacking him. "I want to talk to Mr. Sony right now. That mothafucka is making racist TVs!"

How do you reason with a guy who accuses an inanimate object of being hateful?

Management let him do whatever the hell he wanted for the longest time, as long as they didn't have to deal with him. They could always write off a new TV or a window. It's cheaper than getting a lawyer. And Tyrell was great at defending himself.

Tyrell called the local newspaper a bunch of times claiming mistreatment on the job. "These so-called bosses always tryin' to single me out. Ain't nobody treatin' me fairly 'round these parts!" As soon as the bosses got a dozen calls by reporters, they backed off. I don't think he was looking for a settlement or exposure. I just think Tyrell was a klutz and didn't want to do any work.

"That shit was broken before I touched it, man!" I heard that line almost daily with a few other nuggets sprinkled in. That's part of the reason we called him the Ghetto Urkel. Not only did he look like him, but he had that "Did I do thaaaaaat?" sound almost in stereo. He saved the best excuses for the big accidents, the ones involving almost killing coworkers. Tyrell backed a forklift over a whole pallet of school supplies once claiming he had a mini stroke. Never mind the fact a coworker who hated Tyrell was standing in front of the pallet when he steamrolled it.

"There I was… just moving this here forklift around the loading dock when, all of sudden, wham! I saw my dead momma wave at me from outside the window. I knew I must have been dying at that very moment 'cause I saw the white light and everythin'." When asked if Tyrell had seen his hateful supervisor standing in the path of the three-ton Kubota forklift, he claimed ignorance. "I didn't see shit…" was all he ever said, and no one questioned him.

Two years ago, Tyrell was given a simple task of emptying a floor cleaning machine. It's not hard at all. You simply pull a hose from the machine and let it drain into the sewer. Only thing you could do to screw it up would be if you touched a specific button while operating it. And Tyrell knew exactly what button that was.

The machine, which looks like a small Zamboni, is not difficult to operate. If you can push a shopping cart, you can push a floor-scrubbing machine. It's kind of bulky but manageable if you take your time. After cleaning the cafeteria floor, the night boss instructed Tyrell to take the machine to the loading dock and empty it. This was a five-minute endeavor, which included the time it took to walk down the hallway. Half an hour later, I saw an ambulance and a fire truck pull into the school's parking lot and knew this wasn't going to end well.

If you've never seen a loading dock, it looks like a launch pad made of concrete. A flat area where pallets can be off-loaded from delivery trucks. The drop-off onto the pavement is about six feet. When trucks make their delivery, they need an area for the truck to dip down into when they back up. Well, our loading dock is like many loading docks in that it doesn't have a guard rail to stop you if you get too close to the edge. It's a straight drop onto the pavement if you're not careful. All Tyrell had to do was push the machine to the edge and pull a water hose to drain the dirty water. Damned if that simple bastard didn't drive the fucking machine right off the edge of the dock, sending a helpless floor scrubber to its doom.

I still don't know how he did it. Two simple steps: push machine to edge and pull hose. Tyrell must have moved the floor scrubber near the edge and pushed the Drive button by mistake. Mysteriously, the machine's speed was set to high. Don't know how it was set to high. We never use high because it's too fucking fast. It's borderline running speed at that point. You need to be a track star to operate the machine on high. When we found the machine, it looked as if the Dukes of Hazard took it for a spin.

When the night boss and I got to the scene of the crime, Tyrell was sitting on his ass with a broken, unlit cigarette in his mouth. He looked shaken with his mouth halfway open, the Kool cigarette stuck to his bottom lip. The defenseless floor scrubber lay dismantled on the pavement, twenty feet from the dock, with all its internal parts spilled onto the ground like a gutted fish.

One of the neighbors who lived near the school must have called 911 when they heard the massive collision. It must have sounded like car crash to them because it sure looked like one.

If you're having trouble comprehending the scene, just think about one of those guys who steals a car, puts a brick on the gas pedal, and drives it off a cliff.

Tyrell was mumbling fiercely as the medics put an ice pack on his head.

"Goddamn you, you clunky piece of shit!" Tyrell was on the ground yelling at a machine as it sparked violently. "You stupid-ass mothafucker! Useless as tits on a bull—"

"Calm down, sir, you have to remain calm," said one of the medics. She was taping a gauze to his forearm. "Can you remember what happened?"

"As a matter of fact, I do!" said Tyrell. "This unsafe, hazardous piece of junk almost killed me! Ouch… ouch, my head hurts. Call my lawyer, man. I'm feeling like I might have some sort of long-term damage here!"

The floor scrubber must have been launched off the dock at an incredible speed. It lay on the ground looking as if a grenade went off inside it, its back wheels spinning in place while making a weird buzzing sound. It takes precision, excellent timing, and a knowledge of physics to do what he did. I was convinced Tyrell lacked all three until I saw the carnage. My night boss was the first to address the situation. He stood on the loading dock with his hand on his head, saying "Oh god… Oh god… Damn you, Tyrell! What the hell did you do now, numbnuts!"

I was laughing so hard I almost fainted. I was doubled over cracking up while Tyrell, with his sideways Clippers hat, finally made it to his feet with the help of two firemen.

"What the fuck, Tyrell! How the hell did you drive it off the dock?" said my night boss.

"Aaaah… aaaaaah… I don't know! This stupid-ass bullshit machine just jumped out my hands!"

"You gotta be a complete moron to do what you did. I told you several times not to bring it too close to the edge!"

Tyrell stumbled to gain his footing, all while dusting off his clearly expensive basketball shoes.

"Well, shit on you, sucka," said Tyrell as he polished his red-and-black sneakers. "I almost died tonight, Jack! And look at my damn shoes! That machine of yours scuffed my fucking kicks! These shits are brand-new!"

"Who gives a fuck about your shoes, you fucking asshole! You drove a seven-thousand-dollar machine off a six-foot ramp! I have to call someone and explain this mess!"

As the night boss walked away screaming into the handheld radio, I watched Tyrell stare at the machine. He burped loudly and lit a fresh cigarette, shaking his head and cursing like a fiend.

"Well... I guess we can't finish cleaning the floor now," said Tyrell while he checked his cellphone for missed calls and texts.

"That's all you have to say?" I said, wiping tears from my cheek. "Bossman is coming here now to look at this thing. You're lucky he doesn't fire you!" I was more concerned for Tyrell's job than he was. There he stood watching the machine twitch at random intervals all while he flipped through texts on his phone.

"I don't know what to tell you, man. The machine jumped out my hands and took off. I tried to hold her back now. Oh, yes, Tyrell tried to hold onto her like his life depended on it. But in the end, she just leapt forward and flew off that ramp right there."

He took a drag from his cigarette and blew it out while he shook his head from side to side. I was stunned to see him be so complacent and relaxed. He wasn't sweating or nervously calling a union rep. Tyrell simply finished his cigarette, threw it into the sewer drain, and walked away. Another loud burp followed by a tsk sound from his tongue.

About fifteen minutes after the accident, Tyrell was on the phone gabbing to some random woman, convinced he was going to have sweaty intercourse with her later that night. The machine, just about dead, still buzzed on the ground waiting to die a painful death.

The head department supervisor, Mr. Polotski, arrived shortly after to view the wreckage. For the life of me, I tried not to overhear what they were saying, but their voices carried far down the hall.

Both the night boss and the head supervisor interrogated Tyrell, who was cooler than a cucumber.

"Tyrell, did you drive this machine off the dock?" said Polotski.

"I wouldn't call it driving it off the dock, Mr. Polotski," he said as he leaned back to evaluate the bosses staring him down. "I believe that this machine done drove itself off the dock. The parking break must been broken or something."

"It doesn't have a parking break! Did you push the lever down or push the high-speed button? What the hell happened here?"

"I don't know what happened, Mr. Polotski. The way I see it is that this unsafe machine almost took off my foot. Look at my shoes! I just got these from the outlet store. They new!"

Within minutes, Tyrell had both the night boss and the supervisor tearing out whatever hairs they had left. Plain evidence shows Tyrell was indeed the man who let the machine fly off the loading dock. That poor machine. It was only a week old, if that, so it was in perfect working order before he touched it. Soon after Tyrell got ahold of it, it could have been picked up on radar as an unidentified flying object.

"I don't wanna point fingers here, but I think this machine must be faulty. It went haywire on me," said Tyrell. "My safety and well-being were in jeopardy... and... and... I feel my rights as a worker have been violated, Mr. Polotski, sir." Using large phrases wasn't in Tyrell's daily vocabulary, until his job was on the line. This was a man who said things like *skank* or *trifling* on regular intervals. He danced his way around the issue, blaming a loose wire or bald tires, anything but user error. What began as worker negligence turned into a manufacture's defect in Tyrell's eyes. He insisted the floor scrubber was defective the entire time the bosses questioned him.

At the end of the night, Tyrell was off the hook. The machine, still shiny as if it came off the assembly line, was kaput. Years later, Tyrell insisted the machine almost took off his foot. Each time he told the story, his traumatic injury got worse and worse. Tyrell's version was a bit more drastic than it really was. "That clunky-ass thing almost made me a cripple! I'm talking above the knee, ya hear me?"

Tyrell also has a problem with ladder safety. Each time he went up a ladder, he fell off, usually falling through some expensive copy machine or trophy case. He must've worked as a stunt double in a past life. I've never met a person who can take a header off an eight-foot ladder, obliterate a new laptop cart, and not be seriously maimed. Nothing more than a couple of scratches and scrapes, all covered by workman's comp., I might add. No broken bones or internal bleeding. I'm convinced the man was bulletproof.

For a brief stint of his career, Tyrell was moved to the grounds department. You know, cutting grass and planting trees? He was being punished for flirting with one of the big bosses' secretaries. In true Tyrell fashion, he was able to bypass most of the physical work.

"I'm on blood pressure pills, and I can't be bending down all the time... My doctor told me I'm not supposed to be carrying no damn weed whacker!" In one of the dumbest moves in the history of this department, Tyrell was allowed to use the ride on mowers. Not the small yard roamers your dad uses on Sundays. Picture a huge tractor with whirling blades in front, a giant chainsaw in the back, and the ability to carve trees in seconds. These mowers can reach a top speed of twenty miles per hour. This is a vehicle Tyrell should never have access to.

By far, the most uncoordinated person at my job was given a buzz saw on wheels to operate near children. A John Deere meets Grand Theft Auto kind of terror was what I pictured when hearing Tyrell was in the driver's seat. I couldn't wait for daily updates from my friend Tim in the grounds department. I'd look at my phone to see messages like, "Tyrell just ran over a soccer ball during gym class." Next text, "He just drove the machine into the soccer goal post!" Then later, "Tyrell took the mower down the street to 7-Eleven for a Slurpee! LOL!"

I imagined Tyrell on this massive war machine doing burnouts, chopping up an entire fifth-grade class during a kickball game.

Two weeks later Tyrell walked into my school to start back on his regular job. It was only a matter of time, and Tyrell knew this. See, management thinks they are so slick by punishing people for getting hurt or causing damage while working. Usually it backfires, like when Bugs Bunny would stick his finger in a gun and Yosemite Sam would shoot himself in the face. Instead of working with people or even treating them like humans, management does something asinine, like move you to a position where they know you don't belong. This time, Tyrell really did some damage. He found a way to completely dismantle a huge ride-on mower by driving over a rock garden.

Let me rephrase that: he took a massive grass-eating monster on a destruction derby over a rock pile and turned it into a Gatling gun.

In turn, he destroyed not only a fifty-thousand-dollar mower, but a brand-new Mercedes SLK, which was parked near the rocks. The ironic thing was the guy who owned the car was the same dipshit who was mad about Tyrell flirting with his secretary. Weird coincidence, huh?

I asked Tyrell to tell me the whole story one night at lunch. "What did you do to Big Cheese's car? I heard he was cursing like a sailor in front of the school," I said.

"Well… I drove it just like they said I should. How was I supposed to know where the grass ended and the rocks began? I can't see over the front of that machine. It's too damn big!"

Tyrell began to rub his chin as if he was in deep thoughts about the meaning of life or our purpose in the universe.

"Come to think of it… it did feel a li'l bumpy. Meh, who knows. Next thing I know, this guy was running at me full steam. His face was so red, man… He looked like a cherry tomato, and he was shootin' spit out his mouth while trying to yell at me."

"What did he say?" I said.

"I saw him running after me just as I was getting off that mower, but I couldn't hear what he was saying," said Tyrell. "When I mistakenly ran over those rocks, all I heard was something like a machine gun on full auto. Clanking and tearing up metal and shit. Mr. Big Cheese, that plump, oily-faced tubbo, was yelling at me about his car, but everything was in slow motion." Tyrell was serious as anything trying to get his story straight in case anyone else was listening. "I may or may not have had an out-of-body experience at that time," said Tyrell, all while looking over his shoulder.

"How the hell didn't you know you were mowing rocks instead of grass, Tyrell?" I said. At this point, I was laughing my ass off in between wiping tears out of my eyes.

"It's easy if you just turn yo head for a few seconds!" he said. "I dropped my phone, and as I reached for it, I must have went over a bunch of rocks. You know what, I don't really remember too much of it 'cause I think I must have blacked out or something. You see, I'm on medication for my anxiety, from all the stress this damn job is giving me. So I don't really recall actively running over a big pile of rocks."

I talked to Tyrell for ten minutes about the accident. All he kept saying was how he felt sick and didn't remember all that happened that day. The fact is, Tyrell wasn't lying, but he wasn't telling the whole truth either.

The real story goes something like this: The grounds department supervisor wasn't supervising him like he had been for the last two weeks. It was a Friday, and the head groundsman called out sick. He was probably tired of chasing after Tyrell for all the dumb shit he did.

Tyrell was allowed to work without anyone lurking over his shoulder. That's the first mistake: never take your eyes off Tyrell. When he realized he wasn't being watched, Tyrell sneaked over to his car to grab a few airplane bottles to suck back. After about two hours of ninety-degree-plus weather and eleven shooters of Bacardi, Tyrell started to feel a little loopy. Combine that with the few pills he was taking for an actual medical problem, and you've got one zipped-up soul brother.

It was pure coincidence the car near the rocks belonged to the boss who tried to discipline Tyrell. That's what everyone was lead to believe. Don't forget, Tyrell grew up in the projects. He might not be book smart like some people, but he's a super genius when it comes to street smarts. I imagine Tyrell laughed his ass off, chuckling the whole time as he vibrated in the mower seat with a thousand rocks pelting a brand-new Mercedes.

Tyrell was questioned about the accident by the police. "Nobody trained me on this damn machine" was all Tyrell had to say to the police. Once Tyrell told them he was on medication and showed them the pill bottles, the police cleared him of any wrongdoing. It said right on the bottle: "Do not operate heavy machinery or be in hot weather for extended periods of time." The bosses never bothered to check if Tyrell was telling them the truth about his medications. They were too busy trying to punish him by sticking him in the heat during the summer.

Tyrell's acting out of the whole scenario in front of the school and police was legendary from what I've heard. Just ask the entire building who watched his solo performance after he turned that poor car into swiss cheese. Sure, he was drunk off his ass, but he was also delirious from blood pressure and anxiety pills. Tyrell showed the police the pill bottles, not the rum bottles. They never found any empty bottles either because he kept throwing them in front of the mower's path. "Good luck picking all them pieces of glass off the soccer field and taping them together, sucka!" said Tyrell as he told me the story. "Them dumb-ass bitches can't stick nothin' on me, baby!"

I don't think I can ever forget the sound he made when he described all those rocks hitting the boss's car. "Ping, ping, ping, pong! ping ping, poing!" It was like Tyrell had a "Tommy gun with endless bullets smoking that fuckin' asshole's car" as he put it.

Tyrell always had these types of things happen and never caught hell for it. For eighteen years, he caused considerable damage to machines, vehicles, custodial supplies, etc. I guess I learned from a true master in the ways of debauchery.

More infamous than his exploits was his attendance record. As a state employee, each worker is granted paid sick days for the work year. If you work the entire year, you're given twelve sick days, one per month. Most people use two or three for the flu, perhaps a couple of doctors' appointments a year. Whatever people use sick time for. If you don't use them, they carry over to the next year as earned sick time off. Responsible workers have a majority of their sick time saved up in case of emergencies or early retirement. Tyrell used approximately eighty sick days a year, not counting vacations or personal time. How can this be, you ask? Well, Tyrell simply does not give a fuck and takes off whenever he feels like it. After the first twelve days are burned, Tyrell takes days without pay for a multitude of health problems. I think he's got a friend who's a doctor in Rahway because he has more doctor's notes than a normal individual should.

He once took off four weeks in the middle of the summer because he "didn't feel good." Something about a stomach virus that led to a migraine and other complications. Turns out, he went to Jamaica and spent most of his rent money at Hedonism II. He didn't tell the head office that, but he posted a ton of photos on Facebook with brightly colored drink glasses and string bikinis in his hands. "Cheeeeeeese, mothafuckas!" was the caption, with a thong in his mouth standing next to four women. Another photo showed him nestled between two gigantic pairs of breasts with "Can ya hear me now, bitch!" captioned underneath. He even made a photo album on his page that said, "Tyrell's Snatch and Booze Getaway—2010."

The doctor's note said he was recovering from minor surgery.

Tyrell used to call out sick every Friday and Monday for about three months straight. He kept complaining about his sciatica acting up. Again, his doctor's notes stated things like "Under strict supervision" or "Please excuse from work." He didn't want to come to work, that's all. I didn't blame him. This place will take all the life out of you when you're not looking. Who doesn't love a four-day weekend either?

He called out sick one Friday three minutes before he was supposed to be at work. That night, Tyrell sent pictures of him on a party bus heading into New York for a bachelor party. His bachelor's party. Mind you, Tyrell has never been married or engaged or ever mentioned he was having a bachelor party. He decided one day, after consulting his closest homeboys, that he would like to have a bachelor's party. He felt he deserved it, for whatever reasons. So he threw himself one, complete with decorations, a sash that said "Groom to be," liquor, drugs, strippers, and of course, photographic evidence.

Every half hour, I'd receive texts with some form of lewd behavior happening on or around Tyrell. First came the shots of Hpnotiq, that intense, feel-good drink with its electric-blue glow. Half hour later, Tyrell and his crew of deviants switched to Hennessy while adding large cigars and blunts to the mix. Two hours into my shift, Tyrell made it to the first club of the night, but not before busting out the coke and meeting a few scantily clad women.

Then came the explicit texts: half-naked women now becoming fully naked on a neon-lit party bus. I'm not sure, but I may or may not have seen Tyrell's penis in one of the pictures. It was kinda blurry. After his third club of the night, the texts stopped coming in. I figured he was partied out, facedown drunk on a limo bus with shag carpeting.

The following Monday Tyrell shows up to work with an eye patch over his left eye. Not a pirate's patch, but a gauze-wrapped patch. This wasn't good at all. Did he lose a fregging eye while smashing shots at the club? How in the hell was he going to explain this mess to the boss?

The cover story was Tyrell had a sty in his eye, and yes, he had a doctor's note to prove it. Apparently, one of his buddies on the bus was the very same doctor who wrote all of Tyrell's notes in the past. The official story I got from Tyrell was two girls started fighting over him.

"There I was… having the time of my life with these two fine-ass bitches goin' to town on each other, all whilst sittin' on my lap. I'm tellin' you, I was in heaven, my brotha! Couple seconds later… they start wiggin' out over who smoked the last blunt! Tyrell tried to get up, but not before one of them hood rats jabbed me in the eye. Fuckin' drunk-ass bitches play too hard when they ain't got no weed left. She scratched my damn eyeball with her long fake-ass nails!"

What's truly amazing was how Tyrell gets off for bereavement days. By my calculations, Tyrell's mother must have died six times. About every other year or so, Tyrell calls out because his mother passed away. "She's gone off to a better place, my brotha. Oh, how I'll miss you so very much, Moms." He would come in the next week saying "Thank you" to everyone who sent him a condolence card. Fucking guy lied about his own mother dying. Several times. I'm not sure if the secretary in the office was stupid or just in a coma. How the fuck do you not say something about taking a paid week off for your mother dying six times?

Then he gets off almost every other week for a friend who dies suddenly. All paid bereavement time too.

"My boy Syqetus, may he rest in peace, was my closest friend through grade school. I haven't seen him for like forty years, but I need to go to his viewing this Monday night."

Perhaps the most superb of Tyrell's accomplishments was his conquests of the teaching staff. Yes, indeed, Tyrell had a hankering for teachers, especially the lonely ones who didn't go home after the school bell rang. Tyrell knew within five minutes of meeting a teacher if he would be knee-deep in that sweet poon tang as he called it. "It's all in the approach," said Tyrell. "You gots to feel them stuck-up hoes out. Cast them to the side so you can snag them horny ones."

Tyrell made a life goal to have sex with as many teachers he could. Instead of meeting in a discreet location, preferably off school grounds, Tyrell took an unassuming teacher into the principal's office. "The principal has one of them La-Z-Boy couches that comforts your ass when you fuckin'," said Tyrell. "And them teachers, they think it's dangerous to be fuckin' in the school. They must get all frisky and shit thinkin' someone will burst in and catch 'em. Don't worry, baby… Tyrell will keep you safe! I got the keys to this mothafucka… Ain't nobody barging in on us!"

Think about it: Tyrell had keys to *every* door in the building. All he had to do was wait until the staff left for the day before he took a fourth-grade math teacher into his Dungeon of Doggy Style.

I think deep down Tyrell had sex with teachers not because he could but because he wasn't supposed to do it. "These snooty hoes look down on me, you know what I'm saying? They think they better than us. Who the fuck is you! You stick-in-the-ass bitches! I'll give you somethin' in yo ass, but it won't be no stick! You think because I clean the floors I won't tear up your sweet booty if given the chance?"

Much to his credit, Tyrell had quite a few teachers sprawled out on that couch. I asked him once how many teachers he had sex with in the school, and he yelled out "Fourteen and counting" like he was saying it on record in a court of law. "After I'm done with them, I carve a notch in the back of the couch frame," he said. "Last time I checked, I had fourteen notches on that mothafucka!"

Chapter 13

The Great Janitor Strike of '97

It was the darkest time in all of custodial arts history. The strike of '97 tested the very society of the mop pushing man to his breaking point. Old janitors like to refer to it as the Big No Clean, when a majority of guys didn't work for almost six weeks straight. Toilets overflowed without a plunger in sight. Dust accumulated three inches thick around every door jam. And the smell, oh, the smell was hideous to say the least. I hope, for your children's sake, they never have to live through what those poor children struggled through.

The life of the broom was my calling from a very young age. I didn't know it at that time, but janitoring was in my veins somewhat. I spent a good deal of my childhood rearranging my toy collection in addition to scrubbing them clean after each use. "There you go, Shredder. All clean just like He-Man and T. Rex." My third-grade desk was cleaner than a marine's foot locker. I was constantly organizing my Trapper Keeper in high school regardless of what the cool kids said. I carried those standards through life until I got a job as a school janitor. It was only a matter of weeks until I realized most people are swine and cleaning after them was a true pain in the ass.

It all started in late August during the summer of 1997. I was a green mop then, new to the job. I had to prove myself worthy of donning an extremely heavy set of keys and steel-toed boots. My first summer was full of excitement. The air was clean back then. A man could really take in the breeze just as the sun rose above the horizon. This day, like many before it, began with a fresh application of wax on a newly cleaned tile floor. It was the last of the summer cleaning duties for our group. A majority of the cleaning was done, meaning the crew could relax for a week or two until students came back for September.

The Friday before school began, all the janitors came together for a union meeting to discuss the upcoming contract. Since we were in the teachers' union, we expected the union reps to tell us the contract was signed, thus extending our job for another five years. A hard-fought battle between administration and teachers ended in a deadlock, causing teachers to threaten a strike. I, for one, was happy. Three months into the job, and I had a vacation waiting in the wings. It didn't turn out that way. Apparently, it's illegal for teachers to strike, so the end result was an agreement screwing the new janitors royally. The teachers would still start school in September, but a majority of janitors weren't allowed to work due to a budget freeze. Reduction in force is what the head honchos called it. Therefore, instead of ten people at my post, we only had three when school started. And guess who was lucky enough to be one of the three?

I didn't understand the logic and still don't. Yet since I was one of the low men on the totem pole, I had to pick up the slack while the remaining elders took off. Politics reared its ugly head in my department, causing massive layoffs until a deal was inked. A trio of rookies took to the task with eager dust pails. No one knew just how bad it would get in the schools, not even us new jacks all hell-bent on making a name for ourselves.

The crew consisted of myself, Smitty, and Donna, who now had to cover the work of ten sections. A section is what we called a person's area to clean. Our post had ten of them. That's ten people's worth of work per night with only three bodies to do it. It's simple math here, people. You can't do ten people's jobs with three people. I'm a janitor, not a wizard, for Christ's sake. Try doing those odds at your job. Imagine having five fry guys at McDonald's replaced by one jackass juggling salt shakers and that metal basket you stick in the deep fryer.

Smitty, who had the most experience out of all of us with four months, took the helm in organizing the battle plans. He was a natural-born leader with qualities you'd find in a WWII war hero. Donna played the part of the worker bee constantly striving forward for the betterment of the group. She was rough and sturdy, but not battle tested. With my witty banter and bullish strength, I played the comic relief with muscle able to get the job done. All while putting a smile on everyone's face.

Monday was our first day with the shortened crew, and our plan of attack was simple: run-and-shoot offense with no razzle-dazzle. In other words, we would do the basics and get the hell out of there. Smitty and I would take out all the trash while Donna ran the broom behind us. Over 60 classrooms a night worth of trash bags equals a lot of fregging bags. Donna trailed behind early in the routine, but Smitty and I ran back to help her halfway through the night. That's what a team does. We stayed together as one against the tide of muck. After the garbage was out, we worked on the dirtiest areas next. Bathrooms were cleaned with a hose and a ton of soap all in a sort of running/jumping motion. By golly, our first night was a whirlwind of work! All three of us were high-fiving one another and celebrating like we just hit the lottery.

The job was no biggie during the first week, although I must admit I was exhausted come Friday. Had we been veterans on the job, we might've been able to keep up the pace for months. But as the days progressed, our inexperience was our Achilles' heel. The numbers turned against us, causing a massive backlog of cleaning. All we needed was two or three more workers, and we'd have been able keep our heads above water.

But it was not to be. Three rookies who were thrown into the fire didn't know how truly hot it would get.

We never knew what to do after the first set of toilets backed up. Dear Jesus, we couldn't clean the shit up fast enough. By the time we plunged the first toilet, by God the second and third stalls were packed full. It's as if the children knew we were trailing behind, only to toy with us like buzzards waiting for an old water buffalo to drop. Smitty found the courage to hold his breath and pole vault into each stall with Green Beret–like precision. Our pal Donna, who had a weak stomach, did the best she could. I felt so bad for her, seeing the wave of colors flash across her face as she held in the pain.

Each day would bring more and more trash, considerable amounts of uneaten lunch-room food needing a new home in the dumpster. Then came the daily cleanings: floors, bathrooms, dusting, mopping, and miscellaneous, time-consuming tasks asked by teachers. "Could you move my desk to the far end of the wall? I think the feng shui of the room would be better for my students." We got peppered with too much work, all of which needed to be done or else we'd lose our jobs. Smitty told us we just have "to buck up and git 'r done." Sadly, Donna was the first to snap. Poor girl never had the gumption to stand in a marathon of dirt. She couldn't handle the pressure. The harder she worked, the faster the dirt would accumulate. Donna developed a nervous tick after the first week, leading to a full-on stutter come the following Thursday.

"I can't do it! The t-t-trash just keeps b-building and building and building...," said Donna.

"Get a hold of yourself, woman! We need to focus here. Keep your composure," explained Smitty, all while pulling six trash cans behind him, one tied to another like a family of circle elephants holding onto one another's tails.

"But I can't d-d-daa... do it! These kids are animals. I found half a box of Twinkies in the toilet. It won't f-flush! The plunger keeps m-maa-mashing them to the side of the bowl," said Donna.

"Just take a deep breath. It's going to be all right," I told her. "We can do this together!"

It was no use. She continued to lose her mind as the days passed. I found her sitting in the boiler room rocking back and forth chewing on one of those pink deodorant blocks you'd find in a urinal. She was mumbling the same thoughts to herself as she came unglued, "Twinkies... Twinkies in the f-fucking toilets. Twinkies on the goddamned w-waaa-walls. Twinkies!" I shook her to loosen the grip of insanity.

"Donna, baby girl. Donna! Don't leave me now! You've come too far to turn back. It's only a few more days until they sign the—"

"No!" she screamed. "I can't take it any longer!" Smitty came rushing in with a fresh cup of coffee waving under her nose as it were a smelling salt. It took a few seconds for her to come out of the haze, but the damage was done. From that point onward, Donna seemed as if something was poking her from behind. Whenever I'd look at her, she had this shoulder shrug like she was trying to shake someone's hand off her back.

Two more weeks passed with more requests coming from the powers that be. Clean this faster. Do this job now. It wasn't long before our basic safety was in jeopardy. It was like living in a bio dome and having the air supply cut off a little bit each day. You'd gasp for air not knowing if it was your last breath.

We heard contract talks were moving slow but steady, a light in the darkness known as our lives. "The nightmare would be over soon!" became our motto. It was a little mental uplift to us. Just as our future was starting to brighten, our fellow union brothers and sisters started to turn their wrath toward us.

Those godforsaken teachers, who were fully staffed and didn't give two shits about us, started complaining about the cleanliness of the school. "My desk is filthy! I can write my name in the dust on my ceramic apple. The janitor needs to do their damn job once in a while!" Oh, but we did, sweetheart. We did do our jobs and seven other people's jobs because no one else was there to do them. Once teachers started noticing how disgusting the school was, they set up meetings about unsanitary conditions. Questions were raised at the next school meeting. The heat was on full blast, scorching us until our skin charred. Nobody cared how shorthanded we were. It's as if no one knew a majority of the crew was laid off. How did they not know? They were told the janitors were reduced severely before school started. Hell, I know many teacher union reps who all signed the paper enforcing our cutbacks. But the teachers didn't care what was happening to us. Just as long as they kept their jobs. Fuck the lowly mop swingers, right?

A barrage of questions started pouring in from management. Of course those bastards looked to us and wondered what the problem was. "What do you mean you're doing the best you can? Push that broom faster, boy!" Management pointed their greasy fingers at us saying we weren't working hard enough while teachers continued to complain about our performance. Talk about taking it in both ends. We could've died while cleaning those schools, and no one would have found us until the next morning. Even then those heartless savages would probably nudge us to make sure we weren't faking our deaths. "Sleeping on the job, I see? I know you're still alive! Get up and Windex that door glass!"

The fourth week started with the same labored semantics. No news from the union trenches, and the work was starting to take its toll on us. Donna now drank at work to ease her nerves. I noticed her putting a little bit of Jameson in her coffee mug when she thought no one was around. Soon enough, I'd see her stammer down a corridor with a travel cup in one hand and a dry mop dragging behind her in the other. She was drunk daily and lost the will to care. "I don't give a shit how many teachers bitch about their chalkboards being dirty. You can stick that eraser up your ass, lady!" Donna was a mess, both physically and mentally. Overworking had destroyed our morale. With no end in sight, I started to buckle as well.

"I can't do it, Smitty," I said. "I'm beat up pretty bad, buddy."

"Nonsense, sport. You need to keep it together if we're gonna win this fight. Administration may try our souls, but we need to stay strong and unite."

"I'm near my breaking point. I… I… ain't—"

"*Ain't* ain't a word, my brother. Look it up in a dictionary sometime." Smitty was always my rock. I'd see him buried up to his throat in pencil shavings and know he'd strive onward to clean those rooms like his life depended on it.

But Donna was a broken spirit. Those sticky floors and dusty halls really messed her up.

A week later, I was hauling a ton of trash cans outside. I found her sitting with her back against the dumpster, alone and quiet. The glory had faded from her eyes, and her soul had disappeared within her own body leaving a drab, blank woman to gaze aimlessly at the ground. Her travel cup, with half-dried puddles of whiskey and coffee around it, lay next to her leg.

"Donna? Are you okay?" I said.

"Donna's not here anymore…," said a guttural voice. "She's gone far from this place."

Smitty noticed us outside and came out to help. He knew before he even saw her she was a goner. A dead mop is what the old-timers call it, when the urge to clean has died and only a hardened shell remains. I tried to talk to her, but it was like trying to hug a ghost. No feeling, my friends. No feeling at all.

"Come on now, Donna. We can do this if we all—"

"Save it," she said. "There is no use of fighting any longer." Those were the last words I ever heard her say. Donna rose up from the concrete as if she'd been possessed by Lucifer himself. Those eyes, ugh. The color of those eyes resembled pure evil and lost hope merged into one. She'd been to the edge now, and no one could stop the madness running amuck in her head. Donna dropped her janitor keys to the pavement and slowly walked to her Dodge Daytona. I looked to Smitty for guidance. He only shook his head as if to say "What a shame" out loud.

"Oh, fuck!" I said. "Who the hell's gonna help us now? We still have half a school to clean by ourselves."

"Tough luck, kiddo," said Smitty. "There's no help for us now." He pulled a folded baseball hat from his back pocket and placed it on his head. Looked like he was about to start a war movie quote worthy of the ages.

"It's just you and me, pal. We've got a ton of trash to throw out and not much time to do it in. I need you focused and alert of your surroundings for this mission. No more crying over fallen comrades. Those floors won't get swept with us standing around like a bunch of defeated warriors, will it?" Smitty gazed back at the school with storm clouds amassing in the distance. "Put a fresh set of latex gloves on, solider… it's cleanin' time."

I was moved by his enlightened aurora. Smitty walked past Donna as she drove off into the oblivion. He turned toward the massive pile of black trash bags, snapped his glove tight to his skin, and lunged toward Mount Garbage head first. The last sound I remember was a battle cry worthy of a thousand janitors who worked before us. All of them holding their mops above their heads like Scottish Claymores. I followed him like a trusty sidekick, mounting a shrill, cacophony scream as we took to the bags. We were covered in old milk and smelled like death by the time we finished that night. Smitty and I tore through the remainder of the work like Roman gladiators. We got it done with just enough time to spare. As the boss came to clock us out, he saw one short from the staff. His beady eyes gave us the once over before he spoke.

"Where's Donna?" said Bossman.

"Gone to a better place," said Smitty as he grabbed his metal lunch pail to leave.

"She… she didn't make it," I spoke out with tears in my eyes. I was so nervous my keys shook like a wind chime in a tornado.

"Well… you guys are goin' it alone tomorrow," implored the boss. "Don't forget… you've got an assembly at 6:00 p.m. and a chorus show at eight." He smiled his toothy grin, waiting for us to roar back. Smitty took off his hat, never saying a word. Casually he turned to walk to his truck and said, "I'll be here. And you best believe I'm bringing my second wind with me."

Those last days were pure unadulterated pain. School plays, PTA meetings, carnival night, just to name a few enemies we faced. No rest for the weak. No breaks for lunch or water. Just two cleaning machines hurling themselves into work not knowing when, or if, the contract would be signed. Two men striving against an unprecedented workload somehow managed to get the job done. Smitty never wavered from the mission at hand. Freaking guy put that old dirty Dodgers hat on and polished the school like a ruby glinting in the sun. Each time I'd stop to catch my breath near a filthy locker, he grabbed me like a wounded soldier. "Keep in formation! We've got ten more rooms to disinfect, buddy. We're gonna make it!"

When the dirt finally settled, a contract was signed by the end of the sixth week. It didn't even matter to us anymore. We didn't have a party over it, ordering pizza and toasting to a new contract extension. We had done the impossible. We faced the storm and came out alive. When the rest of the crew came back, the clouds had already parted like the day after a hurricane. The sun shined on us as we welcomed back our fellow coworkers. They were shocked we survived given the conditions. "Did you guys ever stumble along the way? How much garbage did you throw out each night? I bet you two are glad to see us, huh?" The conversation turned to Donna before long. Smitty and I never sugarcoated the truth: "She didn't make it." That's all we said about Donna, never mentioning her name again.

The strike was over with a few strokes of the pen. Life went back to normal. As those fleeting summer weeks passed, the general public never knew how close it was to decimation. Only a handful of troopers witnessed my pain. The other janitors, the laid-off crew who spent those weeks away from the pit, didn't believe my tales. To them, the strike was six weeks of hassle-free downtime. Since they were able to collect unemployment for the time they were off, it was more or less a vacation. For me, Smitty, and the rest of the outcasts throughout the school district, it was a jail sentence with no parole date. I heard a couple of janitors at other schools took the same road Donna did, never to be heard from again. It was a damn shame too. We lost some really good cleaners to the Public School Strike of '97.

To this day, I haven't spoken about the incident with this much openness. Much like a Vietnam POW, I've seen some shit, man. I still have night terrors over it, looking down a scummy hallway with papers floating by like tumbleweeds. Then I see Donna, poor, naive Donna with a box of soggy Twinkies under her arm. I awoke many nights with sweat gushing down my temple crying aloud for her to drop the box. But she never did.

I see Smitty once in a while at staff meetings. We were separated and moved to different posts throughout the district soon after the contract was signed. He doesn't wear his hat anymore. To him, it's a sign of harsh memories buried deep from today's view. I think he might be a little shell-shocked. I heard he took up union mailings, sending workers pamphlets warning them of the dangers in striking. We'd say hi with a head nod and walk away as if we didn't know each other. In the end, I think it's best Smitty and I don't reminisce about the past. No use tearing open those scars.

So be thankful you didn't live through those forgotten times. Tuck your kids in tonight, give them an extra-long kiss on the forehead, and remind them of what others had to go through so they could have a clean school each morning. And please, for the love of Christ, tell them to keep the Twinkies out of the toilet.

Chapter 14

The Three Amigos

As I've mentioned before, the janitorial field tends to be a melting pot of employees. We're well stocked from each continent around the globe. Well, not Antarctica, but you know what the hell I'm saying. When I first ascended to become a main mopper, I was shocked to see so many different nationalities. It was like the Olympics. I was waiting to see janitor carts rolling down the hallway with their country's flag waving high above their heads.

But you see, not all is well in la-la land. That is, much like the real world, when one country gets into a disagreement with the other, a thermonuclear war erupts.

My department has employees from twenty-four countries. I say twenty-four because we have a few Yugoslavians who still say it's one country when, clearly, it's not. Management must be careful whom they assign at a building because of the worldly turmoil. Let's face it, some people just don't get along. We all know the European countries either love their neighbors or loathe them. The Asians? I don't think they like anyone other than their own nationality. And even then it's dodgy. Any worker from the Caribbean is borderline homicidal. We tend to leave them alone as long as they don't threaten to massacre the whole crew at the drop of a hat. The few workers we have from Africa are just plain mystical. I still don't know what country Akua is from, but I guess it's somewhere with a lot of trouble.

One year the boss put an Albanian in the same building as a former Yugoslavian. That shit lasted about two weeks before they came to blows. Haitians don't like Jamaicans either. Found that out the hard way. They both started slap fighting each other near the Coke machine. I almost caught a left hook trying to buy a root beer on lunch break. The Mongolians, or Kalmyks (somewhere near Russia), hate the entire world. Don't even look at them without having a sword and shield in your hands.

Then there's the whole Jews working with Germans thing. I'm not even going to touch that one. When management puts a Jew and a German in the same school, the whole crew must take sensitivity classes on the Holocaust. Even then it goes sour real quick. It's a shit show to say the least. One of these years, we're going to see someone from Iraq or Syria apply for a job, and all hell's gonna break loose.

At my current post, we have seven workers made up from seven different nationalities. I'm mainly Irish with a little French and Danish thrown in, so I make up the American mutt delegation. I should be Swiss because I'm usually the neutral referee between the rest of these schmoes. Next, we have Boris who's from Russia, who hates Ralph the German. They bitch about minuscule items regularly. "Why you don't clean the sink before clean toilet bowl!" "Who you buy sausage from, butcher shop on Route 70? Him meats are no good!" It's like working with children all day long. Half the time they complain about each other to Ingrid, who's from Bulgaria. She's nice in her own way. She simply nods and smiles like a sleepy clown. Deep down, I know she hates both of them for shit that happened to her grandfather during the World War II. Boy, those Bulgarians can hold a fucking grudge.

Next, we have Ethan the Jew, who *nobody* likes. Not because he's Jewish, but because he's a fucking moron. His whiny voice drives right through your ears like a dentist drill. He's a horrible worker too. Most of the time he's on his phone answering calls for his side business. But does he take responsibility for his actions? Nope. He's convinced everyone is an anti-Semite.

As soon as he comes down for break everyone scatters. "Why is everyone leaving?" he'd say. "Are you discriminating against me because I'm Jewish!" Now we all just walk away like we don't know him. "Ralph, I know you hate me, just admit it!"

Lastly, we have my personal favorites, Sophia and Christina, the Sassy Senoritas. Christina's from Mexico and Sophia's from Spain. Don't *ever* call the one from Spain a Mexican and vice versa. They don't like that shit at all. Years ago, one of the drunk maintenance guys called Sophia a Mexican, and she flipped her lid. "I no Mexican, *estupido*! I'm from *Espana*. Don't you ever call me a Mexican, you *cerdo borracho*!"

I'm all for defending your heritage. With so many yahoos working here, you need to defend your borders vehemently. But Sophia pissed off Christina royally. "What's wrong with being Mexican, huh?" said Christina. "You think you better than me?"

That sort of thing happens here a lot. Janitors are very touchy people. They all think someone is out to get them like it's a big conspiracy. Someone will say something in broken English, and another person will get offended. Most of the time it's a miscommunication. You know, seven different people from seven different nationalities with *seven* different native tongues. It's worse at the high school. The smaller schools have less workers because of the size of the building. But the high school is three stories, man. That's a lot of clashing personalities. Last time I checked, they had over twenty workers, with most of them being Haitian, Dominican, Jamaican, Yugoslavian, or Russian. I don't think any of them understand a goddamn word the others are saying.

I experienced my own political correctness back in the day. Yup, had me stammering in all directions trying to get out of the spider's web of monkey shit. A couple of years ago, we had three *cabrons* who said and did things just to piss me off. Three Spanish guys (I don't know where they came from, let's just call them Mexican) caused a shitload of trouble in a short amount of time.

Juan Sanchez, Jose Escobar, and Raul Mendoza (the Three Amigos, if you haven't guessed by now) are one of the reasons management wants to fire us all. This triumvirate happened to be a pain in my ass for several months. I went to war with these bastards. They needled me every step I took. I hated these fuckers because they found a way to screw me and the system at the same time.

A few years ago, the department had to hire a lot of people in a short period. It's nothing new around here. Management does this from time to time, often jerking the rest of the department around. Think of a big shake-up at your job for absolutely no reason at all. Bosses move people from one shift to another, crew members are fired and hired all within minutes. Once the bosses clean house, so to speak, they decide to hire a new batch of janitors. Management will fire five to ten people and then, in a panic, hire a ton of workers to fill the voids. Usually, there is no vetting of the new hired workers either. Management should check fingerprints or do a background check, something to make sure the guy they hire isn't a mass murderer. But they don't.

Let me run you through a hiring boom: my boss, Mr. Polotski, hires a shitload of people to cover a handful of spots. If we have four positions open, the boss will hire ten candidates. Out of the ten people, three of them will have a criminal record, so say goodbye to the jailbirds. Two of the remaining people will not speak a lick of English, so they can't work around children. And the leftover five will either be good workers or morons. Here's a hint: most of the time they're complete and total dipshits devoid of any logic and one quits or dies before their start date.

So hypothetically, we have the four winners to fill the spots, if we're lucky. Like clockwork, one worker will get hurt before their first paycheck. We call these special cases Workman's Comp Queens. The other three jerk-offs are lazy, worthless idiots who can't grasp the concept of sweeping up a pile of dirt. This goes on and on for months. It will take about a year to completely fill four positions. By that time, four more people from around the district will either be fired or quit. We have a tremendous amount of turnover in the janitorial field, if you haven't noticed by now.

The shit cherry on top of the sundae is when HR sticks their nose in the mess. If you don't know, HR stands for human resources. That's the department who evaluates our hiring practices and determines if we have enough of the right candidates. To put it bluntly, HR workers are fresh-out-of-college millennial pussies who think we should all get along. Like we spend our waking moments cuddling puppy dogs and riding rainbows across the sky together.

By law, we need a certain number of ethnically diverse workers. If the boss hires all white people, then HR steps in. Here's where the Three Amigos come in play. My boss was tired of hearing how he didn't hire enough ethnic workers, so he decided to hire three Mexicans at once. The union was happy, HR was happy, etc. It just so happened that a school had three empty spots, so everybody was happy in the end. Well, not everybody. Lucky me, I was told to train the new guys.

These three guys were absolute scumbags. Complete cluster-fucks who looked as if they had the ambition of a frozen tree sloth. Sloppy as hell, moving ever so slowly like their feet were stuck in tar. The entire time I trained them, they spoke Spanish to one another, laughing and chuckling away. I'd show them how to use the chemicals, and they'd be chatting up a storm, ignoring everything I said. I spoke a little Spanish, so I knew most of what they said. Fucking heathens were calling me names you'd only hear in a sailors' saloon. It didn't deter me from doing my job. Hell, I even told them important things in Spanish so they would comprehend it.

That's when the atmosphere changed.

The first time I said something in Spanish, they stopped conversing and listened. But it wasn't a "Hey, let me take this job seriously" listening. It was more of a "Fuck, this guy knows what we are saying" kind of listening.

They became as quiet as a church mouse, no more dialect talk. Simple yes or no answers were all I heard for the next hour. I'd walk ahead down the hallway only to turn around to see them whispering to themselves. Sort of like a group of kids who got caught stealing cookies from a cookie jar.

"Are you guys okay?" I said. "Do you need me to slow down a bit?"

"Ahhh, no," said Raul with his hands in his pockets.

"*Sí*, go ahead," said Juan, also with his hands in his pockets.

But as soon as I went back to walking forward, they'd giggle their asses off by calling me a fat shit in Spanish under their breath. I heard them. You bet your ass I heard them.

Nothing pisses me off more than a worker who pretends to not understand the language just to get out of work. If you're going to be a prick, just own up to it and get it out in the open from the beginning. Don't call me a tub of shit in a different language. Say it in English so I know where I stand with you.

It's one thing if you legitimately don't understand something. I'm a patient guy. I'll try to help. But don't be a coward and talk smack in Cherokee.

You know exactly the type of person I'm referring to. I bet you can name one or two dickheads at your job who pull the same shit. It doesn't have to involve a language barrier either. It could be any dumbass who plays games because they think they can get away with it. Think of Gary in accounting who doesn't get the new computer software. Instead of asking for help, he makes numerous mistakes, which, in turn, makes your job harder. Gary knows he fucked up. Gary's always been a fuckup. That's why Gary is taking an entry-level office job at the age of fifty-two. But he blames you for not training him properly.

Or think of Becky, the secretary who can't answer the phone or take messages without having a panic attack. That's kind of the reason she was hired—to answer the phones. But damned if she didn't screw the whole process up. Someone else had to do the job she was hired to do in the end.

There should be a law to protect people who try to train a fellow employee who doesn't give a shit. It's not right for me to take the blame when someone else doesn't put out the effort to learn. The Three Amigos didn't give a fuck about anything. They'd answer their phones at work, yammering on in Spanish, but God forbid I ask them to help move a set of tables across the room. Each time I gave them a directive, they threw their hands up in a "I don't get it" motion.

Now I know for a fact the job application was in English, as well as the interview and the employee orientation. You think one of these cocksuckers would stop the boss and say, "Help, I don't understand what you are saying to me." Hell no. They pull that "I'm lost" shit when I told them to work.

For almost a month, I'd ask each one individually if they were learning the ropes. Do you understand what to do, Jose? Excuse me, Juan, do you know how to make the floors shiny yet? Each time I'd get what sounded like someone practicing their vowels for a spelling bee. "I... I... ah... ummm... I..." This was followed by involuntary arm flailing as to express a sincere lack of understanding.

Goddamn it. Of course I'd get the deaf, dumb, and blind routine when I told them to stop texting and work. Not on my watch, boys! I got tired of playing Mr. Nice Janitor. It was time to bring out the stern, watchful janitor. I found the Amigos sitting in the break room long after the scheduled break one day. So I put a little bass in my voice:

"Gentlemen, it's time to go back to work. You understand me, right?" But I said it all in Spanish. Full-on, no-messing-around Spanish.

The stares I got from these fuckers! Lord, if looks could kill, I'd be road pizza during rush-hour traffic. They never said a word. All three got up, walked to the door, and continued down the hallway.

All was quiet for the next two days. No hi or even *hola* when I came in. No more polite smiles. My Latin buddies gave me the cold shoulder and stink eye at the same time. The stink shoulder, as I like to call it. Fine by me, gents. Just do the fucking job, which is easy, and go home at the end of the shift, okay? *Comprendes, muchacho?*

But the Three Amigos had other plans.

Since I was in charge of training the Three Amigos, it was my fault when they mixed bleach and ammonia, almost killing half the children in the school. During a school dance on a Friday night, the Spanish speaking dumdums mixed chemicals to mop the floor after the party. Within minutes, the school had to be evacuated and poison control called. It turns out if you mix bleach and ammonia, it creates chlorine gas—bad things happen when you mix them together. The whole school had to go outside because the fumes can burn your lungs from the inside out. It's similar to something called mustard gas, which was used in World War I. By the freggin' Germans, I might add. Google it. It's some serious shit.

Anyway, police and EMTs where called as well as my boss. It was a cluster fuck outside the school, kids screaming and gasping, crying for their mommies. I had no idea what happened until I saw people running for the hills, wheezing for the precious elixir known as oxygen. It was like a war movie scene, only not it black and white.

After the initial ruckus, my boss saunters over to me, with police sirens and ambulances blowing in the background, shaking his head with his hands in the air. I didn't know what the hell was going on. I smelled the fumes, but I didn't know how it happened. One of the other workers, Hector, told me the Amigos mixed bleach and ammonia together in the mop buckets when I turned my back. I specifically told all three of those asswipes not to mix bleach and ammonia. "*No es bueno, no es bueno!*" I told them the first day they started.

I explained to my boss that I showed all three of them not to use these chemicals together, several times over.

"What the hell happened here!" said Mr. Polotski.

"I told them, Mr. Polotski, *do not use bleach and ammonia together.*"

"Well, obviously you didn't explain it clearly enough! What the fuck are we going to do now? Someone's gonna sue us!"

"Look, I told all three of them together at the same time. They shook their heads and said they understood it. They said yes three times. Shit, I even said it in Spanish," I said.

"Goddamn it!" Mr. Polotski said. "Well, maybe… maybe you said it wrong in Spanish or something. I don't know."

"What, am I supposed to be responsible for everything these guys do all night? Jesus Christ, I'm not a babysitter. They don't listen to me anyway!" I said, watching the whole chaotic scene outside. "I trained them and told them what to do. If they don't understand it in English or in Spanish, then it's their problem, not mine."

Later that night, after HAZMAT gave us the all clear to go back inside, Mr. Polotski and I talked to the Three Amigos. They weren't laughing then, but they did play *estupido* when confronted. I asked them what happened, and all they kept saying was "*Yo no se*" or

"*Que.*" Each answer was "I don't know" or "Huh" or "What." After a few minutes, in plain unbroken English, Jose said, "I want a union representative." Right after that, Raul followed by saying, "We want a translator."

Okay. Sure. Let's play that fucking game. Three guys, who almost killed two hundred middle school–aged kids now want representation? Not a word of English the whole first month they worked and now they speak fluently. If I asked them to scrub a toilet, they'd pretend they had a communication problem. But now, when faced with a serious situation, they start blabbing away in a language they supposedly don't understand.

By union law, they have the right to ask for a translator and a rep. In a union, everyone is protected. Just remember that. Ever hear the saying "You're only as strong as your weakest link"? Well, I got three of them saying they "*No comprendo.*" So the boss and I had to call a union rep who spoke Spanish. An hour later, one of the Spanish teachers showed up to help decipher the situation. This guy was making overtime, too, at a hefty price.

At 11:15 p.m., we had a meeting with the union rep / translator, Mr. Polotski, the Three Amigos, and myself. Two hours of horseshit with all three of those bastards saying I never told them it was bad to mix bleach and ammonia.

"Are you fucking kidding me?" I said. "I told all of them not to do that!" I even went so far as to get the chemical containers and show the boss and the rep where it says on the label not to mix bleach and ammonia. "It's in English *and* Spanish in bold letters! Look!"

"It's your job to make sure they understand how to do their job," said Mr. Polotski. "If they make a mistake, it's because you didn't properly educate them."

"You do see they have a difficult time understanding English, don't you?" said the translator, who at that time was getting an earful from Raul in Spanish. I couldn't make all of it out, but I did hear him blame me for being a bad communicator.

"Bullshit," I said. They understand perfectly. I ain't going down for this!"

Here's where the true colors of the union shine brightly. In this case, it's my word against theirs. All three of them blamed me, so it's three against one. Now I'm dead certain I heard Juan tell the translator I was incompetent, which cheeses me right off. I've spent years in college, with multiple degrees, and consider myself well versed in a multitude of things. Suddenly I'm a wet brain.

No matter how much I explained the situation, the report said I instructed my workers wrongfully. No charges were filed by the parents of the kids, but I still had a letter in my file indicating it was at fault.

This place makes me sick to my stomach. I did nothing wrong. Literally, nothing that occurred that evening was by my hand. Yet a couple of dickwads lie to pin it on me because they have some sort of vendetta. What, were they mad I spoke in a harsh tone to them days earlier? Was I a threat to their lazy escapade?

Monday I came in to work to find the Amigos plotting against me in the break room. They sat there around a table, talking in low voices. All it took was a smile from Juan when I walked in the door to set me off.

"It's time to go to work, gentlemen," I said. "It's not break time."

"Excuse me, you don't have a right to talk to us that way," said Raul in a Spanish accent. "I don't like your tone of voice."

"But it's time to work. *Trabajo? Lo entiendes?*"

"This is outrage to me," said Juan. "We don't have to be treated this way."

Jose picked up his Boost mobile phone and hit one button. Guess who was on speed dial? That's right! Mr. Union Translator himself! When he was put on speakerphone, he instructed me to not speak with the Amigos.

"My clients are invoking their right to an attorney or representation," he said. "You do not have the right to speak to them without a union rep present."

"Wait a minute, hold on! I'm just telling them to go to work!"

"My clients do not like the manner in which you are speaking to them. It is insulting to degrade them as you have in the past."

Clients? What the fuck was happening here? Since when did the Spanish teacher become a lawyer? I stormed away angry at the job, yet again. Now I couldn't even look at the Amigos without consulting the translator first. The boss came down that night to reiterate I wasn't allowed to speak to the Amigos without a union rep present. I was only allowed to speak to them for five minutes before the start of the shift, under his direct supervision. What kind of horseshit is this? Now I needed permission from Mr. Translator to tell the workers *to go to work*.

By this time, the translator was making a mint in overtime, and Mr. Polotski started to show up each day to harass me. Like it was my fault this dude was getting 150 bucks an hour.

This same kind of scene played out the entire time the Three Amigos worked. I'd tell them to do a job, they'd cause chaos, and I'd take the fall unwillingly. The next week, I told Jose to wax a hallway, which was well within his job duties. I showed him how to mop the floor with just the right amount of liquid wax so it didn't leave streaks. He mopped it all right. Fucking guy put so much wax on the floor he turned it into an ice rink. You could've had the Philadelphia Flyers practice down the halls. The next morning, six teachers fell ass over tea kettle, and two had to go to the hospital for broken wrists. Sure as shit, when Jose was asked about why he put so much wax down, he said I told him to do it. "He told me to mop it good, so I did what he said," said Jose, by way of the translator. There's that asshole translator again, lecturing me on how important it is to educate everyone on my team.

Two days later, Juan was told to throw out the garbage, which he did. Twenty-seven small plastic garbage cans went into the dumpster. He threw each plastic garbage can out. What kind of shitbird does that? So we had yet another meeting with the union translator, who could've bought a Corvette with all the overtime checks he was collecting.

"Did you tell him to empty the cans or throw them out?" said Mr. Polotski.

"You're joking, right?" I said. "Are you really asking me this?"

"There seems to be a language barrier here," said the translator. "Did you explain how we take the trash out efficiently?"

"You bet your ass there's a language barrier! These morons are playing stupid and you know it. Does Juan throw out his garbage can at home, or does he take the bag out of the can like the rest of the world?" I said.

No one wanted to hear my side of the story. Not a soul listened to me at all during these meetings. Now I won't claim to be a saint. I've had my fair share of run-ins with my boss and the union for that matter. But I'll be damned if I'm going to get gangbanged by a trio of Mexicans who find humor in my demise.

Then came the harassment charges. It all came to a head with the Amigos filing a complaint against me. After messing with me for a month, the Amigos decided to ramp up their attack. A full-on missile deployment was at hand. Whenever I told them to do something, they called the translator and told him I was harassing them. One evening, while eating my dinner, I was confronted by my boss, Mr. Polotski, his boss Mr. Sanders, the union translator, and the Three Amigos. Great. Just fucking great. Here I was sitting down to a nice, homemade bowl of chili, and in walk the hit men, ready to take me out.

"It seems we have a bit of a problem," said Mr. Polotski while slamming down a file folder.

"You bet we do," I said. "What the hell is this?"

"Apparently, you said some rather deplorable words to these three gentlemen," said the translator. "We are here to discuss your potentially racist remarks."

"What? What the hell are you talking about?"

In no way, shape, or form did I call anybody the things they said I did. I'm the very last person to call someone a racial slur. Each person sat across from me with disgust in their eyes, silently judging me for things I never said. Here it was: the top boss was here to take away my keys and throw me to the wolves. The hearing, as I like to call it, began all while my chili was getting cold. I fucking love my homemade chili too. Just the perfect amount of heat and spice.

THE DAY I CLEAN MY LAST TOILET

"On January third," said Mr. Sanders. "You called Mr. Mendoza a racial slur."

"No, I didn't. The only time talked with him on that day was about his bathrooms.

I told him to make sure his bathrooms were cleaner. They looked dirty."

"Well, Mr. Mendoza said you called him a beaner."

"That's ridiculous. I never said that!" I said. "I saw the bathrooms he cleaned were dirty, so I said to make sure it's *cleaner*. It's my job to tell him when he isn't doing the job right. That's all!"

"Okay. Well, he is claiming you said that word to him, so it seems you may have said it," said Mr. Sanders, who was peering at me with his reading glasses on the top of his nose.

Sanders, with his fancy briefcase and pretty leather attaché filled with important-looking papers, was the end of the line for a janitor. This guy was usually called in to terminate employees. This was no good for me. The only thing in front of me was a half-eaten bowl of chili with some oyster crackers on the side. No defense witnesses, no affidavits, nothing. Just that poor, room-temperature, excellently seasoned homemade chili bowl.

"Regardless… on January fifth, you allegedly spoke to Mr. Sanchez in a derogatory manner, referring to him as a wetback? Do you recall this incident?" said Mr. Sanders.

"I never said that! I told him to put a Wet Floor sign out because he was mopping the floors! This is ridiculous. I didn't say these things and they know it!" I pointed to the three buddies who sat there with smirks on their ugly, lying faces.

"Please don't point to them like that," said the translator. "It's offensive. They are not the ones in question here."

"Oh, but it's okay to make accusations about me and ambush me like this. You've gone too far now. I'm calling my lawyer!"

I don't have a lawyer. I don't even have money to pay for a terrible lawyer who's never won a single case. But I needed something definitive to say at that moment in time. Management only brings Mr. Sanders in when they know they have someone targeted. I was scared. Fucking petrified for no reason at all.

It takes a lot to get me riled up, but I was through the roof on this one. I was fuming the whole time, trying to defend against a bombardment from all sides. What did I do to get treated like this? Maybe I offended them by speaking to them in Spanish? I didn't have a clue at that point.

I asked for a union rep of my own during this farce meeting. Here's the bad news: I was told it's a union law only one rep per meeting. Funny how the only union delegate available was the guy making a shit ton of money working with the Spanish guys. To me, that's a clear-cut case of racism, and yet *I* was the one being labeled as racist?

I was beginning to think my time as a janitor was coming to an end. Sure, I'd miss the paycheck, but not the bullshit. This place has been the same heap of shit since long before I started swinging a mop. I'm sure many moons ago, when the first janitors used mastodon-handled brooms to sweep out a cave, it was much the same as it is today. It's just a bunch of unnecessary malarkey from people who think they can get out of doing work.

If I lost this job, I'd be up shit's creek. I mean, I've got tons of student loans outstanding, not to mention all my other bills. But to get fired? I've got too many years in to get ousted over crap like this.

Nah, I wasn't going down without a fight. If you want me gone, you're going to have to nuke my ass off the planet. During the meeting, I took whatever notes I could on a napkin. I didn't have time to get a fancy portfolio. Then I asked for a ten-minute break. It was my only chance to try to call someone, *anyone*! I needed a Hail Mary pass. My phone was the only thing I had except that glorious chili.

But when I walked outside, I didn't have a game plan. *I'm fucking toast*, I thought.

It wasn't like I had any defense for this. I didn't do anything wrong! But I got set up big-time by a couple of guys who beat me on a technicality. Three dudes against one. And they were a minority too. I should've just shaved my head and tattooed a Swastika on my chest. There's no coming out of this alive.

Here it was. My last ten minutes of being employed. No more free dental work. No more longer than the average lunch breaks. Just me, my mind, and my four-year-old iPhone. What the hell was I going to do outside anyway? I didn't think Siri had any answers for "Hey, Siri, I'm really fucked over here… can you find me a hole to crawl in?"

With two minutes outside, I had one of two options on my plate: (1) call my mom and start bitching about how I am going to have to move back home or (2) start bashing the Amigos' heads in with my iPhone. It's not like I was going to need a phone anyway. No one would call an out of work janitor in his late twenties.

Well, folks, a third option landed in my lap seconds later.

When I was outside pretending to call a lawyer, the Three Amigos went outside too. I heard them grumbling behind the door, so I ran around the side of the building behind them. I guess they didn't see me go out the side door. They must've thought I went out the front. So I ducked behind the building real quick with my phone still in hand. They were talking loud with the interpreter in Spanish, laughing like no one was listening. But I was. I peeked around the corner and started the video recorder on my phone.

The four of them were talking so much shit in Spanish, how they were going to sue the district for racial bias, how they would frame me and make me the scapegoat to the whole thing, everything! With my shitty, old phone, I played Big Brother, watching silently from a distance. I had my phone record the whole damn five-minute conversation clear as day. Boy, you've gotta love the cameras on those Apple phones! They were so preoccupied by calling me a *vaca gordo* (that's "fat cow," if you don't know) they didn't see the shiny screen recording their every move.

Once they went back in the building, I had to act quick. Holy shit! What a bunch of fucking dildos! I feared the bosses where ready to shitcan me right there, so I had to act fast. I ran down the hall to my friend Hector, apparently the only Spanish guy in the build-ing I could trust, and told him to come with me. He said "*Sí*" and followed me back into the meeting. Hector's a real sport. I simply told him to stand with me and look menacing. I know he hated the Amigos as much as I did, maybe even a little more. It appears the Mexicans look down on the people from Honduras, where Hector's from. Another unfortunate real-world scenario playing out in the world of janitoring.

The tribunal sat there with a blank look on their faces wondering why I brought Hector to the meeting.

"What's this?" said Mr. Polotski.

"This...," I said with a smile, "is my lawyer." They all had a little chuckle at mine and Hector's expense. I guess Hector wasn't an individual to be known for his sly courtroom demeanor.

"You see, gentlemen," I said while slowly walking around the room, "I need Hector as my lawyer *and* translator. He knows Spanish, and I have a video I want to play for you all."

"What's this got to do with your case and the charges?" said the translator.

"Well, now, everything!" I said and hit the Play button.

Once that video started, the whole room went silent. Dead quiet. Like "someone just farted" quiet. The Amigos and the translator were stunned, their mouths wide open catching flies. The big boss Sanders started writing in his glamourous leather binder. Polotski, that stupid Pollack, was moving his mouth without much in the way of words coming out.

And then there's my hero, Hector. Oh lord, did this guy translate like a motherfucker! His voice rose and fell like he was acting out a scene from *Hamlet*. Hector translated every phrase he could, putting emphasis on the bad parts and highlighting the really bad parts.

"Then they say they going to sue you for the money... Now they calling you all stupid, fat *pingas*, which means penis... right here, see. Now they say you don't know what will hit you... oh, no... now they all say you so stupid and dumb you cannot make them do the work... Oh Jesus... now the one guy he say, 'Fuck those *putos*'... which mean gay traitors!"

My boy Hector saved my skin. Once he saw those assholes on the video, he knew why I brought him in. His translation was more than I could've done. I only knew some stuff in Spanish, but Hector, he was my bright-yellow canary singing the song of my redemption!

Halfway through the video, the crooked translator tried to stop the meeting. "This is an outrage! That's an invasion of our privacy! We… we didn't mean those things. It… it's…"

"It's bullshit!" I spouted. "You lying-ass pricks! How dumb can you be? Now I'm really going to call my lawyer!"

Let's just say the meeting ended shortly after me calling them pricks. Mr. Sanders, who's had it in for me for quite some time, hated not being able to fire me. But he sure did like firing three other assholes at once! It's like he was invigorated. Getting to fire three guys instead of one was a real treat for someone like Sanders.

The Three Amigos were finally booted out of my life forever. Once the big boss saw the video, he couldn't fire me, as much as it would've given him so much pleasure. That crooked Spanish translator, you ask? Well, he didn't get fired. Think about it. Management can't fire four Mexicans in one day. Now that would be considered racist. Management did, however, strip the translator of his titles and union delegation. He was forced to pay back all the overtime he racked up over the weeks. Now he's just a lowly Spanish teacher, which is more than he deserves, that fucking rat bastard.

I don't know what happened to the Three Amigos. My guess is, they are working their scam on some other job filled with non-Spanish-speaking gringos.

It's funny, though. I've always considered myself a pretty intelligent guy. Never thought I'd be inches away from getting fired over some ridiculous crap. Of all the shit I pulled over the years, the massive amounts of dereliction coupled with borderline hazing sarcasm, it took three Mexicans to give me a scare. So I regrouped a bit, buckled down my trust-o-meter, and treated everyone like a potential threat. This way, I'm ready for an attack all the time, much like a ninja.

I can guarantee one thing now: if I'm ever to leave this job, it will be on my own terms. It won't be through some half-assed attempt to bring down the legend known as me. And just for the hell of it, I bought Rosetta Stone, and I'm halfway through being fluent in Spanish. You just never know when you'll need to know what someone's saying about you.

Chapter 15

The Gray Viper

I *have seen pure evil, and it wears a tattered old gray suit.*

Among the many, many levels of upper management lie the realm of the hatchet men. A massive operation such as the board of education needs these slimy Gila monsters just as any other entity would. These individuals are hired for the sole purpose of trimming fat from the budget, employee-wise. Another way of saying it is that these jerk-offs were hired to screw every single person to get a better raise for themselves.

A hatchet man, by definition, is a slicer and dicer. Those self-made backstabbers all employers need to cut costs but deny hiring. He, or she, depending on the job, does the real dirty work. They fire people who are considered unwanted or unneeded at the workplace. A good hatchet man will turn your lights without breaking a sweat. One minute you're having a honey bun on break, and the next, you're sitting in your car holding a box with all the junk you used to have sitting on your desk.

You've seen these turncoats, right? Being all buddy-buddy with you until you drop your guard for one second. Before you can say "Oh shit!" the knife's already in your spine. It may take months or even years of cordial interactions with a supervisor. But don't get too comfy with these dirtbags. Their only mission is to eradicate you just to garner themselves a few more pennies in their paycheck.

My job hired the greatest, and most despicable, hatchet man ever to slither across the face of the Earth. This demon was on point, practically writing the book on being a prick. This heinous hell raiser was so good at being nefarious the board of ed. gave him a lifetime contract, which, giving his questionable heritage, may or may not be forever.

Mr. Sanders was one of the most brutal fucks ever imagined. His entire aura was created to destroy people's lives, a doomsayer destined to vanquish mankind. He's a vile, truly sick individual whom nothing at all is sacred. He fired his own brother-in-law because he called out sick on a Friday. Poor guy had the flu for two days before going to the hospital. Sanders eliminated him because he didn't have a doctor's note. I guess in between shitting your brains out and have a 106-degree fever, the guy might've been a little woozy.

If Sanders was willing to terminate his own family members over a doctor's note, just think what he can do to someone he doesn't even know.

Originally Sanders had two other associates with him. Those poor saps lasted about three months before Sanders convinced the school board to fire them. He chose to do the jobs of three men—because he's that fucking dedicated to being an asshole. He loves to screw people over so much he wanted to do all the terrible acts himself. How do you combat someone who enjoys ruining people's lives for fun? It's just unnatural!

I don't know if you noticed by now, but I like to give people code names. It brightens up my day a little and keeps me from going postal. I'm sure you've got special nicknames for the dicks you work with? Sanders is known as the Gray Viper. I call him this for two reasons. One, he's a snake through and through. From the cold blood in his veins to the scaly skin he sheds once every 90 days, Mr. Sanders surely is a viper masquerading as a human. And two, fucking guy only has one suit! Seriously. He makes almost 190,000 dollars a year, and he stuffs his bony carcass into the same weathered gray suit each morning. Oh, he's got several different ties, I'll give him that. But come on, man! Buy a new suit, you cheap fuck!

It's not even a flattering gray. It may have been snazzy thirty years ago when he first bought it off the sale rack in Jamesway. But now? The hue closely resembles something an old cat would vomit up after giving itself a bath. Yeah, *that* kind of gray. If you pull a loose thread on the sleeve, the fregging arm would fall off.

Sanders's official title is Director in Charge of Revenue Savings. Really? What the shit is that? Why don't they just call him the Penny-Pinching Black Hole because that's exactly what he is. He'll find a way to pull money from any source he can. Need a new school bus? Sanders organized a blood drive where he "sold" the rarer blood types to the community blood bank. Yeah. That happened. I don't know how he didn't get locked up for medical malpractice or something like that. But Mr. Sanders got a nice fat check from the blood mobile for bringing so many high-demand blood donations. All he had to do was a random check of the blood types located in the personnel files. I'm pretty sure that's illegal, but when you have no soul, I guess anything is on the table.

Over the years, Mr. Sanders has become quite amazing at his job. I will give credit where it's due. Sanders is extremely efficient at what he does. Mind-numbingly efficient, as a matter of fact. He probably lies awake all night scheming about how to streamline the business of a school district. He once saved the school board hundreds of thousands of dollars by cutting the food service budget in half. It was an impressive feat until you see how he did it. Instead of laying off a few employees, he fired 100 percent of the school lunch ladies. Every hairnet-wearing grandma was shitcanned overnight. Do you know whom he replaced them with? Prison inmates from the county jail. Yup. He figured since they already have experience in a cafeteria setting, why not just employ convicts? You don't have to pay them health benefits, sick time, or even wages for that matter. Simply have them bussed in from the jail in the morning, serve half-frozen tatter tots, and back out the door when lunch is done.

It might have sounded like a good plan in his demented mind. Once the parents got ahold of the news, they went ballistic at the next school board meeting. "How dare you put my child in danger!" "Do you know how morally wrong it is to have prisoners serving turkey sandwiches to kids!" An angry mob of taxpayers is nothing to him. I bet he faced a tougher crowd during the Spanish Inquisition. Sanders got away with his maneuver by promising he wouldn't have any child molesters in the kitchen. That was his only compromise. "No inmate convicted of a sexual offense of a minor will be permitted on school property," said Sanders at the board of ed. meeting.

But felons, murderers, rapists, thieves, and bank robbers were perfectly okay to start ladling out Jell-O.

The parents and taxpayers were livid. People started screaming at the meeting, throwing crumpled papers at the school board members. It was chaos. When order was restored, Sanders pulled up a PowerPoint presentation displaying the cost versus revenue slide. The bottom line was a serious savings, which many of the taxpaying citizens couldn't argue with. You know those old seniors in your town hate when their taxes go up. They must've shit their diapers when they saw how much their taxes went down instead of going up. A tax break to a senior citizen on a budget is a no-brainer. The old fucks got on board with the plan and gave their support behind the diabolical Sanders.

With a little steam behind the plan, the Gray Viper called for a vote right there at the meeting. The board of ed. authorized the program 5–4 citing a major budget savings as their deciding factor.

Can you imagine how scared those little tikes must have been when they saw Brutus instead of Mildred serving pizza? Talk about nightmares and bed-wetting! You're not supposed to judge a book by its cover, but come on! These guys are actual criminals with only a thin layer of glass separating them from your kids. That and a hairnet.

Weirdly enough, things went smooth for about two months. Prison guards were stationed at each school with stun guns and handcuffs just in case any scuffles broke out. I've never heard such a quite school cafeteria in my life. Usually the café is loud as hell with kids laughing, throwing used milk cartons all over the place. Don't get me wrong, I think the whole program was atrocious. But the place was spotless after lunches and quite as a church mouse. Made my job a lot easier. I'm just saying.

But eventually, it all came crashing down. Food items started going MIA from the school kitchens. You'd be surprised how many of those small juice containers can be stuffed in a pair of orange overalls. The going rate for a peanut-butter-and-jelly sandwich in the slammer has to be worth two packs of smokes. An inmate / kitchen cook can do pretty well for himself if he played his cards right. Then the meatball hoagies started walking off by themselves. Think about how desperate an inmate has to be to stuff a hot sub down his pants to smuggle it back to the clink.

It was only a matter of time until the weapons went missing. Slowly the chef's knives all started disappearing. That's what you get for hiring murderers and kleptomaniacs. The Prisoners in School Kitchens Program ended when two inmates started violently stabbing a cook by the chilled fruit station. Luckily no children were harmed. Emotionally scarred, perhaps. Just a bunch of third graders witnessing Jamal get his spleen removed without anesthesia.

Mr. Sanders never took blame for the whole scandal. I'm sure he made a few phone calls to his lackeys, who paid off a judge or two. He did, however, still manage to save money for the district. He hired all the old kitchen workers back, but at fraction of their salaries. Apparently, when you have a lapse in work, you must start from the bottom all over again. Entry-level pay. All those workers who had twenty years in got screwed royally.

I told you this guy was heartless.

Sanders loves to save on school supply costs too. One year, he bought paint for the schools. It happens once every few years to touch up the parts of the schools that look shabby. But he didn't buy Siperstein's or Sherwin Williams. He sprang for the cheapest shit on the market, filled with stuff like lead and other toxic metals. It was great for the bottom line, saving so much money. Not so much for the children. Do you know what happens to a developing child's mind when it's introduced to lead paint? It's not good, let's just say that. I just hope little Tommy or Suzy doesn't eat any paint chips coming off the wall.

The school buses needed repairs after being on the roads for so long. Do you know how he saved on the repair fees? He sold the seat belts out of the buses to the company who was fixing them. An even swap, apparently. The buses now drive nice and smooth while the kids hold on to one another for dear life. Who needs a seat belt when you've got the buddy system? Again, the school budget never looked so good until the first crash. Those poor kids popped out of the bus like a springy toaster shoots up a slice of rye bread. Who the hell knows how much the legal fees amounted to. My guess is another judge got a kickback from the Sanders slush fund.

No one is safe under the Sanders regime. I told you about the brother-in-law, so you shouldn't be surprised by any of these next stories. A few months back, we had an English teacher named Caleb Masters who was diagnosed with prostate cancer. Nasty stuff, man. My grandfather died from that, so I felt bad for the dude when I heard about him. Mr. Masters had to apply for family medical leave to have the surgery, which I hear is a whole disaster all onto itself. Sanders originally denied his claim, saying his doctor's note was "too vague." You believe this son of a bitch! Denying a sick man time off to get surgery *so he doesn't die.* After having four doctors' notes, from two different physicians, Sanders agreed to allow the poor guy to have *some* time off. "He only gets two months," said Sanders. "The school district can only afford a substitute for two months. That is all!"

Well, Caleb Masters was a trooper. He had the surgery, got the all clear from his doctor, and came back to work a week before the two-month period. Guy is lucky to be alive by dodging one of life's biggest bullets. Don't really know him all too well, but if you can beat cancer, you're aces in my book. Instead of coming back to a safe, secure job, Mr. Masters was met with a letter on his desk from Sanders himself. Take a wild guess what Sanders did? He took away his medical coverage, claiming the surgery cost the districts insurance premiums to go sky high. "Due to your illness, you are now considered a high-risk patient and are now opted out of the health insurance program. If you would like to purchase additional insurance, the rates are listed below."

Isn't that illegal as all hell? I'm sure it breaks all sorts of laws in state and federal courts. Sanders had the balls to stiff the guy on his medical coverage. I'm sure he needs that after-care coverage to monitor how the surgery went. Leave it to a guy like Sanders to upcharge someone who needs medical coverage most. The cheapest medical coverage Mr. Masters could afford was the worst medical coverage in the history of medical coverages. I think the fee for any doctor's visit was five hundred bucks per visit and a twenty-five-thousand deductible for any procedure. Who the hell can afford that? Maybe Sanders, 'cause that fucker makes great money, but not an average Joe teacher.

If I just got through having a life-altering surgery from a disease such as cancer, the very last thing I want to hear is, "Sorry, pal. Your next doctor's visit might cause you to lose your house."

From what I've heard, Mr. Caleb Masters got a lawyer and is fighting it. What I also heard is the cancer came back, and with no insurance, Mr. Masters is fighting for his life as well as his job. Not to mention his legal fees. Sanders, on the other hand, has great medical coverage and an unlimited supply of legal fee monies. Thank you very much, taxpayers. Sanders pulled the same shit to pregnant teachers who went on maternity leave. You only get X amount of days off until you must come rushing back to work. Sanders doesn't give a shit if you have the placenta in a Tupperware container. Your ass better be back to work or else.

One sixth-grade teacher was so afraid of losing her job she worked up until she started giving birth. There she was, being rushed to the hospital in the back of an ambulance with her grade book still in her hands. "Make sure the class takes the science test on atoms tomorrow! Owwwww, oooooo, my contractions!" she yelled to one of her colleagues.

He also likes to sell things to the township to make money for his masters, the school board. Most school districts operate on funds from the state, the federal government, and township taxes. When your taxes go up in the fall, it's because of scumbags like Sanders. He uses a plethora of tools and techniques to suck a community dry like a Buick-sized leech. We had a new elementary school built last year for kindergarten through third grade. All schools have a playground for the little ones to practices running around like nutjobs. The first day of school, Sanders had a surprise for the teachers: he sold the rights to the playground equipment to another school out of district.

Mrs. White's first graders came outside on the first day excited to use the new monkey bars. Too bad the gate was padlocked. "Playground usage must require a permit" read the sign out front, next to a locked gate. He gave a private school priority access to the playground like it was a social club in Beverly Hills. What kind of a monster does that? I've seen some low shit while working here, but this is one is plain evil.

Once the school principal got wind of what happened, he demanded Sanders release the playground. Sanders offered to sell the principal a permit. "I could possibly squeeze you in on Thursday from 10:15 a.m. to 10:30 a.m.?" He was dead serious too. "Brand-new schools do not pay for themselves, you know?" he told the principal, who got fed up and quit at the end of the school year. I guess he was tired of seeing children cry when they walked passed the gate, watching rich kids get to use a brand-spanking-new slide. I'm shocked Sanders didn't have a guard tower built and post armed sentries along the rails. You know, like the Nazis did.

Right about now you're thinking to yourself, how is all this legal? How can one man (or demigod) get away with all this non-sense? Don't workers have rights?" You're right and you're not right. I told you from the get-go Sanders is very good at his job. If he was an artist, he'd have the sharpest pencil in the land. Each time Sanders fired someone or cut their benefits, he knew the federal and state laws for each situation before he dropped the hammer. Christ, he's been doing this for damn near a millennium. Sanders was probably around when the first lawyers of Rome defended their clients in the Colosseum. *Tenacious* isn't the word to begin to describe him.

If you stare into his eyes, you can see how the world will eventually end. Well, technically, you can only peer into one of his eyes. The other eye is fake. Years ago, someone messed him up big-time after a business deal went bad. Some dude smacked old Sanders in the head with a monkey wrench, almost killing him. *Almost* being the pivotal word. The Gray Viper cannot be killed because you can't kill what's already dead inside.

Sanders lost an eye, but he kept on ticking like the goddamn Energizer bunny. Freggin' guy came back to work after only two days off, against doctor's orders. I'm telling you, Sanders is no joke. He makes Rasputin look like a Girl Scout.

I heard a rumor Mr. Sanders has a bullet in his thigh where a bailiff shot him. The Gray Viper wasn't resisting arrest, but he sure as hell did something bad. Maybe he tried to bump off a judge or something? Who knows where these rumors come from. It sounds like something he'd do. And he does have a decent limp along with that fucked-up eye.

You can see it in his face and body, though. Sanders has battle scars from eons of wicked fighting. He's truly a wretched-looking sack of shit. Physically, he looks like Golem from Lord of the Rings fucked the dead guy from *Weekend at Bernie's*. Spiritually, he's Mad Max meets Thor, the God of Thunder. Don't let the withered appearance fool you. The Gray Viper is ready to strike at any time.

It's insane how much of a scumbag he is, yet for some strange and unparalleled reason, the school board loves him to death. Back in the day, when the school district needed to fill the position of Grim Reaper, they had plenty of applicants. People like ex-military Green Berets, psychopathic mailmen, Joseph Goebbels—those types all applied. But when the school board interviewed Sanders, they knew in their heart of hearts he was the most qualified executioner around.

It is a fact that this son of a whore was born to swindle people. Doesn't matter if it's school workers or the board of education itself. Sanders is a natural thief. I bet he's been doing it his whole life. Imagine some runny-nosed second grader hustling his classmates of out their milk money. "If you make it to the top of the monkey bars in under a minute, I'll give you a quarter." Then the greedy bastard has one of his henchmen trip the poor kid halfway to the top. I bet Sanders has hired bodyguards to do his dirty work since he was in pull-ups.

When I first started, my coworkers told me to beware Sanders. "Keep an eye out for him… he'll suck your soul right out of your motionless, pale body in seconds!" I didn't know what the hell they were blabbing about until I came around the corner of a hallway one day and confronted "it." There the sycophant was, in all its cotton tweed putridness. He kind of just appeared right there in the hallway like a fucking ghost. He carried an old leather briefcase in one hand (probably made from the skin of his vanquished enemies) and a pair of cheap reading glasses in the other. It wasn't like he was walking and had to stop. He was in a dead stop as I rounded the corner, perhaps waiting for me.

"May I help you?" said Sanders, his line-ridden face glaring at me with each passing second.

"Ahh… no… I'm just walking to…," I said.

"To do some work, right?" Sanders was intensifying his gaze, trying to intimidate me with all his evil might.

"Yeah, I'm just walking to get my broom," I said, still kinda stunned to run into it so suddenly. He wasn't a tall or a muscular man. But coming that close to him scared the hell out of me. I could smell the sulfur from his breath. His body was hunched over slightly with a bit of a slouch to one side. His skin, sort of dull, resembling the color of a fresh mushroom, had remarkably little in the way of definition to it. Almost like he had just been dipped in marshmallow fluff to be dried out for a few days.

"Good," he said. "I wouldn't want to hold you up from doing you precious work now, would I?"

"No, no, that wouldn't be good," I said, nervously chuckling a bit. Then came a brief ten-second pause from both of us. We stood there like two hardened gunslingers from the Old West in the middle of a dry desert showdown. Sanders, silently judging me in his head, was most likely saving this little encounter for future endeavors. While I, still startled a bit, stood there waiting for something, anything, to be said to break the awkward moment.

"Excellent!" said Sanders. "I shall see you again… Mr.…?"

"Ummm… I'm the new guy. Just… just call me the rookie."

"Very well… rookie." And then he was off, gliding across the shiny terrazzo floor as if his feet never touched the ground

Jesus fucking Christ! What the hell was that all about? I'd heard the gossip about Sanders being a real dick, but I wasn't prepared for an encounter like that. I was so disturbed by our interlude I forgot I had my broom in my hands! Here I was telling him I was searching out its location, and the fucking thing was in my hand the whole time. And good God, who says "I shall see you again"? I didn't like the sound of that at all.

And I'm telling you, he smelled like sulfur. You don't believe me? I don't care. But I was close enough to sniff him. That stench is probably what it smells like at the gates of hell.

It felt as if I had just come face to face with a Bigfoot. Not size-wise, but just the feeling of seeing something you've only heard of in folklore. There's no such thing as a Bigfoot, right? The scientific world doesn't have any definitive evidence like a test subject or a few of those big, hairy bastards running around in zoos. Yet here it was, standing mere inches from my face.

Stupefied and shocked is how I would describe my first Gray Viper meeting. I'm sure he was plotting my termination seconds after running into me. I was just another number to him. Whatever mechanical interface he was operating on was surely scrolling through lines of information while gawking at me. I picture the inside of his head looking like how Arnold Schwarzenegger viewed the world in *The Terminator*.

For the next three years, I had a total of sixteen altercations with Mr. Sanders. Each one of our informal run-ins were staged on his behalf, I'm sure of it. The first time Sanders came looking for me, he wanted help moving something. "Can you move this machine to the other room?" The machine he was referring to was a six-thousand-pound boiler that had been delivered to replace an old, worn model. It was a monster of a machine the size of a Volkswagen Beetle.

"I... I can't move that. I'd need a forklift to move it." Was this guy for real? What kind of shithead asks you to move something like that? Like it was a pile of books or something.

"Oh, so... you can't move it or *won't* move it?" said Sanders.

"I mean I need a forklift or a crane to move it."

"Can't you just put it on a pallet and wheel it away?" He was dead serious. He wanted me to tow it like an ox with a strap in my mouth.

"I can't move that without a machine!" I said. "It's a job you need a heavy-duty machine to move. We don't have a forklift here. If you get me a forklift, I can try to move it..." What the fuck is wrong with this guy?

Sanders just stood there. Motionless and bleak. I could see the anger rising in him, half his face squirming with intensity. He quelled it momentarily.

"Yes... yes... I see that now," said Sanders while he cupped his decrepit hands together. He wasn't looking at the machine. He stared me down as if to say, "How dare you defy me!"

"Perhaps another time then...," said Sanders. And then he walked away. He looked like Mr. Burns from *The Simpsons* as he shuffled away. All he needed was his Smithers patiently groveling under his feet.

Let me ask you this: who does that kind of shit? What type of person asks you to move something they damn well know you can't move? I'll tell you who, a motherfucker who studies your reaction. You see, Sanders is the type of guy who puts people in situations to see how they react. Sort of like a mad scientist who puts a lab mouse in a maze. Eventually, the mouse will die from starvation or find its way to the cheese. Sanders likes to watch people suffer. He's the type of sadistic fiend who puts land mines and laser beams in the maze trying to disembowel the poor little white mousey.

Had I gone berserk and called him a moron for asking me to move the big object, he'd have a right to fire me. But I'm smarter than your average broom pusher. Well, smarter than most of the teachers and administrators in this dump, let's put it that way.

If I've learned anything from years toiling away in this place, it's that each decision you make effects your future. Or rather, make sure you think three or four moves ahead of everybody. Ever play chess? I love chess. I'm a great chess player too. I've beaten old Jewish men in Central Park who do nothing but study chess all day long. I hold my own against most so-called chess masters. Sure, I get beat occasionally. The difference between a good chess player and a great chess player is the things you learn when you get beat.

I weigh each move I make before I make it. Everything I say. Each maneuver is calculated so I don't burn a path before I walk down it. All the times I do something at work it's because I've planned it out. I've beaten people before they even knew they were playing a game. The same applies to Sanders, perhaps the Bobby Fisher of the board of education. This son of a bitch will test you to see how you handle something. If you crack, you're done. He wins by firing you. But if you contemplate the scenario, play it out ahead of time, you can deflect any attack.

Once I started defending myself, I noticed the attacks getting more frequent. Each situation with Sanders challenged my resolve, causing me to use logic and quick wit to combat the fire-breathing dragon. I had a review with Sanders and two of his minion supervisors to see how I was progressing as an employee. As if cleaning up piles of dirt needed a prerequisite. They took detailed notes as they watched me do things like push a broom or empty a pencil sharpener. They'd criticize my work ethic for minuscule details. "I think your mop-handling skills are a little lackadaisical," said Sanders. "You should try using the figure-eight mopping technique. It tends to leave less streaks."

For the record, the figure eight leaves a shit ton of streaks. Just saying. I should know. I've been doing this for close to twenty years.

After a few months of constant checking up on me, the overseers ramped up their attack. Sanders decided to put problematic workers at my post to lure me into confrontation. I'd be minding my own business, silently sweeping a floor, and hear Sanders chatting with a new employee in another room. Sanders doesn't like anybody. Period. Yet here he was gabbing with some new jack about cleaning procedures. Once they'd see me both of them would stop talking, stare at me, and watch me pass without saying a word. Imagine two porcelain dolls with creepy eyes glaring at you when you enter a room. Well, okay. One of the dolls only has one good eye, but you get what I'm saying.

More times than not, these new workers had some affiliation with Sanders. I am willing to bet good money these jokers have buried bodies or cleaned up something Sanders didn't want the public to see. You can tell by someone's body language if they know each other or not. These half-assed lackeys tried to goad me into doing something I could be fired for. "Hey, man… you want a hit from this joint? I won't tell nobody" or the ever so popular "It's okay if you've stolen anything from the school… I've done it too."

It was a little odd to have so many coworkers trying to get friendly with me one minute then offer me weed the next. Rats always have a certain stink about them. With these rats, I could smell them from miles away. I'd ignore their requests while diligently doing my work.

One dumbass tried to fight me over a football team. "If you don't like the Dallas Cowboys, then we got problems, son!" This old crony tried to get physical, shoving me twice. Momma didn't raise no fool, so I calmed myself and called the cops to deal with this hack. The rule around here is if you fight with a fellow employee, you get terminated, no questions asked. It took a ton of composure to hold back from clocking this douche, but I didn't bite into Sanders's trap.

Also, just for the record, the Cowboys fucking suck. Everybody knows that.

It must have burned Sanders crooked ass when I didn't fall for his tricks. I did my job and avoided troublesome workers. Like the once-famous MC Hammer's "U Can't Touch This." I dodged his attempts to set me up all while looking like a model employee to the rest of the staff. "Need a hand with that heavy box, Mrs. Teacher Lady?" I'd say this in front of Sanders when he was surrounded by other administrators.

"Oh, thank you so much!" they'd say. "You're such a gentleman!"

"My pleasure, ma'am!"

"Say, Mr. Teacher Dude, how do you like your classroom? Is it clean enough? I can work extra hard tonight if you think it's even the slightest bit dirty?"

"It's great, buddy! The room looks amazing! Thank you!"

I had these people eating right out of my hand. There I was laying this shit on thick as can be, all while Sanders shot steam out of his wrinkled ears. Here was a man whom all feared, and each time he tried to catch me in a trap, I'd wiggle free. It must've killed him inside to know a janitor was outsmarting him at each turn.

Little did I know how far Sanders would go to try to get me fired.

Come summertime of the next year, Mr. Sanders hired a new nighttime supervisor for the custodial department. The last three ass clowns were fired after about a year. I guess they got tired of me filing grievances and winning all the time. So Sanders got medieval on my ass.

Greg O'Sullivan was perhaps the toughest fucker I've worked with yet. I'm talking level boss in the hardest video game you've ever played. This guy was almost as brutal as Sanders himself. Almost because I don't think a rational human being can be as evil as Sanders was.

Jesus Christ, was this new guy a hard-on! First of all, his eyes were gray, just like the color of Mr. Sanders's only suit. Those cold, steel orbs could cut a hole in the ozone with one look. I'm thinking the gray eyes were a must-have during the job hiring process. Once Sanders found his pit bull *and* he saw he had gray eyes, this was most definitely the guy for the job.

Greg O'Sullivan was grotesque in his own right, another homage to his mentor, Sanders. He had a scar down the side of his face only a machete could've made. Brutally vicious scar too. He wore it proudly like brand-new bow tie. His knees cracked when he walked. O'Sullivan sauntered down a hallway swaying this arms without moving his neck. Only his eyes moved constantly back and forth surveying the land. Think of a muscular silverback gorilla standing on his hind legs strutting around like a jacked-up peacock.

For some reason, he had a pair of toenail clippers on him at all times. O'Sullivan never clipped his fingernails in front of you. He just brought them out during a conversation to fiddle with them. What the fuck is this guy doing with a pair of toenail clippers? Has he used them for torturous purposes in the past?

His thick Irish brogue made me think Sanders actually flew to Belfast and asked the IRA to lend him their most devious man. Once here, O'Sullivan spent a majority of his tenure for the board of ed. as my shadow. I met him around the first week of August, and I tried to be cordial. It didn't work.

"Hi, are you Greg? I'm the evening custodian here at this post. My name is—"

"Yeah, I'm Greg. What you want?" said O'Sullivan. He had his eyes locked on me like an eagle spotting a rainbow trout in a stream.

"Well, I just wanted to introduce myself and say hi," I said. I extended my hand for a handshake only to be met with no hand from the other side.

"Hi," said O'Sullivan. His hands never left his pockets. I heard a metallic clanking sound emanating from where he had his hands. He was fidgeting with what I know now were his toenail clippers.

"Well... okay," I said. "I guess you will be the new super—"

"Enough with the introductions," said O'Sullivan as he glared at me. "You do work now. And I watch to see if you do work good. No more talking, all right?"

Welp. He we go again. Another happy camper. One more jerk-off boss trying to justify his eighty-five thousand dollars a year salary. "Don't associate with the help," said every middle-management boss ever.

I've been here long enough to know when I've being fucked with. Once you've been targeted for extermination, it's easy to spot a setup. Usually the boss with try to get on your good side first. A few casual remarks coupled with positive reinforcements on work ethic.

But Greg O'Sullivan was different. His attitude to me was shitty from day one. Wherever I was, that's where Greg was, spying on me, silently stalking. You know what it's like to have someone watch you, their eyes burning a hole into your back? I'd turn around really quick only to see a deeply scarred face leering from behind a doorway. All I saw was a head seemingly floating in midair peeking at me like Michael Myers from *Halloween*.

I noticed he was a complete prick each and every second he was in my presence. But as soon as he saw another worker, he was a gentleman. People would ask him for a bit of advice or come say hi, and he'd be a sweetheart.

"Hi, Margaret... how's your new Kia Sedona treatin' you? Is the gas mileage as good as I heard?"

"Hey, Mark, how has the married life been? Huh? I hear your wife got a job at the new doctor's office on Maple Ave. Does she like it?"

Mind you, this is the same guy whom when I offered a handshake, he looked at it as if I had impetigo.

Two weeks in, Mr. O'Sullivan laid out his plan for my demise. He walked right up to me, within inches of my nose, puffing out his chest.

"I've been watching you, Mr. Evening custodian, and I see you don't work as fast as other people. Why is that?"

"Ummmm… I don't know. I guess I just take my time when I work," I said.

"Uh-huh," said O'Sullivan. He reared back nodding slightly. "You don't know, huh? That's interesting. Maybe, perhaps, you aren't very good at this job, huh? Maybe you be better working somewhere it is okay to work slowly."

"No, I think I'm doing just fine here," I said. My blood pressure was slowly rising. "Just take it easy and let this blow hard exhaust himself." "I like to be thorough when I work, that's all."

"Thorough, huh?"

"Yes. Thorough. You know what that means, don't you?" I said.

"What?" said O'Sullivan.

"*Thorough*. To be meticulous. Do you know what *meticulous* means?" I said.

He was not pleased with my attempt to show how dumb he truly was. I tend to add a bit of sarcasm to a conversation when I feel attacked. It's my coping mechanism when dealing with assholes. My mouth has, in the past, got me into some trouble before. I'll admit it. I used to let fly with my back talk, so to speak. I've toned it down a tad over the years, but I still defend myself with big words when dealing with mental midgets such as Mr. O'Sullivan.

"Me-ti-cu-lous, huh?" he said. "Hmmm. I'll have to remember that one." He backed up slowly then turned to walk out of the room, no doubt to look up what those words mean.

My new enemy followed me for the next month, constantly prodding me with questions about my work performance. "Do you consider yourself a better worker than Michael?" or "What would you do if you were moved to another post?" I answered him as plainly as possible, always on guard, and above all, I always did my job. This fucking guy wouldn't stop, though. His main objective was to see me out the door. I think that's the only reason Sanders hired him. I never saw O'Sullivan do anything but follow me like a duckling follows its mother.

The long-awaited write-ups came in like an avalanche. O'Sullivan filed numerous papers about me, all suggesting I be terminated immediately. Work write-ups at my job all begin with a basic complaint. Things like improper work ethic, abuse of sick days, things of that nature. Well, Mr. O'Sullivan, finding no real reason to write me up, got creative with his paperwork. "Improper mopping technique" was the title of one report. Apparently, he didn't like the way I held my mop. "He doesn't know how to hold a mop," O'Sullivan said in a brief meeting with the higher-ups. "He's not mopping correctly."

That violation was squashed by the union rather quickly, but not before I had to demonstrate how I held my mop. I had to show three bosses and two union reps how I hold my wet mop. Then they made me pretend I was mopping the floor, all in a mock scenario. There I was, mopping the same spot on the floor with five morons staring at me. I passed the most basic of tests for a janitor.

The following day, O'Sullivan didn't like the way I dusted the window ledges. "You are leaving too much dust on the sill. You need to remove all the dust when you clean!" My blood pressure medication was being put to the test that week.

Days later I had another write-up from the Irish beast. This time, it was for abusing bathroom privileges. "You take too long in the bathroom," said O'Sullivan. He pulled out a notepad to show the two other bosses how long it took me to take a shit on Tuesday. "Nine minutes should be deducted from his paycheck." This son of a banshee was serious too.

What kind of jackal times someone's shits? I am in prison or something?

Again, the union said there wasn't much they could do to impose mandatory bathroom limits. Even though charges were dropped, I knew what O'Sullivan was doing. If a pattern of repeated offenses is shown, then it's only a matter of time before the bosses terminate on the number of write-ups alone. They were all bullshit, but if you have say twelve write-ups in a matter of months, then your ass is in a sling.

Doing my job the right way wasn't working. I was up against a person who didn't follow the rules of engagement. So it was time to bring out the heavy artillery.

The next time I saw O'Sullivan, after he timed my bowel movements, I figured I'd make small talk with the man. You know, to lighten the mood.

"Hey, that's a sweet accent you got there, Greg. What part of the Emerald Isle are you from?"

"I'm from here," said O'Sullivan. He had a clipboard in his hands diligently, taking notes on my trash-collecting abilities.

"Belfast? Cork?" Still nothing. O'Sullivan's unwavering eyes angled toward his notes.

"I've got family from Ireland. Maybe we're related?" O'Sullivan stopped writing. He looked up from his clipboard, and we locked eyes.

"You are not from Ireland," he said. "We are not related in any sense." I made a dent. I found the one thing to break down that wall to his inner defense system. Irish people, true Irish people from the country of Ireland, can't stand a person claiming to be Irish. Oh, you can be Irish now, but if you're not from the country of Ireland, you're nothing to them.

"Hey, I'm Irish, Greg. Look at this red beard? Huh? I'm like a six-foot-four-inch leprechaun, right?" O'Sullivan was pissed. He gripped his pencil firmly. That concrete jawline of his clenched angrily. O'Sullivan didn't say a word. He watched me carefully, trying to stifle his rage.

"Ya know, I did one of those Ancestry.com tests, and wouldn't ya know it… I'm 42 percent Irish. That's a lot. Almost 50 percent of me is from Hibernia."

"No… no, you are not…" O'Sullivan was on fire inside. His left eyelid was twitching uncontrollably. My plan was working.

"I like U2 and corned beef," I said. He made a small grunting sound after my comment, trying to hold back his anger. "Every year I go to the St. Patty's Day parade in Belmar wearing my green pants!"

"You shut your mouth right now, you hear me?" said O'Sullivan. I was towing the line of insanity. His ears were turning bloodred. "We are not related, do you understand me, boy?"

"What?" I said, all coy-like. "All I'm saying is that our families may or may not have been picking potatoes together in the boggy fields of the Old Country."

"Fuck you!" O'Sullivan snapped his pencil inadvertently, dropped his clipboard, and charged me like a Cape buffalo. He grabbed me by my collar and cocked his fist back. All this commotion brought a few people into the hallway wanting to see what the ruckus was. Mind you, O'Sullivan was like a foot shorter than me, but damned if he wasn't ready to level me like a mini bulldozer. He had me up against the wall with his mighty calloused fist locked and loaded.

"You shut your mouth or I'll shut it for you, you hear me!" With an audience of three teachers and another janitor watching, I went in for the kill.

"Is that Guinness on your breath?" I whispered to him. Then I smirked. That was the match in the gas tank all right. A smirk to a livid man pushes him over the edge. O'Sullivan went fucking apeshit.

"Ahhhh! You son of a whore!" He tried to swing at me, but he couldn't reach high enough to strike. Four swings toward my face all missed while I yelled for help.

"Call the police! This guy's trying to kill me! Heeeeellllpppp!"

It must've been a scene worth a thousand photos. Picture a tall guy being pummeled by a fifth grader. I held him back for a few seconds until he tuckered out. He got one decent punch on the left side of my chin, just enough to make a mark. When the cops showed up, the teachers were all freaked out, distraught over witnessing the scuffle. They told the police what they saw: the small man attacked the large man, screaming obscenities the whole time he did it. The police took my side of the story, after which they went to speak to O'Sullivan, who, while in handcuffs, was disorderly at best. He kept yelling in his thick Irish brogue, detailing how he was going to skin me alive with a pair of toenail clippers. "Fucking bastard! You're not blood of mine! I'll cut your fucking nose off and eat it!"

Good thing about the whole situation was I had a witness to how I resisted fighting. Had I slugged him back, I wouldn't be writing this now. Not because I'd get my ass kicked or he'd hurt me. But if I fought back, I'd be out of a job. I wasn't about to let O'Sullivan, or Sanders for that matter, get me that easily.

As they were loading the hobbit-sized Irish brawler into the back of the police car, Sanders appeared at the end of the hallway. He stuck his withered face around the corner just in time to see his latest project being Tased in the backseat of a police cruiser. It was over for O'Sullivan. A police record, even if charges were dropped, meant he couldn't work for a public school system anymore. I turned to see Sanders decrepit face watching me with a combination of disgust and hate. I shot him a look, my "I took your Irish queen chess piece, bitch. Your move." Sanders slowly backed away from the wall, knowing his top henchman was defeated.

The board had no option but to terminate O'Sullivan immediately. That, and I agreed not to sue if they fired him. Sanders tried vehemently to keep O'Sullivan on. He begged the board not to boot him. In the end, the board saved their own asses by shitcanning O'Sullivan, a move all board of education slimeballs will do in a heartbeat.

In retrospect, I should've sued the district. Papa could always use a little extra cheddar in bank account, you know what I'm saying? I didn't want to chance it, though. I did make several racial charged comments after all.

Just for the record, I don't make it a habit about being racist. It's not what I do. But if you're up against the wall like I was, both figuratively and literally, it seemed like my only play. It was either him or me, and I happen to be good at being a mouthy fuck.

The absence of O'Sullivan enraged Sanders. I took down his top crony. He wouldn't forget that, ever. Mr. Sanders hates me. No, scratch that. He despises me, and the feeling is very mutual. Now that I beat his top minion, it would only be a matter of time until he retaliated. Sanders tried other methods of destruction. Things like trying to set me up with other lesser qualified henchmen, but this never worked. I've become very adept at being three steps ahead at all times. I don't trust anyone ever. Each new boss can potentially be the one who takes me out. I've started taking pictures, keeping a daily journal of my work, and I even went so far as to carry a voice recorder with me at all times. This way, if some asshole starts spouting bullshit, I simply pull it out, saying, "I'd like to record this conversation for quality and assurance purposes." It's the same thing all companies say right before you complain to some customer service dick about how you Keurig machine won't brew coffee.

I'd like to say Sanders and I have parted ways from our eternal dance, but I can't. Unfortunately, I'm still working here, and he's still a cocksucking demon.

Fucker just won't die with his withered old self. He's left me alone, for now, but I know in his blackened, shriveled heart he is waiting for the perfect moment. I don't know about you, but I never turn my back on a snake. Even if you think they're dead, it's still very much alive, waiting for the chance to strike.

Chapter 16

The Story of Old Man Winter

I usually won't disclose real names of people I work with for obvious reasons. You understand, right? Most of them would sue the shit out of me for copyright infringement or some legal mumbo jumbo. Some basket cases don't want the world to know just how deranged they truly are. So I have to make up other names, change dates and places, all because some asshole might get offended.

Doesn't anyone believe in the freedom of speech anymore?

Only one guy said I had his permission to use his real name. His name is Mr. Tyrell Jones, and he wanted me to name him so he could get famous. Don't know about all that, but in the case of Old Man Winter, I can use his name, with likeness and stories without getting a letter in the mail from some leech of a lawyer. The reason for my crass attitude? Old Man Winter, a.k.a. James Stevenson, dropped dead three months ago. With no living relatives and not a friend on this planet, I think it's safe to say I won't be hearing any bullshit. Nobody gave a shit about him the seventy-eight years he was alive, so fuck 'em.

Old Man Winter earned his name more than anyone in this book. He was old, like Ramses the Second old. This guy was a frail old prick who did everything in his power to fuck up my day. I have no clue how he got the job in the first place. My guess is someone in HR feel asleep at the wheel and pushed his paperwork through. That's how this joint works. Even if you have a faint pulse, you're qualified. Why anyone would hire someone who looked like an extra for *The Walking Dead* is beyond me.

James Stevenson was born in 1936 in the rural town of Pine Valley, Kansas. The town, much like the man himself, was run-down and dilapidated. It never held more than a hundred people at one time and the people who lived there usually died miserably. Freak tractor accidents happen all the time where corn outnumber people a thousand to one. Wasn't much in Pine Valley except a sawmill, three bars, a railroad yard, and a shitload of pine trees. After a devastating tornado hit in 1965, a majority of the community moved to neighboring White Creek until another tornado hit that town in 1966. It's only fitting Old Man Winter came from a town where even God tried to stamp everyone out.

I love a slice of Americana just as much as the next guy, but Pine Valley is one of the most defunct Midwest towns in history. You know what Pine Valley is famous for? Jack shit.

No one of any importance has ever come out of that trash heap. Unless you love a good view of pine trees and the occasional sagebrush stampede, I suggest you avoid it. The most interesting story about Pine Valley, Kansas, was Burt Reynolds may or may not have stopped to take a piss in one of the bars. Apparently there's a sign in Rusty's Bar to mark the occasion: "This is where Mr. Burt Reynolds relieved himself." It hangs above the Pabst Blue Ribbon sign and a broken cuckoo clock.

I vividly remember the first time I met Old Man Winter. When he came to work, I thought I was looking at a corpse. Seriously, his skin was tight to his bones, like he'd been stuck in Dachau for a year. I took one look at him and almost called Life Alert right there. Scariest person I'd ever seen standing at the front door slowly knocking on the glass.

Jesus Christ, he looked like a ghost, complete with a long, drawn-out face and recessed eyes. This old codger shows up with a clipboard and an old metal lunch pail. He looked like a scarecrow. An old flannel jacket, two sizes too big, hung from his body, and I swear I saw hay sticking out of the sleeves. He was doubled forward knocking on the all glass door. Minus a windy thunderstorm in the background, it felt like I was in the middle of a slasher flick. When I realized he had on a janitor uniform underneath his ragged jacket, I opened the door.

"Can I help you, sir?" I said.

"Is… is… this the high school?"

"Yes, it is," I said. "Are you here to work tonight?" As I said this, he slowly looked in my eyes as if he was a lost puppy begging to be held. He was a deceiving little turd dog. Those eyes were vacant and lifeless. "I… ah… I… ummmm." He was stammering around. "My name is James."

"Hi James. I'm—"

"James Stevenson. I was born in Pine Valley, Kansas, the same year of the Big Drought—"

"Nice to meet you. I'm the lead night janitor here. I can show you the section to clean, if you like?" As I began to read him the new-guy spiel, James continued his story without skipping a beat.

"Nineteen thirty-six. That was the same year my family built the second tallest grain silo in Ricketaw County. My pappaw used two hundred and thirty-seven boards to make the sides of the silo and almost one thousand iron nails. Boy, I never saw such a large silo in my life—"

"O… kay," I said. "Well, James. I can show you around the school and show you the section you'll be working in?" James couldn't care less about work. Or maybe he was senile. I wasn't entirely sure which one. Shit, I didn't know if he was still alive until he blinked. Instead of "Sure, that's sounds like a good idea," he continued to recite his bio.

"I remember growing up along the Spidleway Railroad train tracks and pitching stones at the train. Each day at 1:32 p.m. the Yodleman Coal Train would come through town with its red-and-yellow caboose. Me and my best friend, Hal Johnson, used to hit the train with rocks all the time, even though we shouldn't have."

My problem with James was twofold: (1) I didn't have time to stand there listening to a cadaver yammer about the past and (2) I hate when old people talk for an unusually long time. Don't get me wrong, I respect older folks because they've been around a lot longer and should be respected. But don't tell me the name of your first pet chicken within fifteen seconds of meeting me.

James, or Old Man Winter as he was now known as, loved to talk. At times he could jabber about anything as long as he had a little wind in him. Did I really need to know how much his first bicycle cost in 1942? Odds are I could do without him telling me his high school sweetheart was ran over by an irate bull shortly after prom.

About an hour in, I finally got him situated and into the work routine. This old fuck moseyed down the hall like he had all the time in the world. If I looked as old as he did, I'd be trying to get the most out of my last few days on Earth. Seriously, man, I'd walk as fast as my wrinkled, veiny legs could take me. Not James. His high speed was similar to a snail taking a shit.

This job is not that hard if you ask me. You pick up a trash can, maybe rinse out a shitter or two, and poof, you're a janitor. Perhaps the hardest thing we do is push a big flat broom down the hallway. My new ancient friend was in no condition to walk, much less sweep a floor. Old Man Winter couldn't pick his feet up to move more than a few inches at a time. This guy was haggard, to say the least. His skin was old and rough like an oiled baseball glove left out in the rain for a week and then dried out in the sun for another week. His face, or what was left of it, was so sunken in I thought his eyeballs would fall out if he sneezed. He was such a pitiful creature. I truly felt bad for this guy in the beginning. Who wants to see somebody's great-grand-father bending over to clean up vomit off a gymnasium floor?

I really didn't want him working with me because he was a liability. I'd have to fill out paperwork if this guy croaked under my watch. If I gave him too much work, he might spaz out and trip over a dust bunny.

Old Man Winter was in no condition to work at this job. I've seen quite a few yokels in my day, but this sorry dude took the cake. I found him two hours into the shift sitting in a classroom staring off into space. That's when I felt true pity for him. I bet you this guy worked his whole life, maybe fifty years at some company, then came to work as a school janitor just to get out of the house. Maybe he lost his wife or something? Poor old guy looked as if his entire existence was ending. How can you not feel sorrow for someone who looked like he did? I may be an asshole, but I still have a pit in my stomach when I see roadkill on the side of Route 9.

Each time sad old James came to my post, he looked worse and worse. I told him to do as much as he could and I'd cover the rest. Believe it or not, I'm not a horrible prick as you may have come to think. I have feelings too, and this guy was tugging at my heart-strings. I even listened to his old yarns when he came to work. "Did you know the summer of '54 Pine Valley saw thirteen tornadoes? That's the mark of evil, ya know? Each one was more damaging then the last. My daddy had to rebuild our old silo twice that year."

Old Man Winter went into painstaking detail about life in the flat Earth known as Kansas. "Back in '57, we didn't have sprinklers in our lawns. I had to water everything by hand. My brothers and I would have to feed the cows by 5:00 a.m., collect the chicken eggs by 5:30 a.m., and water the vegetables by 6:00 a.m."

This dude was so monotone and dull. Damn near put me to sleep telling me about the complete workings of a corn planter. I feel comfortable talking about anything pertaining to farm life thanks to Old Man Winter's riveting stories. I bet you didn't know the locust plague of 1874 almost made James's great-grandfather move to another state? If I hear one more shit-ass tale about corn, I think I'll go bonkers. It's like all they do in Kansas is plant and harvest corn. No one listens to music or thinks deeply about life itself in the heartland of America. All James and his family did was contemplate the corn harvest. Go ahead, ask me how many ears of corn a tractor can cut down in an hour. It all depends on the size of the harvester, ya know.

The only time old James didn't talk about his past was when he was trying to get out of work. Whenever I asked if he was done, James would trail off complaining about some random illness. "I'm not sure I can lift that garbage can today. I had a bad head injury in '48 when a wood slat fell off the roof of the church on Cross Street and almost took my right ear off."

Whenever James started complaining, I felt sorry for him. I mean, shit! The guy looked like a mummy minus the wrapping. His aches and bodily grumbles were echoing down the halls like a moaning ghost in a haunted house. I couldn't let this guy work too hard or else he might really drop dead on me. But I was also tired of doing his damn work. Ultimately, the thought of him catching an aneurism scared me, so I let him follow me around while I finished his section. That's when he'd rattle off the really fascinating and vital statistics.

"Did you know the state of Kansas has the most quilters in the country? The last time I checked, we had fifteen people per square mile who quilted or worked on quilts. Forgot about the Amish or those hippy kids putting patches on pants. Kansas quilters are the most skilled in the US of A."

What was I to do? Tell the guy to take a hike? That's what I wanted to do, but he kept following me all over the building. I'd take my breaks in another part of the school, and sooner or later he'd show up talking about how dry the month of August was in 1947. Everywhere I went, within fifteen minutes, I'd see James rounding the corner with his bony index finger pointing at me. "Have I ever told you about the time I found an arrowhead in the school playground?" I was tempted to have dinner on the roof only to find him slowly climbing the ladder ten minutes later, explaining how prairie dogs communicate.

Old Man Winter was in the district for about a year when the boss placed him at my school permanently. Before, he was a fill-in guy. Once, maybe twice a week, I'd see James. Now, he'd be with me all week, all day, unleashing the saga known as Kansas corn life. As you can imagine, I wasn't too thrilled.

Most of the time, my boss would ask how new workers were doing. I really wanted to say everyone he hires is a complete gimp, but I couldn't. So I told him James was okay, hoping the head boss would station him at one of the other schools when a position came up. As luck would have it, my coworker Betty went out on disability after falling off the stage. No one saw her do it, but apparently, she was all by herself and with the lights out. She broke her hip and went out on a medical retirement. If you ask me, I think the crazy bat took a header off the stage just so she could use her three hundred sick days and retire early.

Who else but century-old James to take her place! I only told the boss he was a good worker so he could keep the job. Odds are he was probably living off cat food and Entenmann's Pound Cake. Judging by his tattered clothes and run-down, early-1900s Ford truck, I figured Old Man Winter was borderline homeless.

Since Old Man Winter was at my school permanently and full-time now, I expected him do the job every night, no more favors. This job loves to shorthand you, and I was tired of picking up double work as is. I'm all for helping out the elderly, but not when it cuts into my *Jeopardy* and *Wheel of Fortune* lunch hour. That's the only time I could detox and unravel from this shit storm called work. So I got real on Old Man Winter, telling him since he was full-time now, he had to do the job just as anyone else would. He then proceeded to tell me how he got hurt helping dig the first tornado bunker in Ricketaw County.

"Yes, sir, I still remember the month when my brothers and sisters made lemonade and vanilla iced cakes for the men folk who dug that tremendous hole in the ground… That's the same hole I fell in a week into the project and broke both my ankles. I've never been able to walk right since."

"Look, I'm sorry, James, but you have to do the work like all of us," I said. "We are shorthanded tonight."

"That summer was so hot, most of the wells dried up. I must have fainted twelve times that summer and hit my head on the shovel I was holding. That's why I can't remember to do all the work here. My brain is all scrambled up." After a minute or two, James trailed off about the flies or mosquitoes in the well or some shit.

"Just do the job, James, or I'll have to call the boss." I slipped away to my television, where Mr. Trebek was waiting with open arms. That old fogey kept talking the whole time I walked down the hall. I heard him mumble something as I turned the corner to the break room. I just wanted to watch *Jeopardy* and relax. That's not too much to ask, is it? Just leave me the fuck alone for a half hour so I can guess what the capital of Zimbabwe is.

Soon after I yelled at Old Man Winter, he had his first accident. I was watching *Jeopardy* with my jalapeño cheeseburger when my eyes caught a red light outside. No sooner did *Double Jeopardy* come on when I heard a siren come squealing into the parking lot. "What the fuck now!" I said aloud. I walked to the front of the school to find a medic wrapping James's leg with gauze. Turns out James was sweeping the entranceway when he fell backward into the trophy display case. He went ass first into a glass cabinet, right between the boys' lacrosse second-place trophy and a chorus honorable mention plaque.

"What the hell happened, James?" I said.

"I don't know... I... I turned around after working so hard and..." His eyes started to roll around.

"Did you trip?" I asked.

"I'm... I'm not quite sure. Everything is a blur after all those rooms you asked me to clean. I... I..." Then a rather pale man began slowly collapsing in the medic's arms, and they rushed him to the ambulance. As the paramedics lifted him to a gurney, I knew I had just been butt fucked by a con man. This prick was playing it up to the crowd, all of whom gave me dirty looks like they had just caught be beating him with a cane pole.

Now I'm going to state this for the record: James was not given a lot of work. I simply gave James the section my boss told me to give him. He had a total of four rooms to sweep out, an entranceway to sweep and clean one small bathroom. Shit, James could have told seven and half hours of stories and still finished the job on time. Even for a man who probably was around to see the Pilgrims' land, it wasn't a lot of work. I would literally kill to have that section. I'm covering two sections as is, with four crappers, nineteen rooms, and the gym each night. But apparently, Old Man Winter was so overwhelmed he worked himself into a tizzy.

As the ambulance drove away, I had a thought. Any other time, Old Man Winter would tell anyone within earshot about Kansas or the windmill or whatever else he remembered from the turn of the century. But not today. He was like a canary singing the blues to anyone dumb enough to listen. "Oh, no. Look what this guy is making me do!" Where was story about the 1944 wildfire? Or perhaps, one of my all-time favorites, the time Swamp Pass Road was paved? He didn't venture to elaborate those gems to the medics as they swiftly ushered him to the hospital.

The next day, I had a nice chat with my boss Mr. Polotski about what went down. I told him James was lying, but he couldn't care less. "Well, now, I wouldn't go making accusations like that. He probably tripped over something left in the hall." A five-minute berating of "Take it easy on him" and "Helping out a fellow worker" led me to conclude I was alone in my opinion of James.

Two weeks later, Old Man Winter came back at my school, with his head all wrapped up. He shuffles over to me with a smile on his face and says, "Boy, I remember when the town of Pine Valley got its first fire truck. It was 1956, just after the big mudslide hit town. Those lights and hand-crank siren were something else!"

As with any problem I have at this job, I started out with logical conversation.

"So, James, how are you feeling, today? Are you sure you are healthy enough to work?"

"Well… the doctor told me to take it easy. He gave me a note saying I was to have a smaller workload. I think it's only fair I have someone do half my work from now on."

"But you're cleared to come back in, right?" I said. "That means you are to assume your regular duties? Right?"

"Oh, no, not at all," James said as I heard the squeaky hamster wheel start moving. "I think it's only best if I stay away from that area where I got hurt. I could possibly hurt myself worse than the time I had a paint can land on my right foot. Broke all the bones on the top of my foot. My father and I just started to paint Milo's General Store on Main Street back in 19—"

And there it was, the old fuck was trying to play me like a fiddle. Old Man Winter was going to make my life hell until I just let him sit down all night. What the fuck did I do to this guy, huh? It's not like I worked him like a Georgia plow mule. Hell, I even listened to his tall tales and helped him out many, many times before. Now he had me by the nuts, trying to twist them until I cried uncle. Or so he thought.

Let me give you a little tip about how I operate. I'm normally a decent guy, besides the few minor scuffles I've had on the job. I may be a smart ass, but who isn't? Once you piss in my face, all bets are off. The mean, arrogant, devious, and above all, educated guy comes out. I started doing a little recon on Mr. Stevenson. That night, in the place of watching *Jeopardy* and *Wheel of Fortune*, I busted out my laptop and did some research. I logged on to several websites looking up his full name and used the details of his stories to help me find out who Old Man Winter was. For the next few weeks, I dug deep into his past to find out exactly who I was dealing with.

On the weekends, I worked for newspapers writing sports articles. It wasn't a lot of money, but easy money nonetheless. I went to college all those years, so I might as well use those degrees for something. I had access to a newsroom and all the info-finding databases they had. Census records, public notices, a massive digital national newspaper archive—you name it, I used it. It was only a matter of time until I found out every single thing about Mr. James Stevenson.

I emailed a fellow reporter who has access to national hospital records. Sure, it's illegal and downright immoral. But nobody messes with my *Jeopardy* time. My friend sent me all the info he could on James. Apparently he had a bunch of injuries, but nothing like what he had claimed. A few broken bones, collarbone injuries, concussions, stuff dealing with blunt force trauma. I reviewed his records from all over the world: Minnesota, Iowa, Florida, Alaska, and even Japan. James had two broken fingers and a cracked rib taken care of at a clinic in Osaka, Japan, in 1983. Funny how a guy who said he never left Kansas had a broken wrist in Anchorage, Alaska, back in 1996.

Next I investigated several old jobs James claimed he worked. Places like Milo's General Store, where he said he painted and worked the counter, never existed in Pine Valley or anywhere in Kansas. Of course, he could have been paid off the books, but I never found a registry for Milo's General Store. Several other local Kansas stores like Grady's Family Bakery, where James was head crumb cake maker back in the early fifties never existed. No tax records, no employee payroll, nothing. I even went so far as to pull the local town hall records to check for any evidence saying James had actually worked at this places. Nothing at all came up.

Then it was time to look into birth records for Pine Valley, Kansas. James never had sisters and brothers. He never went to school in Pine Valley or in any Kansas public school. No Susan Wilson or Mark Johnson or any other name James had mentioned from countless stories. The truth was, James was lying about everything. Every useless piece of information he made me listen to was false.

I pulled a favor from a journalist I knew at the *New York Times* and found James's orphanage records. Here's the skinny on Old Man Winter: James had a family for a brief period. His mother and father died in a tornado shortly after he was born. Turns out he stayed in an orphanage until he was old enough to sign himself out. His story starts to take a weird turn from there.

After hitting the road in the late 1940s, James took work as an airplane daredevil. He used to be one of those guys who walked across the wings of a biplane at festivals. Who knows how he got into the business. I read articles from old newspapers about how he used to stand outside the plane while it was doing barrel rolls. Old photos of James showed him as a skinny bean pole with a leather jacket and fish-eye goggles on. He didn't last long in that line of work after one of his copilots crashed in an open field at the Minnesota state fair.

After the daredevil gig, James tried his luck in the circus. He worked as a carnival performer who went by the name the Flying Squirrel. His career as a trapeze artist who jumped through hoops while wearing a gray squirrel suit was a success. Kind of goofy, but it was the Midwest during the middle of the century. I'm surprised they didn't have a fake mermaid in a tank as part of the show. Anyway, I guess he was good because he worked for about ten years traveling all over the country jumping from wire to wire.

After the carnival went bankrupt in the late fifties, James started to work for the independent wrestling circuit. I found several old wrestling promotions where James had performed. He went by many stage names, including the Corn Husker, Jumping Jimmy, the Kansas Killer, Pine Valley Plugger, and someone called Tractor Factor.

Here's the kicker: James was still wrestling while he worked at my job! Long story short, James Stevenson has been wrestling as a jobber for over fifty years in every major wrestling promotion, including his latest company, the Jersey Wrestling Association. This crazy old fuck still wrestles! His latest stage name was Manny the Mopper, a deranged janitor who flies off the turnbuckle with various cleaning implements. He would do backflips off the top rope and smash some guy over the head with a broom handle.

If you saw Old Man Winter, you would have never pictured him as a wrestler, especially at the age of seventy-eight. Each time I saw him looming down the hallway, he gave the appearance of a crippled old man who could barely walk. Here I'm thinking he's on the verge of dying, and the whole time he's in better shape than I was.

I pulled up a YouTube video from a week before his accident, you know, where he was overworked and smashed into a display case? The whole skit was James sneering at this opponent, growling and dressed in green coveralls. He'd come down to the ring with some crazy music in the background, devious eyes searching the room for his next victim. Then he would slide into the ring with a plunger in his hand. Halfway through the match, he'd break out into some sadistic laugh while dunking his mop at ringside. The end of the match was James hitting some guy with a broom while the ref's back was turned.

I don't know how he does it, but this fucking guy has been lying his ass off the whole time. His little stunt with the glass cabinet was probably a scratch compared to what he does each weekend in the ring. I watched twelve videos on this guy, each one showing how not sick he really was. To top it off, he was using my job's equipment in his matches. Two weeks after James started, I couldn't find my toilet brush. It happens from time to time, standard operating procedure in this business. Mops, buckets, spray bottle, etc., simply grow legs and walk away. Most of the time, other janitors pilferage my gear, so I used to carve my initials in the handle. Sure enough, there it was, being pointed at some random dorky wrestler in the hands of Old Man Winter. I could see my initials carved in the side of the damn thing!

Not to take away from the subject, but of course it's was my stuff he stole. The prick has had it in for me since he started. I was nice to this dude, and he pays me back by stealing my toilet brush. In the world of janitorial, that's as low as it gets. It's just as bad as stealing your neighbor's dog and selling it on Craigslist.

In any case, I did all this research, and I finally had his ass nailed.

One fine evening, I came down the hallway to see Old Man Winter slowly rummaging around in a trash can, pretending it was too heavy to lift. I was watching him for about a minute as he slowed his pace to molasses-like speed.

"Evening, James. How are you feeling today?"

"Oh, now… I guess I'm okay," he said as his eyes blinked several times. "My back still hurts a little. I don't think I can throw out that heavy garbage over there." He pointed his twig-like finger to a small black bag on the ground.

"Well, now. I don't think you'll have a problem with it." I was smiling from ear to ear, just like a prick would be smiling if he's waiting for you to hang yourself.

"You know… my back is still hurting from the glass cabinet incident. Maybe I should call my doctor to see if he wants me to be doing all this work." James was reaching for his prepaid Trac phone when I called his bluff.

"But, James, that bag of trash must be lighter than a person. I bet you could slam that bag into the dumpster or give it a DDT without breaking a sweat." I smiled as wide as my bearded face could allow. James stopped reaching for his phone and turned to look at me. He knew. That fucker knew exactly what I was talking about. He sure as hell pretended he didn't know what a DDT was, but deep down he knew right there I had his ass dead as fried chicken.

"I don't… know what that is? I think I'm feeling a little bit—"

"Save it, Gramps," I said. "I know all about your wrestling days, fucker." Still, James carried on his façade of being slow and arthritic, trying to play it off like he was senile or something.

"Ooowwww… owwww. Ouch. I… I think my neck is bothering me now. That silo injury of '46 to my spine must be taking a toll on my—"

"I know all about your past, you piece of shit! I researched all your wrestling videos and circus articles. If you think for one minute I'm going to let you fuck me over by doing your work, you're dead wrong!" I pulled one of the printouts from my pocket, showing James three weeks ago in the ring holding a trash can over someone's head about to hit them. "You're done, pops. Fucking finished here!"

I folded my arms waiting to see what his reaction would be. Calmly, he looked me dead in the face. "Well… well… well. Looks like the fat bastard did his homework. What do you want, a fucking medal?"

"Where's your slow, Kansas, slack-jawed talk now, you old scumbag?"

"It's up your fat ass if you could reach around and grab it." So the cards were on the table as James and I hashed it out right there next to a janitor cart.

"All this time you've been lying to me, making me feel sorry for your decrepit ass. You know how many times I thought you were really sick? You should be ashamed of yourself!"

"I ain't ashamed of shit!" said James. "What are you gonna do now, gum shoe? You gonna run to the boss and snitch on me, you little bitch!"

"I want you gone, old man. I should just let Mother Nature take its course. You'll be dead soon enough anyway. I'll just wait you out until the Reaper comes for you."

James stood back like he was about to cock his fist and swing. But instead, he narrowed his eyes and spoke, "If you think I'm gonna let some fat, lazy, bearded nobody blackmail me, you're crazy. Go ahead, tubby. Spill your guts. But remember this, you tell anyone about those videos, and I'll smack you in the face with a 9-iron. I'll wipe that smug look off your stupid head, boy."

I was flabbergasted. The nerve of this uppity old man, trying to strong-arm me for calling him out. What was I supposed to do, punch him for threatening me? I've already got too many letters in my file for being aggressive toward coworkers. If I turned him in, he would most likely get moved to another building without any punishment. I sure as hell wasn't going to let him talk shit to me, so

I opted to use my authoritative power to work this jerk off into the ground.

"Let me tell you something, you bag of bones. Just because you can pretend to fight don't mean you got the power to back it up. We both know if I turn you in, you'll get away with your shit somewhere else. I'm not gonna give you the satisfaction of screwing me over again. I got all the evidence to bury your ass alive, so you got a choice: you either quit and leave here without problems or stay here and prepare to get your ass worked to the max."

Without skipping a beat, James cracked his knuckles and told me to go fuck myself. "I'm in better shape than you'll ever be, fatty. I can take it if you can dish it out. Whatever you can throw at me, I'll do. Mr. Big Shot… abusing his power to make an old man work to death. You can fuck off if you think you're going to beat me. I've fought bigger and tougher guys than you, and I've kicked their ass all over the globe. So you go ahead, boss man. Give me more work, and I'll handle it no problem. You just better look over your shoulder when you turn your back. You never know when accidents can happen."

He turned and walked away perfect as can be. No hunched-over gait. No moaning or whining. Confident as a motherfucker too. He knew his days on this planet were numbered, so what did he have to lose? I guess he'd rather go out swinging than let me get one over on him. As he walked away, I said something as a comeback, something snarky, but I can't remember now. He just mumbled under his breath cracking his knuckles like he was about to throw down right there.

Over the next few months, I pushed Old Man Winter to the edge. Each day I threw more work on him. From inspecting his toilets to running a finger on the windowsill, I put the screws to him royally. And each time I looked for him to mess up, he would work just as hard to make me look like an asshole. If I told him to wax his floors, he would make those tiles sparkle like diamonds. Anytime I thought I had him dead to rights, James would do the job perfectly just to spite me. He had balls, I had to give him that much.

In turn, if I checked up on him, I would have to have a perfectly clean section myself. If his area was clean and my area looked like

THE DAY I CLEAN MY LAST TOILET

shit, I would get written up or even suspended for not doing my job. It had been a long time since I worked that hard in the system. You remember the *Jeopardy* lunch hour? No more. So I put my fingers to the fire and matched him stride for stride, each mop movement mirroring his. We worked all night cleaning as never before.

For what it's worth, I'll give him credit. He did, in fact, work circles around me. That old bastard had more energy than I thought he did. Must have been all that corn from the forties he ate in that Kansas orphanage. When the summer work started, the heat took a toll on both of us. Each day we sweated while dragging desks into the hallway. "You had enough yet, fat shit?" he whispered to me while no one was looking.

Come July, it was becoming apparent he would win our little campaign. He probably would have worked me into the ground had he not had a heart attack halfway through August. Turns out Old Man Winter had a leaky valve in his heart. The bag of bones dropped to the floor clutching his left side while one of our coworkers called 911. I'll never forget his face as he lay there, reaching toward me, trying for one last time to take a swipe at me. With the other coworker rushing down the hall to get help, I walked by him and gave him one last smirk for the road. "I guess I win this match, huh, old man?" I should've pinned him right there and counted a three-count. Ah, the things you think about after it's too late!

The ambulance took him away, but he was a goner. He died in the truck on the way to Jersey Shore Medical. The story around the schools was that he worked so hard until his last day. The whole district thought he was a hero. Sort of like Batman with a broom. But I know the truth. He was just an old con man who had probably been tricking people his whole life. Do I regret working him death? Not really. I shouldn't have smiled at him while he was on the ground, his life slowly flooding from his body. But at least I won't have to worry about him messing with my *Jeopardy* time anymore. I'll take massive heart attack for four hundred, Alex!

Chapter 17

Roswell Murphy, Conspiracy Theorist, and Activist Hippie

I highly doubt you've ever met anyone like Roswell.

This guy takes the cake for weirdos at my job. He's the one person you'd never want to get drawn into a long conversation with. Why? Because you don't want whatever he's got rumbling in his head to infect you.

I'm sure you've seen these numbskulls on the street typically holding up a sign saying things like, "Don't trust your drinking water!" or "The government is not your friend!"

He also doubles as your friendly neighborhood drug enthusiast, so he'd be the guy holding up a sign saying, "Legalize marijuana now!"

Roswell Murphy is one of those conspiracy theorists. He thinks everyone, and everything, was out to get him. He doesn't own a cell phone, a computer (he uses the library on Saturdays when the government employees aren't working), doesn't trust GPS, and if it didn't mess up his long hippie hair, he'd be wearing a tinfoil hat to block government radio signals.

His legal name was Michael Murphy, and he was born in 1952, in the city of Poughkeepsie, New York. This whacked-out, nervous Nelly changed his name to the town of Roswell because of the supposed alien landing. "I've been there, man," exclaimed Roswell the very first time I met him. "You get this unearthly vibe when you put your ear down close to the sand. It's… its freggin' crazy, man!"

Growing up in the late 1950s and early '60s seemed to have had a vital impact on Roswell. During his childhood, he'd seen things like the Cold War, the Korean War, the Cuban Missile Crisis, the Vietnam War, and the freewheeling late 1960s and early 1970s. Now imagine those times using acid and weed. That's how Roswell, the nongovernment-trusting head case was created. That, and he was at Woodstock in 1969.

"That's when everything changed for me, dude," Roswell once told me. "After that event, man, my eyes were opened, and I'll never be able to close them to the intricacies of our universe."

I'm going out on a limb here, but I believe Roswell ingested an extremely volatile combination of angel dust, weed, cocaine, and fire ant dung while at Woodstock, which fried his brain to the point of no return. That's about the only way I can explain how someone like him could have been created.

Anyway, Roswell was an average-sized guy, six foot one, six foot two, about two hundred pounds. He had long chestnut-brown hippie hair, straight and unwashed most of the time. Holding back his extremely long locks was a bandanna, much like what other hippies use to keep their hairdos out of their face. He never wore work shoes or boots, just sandals. How in the hell can someone wear sandals all year long? As janitors, it's our job to shovel snow when schools are closed. Roswell wouldn't wear snow boots ever. He'd come in with socks and sandals then tie a Shoprite bag over each foot.

Why would anyone want to wear open-toe shoes to mop out a dirty bathroom? Do you know how dirty his feet must've been? If you swing a mop too hard to one side, you're damn sure going to get pissy mop water all over your feet.

As a janitor, you have one of two options for uniforms: you wear the standard Dickies jumpsuit in dark gray or olive green *or* you wear a work T-shirt with jeans. Roswell opted for the jeans, which, judging by their appearance, were older than I was. You know hippies and their jeans, patchworked pieces of art with stitching and burn holes from where the joint hit the denim. Mind you, those jeans were probably as comfortable as a cloud laced with velvet and goose feathers. But Lord knows how in the hell they didn't disintegrate in a brisk wind.

He's protested just about everything, according to him. "Yeah, man… I was there through it all. I stood up against Johnny Law and the government hacks for the past thirty years. The Selma March in '65, the Newark Riots in '67, Viet-fucking-Nam before that. I was one of the first cats to protest animal testing before the damn government said they were doing it. I knew all about it," he said.

I've had brutal first encounters with coworkers in the past. I guess I just rub people the wrong way. This introduction was no different. Mere seconds into our initial meeting, he felt compelled to show me his battle wounds. Roswell had a few old-time scars from his days on the frontlines. No, not war. The picket lines. I didn't need to see all his bumps, but damned if he wasn't the type of guy to show me anyway.

"You see this scar right here, right above my eye?" he said as he pulled back his grungy bandanna. "Well, that's where a fascist cop bashed me over the head with his Billy club for not dispersing from in front of city hall."

"That's quite a gash," I said, wondering whom I pissed off in another life to get sucked into these types of situations.

"Yeah, yeah… it sure was a hellavua brawl, dude! Then the cop's horse kicked me in the back of the head with its hoof. They trained the horses to be fascists too! Goddamn authority and their martial law ways."

"Oh," I said. "Boy… I bet that hurt." I said it like I gave two fucks, which I did not.

"Well, it didn't hurt as much as that one time, I took a spear gun to the abdomen for trying to save the whales," said Roswell, who, at that time, was staring at me. I knew what that look meant. He was casually begging me with his eyes to ask about how he got involved in that sticky situation.

"Wow," I said, indulging him. "What happened?" My eyes were rolling around in my head like a pair of hot Vegas dice.

"There I was," said Roswell, "in the middle of the Sea of Japan on a Greenpeace zodiac boat. We were piloting out to intercept a group of research vessels, who were targeting a pod of gray whales. This mother and her calf were at the surface to breathe when I saw the whale boat shoot its massive harpoon into the baby. I said, 'Not on my watch, you government whaling slimeball!'"

Roswell was getting all worked up as he spoke. After a few seconds of panting, he went back to his tale.

"I told the captain of our boat to pull alongside the baby whale, who was bleeding into the sea. You should've heard it cries for help, man! Goddamned bastards! Anyhow… as we came next to the calf, I climbed to the front of the zodiac, grabbed our protest flag, and took a running leap onto its back. I tried to dislodge the rusty harpoon with our flagpole… but it was too late. When I woke up, I was in a Japanese hospital recovering from my wounds. Those government pigs almost killed me like that poor, defenseless whale!"

"Which government pigs are you referring to?" I said. (Can you hear the inflection of sarcasm in my speech?)

"What?" said Roswell, stupefied from my questioning.

"Well, I mean… you were in Japan, right? Japanese waters? Did you mean the Japanese government pigs or American government pigs?"

"I was legally, on my own accord, volunteering with Greenpeace to stop the whale slaughter," declared Roswell.

"In Japan?" I said.

"Well… yeah, I guess. Even though the ocean belongs to no man, my friend."

"So… you were protesting another country's government, while representing the United States?"

"Hell no!" said Roswell. He was quite worked up now. "I was representing another life-form, pal! Every animal has the right to be here. Don't you get that?"

"I… I agree," I said. Slowly I backed away from within arm's range. Hippies aren't known for their violent attacks, but I wasn't leaving anything to chance. "But… I'm just saying you entered another country's waters. That means you're under their rules and regulations."

"Do you think a gray whale and her calf understand government policies?" said Roswell. He was shaking his head in a sassy motion, with his hands on his hips.

"I doubt they do," I said. "I'm just saying you were—"

"No, I don't think you get it! See… you're one of those sheeple who think the world is full of good people. Well, it ain't, buddy! It's up to real eco heroes, like myself, to stop the greedy corporations and ruling bodies from pillaging our Mother Earth!"

Then he stormed off, throwing his hands up and down, mumbling something about brainwashing.

I learned many things from our confrontation. One, never encourage a hippie / conspiracy theorist. Ever. Just let them yodel on about nuclear waste or the Amazonian albino river otter, but *do not* engage them. You will lose any argument, hands down. These tree humpers spend a lifetime mixing forest ecology with law school, just waiting for an opportunity to make you feel bad about not tying yourself to the last black rhino in Africa.

And two, Roswell was completely fucking warped. I mean, this guy was the real deal: a bona fide space cadet. Picture John Lennon and Fox Mulder from the *X-Files* had a secret love child. He was one of those people who scoured the skies searching for alien vessels while banging on his drum in an Indian medicine circle.

I'd never met a real-life hippie before, but I was pretty sure I pissed this one off. Great. Just fucking great. Don't these kinds of people cast voodoo spells? That's all I needed, a mushroom-eating, didgeridoo-playing shaman to stick pins into my fake voodoo doll nuts.

But alas, Roswell, was never that kind of person, as I found out. Minutes later he came walking up to me with his hand outstretched saying he was sorry. "Look, man… I didn't mean to snap off at you. I'm just passionate about my world, ya know? It wasn't my intention to disrupt your aura as I did. Can I make it up to you by saying a healing prayer in your name?"

What the fuck did this guy just say to me? Was this the black magic I was afraid of?

Tragedy averted, I guessed. I shook his hand saying I was sorry as well, telling him I had a bit of a snarky side.

"Say no more, my friend," said Roswell. "It's all good, and we shall commence our work together just the same."

It took me a few weeks to get used to this bohemian freethinker. Roswell got upset for a moment or two then came rushing back to his spiritual loving self. I'd worked with several janitors in the past who had two or even three personalities, but Roswell was all right by me. I chalked it up to his recreational usage of psychotropic drugs, which he used daily, from what I could tell.

He was forty-six years old when he started working here, just before the job started mandatory drug screenings for employment. Boy, did he dodge a bullet there! I'm not going to say Roswell was the reason the school instituted drug testing, but it does seem peculiar how it happened like two months after he got hired.

Anyone with half a brain cell could see Roswell was permanently stuck in an acid trip. Nobody has Phish and Grateful Dead patches on their clothes willingly. You'd have to be under some comatose, mind-altering herbal supplement to sew a peace symbol onto your canvas backpack. By the way, who uses canvas backpacks anymore? Drug-crunching hippies. That's who.

I worked with Roswell off and on for about ten years. He didn't bother me most of the time, although his incoherent ramblings could be a bit much. On several occasions, Roswell went off topic for minutes on end, discussing why he thought he was being followed by a government agency. "It's a fact that several nights ago, after work, I was being tailed by two guys in a black car. This car had quite a few antennas hanging off it. I wonder what *they* needed so many antennas for?"

He'd trail off, blinking once or twice, and casually walk away. Then he'd come back babbling about the latest juicy paranormal gossip. "Hey, did ya hear? They caught a new species of fish in the Marianas Trench. It's got legs like a human and green glowing eyes. I wonder where *that* thing came from, huh? Think about it."

It was like his brain had a reset button, like on the original Nintendo. Once his mind started to overheat, it would purge the bad vibes, only to start a conversation about how he thought the Loch Ness Monster was "totally a real animal."

"Think about this, will ya? It's the *last* dinosaur trapped in a Scottish lake. We should embrace it and protect it with a benefit concert!"

Roswell always found a way to bring his jilted view of the world into any situation. I'd be dusting a bookshelf in the library, and here comes Roswell with a newspaper under his arm. "Hey, man! Did you see this shit in the *Daily News*?" said Roswell. His eyes were dilated from either pot or hysteria. "The freggin' government wants to shut down parts of Kennedy Space Center to do annual maintenance. Can you believe this crap, man? That's bullshit! I know what they're really do in those areas. They're moving the alien bodies out of cold storage so they can cut them open. That's right, man. I'm talking full on autopsies."

He found daily fuel from anything printed in the paper or "on the line," referring to the internet. "Whenever I do use the computer at the library, I make sure I'm only *on the line* for a couple minutes at a clip. This way, they can't track you if you are just researching a few things."

He was a pretty decent worker when he showed up. Roswell took an ungodly amount of time off. He used a tremendous amount of sick days each year, claiming he had stomach issues. "Boy, I must've had some bad bean tofu last night. My stomach is killing me," said Roswell when he came in the next day. That usually meant he ate a stuffed pot brownie and slept in. I've heard him say that line about ten times a year, usually interchanging the tofu for some other Vegan-friendly dish.

Each time he called out, he had a doctor's note. Not from a traditional doctor, but a natural healer. "My homeopathic practitioner gave me some dried herbs to steep with black tea. I should be all right in a day or two." The job couldn't touch him because each note was from a state-licensed doctor, although I question what his herbologist was really prescribing him.

"I don't trust those so-called medical doctors," said Roswell one time. "I'll get my medicine from my friend Yellow Foot Storm Cloud. He's been healing souls for fifty years."

He was going to witch doctors. Albeit legal witch doctors who wrote on banana leaves instead of a script pad.

Roswell also took a great deal of vacation days to visit what he called sacred places. He's hiked the Appalachian Trail solo, which is an accomplishment by itself, but he did it while baked out of his mind. "Dude, that was the single greatest walk I have ever taken," said Roswell when he came back to work six months later. "It was a special privilege to commune with nature on an intimate level."

A walk, that's what he called it. An almost 2,200-mile walk.

His only camping supplies were a blanket, a walking stick carved from a holy Bayan tree, two boxes of Clif bars, a backpack jammed with Zig-Zag rolling papers, and thirteen pounds of weed. I don't know how the hell he didn't die in the wilderness. Maybe the other animals smelled his dirty hippie feet and thought he was a rotted carcass not worth eating. How does one hike in sandals anyway?

Two years later, Roswell took almost the entire year off to live with the Hopi Indians on preserved land. What does a Whiteman from Upstate New York do in Northwestern Arizona with indigenous peoples? Consume copious amounts of peyote and dance around a tribal fire, that's what. He spent all day praying to the spirits while celebrating the joys of mescaline. He came back to show me each of his scorpion stings he healed with the magic of chanting. "This one here, near my ankle, was so bad I had the village elders sing for three days straight just to get the swelling down. I almost lost my leg, but Mother Earth stepped in to save me!"

Perhaps a trip to the ER with a simple needle might have worked too.

The biggest trip (literally) he ever took was when he went to South America to partake in a two-month-long ayahuasca festival. You heard that right. Roswell traveled to the jungles of Peru so he could ingest a frothy, tar-like substance made from leaves and herbs that can kill you if not combined properly.

"Shaman Vitrovos said I journeyed into the NetherRealm gracefully each time I took in the ayahuasca fluid. I felt a longing for our universe like never before!" said Roswell, who looked and smelled like a dying horse.

Who the hell does that? It's not like Roswell was born a member of an Ecuadorian tribe, where drug consumption is a rite of passage. He did it to get high as fuck.

"How many times did you do this, Roswell?" I asked.

"Seventeen times, and each one revealed another layer of the cosmos to me."

"How are you not dead?" I asked. I was astonished Roswell was still standing, not decomposing under a ceiba tree.

He laughed out loud while tilting his head backward. "My body is my temple. It absorbs only the good and expels the evil."

That was some hardcore shit Roswell said to me. "My body is my temple." More like a petri dish. I bet good money at any given moment Roswell had enough drugs in his system to kill a bull moose.

I think the craziest story Roswell ever told was when he said he met Sasquatch in the Pacific Northwest. During one of his sacred pilgrimages, Roswell took three weeks off to search for an unknown hairy humanlike animal. Yup, that's the type of person Roswell was. He was the kind of guy who spent his vacation time searching for Yeti outside of Seattle.

"People call it Bigfoot hunting, but I wasn't looking to harm the big guy," said Roswell when he told me the story. "It's more like Bigfoot nurturing. That's why I found and conversed with him."

"So… you found a Bigfoot?" I said. Even this was a stretch for a man who took drugs like you or I would take Advil.

"That's the thing! He's always been there, man! You just need to free your mind to follow the clues *they* left us."

"They?" I said. "Who? The government?"

"No way! The Yeti have left us secret paths to traverse to find them," said Roswell, whose eyes were as wide as dinner plates.

"There's more than one Bigfoot?" I asked intriguingly. The way he was explaining it, I got a little interested.

"Exactly, my friend! There's entire colonies of them living peacefully in the forests like the elves of folklore. He showed me his family, his children, and his life partner, female Bigfoot, and we lived together in the lush forests of Washington for almost an entire week."

"So... what did you guys do all week? Play checkers or go fishing?"

"Try to be reasonable with this! Are you taking this seriously? The Yeti don't have games like you or I have. But I did catch a wild sockeye salmon using his guidance and offered it to him. He graciously accepted! That's what his family lives on. Fish, berries, tree nuts, beaver, and sometimes forest mushrooms."

And there it was. That's how Roswell found a community of primitive bipedal mammals. He dreamed it up after gorging himself on wild psychedelic mushrooms. I can see it now, a forest ranger stumbling onto a zonked-out, sandal-wearing hippie with a dark-red fish in his mouth, chanting to an imaginary eight-foot-tall beast.

Most of my coworkers have a tragic ending when they leave this job. Prison is a likely end of the line for some. Others wind up dead or fired. Not Roswell. He's a true success story. He saved his pennies and bought a piece of land out in Montana so he could build a doomsday bunker into the side of a mountain range. Instead of dying in some horrific accident while under the influence of crushed-up moon rocks, Roswell quit this hellhole and lived happily ever after.

Things you or I pay for like internet, new Android phones, brand-new cars, etc., had little meaning to Roswell. Life experiences were his currency. Crude vision quests halfway around the planet were the most expensive thing he bought. He lived in a no-frills tiny shack most of his life, only spending money on the food he couldn't graze for. You can save some serious cheddar when you drive a 1978 Toyota Cressida until it blows up.

Roswell afforded his lavish chemical lifestyle because he never married. No children, no wife, not many friends (other than his drugs), and he outlived all his family. I'm sure he got some inheritance from the mama and the papa when they checked out, but Roswell wasn't much of a spender. To put it bluntly, Roswell was almost like a bum, more like a gypsy with better drugs.

On his last day of work, I said goodbye to one of the better workers during my tenure here.

"Well, buddy… I guess this is goodbye," I said.

"No way, man!" said Roswell, his eyes glossy and moisture filled, although it could've been Visine. "We will always be connected in the Spirit World. You and I have shared time together as one entity. A sweeping entity. Nothing can change that…"

"Okay…," I said.

"Our journeys may take us on different tracks, but we shall meet again, my compadre," said Roswell. "I will look to the stars each night and remember our times of cleanliness as a team."

"You… got that… man!" I said. I had hoped the *man* part was something he'd understand in his language. The lingo of the hippie. "Don't go missing this place too much!"

I put my hand out to shake his, but he had other plans. He came diving in to give me a big bear hug. Jesus Christ, did he stink! Oh my lord, I never smelled his long hair up close before.

"*Adios, mi amigo!*" said Roswell.

"Okay… buh-bye now…" The hug went on for seconds. I was happy he thought that much of me to hug me, but fucking A did he stink.

Was I uncomfortable? A little. Roswell was a decent guy after all. Besides the BO and smell of patchouli oil, he was all right. He might have been a kook and a far-out hippie, but he was an honest soul. One of the more honest and humble people I'd ever worked with.

When he finally did relinquish his vice grip, I was able to gasp for oxygen again. Roswell smiled then reached into his faded jeans pocket.

"Now I know you don't get down on this stuff," Roswell said as he handed me an extra tightly rolled joint. "But if you should ever want to see what I see, light this bad boy up and breathe deep. It's a special blend I picked up the last time I was in Thailand communing with the elephants in a three-hundred-foot bamboo hut."

"Oh… well… Thank you, friend," I said.

"Anytime, my friend. Just look toward the star Nimbru in the eastern sky, and you'll find me."

And then he was gone, like a puff of smoke in the breeze.

I'm not going to tell you if I smoked that joint. As a public school employee, it's unethical and illegal. But to be honest, I couldn't tell you the last time I was given a Wiz-Quiz. Sixteen, maybe seventeen years ago?

But if I were to have smoked his joint, which is still up for debate, it may or may not have been the most amazing experience of my life. I did my time with drugs back in the day. I put away quite a few lines of coke and fat spliffs before. But whatever Roswell put in that special cocoon of happiness was some stellar shit. I couldn't finish it in one sitting. I had to take three naps and two showers, make a trip to 7-Eleven spending 43.65 on snacks, *and then* polish off the J.

I was highly impressed with his horticulture skills, to say the least.

In any case, my coworker and one-time drug dealer left the job a free man. He was paroled into the wild blue yonder to spend his days getting high as a cloud for the rest of his life. As much as he hated government taxes, he took his share of Social Security as soon as he was eligible. That, plus his nest egg of savings from not buying a new car every decade, probably lasted him a long time. I bet he's still kicking out there in Montana under a wide open sky watching the stars and moon faded to gray as the sun comes up.

We should all be so lucky one day.

Chapter 18

Tyrell Jones versus Byron Banks

It's a no-brainer my job has its share of animosity. Working in filth each day can take its toll on a person, ya know. Add in violent criminals and former psych ward patients, and you've got yourself a ticking time bomb. Sometimes small tiffs turn into major blowouts. That's what happened when Tyrell Jones and Byron Banks got into it. I call it the Old Black Man's War.

I was there the moment the feud started, and I witnessed the end of it. My lord, it was a battle for the ages! It went on for the better part of the year, causing turmoil and chaos throughout the department. People had to choose sides over who they thought was right. This thing became the civil war of custodians. Innocent bystanders either chose Team Tyrell or Team Byron, with neither side being right or wrong. They were maddening times.

This rivalry, almost as iconic as the Hatfield and McCoy's, sparked my interest immensely. Since Tyrell was my buddy, I immediately took his side. Byron was a prick anyways, so screw him. From what I remember, Byron fired the first shot, or maybe it was Tyrell? Either way, one of them started it, and since Byron was a jerk-off, I'll just say he did it. Both men fought valiantly until one finally got the upper hand. There can be only one victor in a feud, as you know. I won't bother you with trivial details, just the good stuff.

It all started at the company picnic. The year was 1999, a good year given the circumstances. We we're partying like Prince told us to. With a new millennium around the corner, the world seemed alive, vibrant with opportunity. A lot was happening in the school district

THE DAY I CLEAN MY LAST TOILET

back then. The schools were fully staffed with full-time employees then, not like today. We didn't have to do the work of two and three people like we do now. It was a simpler time, one we all came to embrace as the better years as we look back now.

Anyhow, the picnic was held at a local park on a nice, sunny Sunday afternoon. The whole department was there: the moppers, the grass cutters, and the wrench turners. One day a year we put our differences aside and come together for some eats. A few charcoal grills, maybe some hot dogs and hamburgers, you've been to one before, I'm sure of it.

They had a softball game after lunch, fresh-cut fruit and ice cream sandwiches galore for dessert. That picnic started out nice. It was a really good time, actually. Most company picnics turn into a shit show by noon. This one was different, completely different in the beginning.

For me, the job was slowly becoming more of a reality. I was in the thick of it for my college years. This meant big finals, classes I couldn't give two fucks about, and experimenting with many forms of drugs and alcohol, with a decent amount of sex tossed in for good measure. These are the things I remember most about college. Fuck chemistry. Give me some cocaine and a nice set of tits any day!

So back to the picnic, I came with Tyrell in his beat-up Lincoln Town Car, complete with twenty-inch spinners and fuzzy dice hanging from the mirror. That man was so tacky. It looked like a retired pimp wagon coasting down the street. But he was proud of it, so I let him drive. He had a nice stereo system too, so it wasn't a half-bad ride. Nothing like rolling up to a company picnic blasting Westside Connection! This gets all your coworkers looking to see what delinquents step out of the car.

The only rule for the company picnic was no alcohol since it was a public park. Ya know, so no one got drunk and did something stupid. Most people abided by the rule, except one. Everything was great until Byron showed up. This guy pulled up in a broken-down Lexus, blasting DMX and stinking of liquor. He stumbled out of the car with a smile on his face: "Guess who decided to show up y'alls

217

party! Ha haaaaaaaa!" Byron jogged his way over to the picnic area with a Philly in his mouth and gin on his breath.

Byron Banks was an older black guy who started around the same time as Tyrell. He was about the same age as Tyrell too, late fifties and had the same thug mentality. He was from the South and made it a point to let people know that fact every chance he could. "Y'all don't know a thang about the durty South, ya heard!" Byron said on occasions. "I'm from North Cackalacky. We don't fuck around down there!"

Byron was of average height, a slight beer belly, and always wore young men's clothes. Anytime he wasn't in a work uniform, he had on Southpole jeans with tan Timberland boots. I guess he thought was looked like Timbaland. He didn't.

Byron retired from some government job years before and was working as a janitor to pad his service check. From what I heard about him, Byron was a stone-cold alcoholic, and he loved the ladies and loved the horses and weed even more. He'd been divorced three times and supposedly ran with a gang back in the seventies. That's the best I can gather from my intel. Sometimes it's sketchy even for me to do recon on all my coworkers. Who knows what's real and what's rumor nowadays.

A few coworkers said some outlandish things about Byron. "I heard he keeps a gun under the front seat of his car," said Dana, the kitchen worker. "He's been locked up down in Atlantic City quite a few times," said Bethany from the main office. To me, Byron held himself in a bad way. You ever met someone you knew deep down inside was a punk? That's Byron all right, only add a Southern accent and with a Black & Mild behind his ear.

I had seen him a few times before at in-service meetings, and the son of a bitch was buzzed and stoned then too. Why he wasn't fired years ago is beyond me. Maybe the bosses were afraid of him, playing into the rumors. Tyrell hated him for some reason. Anytime someone mentioned Byron's name, he'd make a pissy face while saying something bad about him. "I don't trust that mothafucka," said Tyrell. "He always givin' me the stink eye. He betta not start that thug shit up in here... I ain't gonna stand for it, man."

So here's the scene: Tyrell was sitting next to me at a picnic table eating a hot dog. Byron was wandering around the party hanging on people, being loud and obnoxious. Typical Byron, only today was Ramped Up Byron. With no bosses to tell him not to be a jerk-off, Byron decided to be the biggest jerk-off he could. The bosses never came to the company picnics. It was beneath them. They wouldn't be caught dead at a social function with us. So technically, it wasn't a company picnic. Just the inmates cutting loose without any prison guards to stop the fights.

On each person Byron went to, you could see their faces scrunching in displeasure. "I haven't seen you in months, Barry! How you be?" Byron had his arm around a very scared Barry who didn't know what to do next. "Hey, Meredith...," said Byron. "Whatchu doin' later? You wanna come hang at my crib? Hehehehe!" It was excruciating to watch. As I talked to Tyrell, he was watching Byron, just staring him down and shaking his head. "I hope that stupid asshole don't come over here," said Tyrell aloud to me. "He betta not come hanging on my neck, talkin' shit to me!"

Not ten minutes after Byron arrived, he came walking over to where Tyrell and I were sitting. "Hey there, boy!" said Byron as he held out his hand to Tyrell. "How come you don't talk to me no more?" Byron had a leather pouch in his back pocket with the out-line resembling a pint of some kinda hooch. He stank so badly of gin you could've lit a fire from his breathe. As God is my witness, Tyrell answered him with a line I will never forget. While sipping his Pepsi, from a seated position, Tyrell looked at Byron and said, "'Cause I don't trust yo ass, that's why!"

"Whatcha mean, Tyrell? What you mean you don't trust me?" said Byron, slurring his words a little.

"You heard me!" said Tyrell. "I said I... don't... trust... you!"

"Boy... who, who you think you talkin' to? You know who I am, sucka?"

"You ain't shit to me, son," said Tyrell, pointing at Byron. "I know you a wannabe thug, but you need to take yo drunk ass out my face!"

And so the war began. It had been brewing for months, from what Tyrell told me later. Nobody really knew how Tyrell and Byron knew each other, if they knew each other at all. I think Tyrell was probably reading Byron like I was reading him: just another punk trying to be a badass.

They yelled at each other for about five minutes before anyone got involved. In those types of situations, two gentlemen usually disperse after a few cuts on each other. Not these two pit bulls. They latched on with vicious one-liners and jokes. Various insults came flowing from each other's mouth. "You and your clothes are fucked up!" was one I remember. "Yo teeth are crooked as hell!" was another. The whole party was huddled around the picnic table watching with anticipation. Before we knew it, the scene turned physical. The Shove Heard 'Round the Park, a defining moment in the history of my job. I don't know who laid the first hand. Only God knows for sure. Tyrell and Byron started pushing up on one another until a crowd formed. It looked like two baseball teams cleared the benches.

Soon an escalating clamor formed. I had Tyrell's arms trying to pull him back while John, the grounds guy, had Byron's arms trying to do the same to him. Shouting elevated to a piercing level. Two older black men, yelling multiple curses and threats, were being held apart so they didn't kill each other. A circle formed around us as a mob mentality sprang up out of nowhere.

The whole thing turned into a fiasco. A red Solo cup filled with some kind of liquid came flying over my head, landing on Byron. Next a plate of macaroni salad was thrown at Tyrell from another direction. Food, sodas, and paper goods, you name it! The altercation caused a stir at a normally quiet community park.

Township park rangers intervened within minutes. Next the cops came shortly after we dispersed. By that time, the whole area was trashed. Litter was strewn all over the ground. How fitting, a group of janitors had to clean up a mess they made! First time in history, I believe. Normally we clean up after other people.

No one was arrested or fined, but that was the last company picnic we ever had. Our permit was revoked by the township three days later. We had Byron and Tyrell to thank for this mess.

At work the following week, we were all sent letters by the head boss about how disappointed he was in us and how this makes the whole district look bad. I personally didn't care about it either way. I was just trying to stop a fight from breaking out. Tyrell, on the other hand, took it to heart.

"That goofy-ass Byron done fucked me over!" said Tyrell. "I'll never forgive him for disrespecting me like this! That drunk ass piece of monkey shit had the nerve to put his hands on *me?*"

"Don't worry about it," I told Tyrell. "It's done with."

"The hell it is! I'ma get him good one day. You watch me!"

Over the coming months, Tyrell and Byron made meager threats through other coworkers. Stupid insults a child would say to another child. "You tell Byron if I see his mangy black ass round my neighborhood, I'm gonna pop his ass like a balloon!" Once it got back to Byron, he made a prompt reply, "If Tyrell ever thinks he gotta chance against me, then all that crack he smoked back in the eighties burnt his fuckin' brain to a crisp!"

It's a good thing they were at different posts in the school system. Most of the threats were empty promises, but you never know. I knew my buddy Tyrell had spent some time in the joint. I bet you a hundred bucks he knows a thing or two about taking someone out. Just looking at Byron leads one to believe he probably spent a few years behind bars as well. If these two ever got together again, it might end up bad.

The next in-service day two months later had them at each's throats again.

During training days, the whole department must come to mandatory seminars for things like chemicals, first aid, Asbestos Awareness Day, etc. I showed up early, which is not like me at all, to get a good seat for the fireworks. Tyrell had been talking so much smack leading up to the seminar I figured he would either clam up or dig into Byron's ass.

Like a scene from a Jean-Claude Van Damme movie, in walks Tyrell, with his head held high, scanning the room for his opponent. The tension was fierce. Stagnant air clung to the bleachers like a musty smell. A few cheers rang out from the audience, not many, but enough to let the whole room know it was about to go down. Then in walks Byron from the other side of the auditorium, his gut hanging out past his knees with his right hand balled up in a fist.

"You gonna talk shit now, punk?" said Byron, while his head nodded from side to side. The crowd chimed in with its "ooooooooooohs," taunting Tyrell to retaliate.

"I ain't the one talkin' smack!" said Tyrell. He had raised his hand to point his finger at Byron, rocking it back and forth. "You the asshole talkin' shit now!" They started to walk toward each other, not too aggressively, but enough to show the crowd they weren't fucking around. As they slowly converged toward the middle of the auditorium, Bossman shouted out a yell over the microphone, "That's enough, boys! Not another step or each of you is suspended!"

Tragedy averted. Both men kept a conversation going while the boss yelled at us all. "There will be no fights or mischief here today, people! Now sit down and get ready for your training seminar."

It amazes me how grown adults revert back to childish ways. I mean, hell. I was there to see a scuffle, just like back in middle school when one kids calls another kid out in the lunchroom. Am I just as bad as these people, ready to fight over careless words told through other people's mouths? The bosses treat us like children, so why not act like children, right?

The remainder of the meeting was spent watching videos about floor wax treatments. Nobody gave a shit about the wax. "Bring on the grudge match," we all thought silently. I hate to admit it, but I don't think I'm any better than the adolescents I clean up after. Since I was so close to Tyrell, and didn't care too much for Byron, I wanted this fight to happen. Having one of my coworkers, a friend, mind you, beat up some drunk bully kind of gave me something to look forward to each day. Let's face it: everyone in the room wanted to see these dudes pummel each other. It breaks up the monotony of cleaning mud off the floor each day.

Don't mind me if I beat a dead horse here, but this job brings out the beast in people. I've been saying it for years: this place is creating monsters out of mice. One day you're happy as a clam, then the next, you snap like a twig. Doing the same, boring uneventful job for long periods of time does something to a person. Look at the United States Post Office. Back in the late eighties, it wasn't uncommon to see a mail carrier going berserk. Hell, they even have a term for it: going postal. What does that tell you about a job when people start turning their workplace into a shooting gallery?

I believe the same mantra applies here. Not so far as the whole shooing thing, but still. Doing the same job, day in and day out, like janitors do, causes a short circuit in your head. Add in cutting of full-time employees, working shorthanded, cutting salaries or raises in half, etc. It's a recipe for disastrous things to happen.

The training seminar ended without altercation, much to everyone's chagrin. I bet the bosses even wanted to see these old-school gents bashing each other to bits. They couldn't admit it, but I know they wanted it to happen. Lord knows if they both fought each other, it would've been grounds for immediate termination. Bosses love those kinds of scenarios. It's the best way to get rid of two troublemakers at once.

When the meeting was done, all the janitors went back to their perspective posts, yearning for a resolution. Byron and Tyrell weren't going to let this thing go. They met in the parking lot to set up a showdown for the ages. I couldn't help but hear their conversation. I was parked only two cars down from where they had their little chat.

"Let's end this, chico," said Tyrell. "You pick the time and the place and I'll be there."

"All right, punk. You got it," said Byron. "How 'bout your school, in the back parking lot, Friday night?"

"Nah, that's no good. See, I got this date Friday night with this little honey from Asbury Park... How about Thursday night?"

"Well... I... I got this thing I have to do down at the docks Thursday night. What... what about Wednesday, your school, right after work at 11:00 p.m.?"

After a few seconds of bartering, the men had their match planed. The fight was happening this week, at my very school! Tyrell and Byron told no one of their planned fight. We all know how well the department holds on to a secret. The only reason I knew was because I ear-hustled my way into the conversation. And because later Tyrell asked me to watch his back.

"Hey, man… ahhh, I need you to do me a favor tonight, if you got a minute," said Tyrell.

"Sure. What's up?" As if I didn't know what he was about to ask of me.

"I got this thing going down with Byron, and ah… I need you to watch my back. Can you keep an eye on this mothafucka for me in case he pulls some shit tonight?"

"I got you, man. I'll be there for you," I said. Tyrell had a look of ease come over him. Back in the day, he was a hardcore dude. Times change after long. Maybe Tyrell didn't have the gusto he once had? Everyone needs a pal occasionally to take care of them in case the situation gets rough. I guess he was happy to have someone in his corner, backing him up like that old guy in *Rocky*.

"Hey, I appreciate that, my brotha! Thanks, man!" said Tyrell, eager to shake my hand in a show of thanks.

The time came to separate the men from the thugs. At 11:00 p.m., the lead night boss drove away, unaware of the melee about to start in the back parking lot. Tyrell and I pretended to drive away as well but turned around to wait for Byron. Twenty minutes later, here comes Byron, with his clunker rolling into the parking lot. With one headlight out, I might add. He gets out of the car, with his little friend John in tow, and walks up to our location under the street lamps.

"I see you brought a friend, huh?" said Byron. "Good, he can watch you get yo ass beat down!"

"You got it twisted. He's here to make sure *you* don't pull any underhanded shit," said Tyrell, who was hyping himself up. Me and the other guy John didn't talk much during their exchange. We were the unbiased refs, there to litigate the transaction. Well, I was biased. Byron was a dick. I was there for moral support. John, who was normally a quiet guy, stood in between both trash talkers. He took over the fight coordinating, discussing the parameters.

"All right. Here's the deal: A simple fistfight. No kicking, no biting, no dirty stuff. Just a clean, quick fight to settle this beef, okay? First one down and can't get up loses. And no weapons! Are we clear?"

"Yeah, man. I'm ready," said Tyrell. "Yup... let's do this," said Byron.

There, under a faded yellow lamp, danced the behemoths. It took them a few seconds to start moving around. I'm not sure when the last time either man was in a fistfight. They looked rusty, to say the least. It's as if they forgot where to put their hands in a boxing motion. I mean, if you haven't been in a fight for, like, ten or twenty years, you might look a little lost. Unless you're throwing down weekly, you lose your edge when you get older.

Insults continued to poor out of their mouths, as if to talk themselves out of the fight. They circled each other twice before Tyrell threw and landed the first jab square on Byron's nose. It didn't break his nose, but it sure let him know this wasn't a game anymore. A few more jabs came from Tyrell, with one making good contact on Byron's right eye.

"Keep your guard up, Byron!" said John. "Don't let that scumbag hit you! Go for a right, he's weak on his left side!"

"Shut the fuck up, John!" I said. "This ain't your fight!" He shot me a look as if to say, "It's you and me next in the ring." What the fuck? I was only there to watch! And to be Tyrell's corner cut man, I guess. Moral support was more of my strong point. Who the hell knows when the last time I was in fight.

"Good job, Tyrell! Give it to him!" I wasn't a very good hype man, but I was getting there.

Stumbling a bit, Byron steadied his feet, going in for a roundhouse right. It struck Tyrell good, a real nice punch.

"That's it! Get 'em, Byron!" said John. Tyrell took a big hit. The roundhouse broke skin on his lip. Without his glasses, Tyrell was at a disadvantage, a slower-than-usual reaction time. He wobbled a bit then came back to center just in time for Byron to land a few solid body shots. Byron had some quick hands for any old beer-gutted sow. He must've landed three or four rib crushers in no time. I heard the "owwws" and "auuufs" from Tyrell, who, at this time, had his eyes closed knowing he couldn't defend against this attack.

"You're all right, Ty! Stay together! Stay focused!" I said. Did I really think Tyrell was holding it together during the fight? No. Not at all. With exception to the first couple of jabs, Tyrell wasn't doing too well. Years of whoring and boozing took its toll. He was gasping for air after those body shots.

Tyrell heard my words of encouragement and came rushing back at his foe. Two rights headed toward Byron's face. Both were blocked, unfortunately. At least there was still fight left in this old dog. The next few seconds were more of a gauging process. Neither fighter planned the fight to go this far. Everyone talks shit until it's time to throw down. With John and I standing there, each fighter had to be a man. No punking out now. But these were old men. Neither of them hadn't seen their prime fighting years since the Apollo missions.

Byron tried to strike next, a failed left roundhouse, which Tyrell dodged easily. This was when Tyrell saw his chance. As Byron was trying to recenter himself after the miss, Tyrell lurched forward with a right haymaker. A solid connection right on the temple. Byron was hit badly. It must've caused him to see stars or at least have a few moments of vision loss. The tide was turning. Tyrell seized another moment. As Byron staggered, Tyrell hit him with a barrage of jabs, followed by a swift roundhouse, knocking Byron back and onto the ground.

"It's not over, Byron! Get up!" said John.

"You got him!" I said. "He's shaken now!"

Byron rolled on the ground for a second or two, realizing he was no longer on his feet. As he got up, he wavered somewhat, with his eyes wide open staring at Tyrell. There stood my Tyrell, still in attack mode, waiting for Byron to make his next mistake. Pride washed over Byron, whose ego was affected more than his body. He lunged forward, trying to come in for a hit, but missed. Tyrell socked him good again, this time in the other temple, busting him open in the process. Again, Byron fell to the ground. This time he rolled a little longer, a few gasps of pain spewing out.

As Byron got to his feet, he dropped his hands around his waist in a half-cocked attempt to defend himself. He was bleeding pretty good now. That last punch stunned him, giving Byron an ever so glossy look in his bloodshot eyes. Tyrell, still poised to deliver another powerful blow, watched as Byron stopped jumping around in place. We all thought the fight was over at that point. Everyone except Byron. He reached around into his back pocket and pulled out a small shiny black object. Then he hit the switch, flopping out a metallic stilettoed blade about four inches long. He smiled as he did it, too. Almost gloating in his display of defiance.

"Almost, mothafucka...," said Byron, still swaying a bit. "You almost had me. I'ma stick my knife in your ass now. Bitch." That sneaky, slimy bastard! I knew Byron was a cheater. And I also knew, deep down, Byron was a real OG who had clearly pulled a knife many times before. Tyrell stopped bouncing back and forth. He kept his hands up in a defensive mode, but he wasn't too eager to rush in that switchblade.

"Hey... hey, man!" I said, like the voice of reason I am. "We didn't agree to this."

"Yeah... come on... this...," John said, back pacing while he said it. "This ain't right."

"Shut the fuck up," said Byron, who had blood spilling into his mouth. "Don't you snitches say a damn thing. This is between me and snaggletooth here." Byron walked slowly toward Tyrell, all while keeping his eyes locked on Tyrell's eyes. "I'ma fuckin' kill yo ass, you hear me, boy?"

It got all too real way too fast. I didn't sign up for this shit, and judging by Tyrell's face, neither did he. Should he run? Should we all run? Remember, I'm just a young man from a trailer park. We don't have a lot of violent altercations there. I live in a nicer trailer park. It's more of a mobile home development, really. We have domestic disputes, drunken disorderly charges, on occasion. Not many knife fights.

Come to think of it, I never wanted to be a part of this anyway. I was only there for moral support. Not only could we lose our jobs, but we might get arrested if the cops showed up. Who knows. Byron might turn his spiky knife on me after he's done carving up Tyrell.

Who cared about the job now. This hoodlum pulled out a fucking knife the same way murderers do. Hell, I wasn't going to die for some pissing contest! When that blade came out, it all changed. I didn't know what the fuck to do.

As Byron pursued his prey, John and I sat there dumbfounded, not knowing what to do.

"Tyrell! Look out!" I said. Really? That's what I came up with? Way to be supportive, dumbass! Like Tyrell didn't see a beer-gutted, knife-wielding black guy slowly closing in on him.

I can't claim to think what Tyrell was pondering at that moment. Whatever was running through his head was his cross to bear alone. He was stone-faced, not moving, but statue-like in his demeanor. Maybe he was playing dead or something. You know, like rabbits do when they think a predator is around? As Byron inched closer, Tyrell continued his stance, ready for whatever came next.

Then it happened.

Byron thrust his blade from overhead, trying to strike down upon Tyrell with all his power. In an instant, Tyrell propped his left forearm out to counter the knife attack. In the same lightning-quick motion, a split second later, he sent his right hand upward, drilling Byron underneath his chin. A direct hit! An uppercut for the record books. Tyrell's fist struck Byron's chin so hard we heard it from twenty feet away. A massive thud much like a baseball bat hitting a brick wall.

Byron left his feet for almost a whole second before landing back first onto the pavement. There, on the ground, lay an out-cold Byron, a small switchblade, and two broken yellow-stained teeth.

"Oooooh, shit!" I said, putting my hand over my mouth. "Woah, buddy!"

With a flash of his fist, Tyrell put Byron down like that time Old Yeller got the bullet. Pure adrenaline surged through Tyrell's body. He was all jacked up, full of himself. And rightly so.

"Yeaaaahhh, sucka!" said Tyrell. His hands were raised above his head, pumping them up and down. "I told yo ass, I wasn't playing wit you, you punk, trick-assed nobody!" Tyrell then pointed vigorously at Byron, who still hadn't moved since getting molly whopped. After a short victory dance, Tyrell came running over to me, shaking my hand with both his hands.

"Thank you, my brotha, for watching out for me. See? You see?" Tyrell said as his voice raised a few octaves. "You see what I mean? This turkey tried to cheat Tyrell out of his life. I told you to watch out for him!"

"Great job, man!" I said. "But... but I really didn't do nothing to help you. I just kinda stood there, not really helping out. I'm sorry I—" Tyrell put his right hand up to stop me from speaking anymore.

"Say no more. You didn't need to do nothing. You bein' here and sayin' you'd have my back was all Tyrell needed."

I'm not going to lie, that line hit me in the feels for a minute. He put his trust in me. It felt good to know I had a buddy who would say something like that.

John came walking over to us with a dopey look in his eyes. He had egg all over his face, not knowing how to talk to Tyrell after his boy tried to stick him like a pin cushion.

"Hey, ahhh. Look. I... I didn't know Byron was going to do that," said John. "He never told me he had a blade on him. That's not cool, man."

"Don't sweat it, baby!" said Tyrell. "It ain't on you, aight?"

"Okay. Cool, man," said John. He seemed a little more relaxed knowing we didn't think he was in on in. "Do... do you think one of you guys can give me a ride home? I came with Byron, and I, ummmm... I really don't want to drive home with him."

As the three of us walked away to leave, Byron started to stir. He moaned a guttural moan, finally coming out of his stupor. Tyrell turned around to watch Byron closely. Then he started to walk toward him.

"I'll be right back," he said.

I hoped Tyrell wasn't going to do anything stupid like finish him. I pictured Tyrell picking up Byron's lifeless corpse, separating his spine in one swooping motion. But he didn't. Tyrell stood over

Byron, looking down on him in more than one way, and shook his head.

"You a sad sack of monkey shit, you know that?" said Tyrell. "Don't you *ever* talk about me again." Tyrell reached down to pick up the switchblade, holding in front of Byron' swollen eye. "If you mess with me again… I'll stick this in *your* ass, you hear me?"

Tyrell flipped the blade back inside the frame and turned around to walk back to his car. Straight gangster, that's what he was! Now I'd seen it with my own eyes, not hearing some rumor. Tyrell was all he said he was, the real deal.

We left Byron there, half dead and embarrassed, on that dimly lit parking lot. My guess is he picked up his teeth and what was left of his pride, dragged himself to his hunk-of-shit Lexus, and drove home.

Byron didn't stay working with us for long. Word got out about his fight with Tyrell, and his crew ragged him for weeks. Nobody knew the fight was on school grounds, but they knew he got his ass handed to him at some point in time, at some location. Weeks later, Byron got into trouble at work. He was piss drunk for a few hours and fell asleep. When his supervisor found him, things got heated, and he took a swing at the boss.

Nobody ever heard from Byron again after he was terminated. I'm positive it wasn't the first, or the last time, Byron had been fired for behavior issues.

And so the war between House Jones and House Banks was over. The hero, my Steve Urkel–looking hero, defeated the scoundrel. Darkness had passed, the evil vanquished from our lives, and everyone was safe once again.

You should've seen Tyrell uppercut that son of a bitch! Goddamn, did he shock the hell out of me and Byron too. He was quick and smooth, like a true old-school street-running survivor. I'm just glad he's my friend and not an enemy.

Chapter 19

Everyone's Got a Story

Picture this, you take a trip the food market. Your list has maybe ten items, ranging from K-Cups to flank steak with a little snacky treat or two mixed in. You speed through the aisles collecting those items with mechanical like precision. As you walk up to checkout, you can't help noticing a moron standing at the head of the line spilling his guts about the latest news in the life of a neurotic loser.

Sound familiar? Hey, man, it happens to all of us. We've all been there plenty of times. The problem is these people are everywhere and each one of them has a story to tell. Some stories, granted, are fascinating and well told (see chapters 1 through 20). Others, sadly, are extremely boring and borderline torture to hear. My main issue is that most of those psychos, degenerates, and scumbags are called my coworkers.

Back in the day, when I made a mental list of people to ignore at work, it was easy to spot a story teller. If a new janitor came to work at my post, I'd know within five minutes if this person was to be avoided at all costs. Have you ever met someone who tells you their entire life history as soon as they shake your hand? Yup. Been there. Two years ago, I met a guy named Douglas Swains, who swore up and down he used to be professional bowler. First of all, is there such a thing as a professional bowler? I mean, I've seen it on ESPN, but can someone make a living knocking down pins? Does the world of late night galactic bowling suddenly turn into a million dollar show down?

Anyway, this guy Douglas wouldn't shake my hand with his right hand. Everyone knows it's proper custom to shake with your right. Fregging Douglas put his left hand out to me. Who does that? I shook it, but I didn't know what to say after what he told me next.

"I'm sorry," said Douglas. "But I never shake with my right hand. That's my money hand. I'm a bowler and I can't risk damaging it."

"Ummmmm… okay," I said.

"It's nothing personal. I just don't want to injury my fingers. I have a huge tournament this weekend in Atlantic City, big payout, if you know what I mean. I don't want to brag or anything, but last year I walked away with a brand-new Cadillac, so it's kind of a big deal."

Here we go. Yet another superstar limelighting as a part-time janitor. Two things: Douglas pulled up that day in a beat-up Nissan Maxima. I saw no year-old Cadillac. And two, he gave me the dead fish. A left-handed Dead Fish, to be exact! For those who aren't hip, the dead fish is when you shake someone's hand but you barely put any effort into the shake. Douglas kind of limped his hand into mine, grasping for the fingers with no tension or force. Had I not known he was a man, I would've assumed he put his hand out for me to kiss like a fancy knight in one of those medieval times movies.

It was less than two minutes since I'd met the famous athlete known as Douglas, and I hated him already. I'm sure people can make some serious money at bowling, but don't start off a conversation with that line. Am I supposed to be jealous of a man who has a 265-bowling average? Also, if someone gives you the dead fish handshake, I take it to mean they don't really want to meet you. Like shaking my hand might jeopardize their well-being. In his defense, he may have had a weaker arm or had some injury to it, but Douglas later explained he was an ambidextrous bowler and was quite skilled with either arm.

Douglas worked as a floater part-time janitor, meaning he went from post to post as a fill-in, as needed. I saw him ten times that year, and each time his bowling escapades got grander and grander.

"Do I look like I got a tan to you? If I do, it's because I just got back from Hawaii, where I bowled in the Waikiki Classic. It's a yearly bowling tourney for us pros. My first time there, I bowled two perfect games in a three-game stretch. Almost took home the Golden Pineapple Trophy, but a darned 7–10 split costed me the last match. Maybe when I go back next year I'll bring home the pineapple!"

Nobody cares, Douglas. Nobody except maybe Don Ho or someone who really loves trophies shaped like fruit.

Two weeks after his Hawaiian showdown, Douglas came back to my post complaining of fatigue. Bowling fatigue, which I'm sure is one of the worst kinds imaginable. He was holding his right hand straight and upright parallel to his chin.

"Don't mind me," said Douglas, his face wincing in pain. "I'll be okay. These twenty-game sets really take it out of me, you know what I mean?"

"Sure," I said. I rolled my eyes.

"That, and the drive back from Peoria. Oh boy, I only got three hours sleep between turn-arounds. I swear, one day, my right arm's going to fall off from over use."

I've seen a one-armed janitor mop a hallway before. Goddamn impressive, to say the least. That guy was a hero if you ask me. Douglas the Wonder Bowler was no hero.

The way Douglas mopped, only using his nonbowling arm, was a travesty. Think about it for a second: a guy dragging a wet mop with his left arm while holding his right arm up near his chest. I don't know where management finds these people.

According to Douglas, his bowling career has been quite impressive. You wouldn't know it by looking at him, but Douglas has bowled with some of the industry's elite ball throwers. You name the bowler, and he's either beaten them or trained them.

"Do you know I worked with Johnny Michelson *before* he won the Grand Rapids Shootout? His spare pickup ratio was terrible. I showed him how to master the viper oil pattern, and now he's a big shot."

I had to google "viper oil pattern." Just a heads-up, it's really a thing.

Douglas also said he spent time training overseas, where he implied the European bowling tours make our bowling tours look like child's play. "I've said it from day one: the Swedish truly know how to roll. Their training routines, the ball hook they can generate. It's a thing of beauty."

About a year into his employment, Douglas left the janitorial field, claiming he got injured while emptying a trash can. Word on the street was Douglas twisted his wrist on a heavy trash can and was now suing the district for workman's compensation. He said his dream of winning the Las Vegas Master Bowlers Cup is out the window now he can't hold his ball. I'm sure he'll get some kind of money from the courts, probably more than he's ever made cracking pins together.

We also had war heroes working here in the past. A couple of dudes used to be in various branches of the military, all solid guys except one jerk. Robert Rukinson, or Private Pissface as I called him, spoke as if he was still deployed. This guy was a true asshole. Everything he did was centered around his previous military career. He spoke in military lingo, called his meals chow, and gave orders to workers like they were in his troop. The problem was Private Pissface was the laziest hunk of shit I'd ever seen. And he tried to make me his grunt.

Had I served in the military and had Robert as my immediate commanding officer, I surely would've shot him in the back during a forced march. I gave him the name Private Pissface because he always had a look on his face like he just took a big gulp of piss. His mug was all scrunched up, his pointy nose and cheeks clenched tighter than a snare drum. Private Pissface was in charge of one of the first posts I worked at, and he went after me the minute I walked in.

"Afternoon, solider," he said to me on the first day.

"Oh, hi. Hi there," I said.

"I'm former Army Sergeant Robert Rukinson, Twenty-Second Division, Jungle Jumpers platoon. I'm the head janitor at this facility. Do you have any questions about your mission here, solider?"

"Ummmm… what mission?" I said, wondering what this guy's deal was.

"You don't look like you're ready for anything too strenuous, chubby. We might have to put you through basic training a couple of times to shed some of that weight, solider!" Pissface laughed a short laugh then eyeballed me.

"Excuse me? What the hell are you talking about?" I said.

"What don't you comprehend? We're here to complete a cleaning mission. I need you to fall in line with the other cadets and do your work, son!" His face was getting beet red.

I don't know about you, but when cornered or yelled at, I tend to get a little testy. This guy was indeed one of my supervisors. Did it give him the right to be all aggressive? Not at all, and I don't take shit from anyone. Even though I was a new worker, I wasn't about to let some shell-shocked ROTC dropout punk me.

"Yeah, I get the whole cleaning part. But this isn't the Army, so why are you calling me solider?" I said.

"Are you defying a direct order? Do you think this is a game, solider?" said Pissface, whose burgundy face had a bulging vein throbbing as he spoke.

"This ain't your platoon, guy. Don't fucking threaten me. We're janitors, not Navy Seals, so back the fuck up!" Oh, I was an angry mopper back then. Still am in some regard.

Private Pissface was not pleased. He stormed over his desk, grabbed his handheld radio, and called for reinforcements. "Unit 38, Unit 38, come in! We got a hostile over at Station 7 and we need immediate action, over!"

Not a good way to start off with a new boss. By the time the head boss came over to diffuse the situation, Private Pissface was writing up what he called my discharge papers, instructing me I should transfer to another post. This son of a bitch actually tried to get me fired for not addressing him as general or commander. What kind of sick puppy does that? I can see if we were at Fort Bragg, but come on! We're janitors in a shitty public school system; this ain't West Point.

For as useless as the teachers' union is, they do step in when a discrepancy is afoot. A union rep came over to speak to us both about workplace morale. Basically, the union has to have a meeting so you can't sue them later in case an employee plugs everyone in the room. We had this big intervention about how to talk to fellow coworkers. I defended my position, saying this guy was a psycho who got in my face because I wasn't buying into his war games theme. Private Pissface, who was ready to line me up on the firing squad, told the boss I was disruptive and should be court martialed "like he did back in Saigon."

Nothing happened to either of us. The head boss told us to chill out and leave well enough alone. The union rep pulled me aside telling me this guy was infamous for this type of behavior. "Just ignore him. He'll calm down eventually," said the rep. "If he gets too pushy, call us." I agreed and went to walk away when the rep called me back. "I almost forgot… he's actually been in the Army and was captured by the Viet Cong, so be careful what you say around him. He's been known to fly off the handle when asked about it."

Naturally, I used this information to my advantage against Private Pissface when he yelled at me. Hey, I didn't start this war. He did so fuck him.

Later that evening, with no one around to witness anything, I began my campaign of terror.

"I think we got off on the wrong foot, comrade. Let's start over, shall we?" I said. Pissface didn't like the comrade comment, but he was receptive to my olive branch.

"At ease, solider. We're both on the same side here. I'm willing to let bygones by bygones if you are willing to get with the program." said Pissface. "Are you ready to fall in?"

"Yeah, sure, Robert," I said.

"It's former Sergeant Rukinson, but you're new here, so I let it slide just this once."

"Gotcha, Sarge. Hey, listen… do you like to travel? I love traveling. Gets my mind away from the old grind, if you feel me? Have you ever been to the *Hanoi Hilton*? I hear it's gorgeous this time of year."

My new boss suddenly dropped his cordial demeanor. I hit a nerve, and now any chance of patching things up went right out the window.

"What did you say?" said Pissface.

"I said," clearing my throat, "have you ever been to the Hanoi Hilton? I hear you've spent some time playing prisoner in Viet-fuckin'-nam."

"Who the hell do you think you are, rookie? Badgering your immediate commanding officer like that! I'll make sure your out of this platoon faster than a M16 bullet!" said Pissface. He whirled around, angry and outraged by my comments.

"Good luck with that, Pops. Why don't you go burn a village or drop some Agent Orange on a rice paddy, you piece of shit!"

For the next few months, I was a thorn in Pissface's side. Each time he went ballistic on me for some asinine thing, I brought him right back to the fields of Ho Chi Minh.

"Hey, Robert... have you ever seen the inside of a tiger's cage? I bet it's cozy in there. Nothing but you and your thoughts to keep you company." He'd storm off to call the bosses, but they didn't believe half the shit he said. Apparently, Mr. Army Guy has been bothering the bosses for years, pretty much crying wolf each time a new worker came to his post.

The union and the bosses ignored Pissface's requests, telling him to go back to work and stop bothering them. Once I found this out, I annoyed him for days. I'd say things in front of the other coworkers in a nonchalant way while I knew Pissface was listening.

"Ouch!" I said, as I took my rubber gloves off. "It feels like I got something under my fingernail. I hope it isn't a bamboo splinter..." Nobody but Pissface knew what I was talking about and I loved it.

Did I take it too far? Yes. Yes, I did. Am I going to hell for torturing a man whose already been tortured? Most definitely. Since this job is hell on earth, I guess I'm exactly where I belong. With countless comments and innuendo Private Pissface went on overload. He called in sick one day and never returned. Turns out my adversary had visions of his past drummed up by my constant pestering. He put in his retirement papers shortly after his second stroke in a week.

Yeah, I know. I'm an asshole, but I'm very good at being an asshole. It's my only redeeming quality according to an old supervisor.

Months after the sarge went AWOL, I met another worker who irked me to no end.

Michael Sangiovese, a.k.a. the Brooklyn Bastard, catapulted into my job. He used to be a New York City pipefitter for forty years. When he retired, he took his $500,000 payout and got a part-time gig with the school district. Now he walks around all night telling people to fuck off.

"What the fuck you lookin' at, dopey!" That's exactly what he said the first time I met him. I don't know what it is about old guys with attitudes, but we're fully stocked with them here. Maybe I provoke people and don't even know it? In any case, the Brooklyn Bastard was a nightmare to work with.

Michael's background was as simple as it gets: I'm from New York, I worked at a real union for decades, and you don't mean shit to me. I tried to tell him how what we do as far as work, but he wasn't having it. After he called me dopey, I tried to keep our conversations quick and infrequent. That didn't work at all. He wasn't interested in work the least bit.

"So, Michael, do you know how to use a mop?" I said. Of course, I was given the task of showing him the ropes.

"Are you kidding me?" said Michael. He looked as if I asked him if he knew how to blink. "It's a mop. How fucking hard can it be?"

"Well, I'm just saying. My boss told me to give you the rundown of what we do here, so that's all I'm doing."

"Listen, small fry. I was a NYC laborer for longer than you've been alive. Don't bother me, okay?"

"But I need to show you how to clean the rooms."

"Yeah, I ain't doing that shit," said Michael, who at this point was looking the other way, checking out a hot teacher down the hallway. When I tried to get him back on track, he walked away. I believe he said this job was "bullshit work" and he "leaves the bullshit work to the dummies."

"Where are you going?" I said.

"Fuck off, you do that crap. That works beneath me," he said.

I think the only reason Michael took the job was so he could hone his arguing skills to a razor-sharp point. The first night Michael did zero work. He walked around the entire evening getting into small arguments with the other coworkers. Unless you count hitting on two teachers and stealing candy from various classrooms, Michael didn't do any real work. The boss found out and came over to discuss why Michael felt it was okay to not do work. Michael laughed in his face.

"Are you serious, asshole?" said Michael. "You expect me to scrub a toilet? I don't even do that shit at my house. I got a Bolivian maid who does that kind of work." After minutes of one-liner insults and threatening to call his old union rep in New York, Michael walked away from my boss the same way he did to me the previous night. Normally if you call your boss a "dumb twat" or "fucking stunod," you'd be unemployed. Michael relished in the discord. He welcomed the chance to argue in front of other bosses and union representatives alike.

Michael had weekly meetings for the remainder of his employment. He squared up with entire rooms full of union reps, council members, and even a few board of education members, all of whom he called useless as tits on a bull. "You people don't know who you're fucking with!" said Michael, who had his lawyer on speakerphone from Queens. "In New York, we wouldn't call what you got here a union. We'd call it a room full of toothless pussies. You people should be ashamed to call yourself union material!"

After six months of constant arguing, and a minuscule amount of work effort, Michael sued the district for harassment, discrimination, and slander. And he won. Shocker. Michael had lots of connections in the New York union system who tore the teachers' union apart. Ultimately Michael left with a nice settlement for simply showing up and being a jerk-off. I'm sure he did very much the same thing for forty some years in the Empire State union system.

On his last day, Michael offered his hand to me with a few words of wisdom as he left with a fat check from the lawsuit.

"This place is a dump, kid. These people are extremely stupid. Get out while you can before you turn into a dumbass like these losers." Then he left, smiling his ass off.

That was almost twenty years ago. I'm still here, complaining about the whole thing, so I guess that makes me a dumbass loser. Michael's story, much like everyone else here, has an ending. Either they leave a happy, rich camper who screwed the board of ed. out of a lot of money or they leave with nothing. They may not have a job when they leave or be alive for that matter, but eventually they leave this place, never to return. Yet I'm still here, withering away like a late season sunflower. I don't know what the means for me. I can't leave even though I want to. I'm stuck in limbo.

If everyone's got a story here, then I surely have one as well. I never gave it much thought until now. I guess my story is the most tragic of them all.

Chapter 20

And Then There's Me

I hope you're still reading at this point. It is a tremendous amount to take in, I know. And I do apologize for any discomfort you may be experiencing or any sort of board-certified psychotherapist you visit once a week due to absorbing this manifesto. I know I sure as hell need one right about now.

My story, not the terrible misgivings of my coworkers, but my saga, is very simple: I'm fucked. Royally and without any lube, "middle of summer in the back seat of a Ford Escort" kind of fucked. This gig was only supposed to be a year or two until I graduated from college. There's where things went totally south, the whole college endeavor. Had I not attended college, I wouldn't have ever applied for this job. Because I went to a four-year school, to better myself in life, I needed a job with these exact hours. Why couldn't I work at Starbucks banging out lattes for a few hours a day?

But there was this little voice in my head telling me to go to school, chase your dreams, and maybe take a bite out of the American dream! Yeah, good luck with that one. Now I'm stuck in stain-covered overalls wondering when the school boiler will blow up and take me with it.

Nobody in their right mind wants to be a school janitor forever. The sheer fact I've made it this far makes me believe it's all just an illusion. Any second now either I'll wake up from this two-decade-long coma or someone will finally pull the plug and put me out of my fucking misery.

I've wasted a better part of my life cleaning toilets and scraping shit off the floor. For what? Not the money, because it's peanuts compared to what your average American worker makes. It sure ain't because I love the job. I'd rather stick needles in my cornea than mop floors for another bloody minute. And beyond a shadow of a doubt, I loathe the fact that I went to college in the first place, landing me in this situation where I can't afford to quit this godforsaken hellhole.

There's an army of people who took the bait of a higher learning, and now they're cemented in a career they can't stomach. Remember your friend Steve who used to do so well in computer class? Now he works at Best Buy part-time and doesn't have dental insurance. When the time comes to get a cavity fixed, he'd rather spend his money on stupid things like rent or gas. His whole mouth of teeth might rot out because he was told he should take Typing 101. Guess what? First graders can ace that class now!

How about your old pal Brenda who said she wanted to work with dolphins down in SeaWorld? So little Brenda went to college for marine biology. Do you know what she's doing these days? She works at the local pet store scooping goldfish for $10 an hour. Last week her old-piece-of-shit Honda blew a transmission costing $2,000. The last time Brenda saw $2,000, it was on a check made out to some ruthless lending company who owns her student loan debt.

And who could forget our old chum Mark. This guy was a genius when it came to home repair. My man Mark spent so many hours working on houses someone told him he should go to school to become an architect. So he did! Now the housing market took a shit, and it flushed old Marky Mark down the drain with it. Nobody's buying houses because they all went to college as well and couldn't afford a $2,300 monthly mortgage. Mark could fix just about anything back in the day. Too bad he can't fix his mediocre credit rating. He's stuck ringing up other people's building supplies in Home Depot.

There isn't a worse feeling in the world then feeling trapped in a dead-end career. You get depressed and angry with yourself thinking you've ruined your life. Where did I go wrong? Why am I stuck in this place? You beat yourself up all the time, but it's not your fault.

You did the right things in life. You thought going to college was the best thing since sliced bread. Now you got your degree and don't have a wall to hang it on. I bet your college degree or degrees are sitting in a box instead of being displayed on a gorgeous office wall. I know mine are.

I guess you can consider me institutionalized. Remember the old guy in the *Shawshank Redemption*? Brooks was his name. Remember how he couldn't handle normal society after he got paroled and decided to hang himself in a halfway house? That's exactly how I see my role in this book. Not the noose part. Although, I can see myself feeding pigeons in a public park when I'm old and feeble. Might be relaxing.

But the fact remains I'm stuck in a place I don't feel welcome. My life has no meaning at this job. If I off myself like Brooks, who's to say anyone would even notice my absence? I just feel all the years I've spent working here were a complete waste of time. Nobody listens to me even though I'm in charge of fifteen schmucks. Not a single coworker or colleague considers me a friend. None of the bosses give a crap if I show up to work anymore (I'm pretty sure they'd prefer I didn't come back ever again). If I left here tomorrow half the people wouldn't care while the other half wouldn't notice I'm gone. Did I mention I know coworkers whom I've worked with the entire time I've been here and they still don't know my name? They call me George or Sal or even something outlandish like Julio. By the way, I look nothing like a Julio. Not even close.

Oh, but some people sure would *love* to see me gone. I know Mr. Sanders, that cockeyed, wrinkly demigod, will finally be able to return to his empty throne next to Satan. Mr. Polotski might pop a bottle of champagne and light an Onyx cigar upon hearing of my leaving. Besides them, maybe a few Mongolians and a teacher or two might notice my departure. That's about it.

I bet you if Tyrell was still here, he'd miss me. But a majority could give a scratch if show up.

It's quite sad, really. You spend half your life at a job where no one cares if you live or die. Do you know how sad it is to hear that out loud? For me to utter those words pains me to my core. Look,

I realize most the world feels mistreated at work. I mean, look at garbage men or grave diggers or even fellow slop moppers in the custodial arts. But this is *my life* and *my story*. It was never meant to be this way, said every disgruntled worker ever.

I'm going to say the truest thing I've ever written in this book: there is nothing wrong with being a janitor. No bullshit. I may loath the duties, but a job's a job. It's still a decent, honest living for someone who wants to support their family. Or someone who owes the government a shit ton of money for student loans. You need some money or health bennies to live on? Hey, this job has some of what you're looking for. But this place, the actual board of education, has destroyed many a soul, and I fear my soul will wither away if I continue to work here.

When I began my higher education, I found solace in working toward a goal, an end to the life of a school janitor. *A college degree.* The first one to be had in my family. I know, it's sounds like a cliché, but damned if ain't all true. It was the happiest day of my life when I graduated from college with a degree in creative writing. It felt as if the world belonged to me and me alone. Millions of people graduate from college each year. But none of them are me. Not one of them knew my secrets or shared in my accomplishments. No other person can look in the mirror and see my reflection. My hard work and sacrifices allowed me to feel important for the first time in a very long time. For that much, I know.

Soon after my ice cream cake with "Congrats!" was eaten and the money-stuffed envelopes were all opened, I still had to face the harshest of realities: nothing had changed. I was still a school janitor. That following Monday, I'd show up to do my duty and toil away at work that neither gave me pleasure nor rewarded me in the least bit. A person who cleans up after other people's children. I was a nanny with a set of keys and a chipped Wet Floor sign. It destroyed me to come to that realization.

It didn't happen overnight, my unraveling. Right after the commencement speech, when I finally threw that hat and got that degree, I still wasn't completely defeated yet. It hit me one day while I was sitting at a keyboard, much like this keyboard, typing out words I wasn't sure anyone would ever read. Instead of an "Aha!" moment, I had an "Oh, fuck!" moment: what was I still doing here, in this place of sadness? I could've quit that night, walked out like a champ, and proceeded to the nearest liquor store to celebrate with a fine double-aged scotch.

But I didn't. Maybe I'm just stuck in the quicksand of a paycheck, realizing I've got student loans, a mortgage, a wife, and a ton of medical bills that need to be paid. Not to mention a little black kitty cat who depends on me to bring her the finest Fancy Feast available.

It's just a hard pill to swallow, you know? I didn't have to like the job, but I still had to do it, night in and night out. That's the part that killed me the most. My dream, not the old one about being a famous writer, but the new dream, is to quit this job and never look back. Throwing my keys on the ground, telling a few choice people "Suck my dick!" and then run as fast as I can out the door, has been a dream of mine for what seems like forever.

I've been asked one question by everyone I meet: "Why do you do it? Why do you stay at a job you hate instead of working somewhere else? You're a smart guy! You can work anywhere else with your degrees and motivation!"

If I could turn back the clock, I would've punched myself in the face seconds before I handed in the job application. Right there in the disgusting hovel of a board office, breaking my nose in front of the secretary might have saved me from this life. At least, after the secretary screamed in shock, I would've stumbled out of the board of education before getting sucked into a never-ending abyss.

I guess I'm afraid of the unknown, to be honest. I'm afraid of where my next paycheck will come from. I'm afraid of losing my house. I'm afraid of not getting my medicine at a cheap price because I don't have insurance. And I'm afraid if I stay here one more second, everything I wrote in this book won't ever see the light of day.

I guess what I'm saying is don't be a dumbass like me. Especially the whole creative writing degree; that shit isn't worth the parchment paper it's printed on. If you're stuck in a job you despise, get out before you can't. I mean, look at me. Where the fuck am I going?

I'll tell you where: anywhere but here. You can't get any lower than a school janitor, right? Well, you could be a janitor in some other place, like a morgue or a hospital with really sick people. Once you've hit rock bottom, you should want to spring upward like a rocket, which is what I plan on doing once I finish this book. I've spent too many years watching the rest of the world speed past me while I'm stuck in reverse. If you've got dreams, brother, keep dreaming until they come true. Quit that useless job and never look in your rearview mirror. If all my years learning in college taught me one thing, it would be this: don't die working at a job you hate.

So I'll stop venting for a minute and let you get back to your life instead of reading about mine. Besides, I've got plenty more stories to write and maybe a few toilets to clean along the way. Not too many more crappers, just enough to keep me humble.

The End

About the Author

J. R. Warnet has been working in the custodial arts for the past twenty years. He also holds a BA in creative writing from Stockton College in New Jersey. JR has been published in over twenty-five newspapers and magazines. Most of his previous work has been focused on news and informational topics. This is his first fiction book with a sequel and an audiobook currently in the works. JR currently lives in Central New Jersey with his wife, Tia Lyn, and their black cat, Salem.

CPSIA information can be obtained
at www.ICGtesting.com
Printed in the USA
BVHW030733310319
544156BV00002B/137/P